Stuart MacBride is ... ...vels
featuring DS Loga... ...ller
Halfhead. The Mc... ...A's
Dagger in the Lib... ...but
Novel, and Best B... ...rime
thriller awards.

Stuart lives in the north-east of Scotland with his wife
Fiona, cat Grendel, about a million spiders (as yet
unnamed), and a vegetable plot full of weeds (called
Frank).

Visit Stuart MacBride's website at: www.StuartMacBride.com

Also by Stuart MacBride

Cold Granite
Dying Light
Broken Skin
Flesh House
Blind Eye
Shatter the Bones

Writing as Stuart B. MacBride

Halfhead

STUART MACBRIDE
Dark Blood

HARPER

This is a work of fiction. Any references to real people, living or dead, real events, businesses, organizations and localities are intended only to give the fiction a sense of reality and authenticity. All names, characters, places and incidents are either the product of the author's imagination or are used fictitiously, and their resemblance, if any, to real-life counterparts is entirely coincidental. The only exceptions to this are the characters of Julie Bultitude, Graeme Danby, Susanna Frayn, Dave Goulding, Allan Guthrie, Ian Haffenden and Fiona Martin, who have given their express permission to be fictionalised in this volume. All behaviour, history, and character traits assigned to these individuals have been designed to serve the needs of the narrative and do not necessarily bear any resemblance to the real people.

Harper
An imprint of HarperCollins*Publishers*
77–85 Fulham Palace Road,
Hammersmith, London W6 8JB

www.harpercollins.co.uk

This paperback edition 2011
1

First published in Great Britain by
HarperCollins*Publishers* 2010

Copyright © Stuart MacBride 2010

Stuart MacBride asserts the moral right to
be identified as the author of this work

A catalogue record for this book is
available from the British Library

ISBN: 978 0 00 724461 4

Typeset in Meridien by Palimpsest Book Production Limited,
Falkirk, Stirlingshire

Printed and bound in Great Britain by
Clays Ltd, St Ives plc

Mixed Sources
Product group from well-managed
forests and other controlled sources
www.fsc.org Cert no. SW-COC-001806
© 1996 Forest Stewardship Council

FSC is a non-profit international organisation established to promote the responsible management of the world's forests. Products carrying the FSC label are independently certified to assure consumers that they come from forests that are managed to meet the social, economic and ecological needs of present and future generations.

Find out more about HarperCollins and the environment at
www.harpercollins.co.uk/green

For Sarah

Without Whom

One of the best parts of writing a book is doing the research, getting out into the real world and speaking to the people who live and work in it. Anything I've got wrong in this book is my fault, anything I've got right is due to the generosity of some very clever people. So I want to thank: Dr Lorna Dawson, Professor Dave Barclay and Dr James Grieve; David Miller, Jane Lund, Margaret McKeen, Barrie Thornton, Gareth Newman, Steve Hillier, Jasmine Ross, and all the forensic gurus at the Macaulay Institute; Mark McHardy, Del Henderson, David Francis, John Angus, and everybody at Aberdeen's Trading Standards Service; DS Alan Findlay, Sergeant Midge Mackay and everyone at Grampian Police who gave generously of their time and experience; my agent Phil Patterson, my terrific editor Sarah Hodgson, Damon Greeney, Fiona McIntosh, Joy Chamberlain, Marie Goldie, Karen-Maree Griffiths, Lucy Vanderbilt, Tara Hiatt, Lucy Upton, the entire Sales team, and everyone at HarperCollins.

I've been out and about a lot this year, and I have to thank Tony Fisk, Michael Moynahan, Frederika van Traa, Al and Donna Buchan, Adrian Hyland, and Michael Robotham for their hospitality; Russell Kirkpatrick for tour guide excellence; Jordan Weaver, Lise Taylor, Sylvia May, Christine Farmer, Amy Neilson, Chris Kooi, and Elsemiek Ariëns for looking after me on my travels; and Jennifer Howard and the crew at Talking Issues for putting up with all the strange noises.

More thanks go to: Aleksander Bogunia, Anna Maria Bojes, Tomasz Zygula, Piotr Kufel; Alex Clark, Erica Morris, Zoë Sharp, Laura Wilson, Malcolm Mackay, Spenser Tait, James Oswald and my brother Christopher; Graeme Danby, Julie Bultitude, Dave Goulding, Fiona Martin, and Susanna Frayn; and to Allan Guthrie for all the feedback.

And saving the best for last – as always – Fiona and Grendel.

DARK BLOOD

1

Run. Don't stop. Keep moving. . .

The big, fat moon makes everything black and white. Frost and shadow. Life and death.

Steve stumbles. The churned-up mud's solid – up and down like a roller-coaster. One foot catches the edge of a rock-hard peak, and he goes sprawling across the icy ground. Tries not to cry out as his arm screams sharp-edged pain.

Somewhere in the darkness a dog barks. Big dog. Fucking scary big dog. You know? Rottweiler, Doberman: some bastard like that. Big and black, with thousands of teeth. Coming after him.

'Fuck . . .' The word disappears into the night sky on a cloud of white breath.

Big dog.

He scrambles upright; stands there, trying to get his balance. Feeling sick. Far too much whisky. Makes everything blurry and warm, even though it's so cold out here his fingers ache with it. Makes the world smell like it's burning.

Steve lurches forward, arm clutched to his chest, hugging

the shadows along the edge of the building site. Trees blocking the searchlight moon.

With any luck no one'll see the trail of blood he's leaving. . .

The dog barks again. Closer.

But then his luck's always been for shit.

Steve speeds up. Lurch, stumble, struggle.

His left foot cracks through an ice-topped puddle, and he stops. Holding his breath.

Steve turns, looking back towards the site office. Torches sweep the muddy ground, muffled voices coming this way. That fucking dog yammering and yowling, leading them on.

Keep going.

Keep moving.

One foot in front of the other.

Follow the eight-foot-high fence: chainlink and barbed wire, skirting the building site.

This time when he trips he goes head-first into a ditch, slithering down the bank, branches snapping, pain ripping through his arm, something raking his cheek with thorny claws. A shatter of ice, and then water so cold it's like being punched in the face again.

He splutters to the surface of the little stream. It's not deep but it's freezing. He thrashes against the brambles, pulling himself out of the water. Shivers like he's got a jackhammer jammed up his arse. Teeth chattering hard enough to chip the enamel.

The dog barks again. Definitely closer now. Probably let the damn thing off its lead. Go on, you dirty bugger, find Steve and tear his thieving, double-crossing throat out.

Steve slumps back against the bank, trying not to cry, frigid water soaking his trousers, jacket, socks, every-fucking-thing. Why do these Scottish bastards call it a burn when it's so fucking *cold*?

Rest. Just for a minute. Rest in the darkness, in the safety of the ditch where no one can see him. Not really so bad. Get used to the cold after a while.

Just close his eyes for a second. Catch his breath.

Rest for a moment. . .

And the next time he opens his eyes something's looking right back at him. A big, muscular shape in the darkness, breath steaming out between sharp teeth. Black coat shining in the moonlight.

Nice doggy.

It barks, lurching forward and back with every terrifying sound, spittle flying everywhere.

Oh Jesus fuck.

Knife. There's a Stanley knife in his pocket, but his frozen, sausage fingers aren't working. They fumble against his torn jacket. Swearing. Tears. Cold. GET THE FUCKING KNIFE!

And then he hears the voice: 'Fuckin' hell, Mauser, this better no' be another bloody rabbit.' Footsteps crunching through frozen grass.

Steve drags the Stanley knife out, holds it in his trembling hand, trying to press the metal slider down. Come on, come on, come on.

And then a man joins the monster. The moon's behind him, hiding his face, making him a thing of darkness that breathes brimstone smoke into the sudden silence. 'Hey Steve,' he says. 'Where you goin', man? We're only just gettin' started. . .'

2

'Inspector?' A shivering constable grabbed the blue-and-white 'POLICE' tape, stretching it up and out of the way. 'They're over there, sir.'

Logan McRae plipped the locks on his mud-spattered Audi, then ducked under the tape and slithered his way across the pale sand, making for the knot of figures gathered outside the SOC tent. It sat between a pair of massive sand dunes, the white plastic sheeting flapping in the frigid wind that whistled in off the North Sea. There wasn't a cloud in the sky, but the low sun hadn't made it over the crest of jagged pampas grass yet, leaving the crime scene shrouded in deep blue shadow.

Balmedie Beach wasn't exactly the Costa Del Sol at the best of times, but at half ten on a cold January morning it could freeze the nipples off a polar bear. Aberdeen – two degrees north of Moscow.

If the city had a zoo they'd have to give the penguins bobble hats in the winter.

'Inspector! Inspector McRae!' An Identification Bureau technician, dressed in the obligatory white oversuit and blue plastic booties, waved him over. 'Same as all the others, sir. You were right.'

Brilliant – the one time he actually wanted to be proven wrong.

Logan signed in with the Crime Scene Manager, then struggled his way into an SOC suit. It fought him all the way, the wind snatching at the legs and sleeves, trying to help it escape. 'Pathologist?'

'Inside, sir. Photographs and samples are done, so just give us a nod when you want us to remove. . .' He pointed at what Logan knew was lurking in the tent. 'You know. . .'

The whole structure creaked and juddered, the wind moaning through the joints as Logan stepped inside. They'd set up a couple of arc lights, the harsh white glare bouncing back off the sand, making Logan's breath steam as he squatted down beside the pathologist.

She looked up at him, her eyes sparkling above the mask that covered her nose and mouth. Then back down at the head, lying on its side in the pale sand.

It was a woman: early twenties; eyes sunken and glassy; ginger hair bleached almost blonde by the arc lights; freckles dark against her porcelain skin; mouth open. A little drift of sand had built up behind her teeth, something golden glittering away in the depths. Just like the other six.

'How did you know?' The pathologist dug the severed head out of the sand. 'She was right where you said she'd be.'

Logan watched them ease Lucy's head into a clear plastic evidence pouch, seal, and label it. One more to add to the collection in the mortuary.

'Time of death?'

Doctor Isobel McAllister snapped off her blue nitrile gloves, removed her mask, and peeled back the hood of her SOC suit, letting her long, dark hair tumble over her shoulders. 'You know I can't tell you that.'

Logan opened his mouth to say something, then shut it

7

as Isobel placed a hand against his chest. Her touch was hot in the cold tent.

She stared up into his eyes. 'I've missed you—'

'Isobel, I—'

'Oh no you don't!' One of the IB techs marched over: Samantha, scarlet hair painfully bright in the harsh lighting. She unzipped her suit, exposing a swell of pale cleavage surrounded by tattoos. 'He's mine. Aren't you Logan?'

Isobel bit her bottom lip. Looked away. 'Oh. I'm sorry, I didn't know.'

'But maybe. . .' Samantha stepped up close and ran her fingertips across Isobel's cheek. 'Maybe I'll let you share.'

Pain jagged across Logan's ribs. 'Ow, what was—'

'Maybe we can all do something . . . *special* together.'

'I'd like that.' Isobel licked her blood-red lips and cupped one of Samantha's breasts. 'I'd like that a – Stop sodding snoring!'

'Mmmph. . .?' Detective Sergeant Logan McRae struggled upright in his seat. 'I'm awake. I'm awake.' Cold. Dark. A lung-rattling cough shook his body, ending with a shiver. 'God. . .' Sniff. He ran his hands across his face, feeling the stubble rasp. 'What time is it?'

DI Steel was almost invisible in the darkness, but he could hear her shifting in the passenger seat of his manky brown Fiat. 'You were snoring.'

The inspector stabbed her thumb on the button for the cigarette lighter, waited for it to pop up, then pulled it out of the dashboard and sparked up a Silk Cut. The orange glow turned her face into a topographical map of wrinkles and shadow. Train-wreck hair hidden beneath a furry hat.

'Bloody freezing. . .' Logan peered at the fogged-up windscreen, then cleared a porthole with his sleeve, looking out at the moonlit countryside. They'd parked down a small lane overlooking a sprawling building site, just off the A90 – Aberdeen to Ellon road. He yawned. 'Need a pee.'

'Shouldn't have drunk all that coffee then, should you?'

'Knew he wouldn't show.'

'I mean, what sort of idiot takes decaf on a stakeout?'

'So where is he then?'

'If I knew that, I wouldn't be sitting here in this crappy car listening to your bloody snoring, would I?'

'Fine, be like that.' Logan helped himself to one of the inspector's cigarettes, lighting it with a Zippo as he climbed out into the freezing night.

'Close the sodding door!'

SLAM.

He stood there for a second, shivering, drew in a deep lungful of smoke, then started down the lane towards a clump of trees. The ground crackled beneath his feet, grass coated in a thick rime of frost, everything turned monochrome in the light of a nearly full moon. Bright as day.

Logan stepped off the lane and into the undergrowth.

God it was cold. Bloody Steel and her bloody CHIS. What was the point of having a Covert Human Intelligence Source if the sodding 'Source' was so 'Covert' you couldn't bloody see him?

Zip, rummage, grimace . . . ahhhhh. Oh yeah . . . that was better.

He stood there, in a growing cloud of bitter-sweet steam, cigarette dangling from the corner of his mouth. Twelve days straight without a single day off. No wonder he was knackered.

You could see the whole development from here: a swathe of frozen mud surrounded by chainlink fencing; piles of bull-dozed earth; a cluster of pale concrete foundations. Twenty or thirty houses looked almost finished, another half dozen were at the scaffolding and brick stage. Eventually there'd be four hundred of the damn things, courtesy McLennan Homes. Nasty, boxy, rabbit hutches for people with more money than sense.

Christ knew how the bastard got planning permission.

The site office was a little Portakabin and as Logan watched, someone opened the door spilling pale yellow light across the churned-up earth. A dog barked. The sound of a radio. Then the door swung shut and the light was gone, replaced by the faint circle of a torch, working its way around the perimeter fence. You'd have to be desperate: taking a night watchman's job on a building site in the middle of winter. Knowing that if anything went missing Malcolm McLennan would have your balls.

Literally.

Logan zipped himself up then hurried back to the car, out of the cold. He clunked the door shut behind him. 'Baltic out there. . .' He cranked the key in the ignition and turned the heater up full, holding his hands over the vents.

DI Steel sat and scowled at the windscreen as it started to clear. 'Sod this, he's two hours late. I'm no' buggering about any longer; some of us got pregnant wives to get home to.'

Logan wrestled the gearstick into reverse, getting a loud grinding noise, then turned in his seat and peered out of the rear window, navigating by the light of the moon. The manky Fiat shuddered backwards up the lane. 'Told you he wasn't going to show.'

'Blah, blah, blah.'

'I'm just saying: no one's daft enough to rat out Malk the Knife.' Logan backed out onto the slip road, flicked on the headlights, then stuck his foot down. Hoping for a bit of wheel-spin, getting nothing but a dull groan as the car slowly dragged its rusty backside towards fifty.

'Stop past Asda on the way home, we're out of ice-cream.'

10

'In this weather?'

'Cravings. Susan wants double chocolate chip, and cheese Doritos. In the same bowl. And before you say anything, I know: I have to watch her eating it.' Steel scooted down in her seat. 'Doesn't this thing go any faster?'

'No.'

They sat in silence as the moonlit countryside rumbled past. Fields of frost-whitened grass, ploughed up earth, miserable-looking sheep, big round bales of hay wrapped in black plastic.

Logan slowed for the roundabout on the outskirts of Bridge of Don. 'Fancy a pint – celebrate my *finally* getting some time off? Dodgy Pete's'll still be open.'

'Pregnant wife, remember?' Steel pulled out her cigarettes again. 'And I want you back at the ranch seven o'clock Thursday morning, bright eyed and bushy tailed. Don't want Mr Knox thinking we're no' pleased to see him, do we? Christ knows what the nasty wee sod would get up to.'

3

The Eastern Airways Jetstream 41 was tiny compared to the British Midlands 737 at the next stand. Logan stood in the shelter of a plastic-roofed walkway outside the terminal building, watching as the little blue-and-white plane edged in from the runway, twin propellers roaring in the drizzly rain, navigation lights winking in the gloom.

The sky it had dropped from was the colour of wet clay, a solid blanket of dark grey that stretched from horizon to horizon, thin slivers of pre-dawn light barely visible around the edges.

'Bang on time.' DI Steel dragged her hands out of her armpits for long enough to produce a packet of cigarettes, stick one in her mouth, and light up. 'Mind you, bet we'll still be farting about—'

'Hey! You!' A little man in a high-visibility vest was scurrying down the walkway towards them. 'You can't smoke here. The whole airport's a no smoking zone!'

Steel took the fag out of her mouth and told him to bugger off. 'Police.'

'I don't care if you're the sodding Pope: no smoking!'

'Oh for God's sake.' She took one last defiant drag and

dropped the cigarette on the concrete walkway, grinding it out with a scuffed shoe. 'There, you happy?'

'Don't let it happen again.' He stuck his nose in the air, turned on his heel and stalked off.

Steel stuck two fingers up at his departing back, muttering, 'Little Hitler dick.'

The Jetstream's engines gave one last roar and the plane rocked to a halt, windscreen wipers slowly squeaking back and forth across the cockpit windows as the propeller blades whined down. Then men in grubby blue boilersuits and ear protectors hauled luggage out of the hold and stacked it onto a buggy.

There was a clunk and the forward door popped open, hinged on the bottom edge, the steps built into the back. One of the cabin crew stuck her head out into the cold morning and a gust of wind whipped her long brown hair into a headbanger's halo. Her expression soured, she ducked back inside. Welcome to Aberdeen.

Logan leaned back against the walkway's cold plastic wall and stifled a yawn.

Steel wrinkled her nose at him. 'How much you have to drink last night?'

Shrug. 'Couple glasses of wine.'

'Aye and the rest. You smell like a tramp's Y-fronts.'

'I was on holiday.' Two blissful days of sleeping in and not having to worry about Aberdeen's assorted criminal tosspots.

'On the batter more like.' She dug in her pocket and came out with a packet of extra strong mints. 'Eat.'

Logan did what he was told, crunching away as the ground crew finished with the baggage.

A uniformed PC appeared at Logan's elbow, carrying three big wax-paper cups, the bitter smell of roasted coffee beans mingling with the fading tang of exhaust and hot metal. PC Guthrie puffed out his cheeks and stared at the rain, pale ginger eyebrows almost invisible beneath the peak of his cap. 'Maybe he'll take one look at the weather and bugger off back to Newcastle?' Guthrie grinned. It made him look like a happy potato.

Steel scowled. 'You took your sodding time.'

'Nature called.' The constable handed over the coffees, then dug about in the pocket of his black fleece. 'Got you a muffin as well. . .'

'Then I take it all back: even the stuff about your granny shagging donkeys.'

The three of them drank their coffee and ate their muffins.

A stream of people clumped down the plane's steps, then huddled along the designated path to the terminal, clutching their laptops to their chests, ties and suit jackets flapping in the wind.

Steel checked her watch. 'Three days' time, that'll be me. Only I'll be in the Canary Islands, no' freezing my nipples off in sunny Aberdeen.'

The last of the passengers picked a small red suitcase from the cart, and trundled it through the puddles and away.

Steel stomped her feet, hands wrapped around her steaming paper cup. 'You *sure* he was on the plane?'

'Positive.'

'Then where the hell is he? It's no' like. . .' She stopped. A large pink head had appeared in the Jetstream's doorway: what little hair remained had been cropped to about the same length as the designer stubble beard covering both chins. The face broke into a wide smile of perfect white teeth.

'Detective Inspector Steel I presume!' There was no mistaking the Newcastle accent, it boomed out across the drizzly morning, easily competing with the distant roar of the delayed BD0671 clambering its way into the dismal sky.

Steel pulled out the photograph Northumbria Police had emailed up, squinted at it, frowned, then leaned over and whispered at Logan, 'If that's Knox, he's really let himself go.' She held up a hand and waved.

The large man hobbled down the steps then stopped at the bottom, turned and stared back into the cabin. 'Well, come on then: this was your idea, remember?'

A thin face peered out: Richard Knox. Pointy nose, pointy chin, and a crooked-teeth overbite that made him look a bit like a partially shaved rat. His hairline was receding, probably trying to get away from his face. 'Cold.'

The big man closed his eyes for a moment, mouth working silently on something. And then he said, 'We've been over this, Richard, you know what I'm saying?'

'Just an observation.' Knox's voice was nearly an octave higher, but still broad Geordie. He took a grip of the handrail and picked his way down the steps to the wet tarmac. 'Not like this all the time, is it?'

DI Steel grinned at him. 'No, most of the time it's a lot worse. Why don't you try somewhere warmer? Like hell? That's meant to be nice this time of year.'

Knox stared back, expressionless. 'Funny. You're a funny lady.'

'And you're a raping wee shitebag.'

'Served me time. Paid me debt to society, like. God has forgiven us.'

'My sharny arse! People like you—'

'All right.' The big man limped between them. 'I think that's enough team bonding for one morning.' He stuck out his hand for Steel to shake. 'Detective Superintendent Danby.'

She looked at the hand for a moment, then grabbed it, her fingers disappearing into the DSI's grip. 'Detective Inspector Steel.'

'Excellent.' Danby nodded, getting an extra chin for his trouble. 'Now, any chance we can go inside before we all freeze to death?'

* * *

15

Knox didn't say much on the way into town, just sat in the back of the patrol car, sandwiched between Logan and PC Guthrie, clutching an Asda carrier bag to his chest while Steel drove.

DSI Danby was a lot more chatty. 'So there we were, half the bobbies in Newcastle, and we still can't find our missing grandad anywhere. We've checked the shops, the post office, every shed and garage for three miles round his house. So it gets dark and we have to give up for the night. Newspaper appeals, radio, even got us a two minute spot on the local telly news. Nothing.'

Knox shifted in his seat, rubbing against Logan in the confined space. Up close he smelled of lavender and peppermint. Like an old lady's handbag. Knox sniffed. 'Do we really need to hear this, again?'

'Three days later, the old boy turns up at the local library, still in his jammies, gabbling on about how he's been abducted by aliens. Course, everyone knows he's got Alzheimer's, you know what I'm saying? So they pat him on the head and get someone to drive him home. Only he keeps going on about how the aliens took him to their underground lab and did experiments on him. Anal probes and all that.'

Danby sniffed, one hand wrapped around the grab handle above the passenger door, staring out of the window. 'So finally his sister calls the doctor and he examines the old man, doesn't he? You know what?'

Knox cleared his throat. 'You're doing this on purpose, aren't you? Spoiling things for us.'

'Just making conversation.'

'Well don't. It's not funny.'

'Suit yourself.' The DSI went back to staring at the drab, grey scenery. On a good day, Aberdeen sparkled . . . but this wasn't a good day. The granite buildings sulked beneath the heavy clouds, their grey walls stained dark by the never-ending

16

drizzle. Headlights shimmered back from the wet road, tail-lights glowering red through a haze of spray.

DI Steel flicked on the radio, breaking the silence. Annie Lennox – Aberdeen's favourite local-girl-made-good – singing about walking on broken glass. The song ended, there was some banal chat from a DJ who obviously thought he was a lot funnier than he actually was, another record, and then the news.

'London grinds to a halt as snowstorms grip England. The A96 is closed between Inverurie and Huntly following a five-car pile-up. McLennan Homes announce jobs boost for the beleaguered North East building industry. And a legal challenge is launched today against a proposed expansion to Donald Trump's golf resort. Hi, I'm Karen MacDonald. Today the Balmedie Dunes Preservation Society confirmed it would be issuing a legal challenge. . .'

PC Guthrie snorted. 'How come every time there's half a millimetre of snow, England goes tits up? What a bunch of wanky. . .' He drifted to a halt, DSI Danby had swivelled round in the passenger seat to stare into the back of the patrol car.

'Er. . .' The constable's cheeks went pink. 'I mean . . . it's. . .' He looked at Logan. 'We. . .'

Logan shook his head. 'No chance: you're on your own, Sunshine.'

Idiot.

'Come on then, Constable,' Danby's voice rumbled through the confined space, 'you have something to say: let's hear it.'

'I just . . . it . . . erm. . .' Cough. 'With the snow, and it's probably, you know, unexpected, and the councils don't grit the roads. . .' He wriggled in his seat. 'Got nothing against the English. Got lots of mates who're English. . .'

Danby looked at him. 'How long you been in the force?'

Guthrie licked his lips. 'Erm. . . Seven years?'

'Take a tip, Constable, if you ever want to make sergeant, practise your lying. Cos right now you're crap. You know what I'm saying?'

4

Grampian Police Force Headquarters was a lot busier at five to nine on a Thursday morning than it had any right to be. By now the CID dayshift should have been out there, keeping the city safe from the people who lived in it; instead they were hanging around the station, making the place look untidy. Logan picked his way carefully down the corridor, two coffees and a pair of tinfoil parcels balanced on a manila folder like a wobbly tray.

DI Steel's office was the last one before the noisy main CID room. Logan stopped outside her door and carefully rearranged his hands so he could knock without spilling scalding liquid all over himself.

Only he didn't get that far.

Someone coughed behind him, and Logan turned to find Detective Inspector Beattie standing there with his arms folded. 'Weren't you supposed to come see me first thing this morning, Sergeant?'

Sodding hell. DI Beattie: sixteen stone of useless with a beard.

'Had to go pick up Richard Knox.'

Beattie looked down at the carpet for a moment. 'We

were supposed to go over those counterfeit goods, remember? Handbags, MP3 players, cameras, perfume. . . What are we doing about them?'

'Have you spoken to Trading Standards yet?'

'No I thought you—'

'I *told* you to go speak to them. Jesus, George, you're supposed to be a DI now, remember? I can't do everything for—'

Inspector Steel's office door banged open, and she lurched to a halt on the threshold, mouth hanging open as if she was about to shout something. She took one look at Beattie, then turned to Logan, 'Where the hell have you been?'

'Had to—'

'Get your arse in here.' She hauled up her trousers, stood back, waited till Logan was inside, then slammed the door in Beattie's face.

Steel's new office didn't look anything like the old one: the knobbly ceiling tiles were still white, not coated in a sticky beige film of cigarette tar; the walls didn't have those greasy Blu-tack acne spots; and the carpet was still a recognizable colour. Logan gave it six weeks, tops.

Steel slumped back behind her desk and Logan handed her a mug and a tinfoil parcel. She unwrapped the bacon buttie and got stuck in, chewing and talking at the same time: 'What we got?'

He pointed at the manila folder, now with an Olympic logo of coffee rings on it. 'Not a hell of a lot. Far as we can tell, Knox hasn't been to Aberdeen since he was eleven.' Logan peeled the tinfoil off his fried egg buttie and bit down. Yolk splurged out into his palm. 'Sod. . .' He transferred the dripping roll to his other hand and licked at the sticky yellow puddle. 'Got them to pull all sexual assaults on OAPs for the three years before he left: two women in their late seventies. No men.'

Steel nodded. 'Good. Means we'll no' have a bunch of angry relatives sniffing about causing trouble.' Another bite, then a scoof of tea. 'Next: Erica Piotrowski?'

Logan went rooting through the folder and pulled out a stack of forms covered in scuffed yellow Post-it notes. 'Trial date's been set for three weeks next Tuesday. She's still sticking to her story, but the PF thinks she'll cop to aggravated assault if we give her the option.'

'Sod that. She went after her next-door-neighbour with a carving knife, I'm no' settling for anything less than attempted murder.' Steel pursed her lips and swivelled back and forth in her office chair for a minute. 'Anything else?'

Logan slapped the papers out on her desk, one at a time. 'Forensics found trace fibres when they did the rape kit on Laura McEwan, and they think they've got enough DNA for a match if we can get them a suspect. Fingerprints have come back on the Oldmeldrum Post Office job. Looks like our friend Mr Maclean is up to his old tricks again.'

'Get him picked up.' The inspector crammed the last two inches of bread and bacon into her mouth then lobbed its tinfoil wrapper into the bin. Mumbling, 'She shoots, she scores!'

'No need – Traffic arrested him for drink driving last night. Out celebrating his "windfall".' Logan stuck the final sheet on her desk.

'Last but not least, another batch of counterfeit twenties turned up. That private bank on Albyn Terrace called yesterday to say someone tried to deposit four and half grand's worth.'

She pursed her lips and went, 'Hmmm. . .' for a while. 'And what did DI Beardy want?'

'Me to do his sodding job for him.'

'All right, settle down, settle down.' Detective Chief Inspector Finnie had the kind of face normally found under a wet rock: wide rubbery lips, floppy Hugh Grant hairstyle, beady little eyes. He stood at the front of the new CID office, with his back to the whiteboards, waiting for silence.

Logan wheeled his office chair out from the walled-off section reserved for detective sergeants, and settled down next to Steel while she fiddled with her phone.

The large room smelled of fresh paint, fresh coffee, and second-hand curry. It wasn't even as if they could open a window: there weren't any. But it was still a lot better than the cramped hovel they used to work in upstairs. The middle of the office was divided up into six cubicles, each lined with beech-veneer desks – arranged so the constables could sit back to back – separated by low walls of purple fabric.

Nine fifteen and the whole CID dayshift was there – eighteen detective constables, four detective sergeants, three detective inspectors – fidgeting as Finnie took them through the usual day-to-day morning briefing. Waiting for him to get to the reason they'd all been allowed to slob about in the office for the last two and a quarter hours, drinking coffee and moaning about the football.

'Next up.' Finnie checked his notes. 'You'll have seen in our *illustrious* local press that we've got a special visitor staying with us for the foreseeable future.' He held up a copy of that morning's *Aberdeen Examiner*, the headline 'SEX-BEAST TO SETTLE IN NORTH EAST' stretching above a blurry photo of a man in a shell suit. Richard Knox.

'Aye,' said someone at the back, 'like we don't have enough perverts of our own to deal with.'

'I'm *sorry*,' Finnie turned a blistering smile on the room, 'did I give the *impression* this briefing was open to audience participation? Did I? Because I don't remember doing that.'

No one spoke.

'Let's *try* and behave like professionals, shall we children? For a *change*?'

He turned and pointed to the large figure sitting at the front of the room. 'This is Detective Superintendent Danby from Northumbria Police, the man who put Knox away in the first place. DSI Danby has kindly agreed to come up here, brief us, and help liaise with Sacro. Superintendent?'

Danby levered himself to his feet, turned, and nodded at everyone. 'Right, Richard Knox. . .' The DSI's big bass voice filled the CID room just as easily as it had the patrol car. He picked up a long, black remote control and pointed it at the huge plasma TV bolted to the back wall between the little kitchen recess and the lockers.

Everyone swivelled around in their chairs.

Knox's face appeared on the screen, staring out at them with a black eye and a swollen lip. It was an old photo, from back when Knox had more hair, but other than that he was still the same weedy-looking rodent.

'Richard Albert Knox was convicted of the illegal imprisonment and rape of a sixty-eight-year-old man suffering from dementia.' Danby pressed the button on the remote again, and an old man's torso filled the screen, covered in bruises, scabs and bite marks. 'William Brucklay was held for three days and subjected to repeated, violent sexual assaults. Chained up in the basement, beaten, abused, forced to eat dog food. A *sixty-eight*-year-old man. . . You know what I'm saying?'

Danby paused for a moment. 'At the trial, Knox claimed the victim was a willing sexual partner who liked a bit of rough. Judge gave him ten years.'

Another click, and Knox's face was back, grinning in front of a bland concrete slab of a building. 'He was out in less than seven, released on licence, and he's been living under twenty-four-hour supervision ever since. We know Knox was responsible for at least six other attacks on older men before we caught him, but we couldn't prove it.'

Danby pressed something else and the TV screen went

blank. 'Don't be fooled by the weedy-strip-of-piss-God-is-my-co-pilot exterior – Richard Knox is a violent sexual predator who gets off on other people's pain.'

There was a moment's silence, then the same voice as before piped up from the back: 'So why the hell are we getting lumbered with him?'

'He's served his time.' Danby folded his huge arms. 'We've got no legal right to restrict his movements any more. If it was up to me he'd be stuck in a little dark hole for the rest of his natural, you know what I'm saying? But as of three months ago he can go wherever he likes.'

One of the uniformed PCs stuck up a hand. 'Yeah, but why Aberdeen?'

'Because blood's thicker than water.'

5

'Hold on, maybe this'll help. . .' PC Guthrie yanked open the curtains, unleashing a cloud of dust. Pale grey morning light oozed in through the grubby bay window. If anything, it just made the place look worse.

Once upon a time the velvet curtains were probably a rich red, but now they were the colour of dried blood. The wallpaper was a collection of faded roses and vines, the room's corners infested with the familiar black spider webs of mildew. Standard lamps with tasselled edging, a sagging couch, a nest of tables, a mantelpiece weighed down with dusty porcelain figurines.

The sour taint of ancient cat pee.

Steel wrinkled her nose. 'No' exactly *Better Homes and Gardens*, is it?'

Logan had to agree. The whole place looked like the contents of a bring and buy sale, circa 1975. 'Could do with a bit of a clean.'

Richard Knox stood in the middle of the worn carpet, one hand on the back of a rickety armchair, and smiled. 'I think it's perfect. . .'

It was a rundown detached house in Cornhill, with an

overgrown front garden, sagging gutters, moss-covered roof, and peeling paintwork.

A pair of black-and-white photographs hung on the wall above the fireplace, one of a dour-looking man in an old-fashioned suit, the other a severe woman with a fifties haircut and scowl.

'I never met me real grandfather.' Knox stared up at them. 'The Lord took him when me mother was still a little girl. But Granny Murray was a terror, you know? Always banging on about Jesus this, and Bible that.' Knox smiled. 'Wish I'd listened to her when I had the chance, like. Bet things would've turned out very different for us if I'd found God before the Devil found me.'

Creepy little bastard. Ever since they'd arrived at the manky old house he'd been practically glowing.

They followed him from room to room, opening the curtains, upsetting the dust and mould, ending up in a double bedroom at the back of the house overlooking a long back garden choked with bushes and weeds. The large bed drooped in the middle, its quilted cover pockmarked and cat-clawed. Knox settled on the edge, clutching the same old battered carrier bag to his chest.

A woman's head poked around the door: John Lennon glasses, chubby cheeks, short curly ginger hair. A hamster in a lumberjack shirt who'd introduced herself as PC Somethingorother from the Offender Management Unit. 'Seems OK to me, location-wise, but I'm still not happy about Richard staying here. Might be a bit risky with it belonging to a relation and all.'

DSI Danby shook his head. 'You don't have to worry about that. Euphemia Murray remarried after Knox's grandfather died. Even if someone gets hold of his mother's maiden name, it won't be the same as the old woman's.'

25

Knox smiled. 'Outlived two husbands, didn't she? You have to admire that.'

The DSI pulled a sheet of paper from his pocket. 'Before we leave you in the capable hands of Constable Irvine and her team, we have to go through the terms of your SOPO.'

Knox groaned, then flopped back on the quilt, provoking another puff of dust from the ancient fabric. 'Do we have to? I mean—'

'Yes we do.' Danby handed the paperwork to Logan. 'Do the honours will you, Sergeant?'

Logan cleared his throat. 'Sexual Offences Prevention Order for Richard Albert Knox, Thirty-Five Cairnview Terrace, Aberdeen. Applied for by Chief Constable Brian Anderson and approved by Sheriff McNab. This order is valid for five years from today's date and lays out—'

'How about,' said Danby, 'we skip the bumph and get to the conditions?'

'Oh, right . . . er. . . You will not go within two hundred yards of any retirement home or recreation centre where older men might congregate. You will not contact any other registered sex offender.'

Knox gave a theatrical sigh. 'You know, the power of God *can* change a man. There's no sinner so desperate that he cannot be redeemed.'

DI Steel laughed, thumbs jabbing away at the keypad on her mobile phone. 'Aye, right.'

'You will not consume alcohol outside of your place of residence.'

'Pffffff. . . I'm surprised you got *that* one past a judge.'

'You will not accost any member of the public—'

Frown. 'What?'

Danby's voice rumbled out from the corner. 'It means if you're alone with anyone, and you make them feel un-comfortable, we can lock you up for five years.'

'That's not fair! I can't control if someone feels uncomfortable, can I?' Knox waved a hand at him. 'Anyway, what about confession? Have to be alone with me priest, don't I?'

Danby scowled. 'You're a Protestant, you don't *have* confession.'

'Well . . . what about the people watching us then? Me keepers?'

PC Hamster fiddled with her glasses. 'You don't have to worry about that, Richard, there's going to be two of them at all times. We've got a specialist team from Sacro who're going to keep an eye on things. You'll be fine.'

'You will not drive any vehicle without a member of your supervisory team present.'

Knox shrugged and collapsed backwards until he was lying down, staring at the ceiling, his legs dangling over the side of the bed. The mattress creaked.

'When I was little, I remember hearing them in here. Granny Murray and Grandad Joe. They must have been in their sixties or seventies, but they still did it every Friday night, regular as clockwork. You could hear the squeak of the springs from me room. . .'

He swung his legs, making the mattress groan in time to the motions.

'The pair of them going at it in here while I was in the next room. Don't think she really enjoyed it like, but it was her duty, you know? Keep the old man's urges satisfied.'

'Right.' DI Steel pushed herself away from the wall and slipped her mobile back in her pocket. 'I've had enough of Creepy Sod Theatre for one morning. We done here?'

Logan checked. 'Two more: you shall not visit any gay bars, clubs, or associations. And you will not obstruct the efforts of any supervising agency. That's the lot. Do you understand these restrictions?'

The weedy little man flopped an arm over his eyes. 'I suppose.'

Logan passed the paperwork back to Danby. 'You want a lift back to the station?'

'What?' Knox sat up. 'You're not leaving us, are you Graeme? You were right quiet on the plane. I was hoping you'd join us for dinner: you know, get a nice curry and some poppadoms? We can catch up a bit, like. Reminisce about the good old days. You, me, and Billy Adams. . .'

Danby stiffened, then turned to look out of the bedroom window. 'A lift would be good.'

'So,' Steel cracked open the passenger window and flicked a disk of chewed gum at a passing taxi, 'you want to tell us why a detective superintendent traipses halfway up the country to babysit a manky wee rapist like Richard Knox?'

Danby shrugged, his huge shoulders going up and down as he stared at the passing scenery. 'Maybe I just fancied a jolly to Aberdeen.'

'Aye, and maybe my arse is made of Toblerone.'

Sitting in the back with the DSI, Logan tried not to picture that.

They'd let PC Guthrie drive. He joined the queue of traffic waiting to turn left onto Westburn Road, juddering to a halt inches from the back end of a bendy bus.

A park ran along the side of the road, complete with pond and bored-looking ducks, the dark scribble of bare trees. Other than that, the place was nearly empty, just a mother and her small child hauling a yapping terrier across the wide expanse of browny-green.

Danby sniffed. 'Can't believe you've got no snow. We were up to our ears in Newcastle this morning.'

'OK, let's try this another way, shall we?' Steel produced a packet of nicotine gum and popped a white pellet out of its foil blister. Chewing with her mouth open. 'Who's Billy Adams?'

'It's not important.'

'Sounded important.'

Danby's face hardened. 'Drop it, you know what I'm saying?'

'That an order, sir?'

'Call it a request.' He turned to Logan. 'These Sacroid people, they up to keeping an eye on Knox?'

'Sacro: Safeguarding Communities – Reducing Offending. It's a charity, biggest provider of supported accommodation for offenders in Scotland, got teams of volunteers watching people like Knox all over the country. Well, maybe not *exactly* like Knox, but yeah, they're up to it.'

Steel rolled her window back up. 'You know, I'm going to find out eventually, so you might as well spill the beans.'

Silence.

'See, I'm what you'd call a tenacious wee sod.'

More silence.

'Seriously, I can be a right pain in the arse when I put my mind to—'

'That's *enough* Inspector. You do your job and I'll do mine, know what I'm saying?'

And this time the silence lasted all the way back to the station.

'I love a good mystery.' DI Steel sat behind her desk, one hand stuffed down the front of her shirt, rearranging the contents of her bra. 'God gave me a nose for a reason – so I could stick it in other people's business. Who do you think this "Billy Adams" is?'

Logan shrugged and dumped the plastic bag from Marks & Spencer on the inspector's desk. 'They didn't have any of the big ones left.' He cleared a space between the burglary reports and trial-preparation documents, then pulled out two little boxes of sushi, a packet of cheese and onion, and a bottle of Diet Coke.

Steel popped open the crisps, stuffed a handful into her mouth, then followed it up with a California roll. 'Maybe he's Danby's boyfriend?'

Logan dug into the bag again: prawn salad and a sparkling mineral water.

Steel scowled at him. 'Salad? Jesus, all this time and I never knew you were turning into a shirtlifter. Still,' a smile spread across her face, 'if that means your tasty IB tart's up for a bit of extracurricular. . .?'

'I'm on a diet, OK?'

'Bout time. You've turned into a right porky wee sod.' Something in her pocket went '*bleep*' and Steel pulled out her mobile phone, frowning at the screen. 'Sodding hell. . . Thought it was my chiz. Been trying to get hold of him all day.' She washed a salmon nigiri down with a mouthful of Diet Coke. 'Finish your gayboy salad, then get digging: I want to know who this "Billy Adams" is, and I want to know how he's connected to DSI Fat-and-Shouty: anything you can find.'

'Beattie wants me to—'

'Don't care.' She stuck her fingers in her ears. 'La-la-la-la-la. Can you see me no' caring?'

'You're not the one he's whinging at the whole bloody time.'

'Which part of "La-la-la-la-la" do you no' understand?' She popped a fingernail of wasabi into her mouth and made dog's-bum faces for a minute. 'Then we're going to have to go do something about these counterfeit twenties.'

'I mean, why did they bother promoting him? My arse would make a better DI.'

'Get onto that bank. Tell them I want security camera footage, see if we can't find out who made the deposit.'

'Do you never read the stuff I give you?' Logan went digging through the pile of paperwork in the inspector's in-tray, coming out with the printouts he'd slapped down on her desk before the morning briefing. 'Here.' He tried to pass them over, but Steel had a cucumber maki in one hand and a bunch of cheese and onion crisps in the other.

'Eating. You read it.'

'We've already got an ID – the guy tried to deposit the cash into his own account. Kevin Middleton. Only prior he's got is for drink driving twelve years ago, wrapped his Jag around a lamppost in Cults after some charity auction.'

Steel smiled as she chewed. 'Perfect. Arrest the silly bugger, then we can all get on with our lives. You thought any more about being Godparent, by the way?'

Logan almost choked on his salad. 'I. . . Erm. . .' Mouthful of water. 'I don't know if. . . Ahem.' Pause. 'Anyway, how come the Perv Patrol aren't dealing with Knox? How come this is our problem?'

The inspector's eyes narrowed, making all the wrinkles stand out. 'Our lord and master DCI Finnie thinks the Offender Management Unit need someone senior to person- ally oversee Knox's case. *Apparently* it's too high profile. *Apparently* I have experience with sexual predators. *Apparently* I'm the best person to support the Diddy Men in this diffi- cult and delicate operation.'

She scrunched up her empty crisp packet and hurled it at the bin. Missed. 'Which means Frog-Face Finnie knows Knox is an odious wee shite, and if anything goes wrong, I'll be the one carrying the can.'

'Maybe it won't be that bad?'

'Course it bloody will: Knox'll need someone watching him till the day he dies. So I'll no' get shot of him till I retire. It's the gift that keeps on sodding giving.' Steel scowled. 'But don't you worry: I *shall* have my revenge. Meantime, you go see what you can get on this Billy Adams bloke Danby's being so secretive about.'

6

'Aw, Jesus, not *again*!' Detective Sergeant Mark MacDonald wrinkled his nose, then slapped a hand over his face, hiding his wee goatee beard. 'Ack. . .' He grabbed a folder from his in-tray and fanned it back and forth, sending paperwork fluttering across Logan's desk.

'What are you. . .' Logan frowned, and then the smell hit him. 'Bloody hell, Bob!'

DS Bob Marshall just grinned. If God existed, He hadn't been paying a lot of attention when He'd put Bob together. Big ears stuck out at right-angles from a square head with a bald patch at the back and a single, thick eyebrow at the front. Arms like hairy string. A monkey in a machine-washable suit.

'Christ!' Mark blinked, then hauled the door open. 'What've you been eating?'

Bob patted the sides of his stomach. 'Can't beat cauliflower cheese and chips.'

'Oh no it's *everywhere*. . .' Logan stood, backing away into the corner of the little walled-off section of the CID office, built to house the detective sergeants. Six desks – four for dayshift, two for night – all but one covered in drifts of paperwork and ring binders, monitor, keyboard, and over-flowing in-tray. The walls were just about visible between the procedural flowcharts, a corkboard covered with mugshots and memos, a whiteboard with each DS's name written above a list of active cases, another one with a schematic of some drug dealer's house scrawled in blue marker pen. And a yellow-and-black biohazard triangle mounted above Bob's desk.

Mark wafted the door open and closed, and open and closed. . . 'Never mind fucking Iraq, bloody United Nations should invade your arse. That's a weapon of mass destruction, right there!'

'I can't help it if I'm talented.'

Gradually the smell faded, and people got back to work.

Logan finished a report on two indecent exposures in Trinity Cemetery – you'd have to be a brave man to wave your willy about in January in Aberdeen – then called up his internet browser and went looking for Billy Adams. 12,900,000 results in Google.

He refined the search criteria, narrowing it down to Newcastle. 358 results. Apparently there was a featherweight boxer called Billy Adams in the fifties, a guitarist with Dexy's Midnight Runners in the eighties, a bunch of businessmen, some football fans. . . Then Logan included Knox's name in the search.

An article from the *Newcastle Evening Chronicle* was top of the list: 'MISSING OFFICER'S BODY FOUND.'

There were more links to the *Newcastle Journal, News Post Leader, Sunday Sun, Morpeth Herald,* and *Whitley Bay News Guardian.* Even a few of the national broadsheets had got in on the act. Logan clicked on the *Chronicle* link.

Under the headline was a photo of a blue SOC tent, the kind you put up to preserve a crime scene. It was surrounded by patchy bushes with some trees and the leg of a pylon in the background, an IB technician in protective gear walking towards the camera, carrying a black plastic box. Further down the article there was another photo: a smiling man with short blond hair, squint nose, blue eyes. According to the caption, it was 'DETECTIVE INSPECTOR BILLY ADAMS (42)'

Apparently they'd found his body in the family Ford Mondeo on a patch of wasteland to the north of Newcastle. The story didn't have a lot of detail on the cause of death – not surprisingly – concentrating instead on how police search teams had been looking for Adams since he'd gone missing from his home the Wednesday before. There was a quote from his wife. One from the detective inspector who'd headed up the search. Another from the young man who'd found the car. And a small potted history of DI Adams's career. Drug seizures, three murder enquiries, one high-profile kidnapping that ended in disaster. . .

Logan dug the phone out from under a pile of partially completed crime reports and called Northumbria Police Headquarters.

'Well?' Detective Inspector Beardy Beattie's office was crowded with box files – piled up on the carpet, the shelves, the windowsill, even the visitor's chair. So Logan had to stand. The only place not covered in boxes was Beattie's desk. That was covered in biscuit crumbs and paperwork.

Logan handed over the indecent exposure report. 'He's done it twice that we know of, probably more. Young mothers with pushchairs every time.'

Beattie sat forward, eyebrows raised. 'Maybe he's not flashing the mothers at all, you think of that? *Maybe* he's flashing the kids!' The DI smiled, obviously pleased with his deductive reasoning. Like a podgy Sherlock Holmes, who'd been dropped on his head as a child.

'Don't be daft George. He's picking victims he knows aren't

going to chase after him. You going to abandon your baby in a graveyard to go running after some pervert who's just shown you his dick?'

'Oh.' Beattie picked at a coffee stain on his new desk. 'What about the counterfeit goods?'

'Did you speak to Trading Standards, like I told you?'

'I . . . erm . . . was hoping we could go over there together. You know, show a united front?'

'Just call them, OK? We shouldn't even be dealing with it: hookie goods is a job for the Shop Cops.'

'Yes, but the sheer volume of—'

'Still their job.'

'Finnie wants us to do that Interagency Cooperation thing: us, Trading Standards and Customs.' Beattie shuffled through some of the mess on his desk. 'It shouldn't take long, just a couple of hours and—'

'You'll have to take it up with Steel. I've got stuff to do for her all day.'

Beattie's bottom lip protruded, his eyebrows pinching up in the middle. The 'lost puppy' look. 'But Finnie wants to see progress.'

'Then go get Biohazard Bob or Mark to help. Or Doreen. Eh? How about giving her some sodding work for a change instead of lumping it all on me?'

'Fine.' The inspector went back to his files, face turning pink. 'I'll call Trading Standards myself.'

Logan left him to it.

'Bloody thing. . .' DI Steel jabbed at the latch of her office window with a fork, digging the tines into the mechanism.

Logan closed the door and slumped in the visitor's seat. 'Tell me *again* why they promoted Beardy Beattie?'

'It's no' safe making the windows so you can't open the bastards more than an inch. What if there's a fire?'

'Useless tosser couldn't investigate a septic tank for jobbies.'

She jabbed the fork into the catch again. 'Give us a hand, eh?'

'Thought you were supposed to be cutting down on the fags?'

'This is an infringement of my human rights. . . Open you bastard!'

They struggled with the mechanism for a minute, before Steel managed to stab herself in the thumb with her fork. 'Ffffffffffffffffffff. . .' She screwed her face up, then hurled the stainless steel thing in the bin. 'FUCK!' Steel slumped into her office chair and stuck her bleeding thumb in her mouth.

'Why can't you go outside for a cigarette, like a normal person?'

Steel just scowled at him.

'Whatever.' Logan pulled out his notebook. 'Billy Adams. AKA: Detective *Inspector* Billy Adams, Northumbria Police. Did a lot of anti-gang stuff, and some undercover work on a big Newcastle mobster called Maitland. Killed himself about six weeks after Knox got sent down. And I mean *seriously* killed himself.'

She pulled her thumb out of her mouth. 'What the hell's that supposed to mean?'

'According to the sergeant I spoke to, DI Adams swallowed enough antidepressants to cheer up a whole bouncy castle full of goths, a bottle of gin, and the barrel of a shotgun.'

'No sodding about for our Billy, then.'

'Blew a big hole in the roof of the family Mondeo, in the grounds of some disused factory. Been there four days in the sun before they found the body. The magpies had been at him.'

Steel went back to sucking her thumb, mumbling around the digit, 'So why's Danby being all touchy about it?'

'No idea.' Logan shifted forward in his seat. 'I went for a

dig in Knox's file too, in case there was a connection there. He's got big chunks marked "restricted". No details.'

'That'll be those other rapes Danby was waffling about. Would've been before the Soham murders, back when we all thought we had to be so sodding sensitive about unsubstantiated accusations going on some dirty bastard's permanent record. Bloody Data Protection Act bollocks.'

Logan shrugged. She was probably right.

Silence.

Then she stood. 'Get your coat, we're off to see a man about some dodgy twenties.'

'Nah, business is shite, truth be told.' The man in the oil-smudged blue boilersuit spoke over his shoulder while a scabby kettle grumbled to a boil. 'Bloody recession barely made a dent in Aberdeen, but suddenly no one wants to buy a car. You know? Hypocritical bastards.'

The office faced out onto what looked like an old cattle yard, the grey concrete floor host to a multicoloured array of second-hand cars crammed in bumper-to-bumper with 'DEAL OF THE WEEK!!!' signs taped to the windscreens. A couple of calendars hung on the white breezeblock walls, all featuring spanners and bits of mechanical equipment. DI Steel finished flipping through one and pulled a face, before perching herself on the edge of the battered desk. 'Whatever happened to nudie women?'

'Milk, two sugars, right?' He ladled coffee granules into three mugs, lined up along the windowsill.

'Aye.'

Logan shook his head. 'Just milk for me.'

'OK. . .' He poured in the hot water, steam turning the window opaque, blocking out the forecourt. The garage was hidden away down a country road, somewhere between Westhill and the Loch of Skene, surrounded by trees and fields full of grumbling cattle.

'Mr Middleton.' Logan watched him sniff a carton of semi-skimmed milk. 'Are you *sure* you wouldn't recognize the man who gave you the cash?'

Middleton sploshed milk into their coffees. 'Dunno. Never saw him before.'

Steel accepted her mug, wrapping her hands around it and breathing in the hot steam. 'If I was a suspicious wee sod – which I am – I'd be tempted to say your mystery man with a handful of dodgy twenties never existed. It was just you, trying to launder the stuff.'

Kevin Middleton stiffened. 'You think I'd be daft enough to pay counterfeit cash into my own bank account? How thick would I have to be?'

Steel shrugged. 'Maybe you thought they'd be good enough to pass the bank's tests?'

Middleton laughed, then settled into the swivel chair behind his desk. 'You're kidding, right? If I wanted to clean some money, I'd go down the bookies. Or the casino. Or to one of them dog nights in Dundee. *Somehow* I get the feeling a bank would know what to look for.'

'Right, right.' Steel looked at him, her head tilted to one side. 'You've obviously given this a lot of thought.'

'What's that supposed to mean?'

'Come on, you don't think it's a wee bit odd: some tadger comes in here with over four thousand pounds in crisp new twenties wanting to buy one of your manky motors?'

'A lot of people doing business in readies now. No bugger trusts them thieving dicks in the banks any more. Safer keeping it under the mattress.'

'And if it's cash, you can *accidentally* forget to mention it to the tax man, right?'

Middleton's face darkened. 'I'm the victim here, OK? Four and a half grand I'm down! Not to mention one Honda Civic.'

Logan took a sip of instant coffee: bitter, burnt tasting,

little beads of fat glimmering on the surface. 'If you sold the car, you've got the buyer's details, yes? On the registration documents?'

Middleton coughed, swivelled back and forth in his chair, stared at a parts catalogue. 'Look, maybe this is all going a bit too far. I mean the bloke probably didn't know the cash was—'

Steel cut him off. 'Don't talk shite. Give us the guy's details, or I'm dragging you down the station and doing you for passing counterfeit money and trying to poison a police officer with crap cheapo coffee.'

Middleton glowered in silence for a bit, then stood and muttered his way to a beige filing cabinet in the corner of the office. He went rummaging through one of the drawers, and came out with a registration document. He held it out and Steel snatched it off him, gave it a cursory glance, then chucked it to Logan. 'Read.'

Logan opened it up and scanned the new keeper section, carefully printed in blue biro. 'You know you're meant to send this off to the DVLA, right?'

'How come you bastards aren't out there arresting paedophiles and bloody muggers, eh?'

'Blah, blah, blah.' Steel took another sip and grimaced. 'We got an address?'

'Car's registered to a Douglas Walker in Peterculter.'

'There you go, wasn't so difficult now, was it?' Steel clunked her mug down on the desk and stood, rubbing the seat of her trousers. 'Come on Sergeant, let's get out of here before Mr Middleton threatens to make more coffee.'

Logan followed her out onto the forecourt, buttoning up his jacket against the cold. Brambles scratched along the dry-stane dyke that bordered the lot, their dark-brown skeletons speckled with frost where the weak sun hadn't managed to reach yet. He dug his hands deep into his pockets, then froze, staring at one of the vehicles: a red Honda Civic.

He checked the registration documents again. 'Inspector?'

Steel kept on walking, pulling out her phone.

Behind him, Logan could hear Kevin Middleton locking the garage up. Then the man was hurrying past, weaving his way between the used cars towards a Range Rover parked at the kerb.

Logan shouted across to him. 'Where, *exactly*, do you think you're going?'

'Erm, dentist appointment?'

Steel leant back against the CID pool car, poking away at her phone's keypad. 'Hurry up; sodding perishing out here. My nipples get any pointier they'll put someone's eye out.'

Logan nodded towards the Honda. 'This is the car he says he sold for four and a half grand.'

'Er . . . no it isn't. Just cos it's the same make—'

'And the same colour, and the same number plate.' Logan held up the registration documents. 'Want to explain that?'

'It. . . Er . .' Middleton sagged back against a Ford Fiesta, staring up at the low grey sky, breath steaming out as he swore. 'I got it back. OK?'

'Oh yeah?'

'Come on, it was four and a half grand!'

'Which you're no doubt claiming back on your insurance.' Logan ran his eyes over the collection of cars on the fore-court. 'Have you had a visit from Trading Standards recently, Mr Middleton? Checking the odometers aren't clocked? All the vehicles are roadworthy? No cut-and-shut jobs?'

'What was I supposed to do? I'm a small businessman, I can't afford to have people ripping me off! You know how it—'

'Oh for God's sake.' Steel stomped her feet. 'Shut up the pair of you. I'm cold and I'm bored and if it's all the same to you, I'd kinda like to get home before the next sodding ice age sets in.' She turned her back on them. 'Logan, get your arse in gear. We're leaving.'

'But—'

'*Now*.' She clambered into the passenger seat and slammed the car door.

Brilliant. Nothing like being supported by your senior officer. Logan pointed a finger at Middleton. 'This isn't over.'

'Thanks a lot.' Logan changed gear and put his foot down, overtaking a minibus on the dual carriageway. 'That was really nice. Empowering.' The traffic was getting heavier the closer they got to the Kingswells roundabout. Rush-hour congealing the arteries leading in and out of Aberdeen like a deep-fried Mars Bar.

Steel cracked open the pool car window and blew a stream of smoke out into the cold afternoon, mobile phone clamped to her ear. 'What did you want to do? Arrest him? Impound all his stock? Spend the rest of the night filling in sodding paperwork?'

'He's dodgy.'

'Shock horror, a dodgy second-hand car dealer. Who would've thunk it? That *has* to be a first.'

'He's—'

'Come on Steve, pick up the bloody phone!' She squinted her face up, cigarette gripped between her front teeth. 'Finnie's getting a DI down from Fraserburgh to cover my cases while I'm away. Try and no' whinge too much when you're working for him, eh? Make it look like I run a tight ship.'

'Brilliant. Bring someone else in.' Logan gripped the steering wheel tighter.

'Steve, it's your mum. Where the hell are you? Call me back.' She snapped her phone shut. 'Voicemail.'

'*I* could've run the caseload. *I* know it all inside out. I'm already doing all the bloody work. Instead of which I'm going to have to hold some Teuchter numpty's—'

'Wah, wah, wah. You're such a bloody moan. Just be thankful I didn't let them hand everything over to Beattie.'

Small mercies.

Steel stuck the phone back in her jacket. 'Can't decide if I'm more pissed off or worried about Steve.'

'Steve who?'

'Polmont, my chiz.'

Which explained the, 'it's your mum' bit – keeping it all secretive, in case anyone else heard the message.

Logan frowned. 'How come you even know his name? Personal info's meant to stay on the other side of the "sterile corridor", or whatever rubbish they're calling it now. Who else knows who he is?'

'No one.' She flicked ash out of the window. 'Just me, Frog-Face Finnie, and now you.'

'Thought all informant stuff was meant to be handled by the Spook Squad? Why—'

'Look it just is, OK? And shut up.' She took an angry sook on her cigarette. 'This is top, top Secret Squirrel. Understand?'

Logan sighed. 'I think I can—'

'I'm no' joking. This gets out, I swear to God I'll wear your wee heterosexual arsehole as a foot warmer. He's a sparky at Malk the Knife's building site.'

'He's the one we were waiting for on Monday? Told you: no one's going to be daft enough to squeal. What is he, suicidal?'

'That's what I'm afraid of. . . Poor wee bugger could be lying dead in a ditch for all I know.'

'So go round his house, pay him a visit.'

She sniffed. 'Don't have an address.'

'Then get a GSM trace on his mobile. If it doesn't move overnight, that's his house.' Logan stuck his foot on the clutch, popped the pool car out of gear, and drifted to a halt at the back of a long line of traffic. 'What about the counterfeit cash? Want to get a warrant organized for the guy who bought the car?'

'Tonight?' Steel stared at him. 'Are you *mental*? Be after five by the time we get back to the ranch. Get some back-shift troglodyte to pick the bugger up. I'm going home.'

'But—'

'Don't make me "La-la-la-la-la" you again.'

7

'. . .celebrations outside the offices of McLennan Homes. Back to you in the studio.'

The picture jumped to a balding anchorman with an unfeasible moustache. 'Thanks, Tim.' That familiar, blurry photo of Richard Knox they'd used on the front page of the Aberdeen Examiner appeared on the screen. 'A convicted rapist took up residence in the Grampian Region today. . .'

Logan turned the sound down, then cracked the ring pull on another tin of Stella. Cold beer after a hot curry. Singing wafted through from the bathroom, Samantha doing her best to murder a Marilyn Manson cover of a Soft Cell version of a Gloria Jones song.

But it was still better than listening to yet another report about Richard Creepy-Pants Knox setting up home in Aberdeen. The anchorman disappeared from the screen, replaced by a lumpy woman mouthing angry somethings at the camera. Probably complaining about Grampian Police mollycoddling perverts when there were drunken yobs hanging about outside her local community centre.

Logan toasted her with his tin of beer.

Then it was over to the weather. Which apparently was going to be crap for the foreseeable future.

A standard January in the north-east of Scotland, then.

'What you watching?'

Logan turned to see Samantha standing in the lounge doorway, wearing a pink fluffy bathrobe and a pink towel turban. She even had pink fluffy socks on. 'You're looking very goth tonight.'

She stuck her middle finger up at him. 'Any beer left?'

'Fridge. And there's a film coming on at half ten, if you fancy it?'

'Got an early start tomorrow.' She plonked herself down on the couch and stole a scoof of his beer. 'Your mum was on the phone earlier.'

Logan groaned.

'Relax, I told her you'd died of dysentery.' Samantha unwrapped the towel from her head, and rubbed at the bright red hair it had been hiding. 'Oh, and some bloke called Reuben called? Wouldn't leave a message.'

Fuck. . . Reuben.

Logan cleared his throat. 'Didn't say anything at all?'

'Nada. Your mum wants us to go round for Sunday lunch to discuss, and I quote, "access to her grandchild".'

What the hell did Reuben want?

Silence.

'You know, if you get over your fatal bout of the squits?'

And how the hell did he get their home number?

'Logan?'

'Hmm?' He looked up. 'Sorry, miles away.'

'Tell you what,' Samantha undid the tie on the front of her robe, 'maybe I've got something here that'll bring you back from the dead. . .'

'What's he doing?'

Mandy wrinkled her nose. 'Praying, I think.'

45

Harry peered around the doorway at the figure kneeling in front of the broken three-bar electric fire. The whole house smelled of damp and mould. Dark and creepy. Dank and creaky. Harry put his hands in his pockets and cleared his throat. 'He's a bit . . . you know? I mean, you saw the papers, right?'

Mandy turned and smiled at him. She was pretty. Brown curly hair. A little black mole at the corner of her mouth. A bit on the chunky side, but that just gave you something to hang onto, didn't it? Not that Harry would ever say anything. Well, you don't, do you? Not when you work together. But still. . . she had tremendous knockers.

She punched him on the arm. 'Worried our boy's going to find you irresistible?'

'Ha-ha.' Harry shifted from one foot to the other. 'Anyway, Knox likes auld mannies. And in case it skipped your attention, I'm in the prime of life.' If you could call a divorced forty-three-year-old man with a receding hairline and expanding waistline in the prime of anything.

'Yeah, yeah.' Mandy went back to staring at Knox. 'Shouldn't you be getting some kip? It's nearly midnight, and you're on at six.'

Harry shrugged again. 'Can't sleep the first night in a strange house. You?'

'Like a log.'

Harry tore his eyes away from the fine hairs at the nape of her neck. 'I hear he attacked more than a dozen pensioners in Newcastle. Chained them up like dogs.'

Mandy put her head on one side, still staring at the praying man. 'Had to watch a paedophile once. Primary school gym teacher. Abusing little girls in the changing rooms. Got away with it for seven years.'

'Jesus. . .'

'Watched him for three weeks, till he slashed his throat with the lid off a tin of tuna. Bathroom looked like a horror

46

movie, blood everywhere.' She sighed. 'Ruined a perfectly good pair of shoes.'

'There's a lovely image.'

'Point is, he was never going to be a hundred percent safe: didn't matter how long it took, he was always going to see six-year-old girls as sex objects. If he hadn't topped himself, I'd probably still be watching him now. Knox is the same. Did it before, he'll do it again.' She shrugged. 'If we're not here to watch him.'

Harry tried a smile. 'Good job I got in a couple packets of HobNobs then.'

She nodded at the man kneeling on the threadbare hearthrug. 'Maybe you should have bought some tins of tuna. . .'

Richard Albert Knox tries not to smile. He can see them, reflected in the dusty screen of the dead television. Standing there at the lounge door like a pair of old women, gossiping.

His knees ache, but that's all right. A little pain never did anyone any harm. Sometimes it did them a lot of good. And after all those years kneeling on the concrete floor of his cell, the tatty old rug's something of a luxury.

But all that time spent on his knees really paid off, you know? Not like some of them dirty bastards in Frankland Prison; the time *they* spent on their knees was for a different reason. Not that Richard had anything to do with that, thank you very much.

No.

Well . . . only once, and it wasn't like he had any option, was it? Not with a length of sharpened pipe waiting for him. They soon learned though, didn't they? Felt the wrath of God. No one bothered him after that.

He sneaks another look at his two minders from Sacro. Harry and Mandy. A right pair of do-gooders. *'Oh aren't we so special, volunteering to look after rapists and paedos?'* How stupid can they be?

Richard can't keep the smile off his face. They have no idea what's coming their way.

8

DC Rennie scowled. 'Is it me, or did the weather just get even crappier?'

Logan watched the windscreen wipers clunk and squeal across the glass. Rain drummed on the roof of the CID pool car, made spreading puddles on the uneven pavements, shivered the branches of a tall leylandii hedge. The little cul-de-sac was quiet, just a few kids being bustled into cars for the last-minute school run. 'You got the warrant?'

Rennie dug it out of his jacket pocket. His short blond hair stuck up in all directions, as if he'd just fallen out of bed, and his face had the kind of unnaturally orange fake-tan glow any D-list celebrity would be proud of. 'Thought nightshift were supposed to deal with this.'

Logan scanned the paperwork – all duly noted and authorized. 'You ready?'

'No.'

'Tough.' He opened the car door and hurried up the path to the semi-detached house, hop-skip-stepping to avoid the deepest puddles, Detective Constable Rennie sploshing along behind him.

They huddled under the little porch while Rennie thumbed the doorbell. 'Argh . . . it's trickling down the back of my neck!'

'Better watch it doesn't wash your tan off. You'll go all streaky.'

'Hey, at least I. . .'

The front door opened. A young man peered out at them: black eye, bruised cheek, and swollen lip, one arm encased in plaster from elbow to palm. The Police National Computer check said he was eighteen, he looked a lot younger. 'Yeah?'

'Mr Walker? Douglas Walker?'

He flinched, one hand coming up to shield his bruised face. 'Don't hit me!'

Logan held up his warrant card. 'Police.'

Walker sagged. Sighed, then turned and limped back into the building. 'Close the door behind you, yeah?'

Inside, it was a study in chintz. Walker levered himself down onto a floral sofa complete with lacy antimacassars. A gas fire hissed away to itself, the mantelpiece littered with glass ornaments, sparkling in the light of a standard lamp. Oil paintings covered the walls – scenes of Aberdeen in OTT gilt frames. Walker grimaced. 'This about that car?'

'What do you think?'

The young man stared at the swirly beige carpet. 'I didn't know, OK? I thought the cash was legit.'

'Let me guess,' Logan edged in front of the fire, letting his trousers steam, 'soon as you found out there was a problem, you were in such a hurry to give Kevin Middleton his car back, you fell down the stairs a couple of times?'

Walker sniffed. 'I'm not pressing charges. And you can't make me.'

Logan let the silence drag out for a while, but Walker kept his face towards the floor.

'You want to tell me where you got four and a half grand in dodgy twenties?'

He shook his head.

'OK.' Logan pulled out the warrant. 'Douglas Walker, it

is an offence to pass counterfeit moneys under section fifteen of the Forgery and Counterfeiting Act 1981, punishable by up to ten years in prison.'

At that, Walker *did* look up. His face pale, mouth working up and down. 'But. . . I. . .'

'I have a warrant here for your arrest. On your feet.'

'You can't. . .'

'Stand up, Mr Walker.'

'Oh Jesus. . .' He struggled upright, trying not to use his broken right arm. 'I didn't know, really I didn't!'

Logan slipped the papers back in his pocket. 'Do you want to come with us voluntarily, or shall we do it the hard way?'

Walker bit his bottom lip, setting it bleeding again.

Rennie took out his handcuffs and the young man whimpered.

'Voluntarily, I'll come voluntarily.'

'Good move.' Logan scribbled that down in his notebook, then got Walker to sign it. He pointed the eighteen-year-old towards the door. 'Anything I should know about before I get a team in here to tear the place apart?'

'My mum and dad are in Corfu. . .' He wiped a hand across his eyes. 'They'll kill me.'

Rennie grinned. 'If I was you, I'd be more worried about my new cellmate.' He made an obscene, pokey-pokey hand gesture.

Logan scowled at him. Then turned back to Walker. 'You got any more counterfeit money on the premises?'

Walker stared at the carpet again, snivelling. He took a deep, shuddering breath. 'There's another three grand in a holdall in my wardrobe.'

He led them upstairs to a medium-sized bedroom at the front of the house, overlooking the surrounding homes and south towards the River Dee, barely visible through the rain. An easel sat in front of the window, with a landscape of

Bennachie sketched out in rough charcoal strokes. The whole place smelled of linseed oil and turpentine.

Walker pointed at the wardrobe sitting next to an unmade single bed. 'In there.'

Rennie snapped on a pair of blue nitrile gloves and went rummaging.

Logan examined the canvas. 'Those paintings downstairs yours?'

'Yeah. . .' The young man sniffed. Rubbed at his eyes again. 'Doing a degree at Gray's School of Art.'

'They're good.'

He shrugged, a blush creeping up his cheeks. 'I was trying to capture the—'

'Got it!' Rennie dragged a black holdall from the mass of shoes and trainers, holding the handles wide apart so Logan could see inside. Lots of little folded bundles made of crisp twenty pound notes.

Logan told him to zip it up again. Then turned back to Walker. 'You sure you don't want to just fess up now? Save us all the legwork?'

'I . . . erm. . .' He sniffed. Looked out of the window at the rain-drenched landscape. 'Think I should speak to a lawyer.'

Logan slumped back in the visitor's chair and rubbed his face with his hands. 'Like interviewing a bloody cardboard cut-out.'

DI Steel picked one of the clear plastic evidence pouches from the pile on her desk and peered at the stack of notes inside. 'There's no' another couple of grand knocking about you forgot to sign into evidence, is there?'

Logan looked at her. 'What's that supposed to mean?'

She dumped the cash back on the desk. 'You any idea how much it's going to cost to put wee Jasmine through a decent school?'

'Jasmine?'

'If it's a girl.' She opened her top desk drawer and pulled out a set of screwdrivers and a pair of pliers. 'Want to help vandalize a window lock?'

'No.' Logan picked up the discarded packet of counterfeit cash. 'You notice it's all in drug-dealer-bundles? Four twenties laid flat, one twenty wrapped around them at ninety degrees, then the whole lot folded—'

'Aye, thanks, Captain Sesame Street, but I do actually know what a sodding DDB looks like. Detective Inspector, remember?'

'Just saying it's a bit odd, OK? Would have thought counterfeit notes would come in big stacks, hot off the presses. Looks like this lot's been done up for junkies and pushers.'

Steel selected a flat-head screwdriver from the set and swivelled her chair around, hunkering over the catch on her office window. 'What's Wallace saying about it?'

'Walker, not Wallace. Douglas Walker. He's saying bugger all, wants to speak to a lawyer first.'

'Jesus, no' again.' Dig, dig, poke, poke. . .

'Says he heard about that case where the European Court decided someone's human rights had been violated by not letting them have a lawyer during questioning.'

Steel sighed. 'Human rights my crinkle-cut arsehole. Tell you, the Americans got the right idea – waterboard the lot of them. Pass me those pliers, eh?'

Logan did as he was asked. 'Still say it'd be easier to go outside and smoke like a normal person.'

'You think this Walker kid's going to crack?'

'Going to let him stew for a couple of hours. Conned him into coming in on a volley, so there's no time limit. Maybe drop a few hints about doing a deal if he gives us his supplier. Usual vague lies.' Logan checked his watch. 'We got that MAPPA meeting in ten minutes. I'm off for a fag. Want one? Or you going to stay here practising your housebreaking?'

Steel sniffed, then dumped the screwdriver on her desk. 'Aye, what the hell.'

Outside, on the rear podium car park, it was teeth-chatteringly cold. The tall, rectangular 'U' shaped bulk of FHQ acted as a windbreak, but the granite buildings it backed onto blocked out the low sun, leaving the whole place shrouded in deep-freezer shadows.

Logan sparked up a cigarette, hands cupped around the glowing tip for warmth, Steel shivering beside him, finger-tips rammed into her armpits. Stomping her feet and swearing out a stream of white smoke and breath.

'Fuck me, it's cold.'

'Any word from your chiz yet?'

She grimaced. 'Bugger's still no' answering his phone. Got the GSM trace though, looks like he's staying somewhere south-east of Balmedie.'

'Want to take a run over after the MAPPA meeting?' Logan took a deep drag on his Benson and Hedges, then spluttered it out in a rumbling cough as the back door opened and the familiar, porky figure of DI Beardy Beattie lumbered out, hauling on an Arctic-explorer-style padded parka. Logan stuck two fingers up in the man's direction. 'Wanker.'

If Beattie heard, he pretended not to, just clambered into one of the CID pool cars and drove away.

Steel pulled the cigarette from her mouth. 'You know . . . people are beginning to notice.'

'Good for them.' Logan took another puff. 'Notice what?'

'Your attitude.' She turned till she was staring out at the little frost-covered stairway down to the mortuary. 'There's been complaints.'

Typical.

'It's Beattie, isn't it? That useless tosser thinks I've got nothing better to—'

'It's no' just Beattie, OK? It's everyone.' She flicked away a nub of ash. 'The DCs are fed up with the sarcasm and the shouting. The DIs are fed up with you complaining all the time and stinking of booze. The DCI's fed up of everyone moaning to him about it. And I'm fed up defending you the whole sodding time.'

Silence.

Logan sucked hard on his cigarette. '*My* sarcasm? *My* shouting? What about that fucker Finnie? And—'

'Enough, OK? Enough. . .' Steel turned and stared at him, eyes crinkled at the edges, mouth turned down. 'It's no' about Finnie, it's about you. Either you pull your socks up, or people are going to start making it official.' She poked him in the chest. 'That sound like fun to you: spending all your time getting hauled up by Professional Standards?'

Logan glowered at her. 'And you agree with them? That it?'

'Fucksake, I'm *trying* to help you!' She stormed off a couple of paces, then turned and stormed back. 'You used to be a bloody good cop, you really did. A team player. But right now you're a fucking haemorrhoid dipped in Tabasco. A broken-glass suppository. A. . .' She paused. Frowned. 'A barbed-wire butt-plug!'

'Oh don't be—'

'Whatever's wrong with you, get over it. Or you're going to end up out on your ear and no one'll be sorry to see you go.'

He dropped his half-smoked cigarette and ground it out with the toe of his shoe. 'Anything else?'

'Get a bloody haircut.'

Logan backed into the boardroom, carrying a tray covered with wax-paper cups and a plate of pastries. He placed it in the middle of the long, polished table and everyone stopped what they were doing to scramble for the jammy dough-nuts. Leaving him with a greasy-looking apple turnover, a white coffee, and a sulk.

Bunch of bastards. Complaining about his attitude, like he was the worst person in the whole bloody place. Hell, he wasn't even the worst person in the *room*.

Like all Multi-Agency Public Protection Arrangements meetings the place was packed with people doing their best to come up with 'defensible decisions'. Decisions they couldn't get blamed for if anything went wrong. Social Services, the Council, Sacro, and Grampian Police, all covering their arses and hoping to God that Richard Knox would eventually get fed up of Aberdeen and bugger off back down south. Become someone else's problem.

Detective Inspector Duncan Ingram – in charge of monitoring every pervert, rapist, and paedophile in the northeast of Scotland – stood at the front of the room, writing up the exit strategy for Richard Knox on the whiteboard in squeaky green marker pen. Pausing every now and then to check his thin, military moustache was still obeying orders.

It was a complete waste of time. Knox didn't need an exit strategy, he needed an exit wound. Preferably from a shotgun to the back of the head.

DSI Danby sat at the other end of the long, polished boardroom table, taking notes. DI Steel slouched in her seat, picking her teeth. And DCI Finnie stood in the corner, holding a murmured conversation with someone on his mobile.

Ingram rammed the cap back on his marker pen, and supervised his moustache again. 'Now, as you can see from the risk assessment matrix, we've got several environmental factors against us where Richard Knox is concerned. The house is within easy walking distance of one sheltered living facility, a bowling green, and Aberdeen Royal Infirmary. All places we can expect old men to be found on a regular basis. . .'

Logan tuned him out.

How could anyone complain about his attitude?

This was so bloody typical of—

Someone kicked him under the table.

'Wh. . .'

Steel was making less than subtle gestures towards the whiteboard. Mouthing, 'Pay a-fucking-tention!'

'. . .and *that's* why,' DI Ingram had written 'HMP PETERHEAD' on the board, 'we have a disproportionately large number of sex offenders to manage. Of the three hundred and twenty-three currently living in the North East, about half are classed as "indefinite". So they're on the list for life. . .'

Logan tuned him out again. It was all rubbish anyway, background info for a nodding DSI Danby. Now *there* was someone with an attitude worth complaining about. But did they? *No*, they had to whinge about Logan instead. Obviously, that cock-weasel Beattie was behind it all. Wanted taking out and—

Steel kicked him again. Then turned and announced to the room, 'How about DS McRae takes us through the surveillance routine?'

Cow.

Logan scowled at her, then stood and marched to the front of the room, snatched a red marker from the tray beneath the whiteboard and scrawled up a rough outline of the house in Cornhill that Knox had inherited. 'We can't put surveillance cameras in the house without Knox's permission, so we're going to set one on the lamppost opposite. . .' Logan sketched in the street. 'Here, and another one here. This gives us a coming-and-going view the length of Cairnview Terrace. He'll get level one surveillance for the first week, then—'

'Just the one week?' Danby shifted in his chair. 'He's not going to suddenly get better, you know what I'm saying?'

Logan shrugged. 'Budget constraints. One week of level one surveillance: round the clock with two officers in an

57

unmarked van. After that we have to downgrade it to level two. We'll try to keep an eye on the live video feed . . . depending on staffing levels.'

'You'll *try* to keep an eye on it?'

'He's going to have someone from Sacro with him round the clock anyway, so it—'

'A bunch of volunteers? That's not good enough.'

'They do more support and monitoring of high-risk offenders than any other—'

'Knox abducts and *rapes* old men.' Danby thumped the table with a huge finger punctuating every word, 'He – needs – constant – *police* – supervision.'

'Yeah, well if you wanted him watched twenty-four-seven you should've kept him in Newcastle, shouldn't you?'

Danby's eyes bugged in his head. 'What?'

'Look, we don't have bottomless pockets up here, OK? Everyone dumps their sodding sex offenders on us and we're supposed to just bend over and take it.' Logan jabbed the whiteboard with his pen. 'This is the best we can do. You want more? Get Northumbria Police to chip in and pay for it. He's *your* pervert.'

Steel buried her face in her hands. 'Oh bloody hell. . .'

DSI Danby was on his feet, face flushed, fists resting on the tabletop. Voice a thick, dark rumble. 'I don't care if everyone here's used to your crap, Sergeant, but my warrant card says, "Detective Superintendent". And if you want someone to bend you over, I bloody well will.'

Silence.

'Er . . . yes.' DI Ingram cleared his throat, straightened his moustache again. 'Anyway, if we're done with surveillance, maybe we could move on to response times and contingency planning?'

9

'Are you out of your bloody mind?' DI Steel slammed the office door behind her. 'Did I say you could sit down?'

Logan hauled himself up out of her visitor's chair. 'He was being a wanker.'

'Course he was: he's a sodding superintendent, it's his *job* to be a wanker! But you . . . you're making a fucking calling out of it!' She jabbed Logan in the chest with a red-painted fingernail. 'What did I tell you outside in the car park?'

'He started it.'

She threw her hands in the air. 'That's it. I give up. You want to screw up your career? Go ahead. Be my sodding guest.' She barged past and collapsed in her chair, running a hand across her forehead. 'Get out of my sight. Go on: bugger off and play with the Diddy Men or something. I don't want to look at you any more.'

Logan let himself out.

The Offender Management Unit offices smelled of new paint and sausages. The walls were papered with mugshots and SOPOs, interspersed with the occasional cartoon clipped out of the *Aberdeen Examiner*. A whiteboard, mounted above a

59

gurgling radiator, was covered with grey magnetic strips, each one bearing the name of someone on the Sex Offenders' Register due a trip to court in the not too distant future.

Logan stood at an unwashed window and stared out, past the dead wasps and fly carcasses, at the rainy streets of Bucksburn. Dual carriageway. A roundabout. Some houses. A McDonald's. Grey clouds. . . Being on the second floor didn't help the view any.

'I hear you went off on one at the MAPPA meeting this morning.'

Logan turned to find PC Hamster from Knox's house standing in the doorway, wearing jeans and a sweatshirt, ginger hair plastered to her head from the rain. What was her name, Irvine? Something like that. 'It wasn't—'

'About time someone stood up to these buggers down south.' She chucked a folder into someone's in-tray. 'Stephen Beech was bad enough – comes up here from Cambridge because he fancies living by the sea, and we have to look after him round the clock. OK, Sacro did the day-to-day stuff, but it still cost a sodding fortune: two hundred grand a year to watch *one* rapist. You believe that? Now every bastard thinks we're the perverts' Butlins of the North.'

She closed her eyes, groaned, then ran a hand through her wet hair. 'God, what a week. . .'

Logan knew how she felt.

PC Irvine sighed. 'Anyway, better get going. I'll drive. Paul's meeting us there.'

Logan followed her out through the door. 'Do you believe Knox when he says he's found God?'

'Doesn't really matter does it? Sex offenders aren't sex offenders because they think it's going to be fun, they're sex offenders because somewhere down the line it's been ingrained into them.' She led the way down the corridor, past a mothballed HOLMES suite, heading for the stairs.

She shoved the door to the stairwell open. 'For Knox, raping old men is normal behaviour. Probably can't understand why everyone's not doing it. *We're* the perverts in his eyes.'

They passed a couple of uniformed officers, humping a collection of dusty file boxes up the stairs.

Irvine smiled. 'Careful there, Jim, don't want people to see you working.'

'Screw you, Barbara.' But he was grinning when he said it.

'And that's kinda the problem.' She pushed out through the back door and into the dreich afternoon. Drizzle drifted down from a slate-grey sky, cold and damp. The rear car park was virtually empty, just a pair of battered patrol cars – front bumpers buckled, side panels a mix of scrapes, dents and rust; a grubby white van with the council logo on the side; a brand-new Volvo estate; and Logan's manky brown Fiat. 'Deep down Knox doesn't really believe he's done anything wrong.'

Irvine pointed a key fob at the council van. Stopped. Gave the fob a jiggle. Tried again. Swore. Marched over and rammed the key in the door lock. 'Bloody thing.'

Logan shifted a stack of paperwork from the passenger seat into the footwell, then clambered in. He hauled on his seatbelt as Irvine started the van up. A rumbling diesel rattle, the gearstick vibrating like an over-sized sex toy.

She wrestled with the wheel and the van inched out of the car park. 'God I miss power steering. . .'

They circled the Bucksburn roundabout, heading along the dual carriageway back towards town.

'So,' Irvine dragged the steering wheel to the left, juddering them around one of Aberdeen City Council's world-beating collection of potholes, 'what's the story? You with us full time now? Just paying a flying visit? Seeing how the other half lives?'

Logan shrugged. 'Let's just say I'm not flavour of the month with my guv'nor.'

'Ah,' her voice was monotone, 'so you're here as punishment.'

'I didn't mean it like that.'

'No, no, it's OK. I mean, what sort of loser *wants* to spend all day dealing with rapists, flashers, and paedophiles, right?'

'It was Steel's idea, I'm just—'

'Slumming it with the Diddy Men?'

'It's not—'

She grinned at him. 'I'm pulling your leg. It's OK, I *like* what I do. Might sound weird, but I get a lot of satisfaction out of keeping people's kids, and wives, and girlfriends—'

'And grandads.'

'—and grandads safe. Someone has to do it, right? And I happen to be good at it.'

'No pervert left behind.'

Irvine shrugged. 'Something like that, yeah.'

'How's it going, Richard?' Constable Irvine settled on the dusty couch, dumped her bag on the floor, and dug out a bundle of badly photocopied forms, held together with a pair of green treasury tags. The blotchy cover read 'ACCUTE-2007 SCORING GUIDE'.

The dusty lounge was silent for a moment, just the tick . . . tick . . . tick of the carriage clock and the creak of floorboards from a room above.

Logan leant back against the windowsill. The place still had that oppressive, throat-clogging taint of mildew, the air cold enough to make his breath steam.

Knox had taken the armchair nearest the broken electric fire. Knees together, arms wrapped around that same tatty carrier bag from Asda. He sniffed. 'OK, I suppose.'

'Good. That's good.'

More silence.

Knox coughed.

Logan checked his watch. God this was exciting.

Finally the front door banged and someone shouted, 'Hello?'

PC Irvine called back, 'In here.'

A short, beefy man poked his head into the room. 'Sorry I'm late. Benny tried tae dee hisself in again last nicht. You ken fit he's like.'

Irvine nodded. 'Slit his wrists again?'

'No, thought he'd gie hanging a go. Neck's one big bruise this morning.' The newcomer stepped forward and held his hand out for Logan to shake. 'Paul Leggett. I'm Barbara's partner. Well, not partner-partner, we work together, like.' He grinned. 'You the boy told that fat prick fae Newcastle tae awa bile his heid?'

'Something like that.'

'Good stuff.' PC Leggett slapped his hands together then settled in the seat opposite Knox, looking him up and down for almost a whole minute before asking much the same question Irvine had. 'Fit like 'i day, Richard?'

Knox straightened the seams on his trousers. 'If it's all right with you, I'd like to get this over with.'

'Fair enough.'

Irvine flipped to the first page of the treasury-tagged sheets. From where Logan was standing, he could see a little printed table, headed 'VICTIM ACCESS'. She cleared her throat. 'So, Richard, have you been out and about yet? Or are you sticking to home for now?'

He shrugged, the plastic bag in his arms rustling as he moved. 'Home.'

Irvine scrawled a zero in the box at the bottom of the sheet, then turned to the next page. 'Must be a bit claustrophobic, just rattling about in the house on your own. . .'

'Not on me own, am I? Got Harry and Mandy to keep us company. 'Sides,' he picked at a loose thread on the armchair, 'house is a hell of a lot bigger than me cell back at Frankland.'

'Hmm. . .' Irvine made a note. 'And is there anyone you'd like to spend more time with. You know, if you could?'

'God. I'd like to spend more time with God.'

Sitting on the other side of the room, Paul raised an eyebrow, but didn't say anything.

Knox sighed. 'I've been through all these tests before, like. Used to do them two, three times a week with this fat bird from Social Services when I got out of prison. "Is there anyone you'd like to spend more time with?", "Has anything made you angry since we last met?", "How did you handle it?" Same questions every time.'

Irvine shifted in her seat. 'I'm only trying to help, Richard.'

'Next up's "Sexual Preoccupations".' Knox clutched his carrier bag tighter. 'Am I masturbating within normal limits? Am I having deviant sexual fantasies?'

She nodded. 'How important *is* sex to you these days?'

He slumped back in his seat, then ran a hand over his eyes. 'I can save you the trouble of quizzing us. My score's going to be "Moderate". Should be "Low", but you probably think I'm being all defensive about it.'

'Aren't you?'

'Wouldn't you be? Someone comes into your home and reads out questions like you're on some sick game show?'

PC Irvine's partner laughed. 'Like *Blankety Blank* for perverts? *Wankety Wank*?'

Knox looked at him for a moment, then smiled. 'I'll have a "P" please Bob.'

Wrong show.

Logan shifted on the windowsill. Knox was right – this was a waste of everyone's time. He'd just tell them what they wanted to hear. Work the system. Screw with the results.

Worthless.

Knox gave a small, humourless laugh. 'You know, it's funny really. All this time and I'm finally at peace. Let God into me heart, chased away me demons. And we're still going through the same questions they was asking us in prison.' The weedy little man went back to picking at the arm of his chair. 'God's forgiven us, surely *that's* what matters. The minister told us all about His forgiveness and love, like. We're all made in His image, aren't we? Even someone like me.' A smile crept across Knox's pointy face. 'God is just like me.'

Now *there* was a creepy thought.

Logan checked his watch. Nearly half two. If they didn't get moving soon, by the time he got back to Bucksburn and picked up his car the Friday afternoon rush-hour would be grinding everything to a halt. And there was no way he was doing any more unpaid overtime for Steel, Finnie, or anyone else.

Logan waited in the hall with PC Paul Leggett, while Irvine was upstairs checking on the two people from Sacro. Knox was still in the lounge, on his knees on the hearthrug, praying to a broken electric fire.

Logan turned his back on the open doorway. 'Ever taken the test yourself?'

A lopsided smile pulled Leggett's face out of shape. 'Apparently I'm a "High Risk" offender.'

'Yeah?'

'Chronic masturbation means mair than fifteen times a month. I'm off the bloody scale on that one.'

Uncomfortable silence.

Logan fidgeted.

'Anyway. . .'

Constable Irvine appeared at the top of the stairs. 'All set.'

Leggett opened the front door, motioning them out into the cold, drizzly afternoon. 'Fit's the live-in help saying till it?'

'He's not been out of the house. Keeps himself to himself. Does a lot of praying.'

'Aye, weel, going to take a lot mair than *that*.'

They hurried down the path towards the grubby van parked at the kerb. By the time they clambered inside Irvine's glasses were opaque with tiny water droplets. She turned the key in the ignition, pumping the accelerator until the engine caught.

PC Leggett cranked up the blowers. 'Fit did *you* think, Babs?'

Irvine took off her glasses and dried them on a corner of her tartan-tea-towel shirt. 'He's hiding something.'

Logan scooted around in his seat. 'Do I need to up the surveillance?'

She shrugged, then pointed through the slowly clearing windscreen at a black box mounted on a streetlight a couple of houses away, then at another rusty van in the old Aberdeen City Council burgundy livery. It was sitting beside a coned-off rectangle of tarmac and looked at least ten years older than the one they were currently sitting in. 'Got level one surveillance, CCTV both ends of the street, two people staying with him full time, regular visits from Paul and me. . . What else can we do?'

Richard Knox stands at the living room window, watching the grimy white van drive off into the damp afternoon.

He checks the lounge doorway – no one there – then pulls the mobile phone from his pocket. The phone he's not supposed to have, just in case he uses it to make contact with other perverts.

Like he'd want to speak to those filthy bastards.

He scrolls down through the address book until he comes to the number of a certain gentleman in Newcastle. A very *influential* gentleman who's not in the least bit gentle. It rings for a while, then the voicemail picks up and Richard leaves a message.

'Hi, Aunty Maggie, just wanted to wish you a happy birthday. Yer present's in the post, like.' Pause. 'It's all going good here, you know? Settlin' in and that. Speak to you later.' And then he hangs up.

Checks the doorway again.

Slides the phone back into its dark hiding place.

Happy birthday.

The police aren't the only ones who've got an exit strategy.

10

The manky little Fiat made a horrible grinding noise every time Logan tried to put it into third. He mashed the clutch to the floor and shoved the gearstick into place, pretending he couldn't smell something burning. Heading back along the dual carriageway towards the Horrible Haudagain roundabout, next stop: FHQ, to find somewhere quiet to hide until his shift was over.

The radio hissed and crackled, never latching onto any station for more than three or four minutes at a time. It gave a burst of static, then music – Katrina and the Waves, 'Walking on Sunshine'. Logan's stomach lurched, his mouth filling with warm saliva. Heart pounding. He stabbed the off button and the radio was silent.

Jesus. . .

He rolled down the window. Cold air, laced with drizzle and exhaust fumes.

Deep breaths.

Just a song. Nothing to worry about. Just a song.

When his mobile phone rang he flinched. Logan checked the display: DI Steel. His thumb hovered over the off button . . . then he hit pick up, holding it to his ear as he pulled into a little layby off the dual carriageway with half a dozen small industrial units in it. Majestic Wines, Pizza Hut, that kind of thing.

'*Where the hell are you?*'

Logan killed the engine. 'You said get out of your sight.'

'*Just . . . bloody. . .*' A pause, then, '*I want you back at the ranch; we're going round to Steve Polmont's place.*'

'I'm stuck in Bucksburn.' Which was a lie. 'Can't you take somebody—'

'*Bucksburn? What the cock-flavoured buggery are you doing in Bucksburn?*'

'You told me to go see the Diddy Men, remember?'

Another pause.

'*Just get your scarred arse back here and pick me up. Now!*'

'You're a bloody idiot, you know that, don't you?'

Logan just shrugged. Outside the car windows, King Street was a study in miserable grey. People clomped along through the drizzle, collars up, mouths down. A few of the more optimistic ones huddled beneath umbrellas: the misty rain just soaked them from the shoulders down.

DI Steel wrestled with the passenger door, winding her window down. 'And could you no' have got a decent pool car?'

'You said come pick you up, I picked you up.'

'Smells like old lady farts.' She dug out a cigarette and lit it, then shoogled the pack at Logan.

'Danby still throwing a wobbly?'

'What do you think? Lucky he didn't have you kicked you off the case.' She dug a sat-nav out of her bag and fiddled some sort of clip thing onto the back, then huffed a smoky breath onto the suction cup and stuck it to the windshield. Where it promptly fell off again. 'Buggering hell. . . you ever clean this thing?'

She breathed on the windscreen, fogging up a patch, then scrubbed at it with the sleeve of her jacket. This time, the sat-nav stuck. 'Nicked it out of lost-and-found.'

'Would a map not have been—'

'Bloody GSM trace on Polmont's mobile came back with latitude and longitude, OK?' She switched the thing on and poked away at the screen, pale-yellow tongue sticking out the corner of her mouth. 'Straight on at the roundabout.'

Logan drove them through the Bridge of Don and out past the Exhibition and Conference Centre, rain shimmering on its bizarre curvy glass bridge and fake airport control tower. Following the green arrow on the sat-nav's screen.

'So, what do we know about Polmont?'

Steel pulled a face. 'Came to me through a DI in Edinburgh who owes me a couple of favours. Polmont was his chiz on another Malk the Knife building site – got themselves half a million in cocaine, twenty illegal immigrants, and one thousand cartons of smuggled cigarettes.'

'Well.' Logan shrugged. 'At least you know he's sound.'

'Aye. . .' Steel picked a flake of ash off her trousers. 'Sort of.'

'What's he done?'

'Polmont's got a bit of a drink problem.'

'He's a bloody alki, isn't he?'

Scowl. 'What, you want to swap tips?'

Logan ignored that. 'He's probably off on a bender somewhere. That's why you can't get him – too pissed to answer the phone.'

'Oh, don't be so—'

'This is another wild bloody goose chase, isn't it?'

'Just shut up and drive.'

Logan put his foot down and the manky Fiat rumbled and rattled up to fifty along the dual carriageway.

All the way out to Balmedie the fields were a soggy

patchwork of green-brown, bordered by pale-grey drystane dykes. The occasional flock of sheep breathing clouds of steam into the cold, damp air. And then they got to the signs saying, 'WORKS ENTRANCE AHEAD', 'SLOW VEHICLES TURNING', 'NO ACCESS TO BEACH'.

It hadn't taken the local press long to nickname Donald Trump's development 'Trumpton'. A vast swathe of coast was due to disappear under the bulldozers: two golf courses, five hundred houses, a four-star hotel, and nearly a thousand holiday villas. Which kind of put McLennan Homes' four hundred semi-detacheds into perspective.

Three hundred yards further on a huge billboard sat at the side of the road – 'McLENNAN HOMES, BUILDING A BETTER TOMORROW FOR YOU'. Photo of a smiling nuclear family holding hands and staring mistily off into the distance. Very aspirational. Or it would have been if someone hadn't spray-painted a big blue penis onto one of the kids.

Logan slowed the car. According to the sat-nav, Steel's map coordinates were off to the left. The Fiat juddered to a halt on the grass verge.

He peered across and through the passenger window at the site entrance – a high chainlink fence, the gates held open with dented oil drums. 'SITE PATROLLED BY GUARD DOGS', 'NO ENTRY TO UNAUTHORIZED PERSONNEL', 'DANGER OF DEATH', 'WARNING: RAZOR WIRE'. A rutted mud track led away into Malk the Knife's development.

Logan checked the sat-nav again. 'You sure you got those coordinates right?'

'Course I'm sure.' She chewed on her bottom lip for a moment. 'Maybe they've got caravans for people living on site?'

'Maybe. . .'

Logan eased the car through the gates. The muddy track bumped and slithered under the Fiat's wheels, taking them closer to the rumble of heavy machinery, the beep-beep-beep of something backing up.

Steel pointed through the windscreen. 'Over there.'

He pulled up beside a long Portakabin with 'SITE OFFICE' stencilled on the side, trying to aim for a bit that didn't look like the battle of the Somme.

'Right.' Steel flicked her cigarette butt out of the window. 'If anyone asks, you and me are debt collectors. I'm the boss, you're the hired muscle. Still a chance we can salvage this cock-up, so no telling anyone you're a cop, understand?'

She pulled the sat-nav off the windscreen and they clambered out into the drizzle.

'Which way?'

She frowned at the little screen, trying to shield it from the rain with her coat, then did a slow three-sixty. Stopped. And pointed out across the churned-up earth.

No caravans, no Portakabins, not so much as a three-man tent.

Steel took a step forwards, but Logan grabbed her arm.

'Maybe we should call for a search team. IB. Pathologist. If Polmont's—'

'Don't be so wet.' She shook herself free and stomped off into the mud.

Logan swore, then followed her.

The going was tough, thick clogs of brown-black earth sucking at his shoes, dirty water oozing in through the lace holes, soaking into his socks. And then his foot disappeared into a puddle, right up to the shin. 'Fuck. . .' Cold and wet, the trouser leg sticking to his skin. He limped after Steel, cursing all the way.

She came to a halt about two hundred yards from the high chainlink fence that surrounded the site, then turned around a few times. The earth here was firmer – still covered in weeds and grass, the vegetation looking pale and unhealthy.

Logan squelched up beside her. 'Hope you're bloody happy, my feet are—'

'Where the hell is he?' She turned around again, then peered at the sat-nav.

'—socks are sodden and my trousers are all covered in—'

'Will you shut up moaning about your bloody feet! He's supposed to be *here*.'

Logan snatched the sat-nav from her – the display read, 'YOU HAVE REACHED YOUR DESTINATION'.

Welcome to the middle of nowhere.

'Well, at least we know he's not stuck in some shallow grave.'

Steel grabbed the sat-nav back. 'Oh yeah, tell me Sherlock, how—'

'Look at the ground. It's not been disturbed.' He pointed at the little black rectangle in Steel's hands. 'What are those accurate to, ten, fifteen feet? And the GSM's about a hundred. . .'

Logan looked out across the tufts of yellowy grass and dark-green weeds. 'Give him a ring.'

'What?'

'Call him on his mobile.'

She did, standing there with her phone clamped to her ear. 'It's ringing. . .'

Logan stood as still as he could, ears straining. A faint metallic warble was coming from somewhere over to his left. He turned and marched towards it, but the sound of his squelching through the waterlogged grass was loud enough to block it out. And then the warbling stopped.

Steel pointed at the mobile in her hand. 'Voicemail.'

'Call him again.'

This time Logan crept across the uneven ground, the ringing getting louder with every careful step.

'Voicemail again.'

He found it on the third go: a scuffed and battered Nokia lying in a patch of greasy nettles at the edge of a burn. He snapped on a pair of blue nitrile gloves and picked the phone up, just as it stopped ringing. The casing had been broken at one point, then stuck back together with black electrical tape.

Steel appeared at his shoulder. 'Is it his?'

Logan stared at her. 'It rang when you called it, what do you think?'

Scowl. 'I'll do the sarcasm, thank you very much.' She stuck out a hand. 'Gimmie.'

'Gloves.'

'I'll bloody "gloves" you in a minute. Give me the damn phone.'

She went stabbing through the phone's menu with her thumbs. 'See what he's got listed as home. . . It's an Aberdeen number.' She pressed another button, and stuck the phone to her ear. Listened for a bit. 'No answer. So he's no' here, and he's no' at home.'

'Probably still pissed.' Logan offered her an evidence bag, but she just stuck the phone in her pocket and marched back towards the building site.

Logan shook his soggy foot and squelched after her.

The rain was beginning to pick up, the thin, leeching drizzle giving way to pattering globs of ice-cold water that kicked ripples across the dirty puddles.

Logan followed Steel down an embryonic street: bare foundations on one side, part-built homes on the other. Wooden skeletons, with blue plastic sheeting stretched between the uprights. A couple of the frames were being skinned with pale orange brick, a radio blaring out *Northsound One* as two teams of brickies built up the next layer.

Further down, half a dozen looked nearly finished – some even had doors and windows. The one at the far end had a big 'SHOW HOME' sign out front, a garage twice the size of the others, and a slightly surreal-looking bright green lawn. No way that could be natural. Probably Astroturf or something like that. A pair of gardeners were planting shrubs and trees around it, hacking out holes in the rubble with a pickaxe.

Bugger that for a job.

Logan stopped in the middle of the muddy street. 'Where do you want to start?'

Steel dug her hands deeper into her jacket pockets. Her nose had gone a fetching shade of pink. With a not so fetching drip on the end. 'Where do sparkies work?'

'Well . . . you wouldn't want to run electrical cables till you'd got the roof on and the place was watertight, would you?'

She shrugged and stomped through the rain towards the little clot of completed houses.

A battered, red Berlingo van was parked outside one of them. It had a crap illustration of Robert Burns on the side, and the words, 'McRABBIE'S FAMILY ELECTRICALS, "YOUR LOCAL BRIGHT SPARKS"'. The address and phone number were for Stirling. So much for being 'local'.

Someone had keyed the paintwork, permanently engraving 'SCABBY' in front of the company name.

The front garden was a mess of rubble and debris, the concrete path littered with clumps of mud. Steel bumped the front door open with her shoulder, hands at her sides, not touching anything. Inside, the house was an exposed framework of raw pine, the outer walls stuffed with pink Rockwool insulation waiting for their skin of plasterboard.

The entryway was carpeted in a layer of flattened cardboard boxes, the brown surface rippled with dirty water and muddy boot prints.

Someone was singing upstairs: a surprisingly tuneful rendition of 'Let Me Entertain You', complete with 'Wakka waaaaa, weeeeeeee-wahhh. . .' guitar solos. Steel nodded and Logan took the lead, up the bare wooden stairs and onto the chipboard landing.

The singer was hunched on top of a folding ladder in what was probably going to be a bedroom, wearing a padded orange boilersuit with that same crappy Robert Burns illustration on the back, tightening the chuck-less bit on a cordless drill. A brief pause for the chorus, then he stuck the huge drill bit against the nearest upright and screeched through it.

Out on the landing, Logan did a quick scan of the other rooms. With no walls it didn't take long. They were alone.

He waved Steel forward.

She marched into the room, drew back her foot, and kicked the ladder. The whole thing shuddered and the singing became a frightened yell. The drill clattered to the chipboard floor and the electrician grabbed at the bare roof joists, swearing as the ladder thumped from side to side. Then he got it stable, looked over his shoulder, teeth bared. 'Are you fucking *mental?* Jesus. . .'

His face was a map of old acne scars, nose a pink-veined golf ball. He hauled out his earphones. 'If you bastards are here about the—'

'Shut the fuck up.' Steel jabbed a finger at him. 'Looking for a sparky.'

His eyes narrowed. 'I don't do homers.'

'Steve Polmont.'

'Not seen him.'

Logan stooped and picked the drill up off the sawdust-covered floor. 'You McRabbie?'

'Why?'

Steel grinned up at him. 'We represent a certain gentleman Mr Polmont has a . . . business arrangement with.'

'Oh for fuck's sake.' Scabby McRabbie sighed. 'Dogs or horses?'

'Where is he?'

McRabbie held his hand out. 'Buggered off and left us in the shite, didn't he?'

Logan kept the drill just out of reach.

Sigh. 'He was a dick, OK? Barely sober, aye and that's when he bothered to turn up. Wouldn't trust him to change his socks, never mind a plug.' McRabbie swung his arm around at the semi-skeletal house. 'Spent half the day rewiring the shite job he did in the first place. Supposed to be on a team bonus, and—'

'When'd you last see him?' Steel dragged out her fags and sparked one up, then moved the burning lighter towards the nearest clump of Rockwool. 'Be a shame if something happened. . .'

'It's flame retardant.' McRabbie stuck out his hand again, and Logan passed him the drill.

'Ta.' He made the hole he'd been drilling slightly bigger, then rested the drill on its large battery pack and hauled a thick bundle of orange cables through the upright. 'Used to be you could get away with a couple extra sockets in the living room, now every other bastard wants their whole house done with Cat-Six.'

Logan watched the electrician pick a single strand out of the bundle and mark it with a blue plastic tag, then loop it over a ceiling joist. 'Where is he?'

'Fuck knows. Haven't seen him since . . . what, Monday? Probably lying drunk in a gutter, or dead in a fucking ditch. Long as the useless bastard don't come back, I don't care.'

McRabbie picked up the drill again. 'You know they make

me buy my own kit now? Two-five, one-five, fucking boxes, fronts, light switches, you name it: got to claim it back on expenses. That's Steve Bloody Polmont's fault.'

The drill screeched through another upright, sending a shower of sawdust flying. Then McRabbie thumped it back down on the top step of the ladder. 'You know what. . .' He dug a fiver out of his overalls and chucked it at Logan. 'Here: you catch up with the wanker, you give him a kick in the nads from me!'

Logan picked the note off the floor and pocketed it. 'Deal.'

Steel stomped down the stairs, with Logan bringing up the rear. Up in the bedroom the singing started again, accompanied by the whine of the drill.

She stopped at the front door, looking out into the rain. 'Well, that was a waste of sodding time.'

'Look on the bright side, at least we know he was here Monday.'

'Fat lot of good it does us.' She took a long draw on her cigarette, pinching her mouth into a chicken's-bum pout. 'Bloody Polmont.'

'Well, maybe—'

Steel slapped a hand against his chest. 'Shh. . .' She pointed out through the open door, where a small crowd was gathering around a dented white Transit van. The driver's door creaked open and a huge man in dirty blue overalls stepped out into the rain. 'Here, isn't that Wee Hamish's right-hand thug?'

Reuben.

He was big in all directions – massive fists clenched either side of his straining stomach. His face was twisted with scar tissue, a patchy beard making little islands of dark fur on the swell of his cheeks. Freddy Kruger meets the Michelin Man.

Logan took a step back, making sure he couldn't be seen. 'What the hell's *he* doing here?'

Reuben lumbered round to the van's side door, clunked the handle and hauled it open. Then reached inside and dragged a body out onto the muddy road. The body twitched, tried to roll over. One of its legs bent in three different directions, all at the same time. Face covered in blood. Hands curled up like deformed claws.

Reuben just stood there.

Silence.

Logan flipped his phone open. 'I'll call for backup.'

'You'll bloody no'!'

'But he's—'

'What do you think Finnie'll do if he finds out we tried to meet up with a chiz without his approval?'

Logan stared at her. 'You didn't clear it with him?'

'Might have slipped my mind.' She coughed. 'Now shut up – can't hear what's going on.'

'Oh that's just. . .'

Steel hit him again. 'Three o'clock.'

A large man emerged from the show home: six-two; arms held out from his sides, as if he was carrying a couple of beer barrels; jeans, leather jacket, bald head glistening in the rain. Something dark and muscular trotted along beside him. Pointed nose, lolling pink tongue.

The little crowd of joiners and plumbers backed off, giving him room.

He stopped, stared down at the body quivering in the mud, then up at Reuben. 'Problem?' Scottish, but not local.

Wee Hamish's man pointed one huge sausage finger at the battered figure. 'This yours?'

'What if it is?'

'Had a bit of an accident, didn't it?'

'Oh yeah?'

79

Reuben smiled, showing off the hole where a tooth used to be. 'Accidentally tried to sell his shit in the wrong part of town.'

The bloke with the dog stripped off his leather jacket and handed it to the nearest bystander. No wonder he couldn't get his arms near his sides: he was a solid slab of muscle, straining at the fabric of a white T-shirt. He cricked his head from side to side. Flexed his shoulders. 'Think you, me, and Mauser here need to have a wee chat.'

The dog's ears pricked up, a rumbling growl coming from its throat.

Reuben undid a couple of buttons on his overalls, down by his huge waistband, held one side open.

'Can't see.' Steel shifted, peering. 'He getting his cock out?'

'Why would he be . . . what's *wrong* with you?'

Big-and-Bald stared at whatever was in Reuben's overalls, then nodded. Took a step back. 'Maybe later.'

'Wee message for your lord and master.' Reuben waved a huge hand, taking in the part-built houses. 'Keep it legitimate and we'll all get on fine. Disrespect,' he paused to kick the man lying at his feet, 'well, that's gonnae land us *all* in a world of shite. We clear?'

Mr Big-and-Bald folded his huge arms across his chest, saying nothing.

Reuben slammed the Transit's side door. 'Fair enough.' Then he clambered back behind the wheel and cranked the engine. The van's tyres span in the mud before they finally grabbed traction. He drove off, slowly. Not so much as a jaunty wave.

Logan watched him go, staring after the van like everyone else. And then Big-and-Bald nudged the man lying on the ground with his foot.

'Get this fucker out of here.' He turned and strode off towards the site office, snapping his fingers, 'Mauser, heel!'

The huge black dog raised its snout, sniffed, then turned and loped after its master.

DI Steel took the last gasp from her cigarette and ground the butt out against the nearest chunk of pink Rockwool. 'Think we'd better go pay baldy a visit, don't you?' She stepped out into the rain.

The site office was divided into cubicles by chest-high partitions, each one covered with pinned-up spreadsheets. A large architectural plan covered one wall, 'Camberwick Green' in all its proposed glory.

The office was tidy: no mounds of grubby paperwork, no piles of half-read tabloids, no Turner-Prize-winning installations of discarded polystyrene cups. Just laptops, graphics tablets, printers, and something classical playing from a portable stereo. All overlaid with the dirty stench of wet dog.

A kettle sat on a wee table opposite the door, curling steam into the tidy room. Someone was making tea – blue jumper on over a shirt and tie, carefully arranged combover, ridiculous little beard, as if he'd drawn around his chin with a magic marker.

He looked up as Logan thumped the door closed behind them.

'Are you here about the drainage?'

Steel sniffed. 'I look like a fucking plumber?'

Frown. 'There's no need to—'

'Steve Polmont.'

Big-and-Bald stood up from behind one of the partitions, a hands-free headset stuffed in his ear. 'There a problem here?' Up close he reeked of aftershave, a cloying musky smell with chemical overtones.

Steel perched on the edge of a desk. 'Polmont had an arrangement with our employer. But he's no' been keeping his end up. Know what I mean?'

Jumper-and-Tie went back to making the tea. 'Well, I don't see how that concerns us, Miss. . .?'

'We're talking three big ones here.'

'Ah. . .' He stuck a teaspoon in and swirled the bags around for a bit. 'You should really be taking this up with Mr . . . Polmont, was it?'

'Where is he?'

Milk. Sugar. 'Andy, do we have a Mr Polmont working for us?'

The big man shook his head. 'He was that sticky-fingered sparky, did a runner.'

'Ah, yes. . .' Jumper-and-Tie handed a mug to his colleague. 'There was a problem with missing electrical equipment. Wire, cabling, junction boxes, that kind of thing. Mr Polmont made himself scarce before we could contact the police. Sorry we can't be of further help.'

The inspector nodded. 'He got any wages outstanding? Something he could be putting against his debt?'

'I really think anything outstanding should go to pay for the equipment he stole, don't you?'

'Nah, that's no' going to—'

'Think it's time for you to leave, yeah?' Big-and-Bald, AKA: Andy, came round the corner, towering over Steel, that huge scary dog trotting behind him, claws making skittering noises on the linoleum floor. 'Got a buildin' site to run here.'

She looked up at Andy. Then round at Logan. Raised an eyebrow.

I'm the boss, you're the hired muscle. . .

Logan stared at the huge slab of a man. Screw that.

He stuck out his hand for Andy to shake. 'No hard feelings.'

The big man paused for a second, then took it, his thick fingers dwarfing Logan's, *squeezing*, a vice made of flesh and bone. Logan grabbed the hand with his left, digging his nails in. 'Woa, easy, Tiger!'

Andy grinned. 'You have a nice day now, Officer.'

'You're a big, sodding, wet, Jessie bastard, you know that, don't you?' Steel stomped to a halt at the Fiat's rusty passenger door. 'Couldn't throw your weight around for two bloody minutes!'

'Did you see the size of him?' Logan stopped behind her, both hands held up like a surgeon, waiting for a nurse to glove him up. 'He'd've torn my head off and crapped down the stump. Anyway, he *knew* we were police.'

'You're such a girl.' She nodded her head at the car. 'Well? Unlock the sodding thing; bloody freezing.'

Logan stuck one hip out. 'Keys are in my front trouser pocket.'

She glanced down. 'So?'

'You're going to have to drive.'

Her top lip curled. 'Aye, that'll be shining. Detective *Inspector*, mind? You drive, I . . . passenge.'

'Can't. Did the hostage trick when I shook with Baldy Andy. You need to bag my hands till we get back to the station.'

Steel took another look at his trousers. 'I'm no' going digging about in your breeks, what if you get a stiffy?'

'Just . . . don't flatter yourself, OK?'

11

'Bloody hell.' Logan had one last bash at getting a cigarette out of the packet, then gave up. 'Can you. . .?'

Steel shifted down and the Fiat whined around the outside of a massive tractor hauling a trailer full of cattle down the dual carriageway. 'You're like a wee kid.' She took the pack from his slippery plastic-bagged hands, tapped one out against the steering wheel, stuck it between her teeth, and lit it with the car's cigarette lighter. The edges of her scarlet lips cracked out like spider veins as she sooked. Then she held it out – a bright-red print on the filter – so Logan could sit forwards and pluck it from between her fingers with his mouth.

It tasted of burning perfume and Vaseline.

'Thanks.'

Steel went back to squinting into the rain, windscreen wipers squealing and groaning across the pockmarked glass. 'Either Polmont's buggered off, or he's dead.'

'And if he was stealing electrical supplies from Malk the Knife, doesn't matter where he runs to. Sooner or later. . .'

'Silly bugger.'

'You know,' Logan tried to take the cigarette out of his mouth to tap the ash off, but couldn't work the clear plastic bags into a position that wouldn't burn a hole in them, 'if you were going to kill someone for nicking your electrical wiring, there's plenty of places to bury the body on a building site: mechanical diggers, concrete. . .'

'Aye.' Steel reached over and took the fag from Logan's mouth, flicked the ash out of the open window, took a sneaky puff, then stuck it back between his lips. 'Get onto Strathclyde when we get back, tell them I want a cadaver dog up here first thing tomorrow morning. And don't take any crap. Rotten Weegie bastards never want to travel north of Perth. Better get the Time Team organized too: ground-penetrating radar, trowels, beards and silly hats. You know the drill.'

'Warrants? Budget?'

Steel pulled her mouth into a thin line. 'You do your bit, I'll sweet talk Finnie. Worst comes to worst I'll go rummaging through *his* trouser pockets.'

'Yeah,' Logan nodded. 'That's the kind of threat that'll make him cooperate.'

'Still say this is a bad idea. . .'

'Just shut up and keep an eye out.' DI Steel squatted in front of the dark-blue door and peered in through the letterbox. It was a nondescript tenement building in Northfield, three stories of damp grey granite with six flats arranged either side of a central stairwell.

Logan leant on the balustrade, the plastic bags on his hands crinkling as he peered down from the top floor. 'We need to get back to the station before the samples deteriorate. And you know what else we need?'

Steel stuck her hand through the letterbox, then her wrist, then as much of her arm as she could, tongue sticking out the side of her mouth. 'You to shut up?'

'A *warrant*. We need a warrant.'

They'd got the address on the way back into town, Steel

telling Control to do a reverse lookup on the telephone number they'd got from Steve Polmont's mobile.

'Come on you wee bugger. . .' She had her face flat against the door now, teeth clenched, one eye squinted shut. 'Shitebags.' She slumped. 'Can't reach.'

Logan nodded. 'Good, now we can go get a warrant, and come back and do it properly.'

Steel wriggled her arm free. 'Don't need a bloody warrant. Polmont could be in there, dying right now.'

'But—'

She stuck a finger to her lips and shushed him. 'Did you hear that? Someone crying for help?'

'God, you are such a cliché.'

Steel stood, took two steps back, then slammed her high-heeled boot into the door, by the lock. She hopped away, swearing and clutching her ankle. The door hadn't even moved. She crumpled against the wall, wobbling on one leg. 'Well, don't just bloody stand there!'

Sigh. Logan squared up to the lock, raised his damp, mud-spattered foot, and kicked. The door juddered. On the second go it flew open in a burst of splintered wood. 'Happy now?'

Steel limped forward as the front door to the next flat burst open. A man in a tatty blue dressing gown lurched out onto the landing, brandishing a massive monkey wrench. Hair flat on one side, sticking up on the other.

'Right, you little bastards. . .' He staggered to a halt. Stared at Logan and Steel. Then at the kicked-in door. Backed up a step.

The inspector jerked a thumb at Polmont's flat. 'When did you last see the guy who lives here?'

He let the arm clutching the wrench fall to his side. 'I work nights.' He shuffled backwards until he was inside his own flat. 'Try to keep the noise down, yeah?' And closed the door.

'So much for Neighbourhood Watch.' She hobbled past Logan into Steve Polmont's home.

It looked like the kind of place that got rented out fully furnished, which meant a random collection of shabby furniture and mismatched crockery scrounged up from second-hand shops. No paintings or pictures on the walls. Carpets that hadn't seen a hoover since the turn of the century. Just about bearable if you were going to be working on a building site for the next year and a bit.

The lounge and kitchen were two halves of the same room, filled with a sharp, rancid smell. Two clothes horses sat in the middle of the carpet, covered in socks and pants, a pair of jeans, and a threadbare checked shirt.

Empty whisky bottles stood guard along the kitchen work surfaces, a regiment of empty Grant's vodka bottles on the greasy windowsill.

A dirty bowl sat on the little kitchen table with the pale pink husks of shrivelled Rice Crispies clinging to the edge, a half-full bottle of Bell's sitting next to it.

The breakfast of champions.

Logan fumbled the fridge door open with his plastic-bagged hands. A couple of microwave ready meals, a carton of milk past its sell-by date, a block of cheddar going green and hairy. 'Polmont's not here.'

'Shut up and help me look for clues.' She limped back down the corridor. The first door opened on a small bathroom thick with the bitter tang of old sick. Next was a bedroom, with an unmade double bed, an overflowing ashtray, a tub of hand cream, and a copy of *Butt-Mania* magazine – a couple of used tissues lying by the side of the bed.

A little boxroom lay behind door number three. And it was actually full of boxes: iPods, hair straighteners, cartons of cigarettes, portable DVD players, drums of electrical cable, strange rectangular things with wires sticking out of them, a couple of fuse boxes. . .

Steel gave a low, breathy whistle. 'Must be, what: three, four grands' worth in here?'

Logan nudged a large brown cardboard box with his foot. It clinked. 'What about this lot?'

'I don't know, do I? Open it.'

He held up his bagged hands. 'How? You wouldn't let me go back to the station.'

'God's sake, got to do *everything* myself. . .' She ripped the top flap back and hauled out a bottle of Grant's vodka, just like the ones in the kitchen, only full. Another three boxes were stacked underneath the window. Steel checked – more vodka. 'What do you think, nicked?'

Logan nodded at a dozen multipacks of Durex condoms. 'That or he was planning one hell of a weekend.'

Steel peered into another box. 'Journals.' She dumped one on top of a crate of rolling tobacco and flipped it open. The pages were creased and grubby, covered in a dense web of dark-blue biro. She peered at it, then backed off, and tried again, one eye squinted shut. 'Bloody handwriting's appalling.'

Logan looked over her shoulder. 'Get your eyes tested.'

'I don't *need* glasses.'

'If you say so.'

To be fair, Steve Polmont's writing *was* appalling. The letters all ran together with lots of crossings out and scribbled annotations. 'Listen to this: "G and Y went on the rampage today – found out someone's been helping themselves to the shipments. Saw A give J a kicking for it. Have to lay off for a while." It's dated Sunday.'

'What else?'

'Something about a telephone conversation. . .' The writing grew increasingly erratic, until it was little more than a collection of random scribbles. 'Must've been drinking while he wrote it.'

Steel slapped Logan on the arm. 'Told you I didn't need glasses. Who's "G and Y"?'

'No idea. "A" might be Andy? The big bald bloke?' Logan tried, and failed, to turn the page with his bagged hands. 'Little help?'

'What did your last slave die of?' She was rummaging through another box, pulling out bundles of computer games, still wrapped in shiny plastic. 'Fancy the new *Resident Evil*?'

'That would be unethical.'

'You're quite right, Sergeant, what *was* I thinking?' She stood and slipped a copy into his jacket pocket, then stuck a couple more in her handbag. 'Let's face it, if Polmont's nicked them off Malk the Knife, Malky's no' exactly going to come round the station asking for his gear back, is he? This stuff'll sit in evidence for six months then get turfed into the police auction. Or chucked through an industrial wood chipper. It's win-win.' She snapped her bag shut. 'Right, back to the station. We'll get a warrant, then come back and find this stuff officially.'

Logan stood for a moment, looking at all the bottles of vodka, wondering if he shouldn't take a couple into custody while he was at it.

'You coming?'

'Oh . . . yes.' He struggled with his jacket pocket, pulling the video game out with his slippery hands, and dumped it back in the box. 'Already got that one.'

Steel rolled her eyes. 'You are *such* a goody two-shoes.'

She really had no idea.

12

Logan tumbled another handful of dried penne into the pot of boiling water. The ivory shapes looked like little segments of finger-bone in the light from the extractor fan.

Through in the lounge, the TV was babbling away to itself, the *Channel 4 News* covering the latest round of scandals from the Scottish Parliament, as Logan had a bash at making tea for a change.

A little after half six and there was still no sign of Samantha – probably pulling another green shift – but he was going to bloody well impress her when she finally got in. Baked pasta with some sort of sauce and cheese. A thank you for her promising to rush through the DNA samples she'd scraped from under his nails in the little lab back at FHQ.

He checked the recipe he'd downloaded, then excavated a dust-covered casserole dish from the cupboard. A home-cooked meal, how hard could it be?

Chop an onion, fry it in olive oil, chuck in a tin of tomatoes, couple tins of tuna, some mixed herbs. Easy. What was all the fuss about?

Right now Steel was probably breaking back into Steve

Polmont's flat, acting all surprised at the boxroom full of stolen goods. At least Logan didn't have to worry about his fingerprints being on anything.

He checked the recipe again, went to the wine rack for the last bottle of red in the house and glugged in about a glassful.

Move over Gordon Ramsay.

Should have taken a bottle of that vodka when he'd had the chance. *And* the video game. Be nice if the job actually came with some perks for a change.

He let the sauce simmer for a bit, then helped himself to a glass. Chef's prerogative. It wasn't as if he was planning on getting hammered, just having a civilized glass of wine. Then another one. And another.

Bloody Steel. Lecturing him about *his* attitude, and *his* drinking. How many times had she turned up at the station hungover and reeking of stale booze? Not to mention helping herself to evidence from Steve Polmont's flat.

Hypocrite.

Logan chucked everything together in the casserole dish, then covered it in a wodge of grated cheddar. Whacked it in the oven.

Maybe have another glass of wine to celebrate. . .

Not every day you cook a five-star meal, is it?

Might as well finish the bottle. No point letting it go to waste.

He clunked back into the flat. 'Sam? You home?'

No answer.

'Sam?'

Logan kicked off his shoes, then dumped the bag from Oddbins down on the kitchen table. Two bottles of Shiraz, and a Sauvignon Blanc. He dug out the corkscrew – got to let the wine breathe, right?

91

Maybe try a glass, just to check it's OK.

He toasted his reflection in the kitchen window and drank.

Drank some more.

Pasta bake smelled good.

He shrugged off his jacket and rolled up his shirt sleeves. Maybe have some crisps to keep him going till Samantha got back.

Logan topped up his wine again. Raised it to his lips. Then swore as the doorbell went.

Why could she never remember her damn keys?

He placed his glass carefully on the working surface, then unlocked the flat's front door and hurried down the communal stairwell. Unlatched the deadbolt and threw the door open. 'You'd forget your head if it wasn't. . .'

A large man stood on the pavement outside, scarred face pinched into a disfigured scowl.

Reuben.

He hefted his thumb over his shoulder at a black BMW, its hazard lights winking on and off in the cold, crisp evening. 'Mr Mowat wants to see you.'

Fuck.

Logan looked down at his own feet. Black socks with a hole in one toe. 'I'm kinda in the middle of—'

'*Now.*'

Logan blinked, the wine making his teeth itch, the mellow buzz turning into an unpleasant fizzing behind his eyes. 'But—'

'I'm not telling you again.'

'Can I at least put my shoes on?'

Skeletal trees hunched over a collection of potholes and cracked tarmac, winding through the darkness. The BMW bumped along the rutted track, the occasional grinding noise from under their feet making Reuben grit his teeth. 'Fuckin' thing. . .'

Logan looked out at the darkened countryside. Two days ago these fields were bathed in the moon's glow, now there was just the car's headlights as they headed down the side road overlooking Malk the Knife's building site, not far from where Logan and Steel had parked on Monday night. Waiting for Steve Polmont to turn up.

The BMW's headlights picked out one of those big, ugly Porsche 4×4 things at the end of the lane, its exhaust spiralling out into the cold night air. Reuben stopped, hauled on the handbrake, then killed the engine and the lights.

Darkness.

Reuben turned and glowered at Logan. 'Listen up: you upset Mr Mowat tonight and I'll tear your cock off and make you eat it. Understand?'

'Why would—'

'You fucking watch yourself, McRae.'

'God's sake. . .' Wanker. Logan popped open his door and stepped out into the overcast night.

Bloody *freezing*. Right through the soles of his holey socks. Bastard could have let him grab his shoes. . .

At least it had stopped raining.

Logan hobbled through the darkness to the Porsche Cayenne, breath trailing along behind him, then clambered into the passenger seat and clunked the door shut. Shivered.

'Ah, Logan, glad you could make it.' Wee Hamish Mowat sat hunched behind the wheel, gnarled hands held over the vents. His face was caught in the glow of the dashboard lights – that big hooked nose, the deep crevasse wrinkles, eyes sparkling like something sharp and dangerous at the bottom of a toy box. 'Will you take a wee dram?'

'Er . . . yeah. Thanks.'

The warm interior carried the smell of Old Spice, underlaid with something else. Something sour and sickly.

Wee Hamish pulled a silver hipflask from his jacket pocket, unscrewed the lid, then passed it over.

Logan looked at it. 'Actually, Mr Mowat—'

'It's all right, Logan, what I have isn't catching.' His voice was a gravelly mix of Aberdonian and public school. Sounding tired. 'And after everything you've . . . *helped* me with over the last six months, I think you can call me "Hamish", don't you?'

Logan accepted the flask. Forced a smile. 'Thank you. Hamish.'

He wiped the neck and took a swig. Whisky. It started a low fire in his innards, spreading its warmth up through his chest. 'Good stuff.'

'1974 Ardbeg.' Wee Hamish took the flask back and drank. 'Can't take it with you. . .'

They sat in silence for a moment, just the rumble of the engine and the whine of the air vents. Then Wee Hamish pointed through the windscreen at the building site laid out on the fields below. 'Four hundred houses, just like that. Planning permission for a hotel. Going to have a swimming pool. All legitimate and above board.'

Logan kept his mouth shut.

'Course, wouldn't be happening if it wasn't for Donald Trump.' He took another hit of whisky. 'What do you think, Logan: for it, or against it?'

'Er. . .'

'Keeping an open mind? Good. Good. Some say it's a bad thing, that Trump steamrollered local opposition, then went blubbing to the Scottish Parliament when the planning department said he couldn't have his golf course. Got them to overturn the decision. Others say it's a good thing – it shows that Aberdeen's open for business. Welcomes investment. Is looking to the future. . .'

He stared at the hipflask in his hand. 'The future's a funny thing, isn't it?'

Logan shifted in his seat. 'We're pretty sure Malk the Knife's development's just one big money-laundering exercise. He's using it to get a foothold in the North East. . .' He trailed off to a halt. Wee Hamish was staring at him.

'Do you play chess, Logan?'

'Er . . . no. Not really. More of a *Grand Theft Auto* kind of guy.'

'Shame. We shall have to do something about that.' He tapped his fingers on the steering wheel. 'Mr McLennan is the Black King. He moves his pawns around the board, always pushing forwards. Drugs. Prostitution. Counterfeit merchandise. Then he has his bishops. Moving diagonally, back and forth from Edinburgh. Keeping an eye on the souls of his flock. His knights taking care of the opposition.'

'I see. . .'

'Do you?'

Logan wriggled his toes in the warm air of the footwell. 'It's no secret Malk the Knife's pushing in on your territory. We're getting a huge influx of dodgy goods, forged money. Car theft's up about three hundred percent. There's more drugs out there than ever before.'

The old man drank from the flask again, then screwed the cap on and slipped it back into his jacket. 'You shouldn't call him "Malk the Knife", it's disrespectful.'

Logan opened his mouth, but Wee Hamish held up a crooked finger.

'Never treat your opponent with disdain, Logan. When you do, you underestimate them. And when you underestimate them, you give them an advantage. Take it from me: it's a lesson learned from many, many games of chess.'

Pause.

'OK. Mr McLennan it is.'

Wee Hamish reached over and patted Logan on the shoulder, his hand unnaturally hot, making Logan's skin prickle through the fabric of his shirt.

'That's good.' The old gangster smiled. 'I don't like people trying to take advantage of my city, Logan. It worries me. Especially now.' He went back to staring out through the windscreen. 'A city needs a White King. Otherwise, how can it go to war?'

Logan hobbled back across the cold, damp ground and jumped into Reuben's BMW. The fat man turned and glowered at him. 'Well?'

Logan shrugged. 'You could've let me put on a pair of bloody shoes. Feet are freezing.' He fiddled with the climate control buttons. 'How do you put on the heat?'

Reuben slapped his fingers away. 'Did I say you could touch my car?'

Logan held his hands up. 'Fine. Don't mind me. I'll just catch pneumonia and die. Perfect.'

The little lane snapped into focus as Wee Hamish's Porsche headlights came on, then the huge 4×4 backed up, swung around, and squeezed past them, half up on the grass verge.

And then it was gone.

Reuben performed a clunky seven-point-turn, and headed back the way they'd come.

They bumped off the cracked road and onto proper tarmac, roaring back into town at well over the speed limit. The sky had an ominous dark-orange tinge, low clouds reflecting back the streetlights as they drove down the Ellon Road and across the Bridge of Don.

Reuben broke the silence. 'Glove compartment.'

Logan looked at him. 'What about it?'

'Open the fucking thing, you moron.'

Inside, there was an AA card, a Scottish road atlas, and a standard white envelope. The thing was sealed, stuffed full to bursting. Logan pulled it out. 'What's this?'

'Mr Mowat says it's relevant to your interests.'

Logan eased up one side of the flap, but Reuben smacked his hand.

'Don't open that in here! Fuck's wrong with you?'

Logan hit him back, whisky and wine burning in his stomach. 'I'm getting pretty bloody sick of you acting like a dick the whole time!'

Reuben jammed on the brakes. 'Who the fuck you think you're talking to?' This time it wasn't a smack it was a slap, a backhand right across Logan's cheek, hard enough to bounce him off the headrest. 'Clean out your lugs, *Officer*, you never, ever speak like that to me again. Understand?'

Logan leaned forward in his seat, feeling his cheek starting to swell up, the taste of blood in his mouth where he'd bitten his tongue. 'Fuck. . .' Bastard. Fucking fat bastard. Fucking—

'Better learn to show some respect, McRae, or I'll—'

Logan slammed his elbow into the bridge of Reuben's nose. The car lurched forward and stalled as blood poured down Reuben's face.

Oh . . . *fuck*.

Reuben was going to kill him. He was going to drag him out into the middle of nowhere and fucking kill him.

DO SOMETHING!

The big man's hands came up, but Logan hit him again. Another elbow in the face, splitting his lip. Again. And again. Fast. Furious. Vicious. Not giving the fat bastard time to recover or fight back. Hammering into Reuben's skull as he tried to cover his bleeding face with his hands. The big man didn't cry out, didn't whimper; the dull thunk, thunk, thunk of bone on broken skin and Logan's grunts the only sound.

A car horn blared from somewhere behind them.

Logan slumped back in his seat. Teeth gritted. Elbow aching as Reuben curled forwards, shuddering, dripping bright-red on the leather upholstery, his breath a harsh bubbling wheeze.

'I'm a *police* officer.' Logan wrenched his seatbelt free. 'You EVER touch me again, I'll fucking kill you!'

He hauled the door open and staggered out.

That car horn sounded again, the driver mouthing obscenities through the windscreen. Logan stuck two fingers up at him, stuffed the envelope in his back pocket, and marched away up George Street in his socks.

Fucking Reuben.

He ran a hand across his eyes. His fingers were trembling, heart pounding, feeling sick as the adrenaline rush slowly faded, leaving nothing but the booze behind.

Now what was he supposed to do? No way Reuben would ever let this go. Hitting him *once* had been bad enough, but panicking and doing it again and again?

God, his elbow was really sore. . .

The first drop of rain slapped against the back of Logan's neck, getting heavier as he hobbled along the cold pavement. Brilliant. As if the day needed to get any worse. By the time he was passing the university playing fields, it was chucking it down, a freezing deluge that soaked right through his shirt, socks and trousers.

The Bobbin was just up ahead, lights blazing from its windows, a little knot of smokers huddling in the lee of the porch over the front door. Banished to lung cancer and pleurisy. Logan hobbled inside.

The pub was getting busy – students from the university clustered around low tables, vintage Meatloaf pounding out of the jukebox.

Logan squelched his way to the bar, then closed his eyes and swore. No wallet. Reuben wouldn't let him go back for his coat.

And Logan hadn't said a bloody word about it, had he? No, he just got in the car like a good little boy, because Reuben was a big, fat, scary bastard. . .

Oh, he was *so* screwed.

He rummaged through his trouser pockets, coming up with a couple of pound coins and some smush. Just enough for a pint of Stella. A young woman with a pierced eyebrow and a ring through her nose stopped reading the job section of the *Press and Journal* for long enough to serve him. 'Anythin' else?'

He took a deep gulp, the cold lager making one of his teeth ache. 'Got a payphone?'

She frowned. 'You OK? Your arm's all, like, bleeding and stuff.'

He looked down – the dark-red stain started at his right elbow, fading to pink at the cuff. Reuben's blood. Shirt was probably ruined now. 'Phone?'

She pointed towards the back of the bar. 'Out of order. Some "funny bastard",' she made finger-quotes, 'superglued the receiver into the cradle last night. . . Look, you need an ambulance or something?'

'No.'

That must have come out sharper than he'd intended, because she flinched back.

He closed his eyes and rubbed at the bridge of his nose. 'Sorry been a crappy day. Any chance of a taxi?'

She sucked her cheeks in for a moment, then nodded. 'Give us a second.'

She went off to serve a big woman with a bad perm and a Six-Nations rugby top, then made a call on the cordless phone behind the bar. By the time she returned, Logan was halfway down his pint.

'Fifteen minutes, OK?'

'Thanks.' He took his drink and squelched over to the only free booth in the place, collapsing onto the faux-leather bench. Shifting about, trying to get comfortable. There was something lumpy in his back pocket. . . Logan pulled out the envelope Reuben had given him.

He peeled back the flap and peered inside. Money. A *lot* of money. 'Sodding hell. . .' It was full of fifties, twenties, tens, and fives.

A quick look around to make sure no one was watching, then he counted out the notes onto the seat beside him, keeping his body between the cash and the rest of the bar. Three grand in fifties, five hundred in twenties, two in tens, and a dozen fivers. Three thousand, seven hundred and sixty quid in used, non-sequentially numbered bills.

Just when he thought the day couldn't get any worse. . .

13

Logan mashed his thumb against the flat's doorbell again, then turned and waved at the taxi sitting at the kerb. Engine running. Driver staring back at him. Safe and dry out of the rain.

'Come on, Samantha. . .'

Finally the building's door swung open. She stood on the threshold, frowning at him, eyebrows shooting upwards. 'What happened to you?'

'I need some cash for the cab.'

She sighed. 'Hold on.' Samantha limped back upstairs, returning two minutes later with a dog-eared twenty. 'This do?'

'Thanks.' Logan paid the driver then squelched after her up to the flat, leaving wet-sock footprints on the steps. 'Christ, what a day. . .'

'You're wringing.'

He peeled off his soggy shirt and chucked it in the kitchen sink, then did the same with his trousers and socks till he was standing there in nothing but his pale, goose-pimpled skin and damp, grey underpants.

She handed him a stale-smelling towel from the washing

basket and he scrubbed at his hair on the way to the fridge-freezer. The Wyborowa nestled between the frozen sweetcorn and the fish fingers – Logan pulled the bottle of vodka out and clunked it down on the working surface, followed by two shot glasses covered in frost. 'Want one?'

'Sure you wouldn't rather have a cup of tea or something? You look frozen.'

He filled one of the chilled glasses to the brim, then threw it back. His hand only shook a little.

'Are you OK? I came home and the flat door was lying wide to the wall.'

'Been better.' He made another vodka disappear. Every time he bent his arm, pain radiated out from his battered elbow, a livid purple stain already spreading across the pale skin. He made another trip to the freezer for the bag of sweetcorn, holding it against the swollen joint.

'Where's your shoes and jacket? You trying to catch your death?'

Logan dropped the towel around his shoulders, feeling the Wyborowa work its numbing magic. 'I made pasta bake.'

Samantha pointed at the casserole dish sitting on a trivet next to the microwave. His culinary efforts were all shrivelled and brown. Blackened in places. She hadn't even tried it.

And he couldn't blame her. It looked bloody awful.

'Was a nice thought, though.' She peered into the sink, then pulled out his shirt, staring at the bloodstained sleeve. Then at him. 'What happened to your arm?'

Logan shrugged. 'You wouldn't believe what that cow Steel said to me today: apparently my attitude's crap and everyone hates me. Oh, and I drink too much.' He polished off another shot of Polish vodka. 'Can you believe that? *She* thinks *I* drink too much.'

Samantha didn't say anything.

Logan groaned, slumped in his seat. 'God, not you as well!'

'Well, maybe—'

'Oh come on! So I have a wee drink every now and then.'

'It's not now and then, it's every night.'

'I give up.' He poured himself another drink.

She stuck her hands on her hips. 'You asked.'

'And it's not every night.'

'Really? When was the last time you went to bed sober?'

'Look, it's not like I'm an alki, OK?'

Samantha's chin came up. 'Prove it.'

'I don't have to prove—'

'Go a week without getting hammered every night.'

'Just. . .' He closed his eyes. Counted to three. 'Can we not do this, please? I've had a really, *really* crappy day.'

'Oh, you've had a bad day? Well you know what, mine was just fucking great. I got to spend eight hours scraping a thirteen-year-old girl's internal organs off the underside of an articulated lorry.'

Silence.

Logan put the top back on the vodka bottle. 'I'm sorry.'

She settled back against the sink. 'Go a week.'

A week. No problem. Could do that easy. 'OK.'

He waited until she disappeared off to the bathroom to do her teeth, then opened the bottle again.

Logan surfaced with a gasp, the duvet wrapped around his chest like a fist. Jesus. . .

He struggled free and sat on the edge of the bed, shivering in the light of the clock radio. 04:21. Another happy night full of sand and severed heads. Only this time it had been Samantha buried out in the dunes.

He turned and looked at her side of the bed. Empty again.

Brilliant.

Logan dragged himself through to the bathroom for a sulphurous pee. He stood there for a minute, trying to decide if he wanted to be sick or not. Mouth dry. Still a bit drunk. . .

He coughed, retched a little, then bent over and howched a purple and black splatter into the sink. Red wine and saliva, looking like a tumour on the white porcelain. Logan washed it away with the cold tap, before splashing some water on his face. His cheek had taken on an angry purple-and-yellow tinge where Reuben had hit him – top lip swollen, split and stinging. Could barely bend his right arm.

Why did everything *always* have to be so screwed up?

He knocked back a couple of paracetamol, then dumped the empty blister pack in the little stainless steel bin with all the blood-soaked toilet paper.

He killed the bathroom light, hobbled back down the hall, eased the lounge door open and peered inside. Samantha was on the couch, stripy-socked feet sticking out from beneath the spare duvet.

Logan shut the door as quietly as he could then slouched through to the kitchen for a pint or two of water, trying to sabotage the coming hangover.

The sink was still full of his clothes, so he dragged everything out and stuffed them in the washing machine. Then remembered the envelope full of cash in the trouser pocket.

It was all damp and wrinkly, but the contents seemed to have survived OK. All three thousand, seven hundred and sixty pounds of it.

Could have used it to pay for the taxi, instead of standing out in the rain like an idiot waiting for Samantha. Should've used it. Stupid not to. What did it really matter anyway? Just because it came from Wee Hamish Mowat.

Six months now he'd been doing . . . *favours* for Aberdeen's biggest crime lord. Nothing illegal – he wasn't getting people off with murder, tampering with evidence, or tipping Wee Hamish off when there was a raid on the way – just acting on information. Arresting rival drug dealers, shutting down someone else's brothel, a dog fighting ring in Ellon. Taking other players' pawns off the chess board. Pawns who needed locking up anyway.

And not once had Wee Hamish felt the need to hand over envelopes stuffed with cash. To *buy* him.

£3,760.

'Fuck. . .' Logan let his head thunk against the kitchen cabinet.

Eighteen months ago he'd been the golden boy of Grampian Police and now look at him: everyone down the station thought he was a foul-tempered, alcoholic tosser; he'd just battered a mob enforcer half to death in the middle of King Street; and Aberdeen's biggest crime lord thought he should be on the payroll. Woo hoo. Way to go. Fan-fucking-tastic.

A new personal low.

Logan stacked all the notes together into one pile, wrapped it up in kitchen paper, then crept out into the hallway and hid the lot in the airing cupboard, behind the hot water tank.

It wasn't perfect, but it'd do till he figured something else out.

The black Range Rover winds its way slowly north. Newcastle to Edinburgh is the worst bit: the A1's a fucking disgrace, isn't it? 121 miles of twisty tarmac with the occasional crawler lane and tiny patches of dual carriageway. Get stuck behind a caravan on this thing and you're screwed, like.

Not that it's a problem at twenty to five on a Saturday morning. Wipers going at a steady creak, keeping the snow confined to the edges of the windscreen. Winter wonderland in Newcastle when they left. Six inches in places.

They're making good time, even though Tony's taking it easy – iPod hooked into the huge car's stereo, dribbling out that jazz stuff Julie likes so much. It's not too bad, once you get used to it.

She's asleep in the passenger seat, and Neil's curled up in the back with a coat draped over him like a blanket, mouth open, snoring in time with the bloke playing the saxophone. It's funny how even the most violent, dangerous bastards can look like little kids when they're asleep.

The sat-nav says 102 miles to Aberdeen.

Tony keeps the needle at a steady sixty-five. No speeding. Nothing that would draw attention to them. Playing it cool. Heading north through the snow.

Bringing a whole shit-heap of trouble with him.

14

'Lying *bastards*!' A porcelain dog hit the faded wallpaper, and became a starburst of pale shards. 'All of it. . .' Richard Knox grabbed a ballerina from the mantelpiece and sent it crashing into the far wall. Face flushed, teeth bared, spittle flying from his lips. 'Bloody lies!'

'Jesus, Richard, calm down!' A large woman – one of Knox's minders from Sacro – was crouching behind the sofa, popping her head up over the dusty fabric, then ducking down again as a shire horse turned into porcelain shrapnel.

'They've no right!'

Logan froze on the threshold, head pounding. 'What the hell's going on here?'

Knox snatched a Scotty dog from the mantelpiece and drew his arm back to send it flying. Logan stepped forward and grabbed it off him.

'All right, that's enough!'

Knox span around, eyes wide and shiny. Lips twitching across his gritted teeth. 'Give it back!'

'Constable Guthrie?'

Guthrie bumbled into the living room, clutching greasy paper bags from the baker's they'd stopped at on the way over here, a wodge of flaky pastry in his other hand. 'What?'

'Lying. . .' Knox's eyes darted left, then right, then he snatched up a fishing teddy bear and sent that flying instead. 'BASTARDS!'

The constable dumped his baked goods on the ancient couch and grabbed Knox's arm, twisting it up behind his back, then slamming him into the wall. 'Behave yourself!'

Knox struggled, screaming abuse. Guthrie glanced over at Logan, and got the nod. He pulled Knox back a couple of feet, then rammed him forwards again. Making the photos above the mantelpiece rattle.

'Aaagh . . . get off us!'

'You want another one?'

Knox didn't reply, but he did keep wriggling, so Guthrie introduced him to the wallpaper again.

This time the struggling stopped.

'You want the handcuffs?'

Silence.

'OK.' The constable let go and stepped back.

Knox staggered towards one of the cat-shredded armchairs and collapsed into it, rubbing his wrist and staring at the dead television. 'Liars. . .'

The woman crept around from behind the sofa. 'Thanks.' There were little flecks of white china in her hair.

Logan pulled out his notebook. 'Richard Knox, I'm arresting you for assault. You do not have to say anything, but if you fail to mention—'

'I didn't assault anyone.' He kept his eyes on the ghosts in the TV screen.

Logan glanced at the woman, raised his eyebrows.

She shook her head. 'Didn't touch me.'

'Where's your partner? Thought there was supposed to be two of you.'

Knox shifted in his seat, muttering, 'Got me rights. . .'

'Harry's stuck in the bog. Had a dodgy chicken chow mein

last night. I was going to send him home if he doesn't get any better.'

Logan looked around at the wreckage, then rubbed at his gritty eyes. 'You want to tell me what the hell this was about then?'

She pointed at a tattered copy of the *Aberdeen Examiner* lying against the skirting board. Half the pages were sprawled across the carpet, but the lead story was clearly visible from where Logan stood: 'SEX-BEAST STRIKES FEAR INTO COMMUNITY'. The photo of Knox was more up to date than the last one the papers used. Someone had been digging.

Logan bent down and picked up the front page, letting the rest of it fall back to the floor.

> ### Exclusive by Colin Miller
> Everyone knows a leopard can't change his spots: once a dangerous animal, always a dangerous animal, but the people of Aberdeenshire are being expected to believe that convicted serial rapist Richard Knox can live amongst them without posing a serious risk to the population. Knox (39), a vicious sexual predator, served eight years in a high-security prison for the brutal abduction and rape of Newcastle grandfather William Brucklay (68). . .

It wasn't exactly the journalist's best work. Sensationalist, melodramatic, and obviously designed to whip up outrage and panic. Further in it got even worse, with quotes from people in Newcastle, and William Brucklay's grandchildren: teenagers more than happy to share the family's anger. Castration's too good for him, they should bring back hanging. That kind of thing.

And in Richard Knox's case, they were probably right.

Logan folded the page up, then dumped it on the coffee table.

Knox was clutching his carrier bag again, the thing rustling as he rocked back and forth in his seat, muttering. 'It's all lies.'

'All of it?'

'"Convicted serial rapist".' He scowled at the TV. 'Was convicted of one rape. *One*. Not a series. Served me time. Found God, didn't I?'

'Well. . .' Logan looked at the chunky woman from Sacro – Margaret, Marge? Something like that. 'Maybe you'd be better off trying your luck somewhere else? We could organize a midnight flit: get you somewhere further away, where they don't know you. Devon, Cornwall, something like that?'

Get you the hell out of Aberdeen before you cause any more trouble, you creepy little bastard.

'This is me home!' Knox drew back his foot, then lashed out, crashing his heel into the TV screen, shattering it, sending the whole thing clattering over backwards to the floor.

Marge/Margaret flinched. Swore.

PC Guthrie loomed over Knox. 'All right, on your feet.'

The man didn't even look up at him, just sat there, clutching his foot. 'What you going to do, like, arrest us for smashing me own telly? Bloody thing didn't work anyway.'

The constable flopped his hands about for a moment. 'Sarge?'

Logan shrugged. 'He's got a point.'

Knox closed his eyes, lips pinched tight, breathing in and out through his pointy nose. Then stood, and knelt in front of the ancient electric fire, head bowed, hands clasped together. Mouth moving silently.

They left him to it.

'Tell you.' Margaret/Marge filled a new-looking kettle in the sink, and plugged it in. 'He's really starting to creep me out.'

110

Logan shrugged. 'Sex offenders can be a bit—'

'Trust me, I *know* sex offenders. Did six years as a prison officer in Peterhead, I've seen every flavour of mong and stot you can think of and none of them weirded me out like Knox.' She picked four mugs off the draining board and sniffed them, then plopped a teabag in each. 'There was this one guy done for snatching women off the streets – blondes usually – bundled them into the back of an old van with the windows blacked out. Liked to rape them while he burned them with the cigarette lighter. Apparently nipples were a particular favourite. Never looked you in the eye when he spoke, always stared right here. . .' She pointed at her not inconsiderable breasts. 'You just knew he was thinking about it: the smell, the sizzling sound. The screams.'

'Christ.'

'Yeah, and even *he* wasn't as creepy as Knox.'

She rinsed a teaspoon under the tap, peering at Logan out the corner of her eye. 'So . . . what happened to your face?'

Logan reached up and touched his right cheek. The skin was all swollen and tender. 'Cut myself shaving.'

'Right. . .'

The sound of flushing came from upstairs.

Marge/Margaret looked up and smiled. 'Harry's arse must be in tatters by now.'

She was fishing the teabags out of the mugs when a balding, middle-aged man groaned in through the door, clutching both sides of his little pot belly. Face all pale and sweaty. 'I think I might have died. . .'

'You want tea?' She pointed at the greasy paper bags, sitting on the work surface. 'The nice policemen brought doughnuts.'

He grimaced. 'Mandy, please, just dig a hole in the back garden and bury me.'

'Told you that chow mein looked dodgy.'

'Bloody thing wasn't even past its sell-by date.' He forced

a smile, then held his hand out to Logan. 'Hi, I'm Harry—' Something deep inside him gurgled, and he grimaced. 'Oh God, not again. . .'

And then he was off, scurrying back up the stairs, moaning and swearing.

Logan leant back against the cooker. 'If you're worried about Knox, maybe—'

'It's not like I'm scared of him, or anything. I mean, come on.' She pointed at her breasts again. 'These are "get out of jail free" cards, far as he's concerned. He's just . . . not right, you know?'

'Yeah, but he's going to— bugger.' Logan dragged out his warbling phone. 'McRae?'

DI Steel's voice came through from the other end. *'Did you chase up that cadaver dog like I told you?'*

'Did it first thing. Should be here round about eleven.'

'Believe it when I see it. Tell you, those Strathclyde bobbies—'

Logan put his hand over the mouthpiece, mimed smoking a cigarette, and pointed towards the back door. Mandy nodded and offered him a doughnut.

The handle turned, but the door wouldn't budge. Logan balanced his tea on the windowsill and gave the wood a bump with his shoulder. It bounced, but didn't open.

'What about that fat tit Danby, you manage to dig up any dirt on him?'

'No. You told me to look into his mate, Billy Adams.'

Another shove and the door creaked in its frame. One more and it popped open. The back garden was a riot of dead thistles and knee-high yellowy grass, the broken brown spears of docken flowers jabbing up into the grey morning. A holly bush sprawled out from the back corner, beside a bloated and crumbling shed.

'You have actually heard of the word "initiative", right?'

Logan stepped out onto a patio made up of cracked

112

concrete slabs, wet grass poking up through the joins. 'There's no way Danby came all the way up here just to hold Knox's hand: he's a *superintendent*, they don't babysit rapists, doesn't matter how well known they are. Something's up.'

He balanced the doughnut on top of his tea and lit a cigarette, the smoke spiralling away into the cold air.

'You thought about what I said yesterday? The attitude, the drinking, the being a pain in the arse?'

'I am *not* a pain in the arse.'

'It's my arse and you're in it. Being a pain.' There was a pause. *'Case in point: Douglas Walker's brief's downstairs right now, kicking up shite about his client being denied his human rights.'*

Logan closed his eyes and massaged his pounding forehead. 'Sodding hell – *please* tell me you didn't just leave him in the interview room!'

'Oh no you don't: he was your bloody arrest! Why didn't you charge him?'

Bloody typical.

'Because you ordered me to go supervise the Perv Patrol after the MAPPA meeting! Then you dragged me off to the building site and Polmont's flat. . .' He let his head fall back until he was staring straight up into the low grey sky. 'Walker was only in on a volley, his lawyer's going to have a field day.'

Steel let the awkward silence drag out for a couple of beats. *'Don't be so sodding daft: course I didn't just leave him there. What do you think I am, an amateur? Interviewed him, charged him, packed him off to a cell for the night.'*

'Oh . . . OK.'

'Point is, you should've bloody well checked first thing this morning, shouldn't you? 'Stead of waltzing off with no' a care in the world.'

'I didn't waltz anywhere! You *told* me to go check up on Knox, so I checked up on Knox. How am I supposed to sodding do everything?' Logan flicked the ash off the tip of

113

his cigarette. 'And in case you're interested, Knox threw a wobbly when he saw the morning paper.'

'Aw, boo-hoo. Is the widdle wapist upset? Diddums. Tell him I'll come over and kiss it all better with the toe of my boot.'

'You know, you could *help* for a change: get the Press Office to tell the media to back off Knox for a bit.' Logan dropped his cigarette and ground it out against the wet paving slab with his foot.

'Fuck him.' Steel sniffed. *'Get your arse back to the ranch and deal with Walker's bloody bum-faced brief. I want it all sorted out by the time I'm finished at Polmont's flat.'*

Logan hung up and slid the phone back into his pocket. The doughnut had left a greasy film on the surface of his tea. He poured it out onto the waterlogged grass, not in the mood any more.

Bloody DI Steel – why did *everything* always have to be his fault?

Back inside, he dumped the mug on the draining board, said thank you for the tea, then made for the front door. He glanced in through the lounge door on the way past, and stopped. Knox was standing in the bay window, looking out at the dreich clay-coloured sky, hugging that carrier bag of his like a hot water bottle for the soul.

He turned, saw Logan watching him, and looked away. 'I'm sorry about acting the spaz, like. Just gets a bit much sometimes, everyone hating us, you know?'

Logan did. 'It's. . . Don't worry about it.'

Knox nodded, and turned back to the grimy glass. 'Do you have a guardian angel, Sergeant?'

Logan laughed. 'If I do he's shite at his job.'

'I've got one. God sent someone to look after us. Even when I was in prison he kept an eye out. Kept us safe so I could learn me lesson.'

Logan took his car keys from his pocket. 'Yeah, well—'

'See, God's always testing us, isn't He? Getting caught, going to prison, that was all part of His plan for us. If He hadn't done it, I wouldn't have found Him, would I?' Knox reached out a hand and drew something on the dirty window with a fingertip. 'He's made us the man I am, like.'

Now there was something to be proud of.

The snow's coming. Richard can feel it in his bones. His arm aches where they broke it at that first group therapy session. Doing all the STOP programme bollocks: everyone sitting about like a bunch of fannies, whinging on about how their mummies and daddies didn't love them. Didn't like him taking the piss, did they? No. And ever since then, his arm aches when it's cold.

The first lesson from God: know when to keep your mouth shut.

Course, then they all had little accidents, didn't they? And God said unto them, never fuck with a man who works for Mental Mikey – the holy word delivered by a couple of screws who owed the big man a favour.

Guardian angel, see?

Richard watches the policeman hunch his way down the garden path, through the rusty gate, and into a little brown Fiat that looks like a motorized turd.

Stared at him like he was mad, didn't he? Didn't believe Richard was telling the truth, the whole truth, and nothing but the truth. So. Help. Him. God.

It's all a test. It's all a lesson. How you deal with things is important to Him, isn't it? Stands to reason. Otherwise He wouldn't make things happen the way He does.

And God loves Richard Knox.

Richard places his hand against the glass and scrubs away the picture he drew in the grime. Smiles to himself.

Soon. Very, very soon. . .

15

It was nearly half ten by the time Logan got back to the CID room. The place was packed – plainclothes and uniformed constables sitting in every seat, working the phones. The almost constant murmur of conversation and electronic ringing.

'Yes, sir, I know you're worried about your father but—'

'In Kincorth? I see. . . And what makes you believe it was Richard Knox?'

A constable stuck her hand over the mouthpiece and offered the phone to Logan. 'Sarge, there's a bloke on the phone says he was attacked by Knox last night, do you want to deal?'

Logan looked out across the crowded, noisy room. 'Is every nutjob in the city calling in?'

'Pretty much. So, you want it?'

'Do I buggery.' He hurried through into the little sergeants' alcove, before anyone else tried to lumber him with their loony, closed the door – shutting out the babble – and collapsed into his seat. Rubbed at his thumping forehead.

He had the little office to himself, no one to see him rummaging through everyone's desks on the hunt for painkillers. OK, so he was a bit hungover but after Reuben and everything he'd deserved a drink, hadn't he? Even if the late night vodka hadn't been the best of ideas.

DS Mark MacDonald had a packet of ibuprofen hidden in a drawer. Logan helped himself to two, washing them down with the pint of orange juice he'd bought on the way back to the station. His stomach gurgled as the liquid hit, bitter acid at the bottom of his throat.

There was a Post-it note stuck right in the middle of Logan's computer screen: a summons in block capitals. 'MY OFFICE AS SOON AS YOU GET BACK!!!' Signed, 'DI BEATTIE!' just like that, with an exclamation mark. Just in case Logan didn't know he was a dickhead.

Logan peeled it off, scrunched it up, and hurled it at the bin.

Someone shouted, 'Shop?' and Logan looked around to find PC Butler standing in the doorway. She wasn't exactly the tallest officer in Grampian Police: petite, with cropped blonde hair, Butler looked like the kind of person who helped little old ladies across the road; raised money for under-privileged kittens; couldn't pull the skin off a boiled tattie. Which just went to show how wrong you could be.

She waggled a manila folder at him. 'You in for an armed robbery?'

'Dump it on Doreen's desk.' He jerked his thumb towards a neatly ordered workstation, with law books alphabetically arranged on a shelf above the computer.

Constable Butler pulled a face, wrinkling her nose, and puckering her mouth. 'You sure you don't want it?'

'Positive.'

'Oh come on.' She settled onto the only clear patch on Biohazard Bob's desk. 'DS Taylor's being a right cow at the moment. Ever since her husband ran off with that accounts assistant, you can't do anything right.'

117

'Give it to Bob then.'

Butler shuddered. 'I'd have to drive him about, and it's too bloody cold to have the windows open all the time.' She batted her eyelashes. 'Please?'

'DS MacDonald?'

'Wandering hands. He does it again I'll have to castrate him. Don't want that on your conscience, do you?'

Logan turned away and jabbed the power button on his computer. 'Thought you lot in uniform were all whinging about me being shouty and sarcastic.'

He could hear her shifting on the desk behind him. 'Yeah, but you're kinda the lesser of four evils. So . . . armed robbery?'

Logan slumped back in his seat and swore at the ceiling tiles. 'Tell me about it.'

'Great.' She slapped the folder down on the desk in front of him. 'Henderson's the Jewellers, on Crown Street. Bloke wanders in with a wee kid in a pushchair, asks to see the engagement rings, and when the assistant hauls them out, our boy produces a sawn-off sledgehammer.'

'Who the hell holds up a jewellers with a sawn-off sledge-hammer? You sure it wasn't a shotgun?'

'Positive.'

Logan flicked through the file. 'Time?'

'Nine fifteen this morning.'

'Anyone hurt?'

'One witness peed herself, that count? Said she was only in to pick up her husband's watch.'

Logan pulled out the witness statements, skimming them as PC Butler waited. At the back was a list of items the jewellers claimed their mystery shopper had got away with. It had an estimated value of just under five hundred pounds. Not exactly worth getting banged up for. 'Is that all?'

Butler shrugged. 'Apparently. Went on a bit of a rampage,

118

smashed open display cabinets, stuffed his pockets with shiny tat, then legged it.' She paused. 'Got the security camera footage upstairs if you want to see it?'

'What the hell.' Logan thumped the folder on top of his heaped in-tray. 'Fingerprints?'

'Gloves.' Butler smiled. 'Thanks, Sarge.'

Logan checked his watch. 'You've got twenty minutes, then I'm out of here.'

'But Sa-arge—'

'Got an appointment with a cadaver dog. Take it or leave it.'

'Done.'

They'd got as far as the corridor outside the CID room when Beattie appeared. Face pink and shiny, nose red, all bundled up in a duvet-style puffy jacket. There were droplets glittering in his moustache and as he saw PC Butler and Logan he wiped them away with the back of his hand. 'DS McRae, I need to see you in my office.'

Logan didn't move. 'Got an armed robbery to look into.'

Beattie frowned. Looked at PC Butler. Sniffed. Rubbed at his beard. 'Constable, will you excuse us for a moment?'

She made herself scarce.

'You were supposed to help me with the knock-off merchandise enquiry.'

Logan slumped back against the wall. 'Did you phone Trading Standards yet?' Knowing full well that there was no way the beardy tosser—

'I did it yesterday.'

'Oh. . . Right.' Pause. 'And?'

'It's getting worse. We've had fifteen complaints about dodgy DVD players this week, then there's the hair straighteners, and the vodka, and the perfume, and the iPods. Whole city's awash with counterfeit goods.' Beattie sniffed, then hauled out a lumpy grey hankie and blew his nose into it.

Paused to check the contents. 'Talking of which: Big Gary tells me you've got a lead on those dodgy twenties?'

Logan shrugged. 'We arrested someone, if that's what you mean.'

'Still in custody?'

'Far as I know.' Because he hadn't bothered to check. Sod DI Steel, there was no way he was running about just to keep some jumped-up solicitor happy. Whoever Douglas Walker's lawyer was, he could bloody well wait.

Beattie chewed on the edge of his moustache for a bit. 'Right, about these fake handbags and things. . .'

There was more, but Logan wasn't really listening. DI Steel had just limped through the double doors at the end of the corridor, legs bowed, face all pinched up on one side, showing gritted, yellowy teeth as she hobbled towards them.

'. . .do you understand?' Beattie paused, obviously waiting for a response.

'Erm.' Logan frowned. 'In what way?'

Beattie rolled his eyes. It made him look even more of a tit than usual. 'Will you sort it out or not?'

Steel was getting closer. Limping and wincing all the way.

'Erm, yeah, sure.'

'Monday. Don't forget.'

She hissed to a halt and scowled at Beattie blocking the corridor. 'Move it or lose it, beardy boy.'

Beattie stiffened. 'There's no need to—'

'Blah, blah, blah. Out the way before I introduce Mrs Boot to Mr Testicles.' She winced, paused, hauled at the crotch of her grey trouser suit. 'Second thoughts: McRae, kick his knackers into orbit. Then get your scarred backside down to Interview room three, Douglas Walker's brief's waiting for you.'

'Actually,' Beattie stuck his hairy chin out, 'Sergeant McRae already *has* a job to do. Don't you Sergeant?'

Steel limped closer. 'Aye, he has: working for *me*.'

Beattie glowered. 'I'm not some wee DS for you to push around any more, I'm a *detective inspector*. And I say McRae's working for me!'

Logan groaned. It didn't matter how this went, he'd be the one who'd end up getting the blame. He turned and looked back towards the CID room.

Steel and Beattie were shouting at each other, nose to nose in the middle of the corridor, so Logan crept back through the door, leaving them to it. With a bit of luck he could sneak out the other side of the CID room, down the bare concrete stairwell and away before they even noticed he was gone.

Logan swore, told PC Butler to pause the tape, and dragged out his phone. 'McRae.'

DI Steel's gravelly voice crackled in his ear, *'Where the sodding hell did you disappear off to? I've got an angry solicitor wanting someone to shout at, and he's no' bloody doing it at me!'*

The review suite was a tiny room on the ground floor of Force Headquarters: two creaky plastic chairs, a storage cabinet for the police van CCTV hard drives, and the rancid-fatty smell of stale chips coming from somewhere underneath the little Formica desk.

Butler fumbled with the remote, and the image on the screen froze: Henderson's the Jewellers in glorious black-and-white.

A woman stood by a display stand of porcelain figurines, a small boy clutching at the hem of her skirt. A shop assistant slouched behind a long glass counter. A lumpy man was halfway across the shop floor, flat cap on his head, pushing one of those mountain-bike-style strollers – all chrome and big chunky wheels. He had a little child strapped into the seat, wearing a knitted bobble hat, sooking on the floppy ear of a cuddly bunny.

They didn't exactly look like a crack team of armed robbers.

Logan put a hand over the mouthpiece of his phone as Steel ranted away.

'. . .is it no' bad enough I've got idiots like Beattie to deal with, without. . .'

He pointed at the screen. 'This digital, or DVD?'

Butler shook her head. 'Tape.'

'. . .show some sodding responsibility for your actions? And another thing. . .'

That meant the image probably wouldn't be good enough to enhance beyond an indistinct blur. 'OK, let it play again.'

The man stepped up to the counter, head down – looking at the shiny things arrayed beneath the glass. He'd been in the shop two minutes now and the camera still hadn't got a decent shot of his face.

There was a moment's silence from the phone, then, 'McRae! Are you listening to me?'

'Uh-huh.'

Logan tapped the screen again. 'Look at the front door.'

'I swear to God I'm going to snap my foot off in your arse if you don't start. . .'

Butler leaned in closer, face screwed up. 'What?'

'Bottom right corner. He's dropped something where the door meets the jamb, so it won't shut all the way.'

'. . .bastard Beattie: see how you like that!'

The man pointed at something glittering away beneath the counter's glass surface, and the shop assistant nodded. She undid some sort of catch, then opened the back of the display, pulling out a black velvet tray. There was no audio, everything happening in complete silence.

Outside the shop window a bus juddered past. The time stamp in the corner of the screen read '09:14'.

'. . .bloody solicitors crawling up my. . .'

The assistant held up one of the items from the tray.

The man in the flat cap nodded, then reached into his long black overcoat.

PC Butler smiled. 'See, told you.'

The sledgehammer was about half the length it should have been, but that didn't stop it shattering the glass counter top into a million glittering fragments. Another swing and the cash register went flying. Another, and a display case exploded. A silent ballet of destruction.

'. . .should know better by now! Honestly, you're no' a child so stop acting. . .'

The woman in the corner scurried back against the wall, hauling her little boy with her. Mouth open. Screaming.

'. . .your own. That what you want?'

The man hoisted the sledgehammer over his head and brought it crashing down, double handed, into the counter again. The flat cap went flying, exposing a swath of bald head hiding beneath a thin comb-over.

'. . .but no, you *have* to play the bloody idiot. . .'

A scramble of black gloves through the wreckage, stuffing rings and bracelets and necklaces and bits of broken glass into his pockets, then the flat cap was snatched up and rammed down on the balding head again. Not once had he looked at the camera.

The man backed away through the open door, pulling the stroller with him, and—

Logan sat forward and poked the screen. 'There: the cuddly rabbit.'

The little kid in the stroller must have lost its grip, because the rabbit went tumbling to the glass-strewn shop floor. Bounced once. Then lay there.

'The kid was sooking on it, we'll be able to get DNA from the saliva.'

Butler stared at him. 'The kid didn't rob the shop, it was—'

'You don't hold up a jewellers with someone else's kid, do you? What sort of crappy babysitter would that be? It's his. Or maybe a grandchild, but it's definitely related. We'll get a familial DNA match.' Logan sat back in his seat, pleased with himself. 'Get round there and pick up. . .'

He drifted to a halt, then swore as a hand reached back into the shop from outside and grabbed the fallen bunny. Then kicked away whatever had been keeping the door ajar, allowing it to finally clunk shut.

So much for that.

And then Logan realized Steel had stopped ranting in his ear. 'Inspector?' Silence. 'Hello?' He looked at the phone's display. She'd hung up.

Couldn't have been that important then.

Logan sat back in his seat, tapping the mobile against his chin. 'There's something not right about this.'

He told Butler to wind the tape back to the start, then sat and watched everything unfold again. 'See, he blocks the door from closing, so he obviously knows the first thing jewellery shops do is trip the silent alarm. Bang, all the exits lock till the police turn up. But when he does the smash and grab, he goes for sparkly, worthless crap. . .'

PC Butler shrugged. 'Maybe he watches too much telly? *CSI*, *The Bill*, that kind of thing?'

'Could be. Get the shop assistant in front of an e-fit artist, maybe we can—'

BANG. The viewing room door flew open, and there she was: DI Steel, face flushed, teeth gritted. 'You!' She threw a finger in Logan's direction. 'Where the bloody hell do you think you've been?'

Butler shrank in her seat, trying not to make eye contact with anyone.

Logan opened his mouth, but Steel wasn't finished yet.

'Interview room three, *now*.'

'But—'

'NOW!'

'The treatment of my client has been appalling!' The little man shifted in his seat and poked the tabletop with a finger. 'It's an absolute *outrage*!'

Sitting next to him, Douglas Walker was a mass of bruises and misery. He cleared his throat, but the lawyer placed a hand on his shoulder.

'It's all right, Mr Walker, I'll deal with this.' The little man glared at Logan, the strip light shining back off his little round glasses and bald head. 'You held my client for hours, without *any* sort of formal charge, then you forced him to submit to interview without legal representation!'

Logan stared at him in silence for a while. Jumped-up baldy little git. All squint teeth and Armani suit. DI Steel was slouched against the side wall, scowling, playing the disapproving senior officer. Making sure he didn't duck out of being shouted at by Douglas Walker's brief.

'Well?' The lawyer poked the table again. 'We demand an immediate apology and an independent investigation into your—'

'You've not done a lot of criminal work, have you, Mr. . .?'

The little man flushed, pulled out a business card and slapped it down in front of Logan. 'Barrett. Of McGilvery, Barrett, and McGilvery. And I suggest—'

'What are you: friend of the family? I bet you normally do conveyancing, don't you? Maybe a few wills every now and then to keep your hand in. But mostly it's the legal side of buying and selling properties, right?'

'What does that—'

'So basically, you're just a glorified estate agent.'

'How dare—'

'You see, if you knew anything about criminal law, you'd know we can question your client as often as we like and we don't *need* a lawyer present. Look it up.'

Barrett of McGilvery, Barrett, and McGilvery was going an unnatural shade of deep pink. Spittle flying from his mouth, 'You held my client for seven hours without charge, in direct breach—'

'Your client came in voluntarily. Didn't you, Douglas?'

The lawyer gripped his client's shoulder again. 'You don't have to answer that, we've only got his word—'

Logan dropped his notebook on top of the little man's business card. 'Your client signed a declaration that he was happy to help us with our enquiries.'

'You. . .' Barrett looked from Logan to the young man sitting next to him, then back again. 'You conducted an illegal search of—'

'Your client volunteered the location of a holdall full of counterfeit money in his bedroom. And even if he *hadn't* the arrest warrant gave me the legal right to search the premises for anything relating to the offence he'd been charged with.'

Silence.

The lawyer took a deep breath. 'My client is only eighteen, his parents have a right to be—'

'He's old enough to be tried as an adult. And you're old enough to know better.' Logan stood, staring down at the little man with his little round glasses and little triple-barrelled business card. 'Right now Douglas is looking at a ten stretch. Craiginches only holds people serving a maximum of four years, so he's going to be doing his time somewhere exotic. Like Barlinnie, or Shotts.'

A sinister lurching warble cut through the silence – Logan pulled out his phone and cut off the 'Danse Macabre' mid-Wurlitzer. 'McRae.'

Barrett spluttered. 'This is outrageous, we're supposed to be—'

Logan silenced him with a hand. 'Sorry, Gary, there's an idiot here shouting his mouth off.'

'How *dare* you!'

'I said, there's a wee Weegie constable down here for you, with a really big dog. Do me a favour and come get her before it squats one out on my floor.'

'Be right down.' Logan snapped the phone shut.

Barrett jumped to his feet. 'I *insist* you apologize for—'

'We're done here.' Logan turned his back and marched to the interview room door. Hauled it open. Stopped on the threshold. 'You might want to have a wee word with your client about cooperating, *Mr* Barrett. Then you can get back to selling houses, or whatever the hell it is you do when you're not pretending to be a lawyer.'

16

There's three huge seagulls squabbling over a puddle of vomit – darting forwards to snap up the chunky bits. Filthy fuckers. Not natural, is it?

Tony sniffs, chews, then spits out of the Range Rover's window.

Neil's in the back, plugged into his iPod, little white cables coming out of his ears like his head's been wired wrong. Which it probably has.

'You know what I think?' says Tony, even though he knows Neil isn't listening. 'I think this is completely fucked up. Waste of time. And effort.'

He flicks the windscreen wiper and the blades squeak once across the glass, clearing away the speckles of drizzle. Typical Aber-fucking-deen: always bloody raining. Cold as a nun's tit too. Was warmer back in Newcastle, aye and it was snowing there.

The passenger door opens, and Julie climbs in, blonde hair all frizzy from the rain. Five-foot-five of Home Counties English, in jeans, cowboy boots, and a black leather jacket. 'Miss me?' She dumps a white carrier bag on the arm rest between the heavy leather seats, then digs a brush out of that huge handbag of hers and has a go at taming the beast.

Tony checks the rearview mirror, watching one of them parking wardens grumping along the line of cars in the rain. 'Any joy?'

Julie points at the bag. 'Chicken Rogan Josh, balti lamb, king prawn korma for the big girl's blouse in the back—'

Neil sticks his middle finger up at her. So he must be listening after all.

'—three pilaf rice, and a couple of naan bread. One garlic, one cheese.'

Tony groans. 'Not curry *again*.' No wonder his guts are giving him grief. 'What about Danby?'

Julie's face turns down at the edges: it takes a lot of the pretty away. 'Bloody Sacro wouldn't talk to me. Said anything to do with Richard Knox was strictly need-to-know.'

Neil leans forwards, sticking his big head between the seats. He's done that thing with his hair again, makes him look like a greying Geordie Elvis, only with a much bigger nose. 'Sort of fuckin' name is "Sacro" anyway?'

'Don't get me started. . .' She rummages in the plastic bag, tearing free a chunk of greasy naan. 'Who's hungry?'

'Ta.'

She hands the wodge to Neil, while Tony gets the car moving before that traffic warden comes close enough to take a note of their number plate. 'Why didn't you flash one of those warrant cards of yours?'

'Sweetheart, there's no way I'm letting a bunch of sodding Sweaties know I've been asking questions. Got no intention of *anyone* finding out I'm up here. Can you imagine the shit-storm if Northumbria plod got wind of it?'

Neil nods. 'Point.'

'So I went in as Jocelyn Bygraves, social worker.' She

flashes one of the collection of fake IDs from her handbag. 'Think there'd be a bit more honour amongst lefty tree-huggers, wouldn't you?'

'Nah, never trust a social worker.' Neil reaches forward and helps himself to another chunk of bread, speaking with his mouth full. 'So what we going to do about Danby, like?'

Julie frowns for a bit. 'The fat bastard's going to be around here somewhere, right? Hotel, B&B, something like that?'

'No chance,' Tony eases on the breaks, coasting up to the red lights, 'you got any idea how many B&Bs there are in Aberdeen? *Thousands*. It's all these buggers coming up to work in the oil, isn't it?'

Neil nods again. 'Point.'

Bloody right – point. 'What's Knox saying till it?'

Julie pops the lid off a plastic container, filling the car with the rich smell of Indian spices. 'Says he doesn't know where Danby's staying.'

'What, so we've got to go grubbin' all round town, cos that OAP-rapin' bastard can't keep his end of the bargain?' Neil licked the grease off his fingertips. 'That's bloody typical, that is.'

'It is what it is, Babe. If *you* were Danby, would you tell someone like Knox where you were staying?'

'Point.'

'Anyway, Detective Superintendent Danby's bound to turn up at the local cop shop sooner or later.'

Sitting in the back Neil laughs. 'You wanna stake out police headquarters?'

She shrugs. 'Why not? Bunch of Sweaties won't notice, will they? Be too busy shagging sheep, or whatever it is they do up here.'

'Just cos they're jocks, don't mean they're idiots. They're gonna spot a fuckin' huge Range Rover parked outside the front door for a week.'

Julie swivels around in her seat. 'You want to just give up? Turn round and go home empty handed? That sound like a better idea to you?'

Oh God, here we go.

'I'm not saying that, it's—'

'You any idea what the boss would do to us?'

'Yeah, but—'

'But *what*, Darling?'

Neil shuts his mouth, sharpish. They all know what that tone means: that cheery, everything-in-the-garden's-just-peachy tone Julie always uses before she goes off like a Rottweiler on acid.

Tony keeps his eyes on the road, dead ahead.

Never, *ever* get involved.

'Well?'

Neil clears his throat. 'Sounds like a plan, like.'

'Good boy, knew you'd see sense.' She tears another handful of naan from the bag and passes it back between the seats. 'We stake out the cop shop, we follow Danby home, then we beat the living crap out of him till he talks. Piece of piss.'

'Hmm.' The cadaver dog-handler wrinkled her nose, staring out at the building site. 'Gonnae be a lot more difficult with all that frost and ice.' Police Constable Fiona Martin dragged her hair back from her face and secured it with a little elastic thingy, leaving a peek-a-boo fringe over her forehead. She turned and wiggled her fingers through the metal mesh separating the two front seats from the back of the little van. 'Hey Sleepyfish, ready to rock?'

The huge yellow Labrador raised its head from the tartan dog bed and licked her fingers. Then had a yawn, and a stretch, followed by an almost inaudible, *'Pffffffffffrrrrrp.'*

'What's his name. . .?' Logan stopped, wrinkled his nose.

'Oh . . . *Jesus*!' It was like a rotten herring wrapped in a rancid nappy. 'God! Aw, you can *taste* it!'

He scrabbled at the door handle and clambered out into the cold morning, breathing deeply.

PC Martin stared at him from the driver's seat. 'Wardrobe. And it's no' his fault he's got a delicate stomach.'

Logan backed off an extra couple of paces, frozen mud crunching beneath his feet. 'What have you been *feeding* him?'

The constable climbed out, wandered around to the back of the filthy van – the Strathclyde Police Crest emblazoned down the side – and popped the double doors open. 'Yeah, like your farts smell of lotus blossom and strawberries.' She rattled a choke chain. 'Come on, you.'

The Labrador's front end bounded upright, booby-trapped bum still in the dog bed, tail thumping.

'Who's a clever boy? Who's a clever boy? You are, aren't you?' PC Martin ruffled the dog's ears, making the skin shift from one side to the other, as if it wasn't properly attached to its head. 'Yes you are!' She slipped the chain over Wardrobe's head and clipped on a thick red leather lead.

The dog bounded out into the cold afternoon, turning its handler round in a complete circle, before sweeping its nose across the frozen mud, making snuffling sounds.

Impressive. 'He's picked something up already?'

PC Martin stared at Logan, then clunked the van's back doors shut. Locked them. 'He's been cooped up in the back of a van most of the morning, he's looking for somewhere to pee.'

Wardrobe finished sniffing, then cocked his leg on the van's rear tyre, making a little cloud of steam.

PC Martin looked over at the building site. 'It just us?'

'Trust me: we get something, you'll be fighting the IB off with a stick.'

She jammed her free hand in her pocket, as Wardrobe raked his front and back paws on the rough ground. 'Can't believe you're *still* calling them IB. Sarge was right, it's the bloody dark ages up here.' She grinned. 'Shagging sheep rots your brain, eh?'

'They all cheeky buggers where you come from, Constable?'

'Pretty much.' She gave Wardrobe's lead a little tug. 'Come on Slobberchops, time to go to work.'

It was like someone had flicked a switch in the dog's head: sudden stillness, ears pricked.

'Anyway,' Logan followed her towards the crescent of part-built houses, 'calling them "CSI" sounds like wanky Americanized TV bollocks. I mean, have you ever *watched* that show?'

'If it's not *EastEnders*, Corrie, or *Strictly Come Dancing*, don't want to know about it.'

They started at the far end of the street, where the houses were just concrete foundations, PC Martin following behind Wardrobe, the dog's nose to the frosty ground as it circled the edges of the huge slab.

'Can he really smell a dead body all the way through concrete?'

Martin didn't look up. 'Anyone tells you they can is talking bollocks – most bodies aren't buried *in* concrete, they're buried *under* it. What he smells is the liquids leaching out of the corpse into the soil. That oozes up through where the concrete meets the earth, and Bob's your body, Colin's your cadaver, Sam's your stiff. . .'

They moved onto the next set of foundations. 'If he can smell that, how come he doesn't choke on his own farts?'

'How long's your plumber been missing?'

'Electrician. And he disappeared Monday.'

She let Wardrobe finish, then led the way through the

133

rutted mud to the next property-to-be. 'Four days? Not asking much, are you? When it's cold like this, slows down the decay. Probably won't be enough putrescence to detect. No leakage: nothing to sniff.'

A line of concrete rectangles stretched ahead of them, each with short lengths of pipe sticking out from the grey surface, capped off with blue plastic.

Further down, the plots actually started to resemble houses, timber frames with that blue plastic sheeting stretched between the uprights.

PC Martin chewed on her bottom lip, looking out at the frozen earth. 'Might have to come back in a couple of weeks, see if your missing sparky's rotted down a bit. Four days just isn't long enough.'

So much for the almighty power of the cadaver dog.

Logan cupped his hands and blew, filling them with steam. 'Just do your best, OK?'

She shrugged. 'What the hell, we're here anyway.' She set off for the next set of foundations as Logan's phone started ringing. He pulled it out and peered at the screen.

Don't let it be Steel, don't let it be Steel. . . It wasn't. It was even worse.

He took the call. 'McRae.'

'*LoganDaveGoulding.*' Said like that, in a flat Liverpudlian accent, as if it was all one word. '*What's up? You running late?*'

Logan checked his watch. Sod. 'Sorry, something came up.' Which was only partially true – mostly he'd forgotten all about his appointment.

There was a pause, as if the psychologist was trying to decide whether to believe him or not. '*You got a moment now?*'

Logan watched the cadaver dog and handler sniffing their way around the next set of foundations and thought about lying. What the hell. 'I've been having that dream again.'

'Which one: giant lizards, or the talking shark that steals all your clothes?'

'Severed heads on the beach.' Logan could hear his own voice echoing back at him. Dr Goulding must have put him on speaker-phone.

'I see. . .' Pause. 'We've not had that one for a while.'

Logan could hear him scribbling something down.

'You know, I have a recurring nightmare where all the people turn into frogs, and all the frogs turn into people. And the people forget that they used to be frogs, and the frogs forget they were ever anything else. And I'm the only one who knows. Living, surrounded by reptiles. . .'

Logan didn't know what to say to that. 'Erm, did you get a chance to look at the assessment matrix for Richard Knox?'

'You know, the fact that you've not had the severed heads dream for a while probably means something's unresolved in your psyche. Is there anything causing you stress?'

Logan rubbed a hand over his bruised face. 'Everything causes me bloody stress. Everyone causes me stress. It's like they're holding a competition to see who can piss me off the most.'

'I see. . .' More scribbling. 'Have you been doing your breathing exercises?'

'Course I have.' Which was a lie.

'Knox strikes me as a rather conflicted character.'

'No shit.'

'He's got this deep-seated religious belief system which has to be in complete contradiction to his psycho-sexual landscape.'

Logan watched Wardrobe drag his handler on to the next plot. 'You don't think the whole God-bothering thing is just a front?'

'Don't see what he'd gain from it. To be frank, I'm more worried that he's gone out and got himself an omnipotent invisible friend.' There was a pause. 'Who's stressing you the most?'

'Bloody DI Steel. She's got it into her head that I've got an attitude problem. That I'm too cynical. That I drink too much.'

Silence.

Logan scowled. 'What?'

'And how does that make you feel?'

'Stressed. Remember? That was the point of the—'

'Do you drink too much?'

'No! OK, so I have the odd glass of wine, but—'

'Maybe you're angry with her because you think she's right.'

'She is *not* right!'

'Well, we can always talk more about that at your next session.' There was a click and the line became a lot clearer – Goulding must have taken him off speaker-phone again. *'The thing about religious obsessives – I mean the proper card-carrying have-you-accepted-Jesus-into-your-life neurotics – is that they're often buying into a belief system that justifies their lifestyle choices. Homophobia, misogyny, exclusion. For Knox to join in, given his past is . . . well, let's call it "worrying".'*

'I mean, I don't wake up wanting to get blootered, do I? Just been under a lot of pressure recently.'

'I think there's a very real chance he's going to offend again, and sooner rather than later.'

'It's not like I'm an alcoholic or anything.'

'Can you get me in to see him?'

'What? Oh, erm . . . possibly. I'll have to check.'

'Good. Now you and I need to get a proper session organized. I've got a cancellation on Monday you can have.'

'Do we have to?'

'Yes, twelve noon. And don't forget – I need to see Knox ASAP.' Another pause. *'And maybe it wouldn't hurt to try laying off the booze for a bit, OK? Might make you a bit less edgy.'*

Logan hung up and rammed the phone back in his pocket. Liverpudlian git. Why did *everyone* have to bang on about his drinking? OK, so he was only just crawling out from under a gargantuan hangover, but that wasn't his fault, was it? Having to deal with Knox, Steel giving him a hard time, beating Reuben up, the bribe. . . Enough to turn anyone to drink.

God it was cold.

He stomped his feet, scanning the building site for PC Martin and Wardrobe the Wonder Dog. The pair of them had almost made it to the first part-built house – a bare timber frame reaching up into the cold grey sky.

Logan wandered over, hands twitching through his pockets, looking for a pack of cigarettes. Only the second one today. Which was a bit of a record, considering how crappy—

'Excuse me, exactly *what* do you think you're doing?' It was the man from the site office, not Big-and-Bald, but the other one: ridiculous trimmed beard, comb-over hidden beneath a bright orange hard hat.

Logan pulled out the sheet of paper they'd picked up at the Procurator Fiscal's office on Guild Street on their way over and kept walking. 'Mr. . .?'

'This is a private development. I'm going to have to ask you to—'

'I have a warrant here to search—'

'—leave, or do I have to call site security. . .?' The man trailed off, staring at the handcuffs dangling from Logan's index finger.

'Police.'

He curled his top lip. 'I thought you said you were a debt collector for some sort of local bookies.'

The man obviously thought Logan was an idiot. Mr Big-and-Bald had looked him straight in the eye and called him 'Officer'. They knew fine what he was.

'Speaking of "site security", where is he? Your bald mate with the big dog?'

137

'I don't see what that has to do with—'

Logan thrust the warrant at him. 'I think I'll decide what's relevant, don't you, Mr. . .?'

'Joseph Brett, project manager.' He raised his chin. 'And may I ask exactly *why* you feel it necessary to search a perfectly legitimate—'

'Don't mind me.' PC Martin clumped past, dragged along behind a panting Wardrobe, then disappeared around the corner. Doing a lap of the perimeter.

'And you say you haven't seen Stephen Polmont since Monday?'

Pink rushed up the man's cheeks, clashing with his orange hard hat. 'I didn't say anything of the sort. I said he was suspected of stealing electrical equipment and disappeared before we could contact the police.'

'Right. . .' Logan turned and watched the constable and the Labrador work their way across to the next house in line. The ground floor was already clad in a skin of pale-yellow brick, partially hidden behind a web of scaffolding. Two men in padded overalls and thick woolly hats were laying down the next course, their paint-spattered radio blaring out Radio 2. 'Big development: four hundred houses. That's a lot of money.'

'It's—'

'Course, it's nothing compared with how much your boss rakes in from drugs, loan sharks, and prostitutes, is it?'

The project manager stared out across the rutted mud. 'Is this little search of yours going to take long? A development this size doesn't run itself.'

'Might want to tell Mr McLennan it's not a good idea to go muscling in on someone else's territory. Burning bridges with the local community.' Logan jammed his hands deeper in his pockets. 'Aberdeen doesn't need any more scumbags, Mr Brett, we've got enough of our own.'

The project manager straightened his hard hat. 'McLennan Homes is a law-abiding company. We build family homes, community centres, libraries. We do *not* deal drugs or start gang wars. And anyone who says we do is going to be looking at a lawsuit.' He turned a cold smile on Logan. 'Are we clear?'

PC Martin appeared around the other side of the house, no Wardrobe. She grinned at them. 'He's got something!'

Logan hurried over through the ruts of dirty brown earth. The Labrador was lying down beside the wall at the rear of the property.

PC Martin bent down and ruffled the dog's ears again. 'Who's a clever boy? You are. Yes you are!'

Wardrobe's tail thumped against the frozen earth.

'Well, well.' Logan turned and smiled at the project manager. 'Looks like we might have found your missing sparky after all.'

'There's definitely something there.' The IB technician pulled his white facemask off, revealing a big salt-and-pepper moustache and a face like a squeezed sponge.

They'd had to rip the chipboard floor up to get at the concrete underneath, piling the wooden sheets against the walls in jagged layers so he and his assistant could wheel the ground-penetrating radar kit slowly around the part-built house.

Logan peered at the GPR screen. It was a ripply mix of blacks, dark blues, and greens, with an orange and white blob in the middle. Squint your eyes and it could almost be a body, lying curled up on its side. Or a squid. Or a radioactive amoeba. 'What if it's not?'

Mr Moustache tapped the screen. 'Head here, legs, and that's an arm.'

DI Steel shoved Logan out of the way. 'Let me see. . . You sure?'

The man shrugged. 'Eighty percent.'

'Dig it up.' Steel hauled at the crotch of her SOC suit. 'Don't see why we've got to wear these bloody things, like huge great albino bloody Smurfs. Poor sod's buried under three feet of concrete, what the hell are we going to contaminate?'

'Because, Inspector,' came a voice from the doorway, 'we do not treat our crime scene as if it were the January sale at Primark.'

Dr Isobel McAllister stepped down from the front door onto the bare concrete, carrying a small stainless steel briefcase. She wore the same white paper oversuit as everyone else, but somehow she managed to make it look stylish. She nodded at the moustachioed IB man. 'Where is it?'

He described a rough oval with his finger.

'I see. And are we certain the remains are human?'

Mr Moustache shrugged again. 'Cadaver dogs react to decaying meat, so it could be anything.' He stomped a bootied foot on the grey floor. 'Might be a pig, might be a deer, but there's something dead under all this lot.'

Steel scowled at him. 'You told me eighty percent!'

'Yes, but—'

'Peter,' Isobel placed her metal case on the floor and popped it open, 'I need you to help me mark out the body.' She produced a measuring tape, a box of white chalk, and what looked like a bag full of ten pence pieces. Then she and Mr Moustache laid out a six-inch grid in pale-blue chalk over the rough area of the body, and marked each intersection with one of the shiny silver coins. When that was done they ran the GPR kit carefully across it, Isobel taking notes in a small pad.

'The body is. . .' She pulled a stick of white chalk from the box and, checking her notes, outlined a crouching figure at her feet. 'Here.' Isobel smiled down at it. 'You know, in all the time I've been a pathologist, I've never seen a body chalked up at a crime scene. Like being on the television, isn't it?'

Steel leant over and whispered in Logan's ear. 'Aye, only a hoor of a lot more boring.'

Isobel selected another stick of chalk. 'So we need to cut . . . here.' A perfect rectangle of red, never closer than twelve inches from any point on the body.

The inspector rocked back and forth on her heels. 'Right, McRae, you nip out and grab a couple of jackhammers, and—'

'You'll do no such thing!' Isobel clunked her case shut again. 'I will not have my crime scene turned into a building site.'

Steel cast an eye around the ripped-up floor and exposed wooden frame of the part-built house. 'Hate to break it to you. . .'

'You know what I mean. I want this section of the floor cut away and brought back to the mortuary. We'll create a secondary crime scene there to examine the remains.'

Logan looked down at the slab. 'Don't think that's going to be possible.'

The pathologist narrowed her eyes. 'We need a secure and *sterile* environment, Sergeant. Otherwise—'

'It's got to weigh, what, half a ton?'

The IB Tech ran a hand across his bristly moustache. 'Actually, that much concrete's going to be closer to two and a bit.'

'About three times as much as my car. Can you imagine trying to get it down the corridor and into the cutting room?'

Isobel cocked her head to one side for a moment. 'Agreed. We'll need a second location. Somewhere with forklift access. Running water. And refrigeration.' She grabbed her metal case and stood. 'In the meantime, I want this block *cut*, not hacked out of the foundations.'

17

A thin stream of misty rain fell through the gaping hole in the ceiling, sparkling in the harsh glare of the IB's arc lights. Logan peered up through the severed joists at the heavy sky and the huge metal hook lowering down into the house.

Outside, the roar of the crane's diesel engine had replaced the deafening judder of the jackhammers. So much for Isobel's insistence that her crime scene wouldn't become a building site. The foundations were too thick to cut through cleanly, so they'd had to excavate the rectangle she'd marked out on the concrete by hacking a foot-wide trench around it, the rubble all heaped up in the corner against a mound of pink Rockwool insulation.

Nearly a dozen IB technicians stood in little clumps around the outside of the room. A pair of them wandered the ground floor, one with a high-definition video kit, the other with a huge digital camera – its flash flickering in the confined space.

Two IB technicians threaded thick steel rope through four heavy eyelets bolted into Isobel's concrete slab, then fiddled about with connectors and spanners, fitting a big metal ring to slip over the big metal hook.

DI Steel's stale cigarette breath washed over Logan's cheek. 'Wish they'd get a shift on, I'm bursting for a slash.'

Logan shifted his feet, watching as the IB hooked the block up to the crane. 'You think it's him? Polmont?'

'You'd better pray it is, amount of man-hours we're wasting on this.'

'Just seems a bit quick, doesn't it? They kill him Monday, bury his body in the foundations . . . what, Monday night? Leave it to set. The soonest they can start building is Tuesday.'

He pointed at the house, the brick-clad ground floor, the gaping hole in the roof where the IB team had to cut away the joists. 'How did they get all this built in four days?'

'Kit houses, aren't they – all prefabricated units. They're no' building the thing from scratch, just sticking it together like a big fuck-off Lego kit. Good team of builders, and you'd be moving in before the end of the week.'

'Right, before we begin,' Isobel took her place at the head-end of the hooked-up slab, 'I want you all to remember that any evidence we have here will be clinging to the under-side of the concrete. *Everything* is to be collected and analysed.'

She nodded at one of the albino Smurfs, who unfurled a long sheet of the ubiquitous SOC blue plastic. Another Smurf grabbed the other end, then they both held up a thumb.

'Norman?'

The tech with the HDTV camera squatted down, focussing on the jagged edge. 'Rolling.'

'You may begin.'

One of the IB team mumbled something into a bulky radio handset and the rumble of diesel got louder – the hook slowly pulled upwards, hauling the steel ropes tight. There was a loud *crack*, then the slab of chalked-up concrete juddered out of the foundations. It had to be at least three feet deep.

143

Smurf Number One shouted, 'Hold it!' and the crane's engine eased off, the slab hanging two feet above the rest of the foundations. Then Smurfs One and Two slid the blue plastic sheet under the rectangle, pulling it tight. 'OK. . .'

The engine roared again, and the block rose jerkily into the air, clumps of black-brown earth falling in stinking clumps.

The two cameras swarmed in, taking shots of the block's underside. Clack, flash, whine. . .

A large chunk of sticky earth gave way, thumping down on the stretched plastic sheet, exposing a leg, dangling out of the concrete from the knee down. Blue jeans stained almost black. A battered Nike trainer, the filthy white plastic stained with dark brown blotches. A flash of ankle, porcelain white on one side, a tidemark of reddish-purple on the other with a smear of waxy-yellow – pressure pallor where the skin had been in contact with the ground, the cells and capillaries too compressed for blood to pool.

Definitely a body.

Thank Christ.

Isobel waved, and the slab jounced to a halt, swinging gently back and forth. She put a hand out and steadied it, then peered up at the underside. 'Hmm. . .'

Steel hunched over, hands on her knees, looking at whatever Isobel was looking at. After a beat, Logan joined them.

Between the clumps of mud and concrete was the partial outline of a man, lying twisted, three-quarters hidden by the grey mass, that one leg dangling free. A thin trickle of yellow-green liquid spattered onto the blue plastic below. It smelled like meat left too long in the fridge.

'So. . .' Steel's voice was muffled behind her mask. 'You fancy declaring death so we can get this circus on the road?'

Isobel didn't even look around. 'We will proceed at the

pace required for the proper preservation of evidence, Inspector. Now, if you don't mind, I'd—'

'You think it's our bloke?' Steel scooted forward, probably trying to get a better look, getting a face full of tumbling dirt instead. 'Sodding monkey bollocks. . .'

One of the IB laughed – the sound quickly dying as Steel glowered around the room. Much shuffling of feet and looking at something else.

That last fall of dirt had exposed a hand, the fingers nearly white, the knuckles stained purple with hypostasis.

Logan stepped in close, staring at the grubby hand. A pair of small ragged holes punctured the palm, surrounded by dark purple bruising. Black earth and grey concrete were wedged in under the fingernails.

'Sergeant.' Isobel pushed him firmly to one side. '*Please* try to stay out of the way.'

'He tried to claw his way out.' Logan turned his back on the body. 'He was still alive when they buried him.'

18

It was getting colder. Logan stood in the open doorway, his SOC suit covered in dust – going dirty grey in the misty drizzle. The crane was a huge scuffed yellow thing, borrowed from the building site, a yellow light on the cab roof flashing gold and darkness through the rain. The bitter smoke tang of diesel exhaust pulsed out in great clouds as the foundation slab was slowly lowered onto a waiting flatbed truck.

Smurfs One and Two had secured their blue plastic sheet to the block with at least three rolls of silver duct tape, wrapping the whole thing up like a morbid Christmas present. Now they guided it carefully onto a framework of wooden posts, keeping Steve Polmont's remains from being crushed against the metal truck bed.

The truck's rear end sank as the huge chunk of concrete settled into place, the suspension groaning. Two more techs unhooked the crane, strapped the block into place, and drove it away.

Smurf Number One peeled off her mask, then her SOC suit hood. She ran a hand through her brown and grey hair, letting it fall around her shoulders, then looked up to see Logan watching.

'You're that DS aren't you?' Her voice steamed out around her head and a smile creased her round face, wrinkling up the eyes. 'The one who had to eat human flesh?'

Logan tried not to grimace, he really did.

She stuck out a gloved hand. 'Doctor Jessica Frampton, forensic soil science. This is Tony, my assistant.'

Smurf Number Two nodded, one eye not really pointing the same way as the other. 'Wassup?'

'Right, yes.' Logan shook the proffered hand, then nodded at the truck's taillights, fading into the distance. 'So, you're the concrete specialists?'

'Soil. They won't get a lot of trace evidence off the body – any fibres will be all on the outside of the clothing, bound up in the concrete – but the soil. . .' She winked, not letting go of his hand. 'The soil always has a story to tell, don't you think?'

'Erm, OK.' Logan tried to back away, but her grip was solid.

'Tell me, do we really taste like chicken?'

Awkward silence.

'I think I'd better. . .' He pointed over his shoulder, back towards the house. 'You know.'

Smurf Number Two, nodded. 'Later.'

Dr Frampton finally released Logan's hand. 'The soil never lies.'

'OK. . .' And he was free.

DI Steel was waiting for him in the CID pool car, dribbling smoke out of her nose. She flicked a nub of ash into the footwell as Logan stripped off his SOC suit and chucked it in a bin-bag. He rolled the whole lot up and threw it in the back.

'Who you speaking to?'

Logan slid in behind the wheel. 'Some creepy soil science woman and her pet monkey.'

'Ah, Dr Framptonstein and Igor the Dude.' Steel shrugged and had a dig at her crotch. 'She's no' as bad as she seems, just a bit enthusiastic, you know?' Putting on a *Hammer House of Horror* accent for, 'De soil is de life! Bwahahahahaha. . .'

They watched the pair shuffle back into the crime scene house, both carrying shovels. Off robbing graves.

Steel pulled her seatbelt on. 'Did a kidnap case with her, must've been seven, eight years ago. Banker's wife got grabbed on the way home from Markies.'

Logan cranked the key in the ignition, and sent the pool car crawling down the rutted road, making for the site exit, drizzle gleaming in the headlights.

'Course we knew who did it: Ronny Maguire, a scrawny wee shite with a face like a ruptured scrotum. Swore blind he was in Dundee when she went missing, but we found this muddy pair of boots in his garage. Frampton takes samples, and next day she's back with three possible locations, all within about a hundred feet of these lay-bys on the A96.' Steel took a long puff, rolling the cigarette from one side of her mouth to the other. 'Bang on the money too.'

Logan drove past the last set of foundations, rear tyres squirming in the mud. 'You found the banker's wife?'

'In a drainage ditch: all tied up, covered with a chunk of old carpet, raped and strangled. Ronny'd got the kidnap idea off the telly, thought he could make a bit of easy cash. . .' Sigh. 'Daft bastard never could keep his hands to himself.' Steel slumped further into her seat. 'Still, look on the bright side – only lasted three days in Craiginches till some public-spirited junkie kicked him to death.'

The car's headlights swung past a grubby van with the Strathclyde Police logo on the side, windows glowing an opaque gold. 'Hang on a minute.' Logan bumped the car to a halt, undid his seatbelt and clambered out into the soggy gloom.

Steel leaned over in her seat. 'Hoy, where do you think you're—'

'Just be a tick.'

'Don't—'

He clunked the door shut, muffling whatever came next, then hurried across and knocked on the van's steamed-up window. PC Martin cracked the door open.

'Can I not even get. . . Oh, it's you.' She pointed at the passenger seat, where Wardrobe was sitting, tail thumping against the dashboard. 'I'd invite you in, but. . .' Shrug.

'Should he not be wearing a seatbelt?'

'You're letting all the heat out.'

'Did you get anything else from the other houses?'

The constable raised an eyebrow, then turned to her dog. 'Hear that, Wardrobe? Local plod think we're holding out on them. Did you find another deid body and not tell anyone about it?'

Wardrobe's mouth fell open in a huge grin, tongue hanging out the side like a soggy pink bathmat.

PC Martin looked back at Logan. 'Nope, looks like one corpsicle is all you get.' She pulled a handful of prawn cocktail crisps from the packet in her lap, feeding them one at a time to the big yellow Labrador. 'He likes cheese and onion, but it makes his breath stink. Doesn't it, Mr Stinky?'

Bark.

She gave him another one. 'Sniffed out every plot in the place and as much of the site as we could. Might be more remains out there, but with the weather that cold, frozen earth. . .' She dug out more crisps. 'Give it three weeks and you might get more seepage – aye, if there *are* any more out there.'

'What about blood? Would he pick up blood?'

'Not unless it was in a big bucket going fusty. Wardrobe's a cadaver dog, he only does dead bodies. Now, if you don't

149

mind, it's sodding freezing and we'd like to finish our crisps in peace before hitting the road. Long way from the Land Of The Sheepshaggers to God's own Clydeside.'

'I really don't see how I can possibly help.' The project manager ran a hand across his comb-over, straightening up the trailing strands as Logan eased the interview room door shut.

A gust of rain hammered the window, making the vertical blinds rattle. The misty drizzle had given up on the way back into town, replaced by driving needles of icy water. Making the streetlights bob and sway.

DI Steel looked up as Logan dumped the manila folder on the scarred Formica table and settled into the seat next to her. 'Detective Sergeant McRae enters the room.' She sniffed. 'This it?'

Logan nodded.

Silence.

'Are we nearly finished here? Because I have a development to run.'

Logan opened the folder and pulled out a handful of printouts. 'We found a body buried under the foundations of one of your houses, Mr Brett. How many more are there out there?'

'I have no idea what you're talking about.'

'How many more bodies? You've got planning permission for four hundred houses, that's a lot of concrete. The whole place could be a graveyard for all we know.'

The project manager took off his glasses and sighed, pinching the bridge of his nose. 'We've been over this. McLennan Homes had nothing to do with—'

Steel banged the table. 'Then how come there's a dead body—'

'—actions of a disturbed individual, who—'

150

'—no' supposed to believe you don't know—'

'—had access to the site. It's not—'

This was all they'd done for the last hour and a bit, go round and round with Brett denying any knowledge or responsibility, and Steel trying to wind him up. It didn't seem to be working.

The latest bout over, the project manager smoothed the hair over his bald patch again. 'Now, I think I have been extremely patient with your questions, but I'm going to have to draw this conversation to a close.' He stood. 'If you wish any further statements you can contact our legal team.'

Steel glowered at him. 'Sit your arse down.'

Another sigh. 'Inspector, I came here voluntarily to assist with your enquiries. And now I'm going back to work. Good day.'

Logan tapped the sheet of paper. 'Tell me about your site security, Mr Brett. The large, bald man with the big dog.'

Brett raised an eye brow. 'What about him?'

'How about we start with his name?'

Pause. 'Andy. Andy Stephenson. It says that on the—'

'The list of employees you gave us?' Logan made a show of scratching his forehead. 'That's odd, because the DNA sample I took came back belonging to a Mr Andrew Connelly.' He held up the paperwork he'd just printed out. 'According to the police national computer, Andrew Connelly served three years for aggravated assault. Two years for demanding money with menaces. Got a suspended sentence for his part in a security car heist. . . There's more if you want to hear it?'

The project manager sniffed. 'At McLennan Homes we believe *every* large organization has a responsibility to help integrate people from troubled backgrounds into society. It's part of our Community Commitment Programme to—'

151

'Blah, blah, blah.' Steel hauled at herself under the table. 'He's a bloody enforcer for Malk the Knife and we all know it.'

'That's *slander*, Inspector.'

'And my arse is—'

'Where is he?' Logan ignored Steel's glare. 'Andrew Connelly wasn't at the site when we recovered the body. Our teams have spoken to everyone else.'

Brett's eyes narrowed. 'Andrew is on compassionate leave, Sergeant. His mother had a stroke yesterday.'

'Well, *that's* sodding convenient.' Steel actually stopped rummaging for a moment. 'You expect us to believe his dear old mum's no' well at exactly the same time we dig Steve Polmont's body out from under one of your bloody houses? Four days after you catch the silly sod nicking electrical supplies? No way Malk the Knife—'

'I repeat, Inspector, McLennan Homes had nothing to do with—'

'Someone had to operate the bloody cement mixer—'

And they were off again.

Logan slouched his way downstairs, with yet another report wedged under his arm so he could burn his fingers carrying the two coffees from the canteen back to Steel's office. He tried using his elbow to work the door handle and instantly regretted it as the metal dug into the bruised joint, making it ache again. He used his other arm, and froze as the door swung open.

Buggering hell. . .

That big git Danby was sitting in one of the visitor's chairs, craning his thick neck around to see who was coming into the room. Steel sat behind her desk, which was actually tidy for once. Something had to be up. And then Logan saw the battered journals they'd taken from Polmont's flat – the ones full of barely legible, drunken scribbles.

Logan stopped and nodded at the pair of them. 'Ma'am, sir. You want me to come back later?'

One of Danby's eyebrows climbed up that huge pink forehead. 'So it's "sir" now, is it?'

Might as well get it over with. 'I'd like to apologize for my earlier comments, sir. It was unprofessional of me to let my personal feelings interfere with the meeting.'

Danby actually smiled. 'Dear God, that was stilted. You been practising that?'

'Erm, not really.'

'Trust me, it shows, know what I'm saying?'

'Yes, well. . .' Shrug. 'Sorry.'

'So you should be.' The man waved a huge hand at the other visitor's chair. 'Sit.'

Logan looked at Steel. 'Ma'am?'

'Park your arse.' She stuck out a hand. 'What did Fingerprints say?'

'It's Polmont.' He held out the report and she snatched it from him, eyes flicking across the page. He pointed at the diagram. 'They got a sixteen point match off the prints we lifted from the hand.'

She nodded. 'Post mortem?'

'Isobel. . . Dr McAllister's got it scheduled for half nine tomorrow morning. They're getting an archaeologist in to help dig the remains out of the concrete.'

Danby shifted in his seat, then reached out to take one of the coffees. Thieving bastard. 'What did your project manager friend say?'

Logan looked at Steel. 'Guv?'

'Tell him.' She took a sip of her cappuccino. 'This got cinnamon on it? I don't like cinnamon—'

'It's chocolate. According to Mr Brett, they poured half the new foundations on Monday night and the rest on Tuesday morning, due to some sort of equipment failure.

Claims anyone could've sneaked onto the site after they shut up for the night, and buried the body in the damp cement.'

Danby frowned. 'I see. . .'

'All bollocks, of course.' Steel wiped away a foam moustache. 'If Polmont was dumped in wet cement it'd be all over him, 'stead of down one side. It was poured in on top.'

The huge DSI drummed his fingers on the arm of his chair. Then stood. 'Better be getting on, got the Sacro report on Knox to wade through.' He picked up one of the journals on Steel's desk and tucked it under his arm. 'Don't forget to keep me up to date.'

Logan waited until the door clunked shut. 'Why's he sticking his nose in?'

'Never you bloody mind.' She dug something out of her in-tray and threw it to him. 'You'll be happy to know, you've had papers served on you *again*. Douglas Walker's brief thinks you're unprofessional, overly aggressive, and offensive. How many times is that now?'

Logan scanned the official complaint. 'Stopped counting when we got into double figures.'

'Funny. It'll be even funnier when you're up in front of the rubber-heelers in half an hour, won't it? You silly bastard.'

'He was an idiot.'

'I don't care. As of tomorrow you're someone else's problem. I'm off on holiday and you can try your luck with whatever banjo-playing inbred loony they send down from Fraserburgh. Meant to be here today, but they've got some sort of big drug-raid-stakeout-thing tonight, so you'll have to give him the handover tomorrow. I want you in the office seven sharp: *sober*. Understand?'

Logan dumped the complaint on the desk. 'Yeah, so I can hold his bloody hand when we both know—'

'Do you still want to be a police officer? I mean really?

Or are you behaving like a tosser because getting fired is easier than quitting?'

Logan stared at the carpet.

'I'm getting tired of going through the same bastarding crap every time you have a bad week!'

He cleared his throat. 'Dr Goulding wants access to Knox.'

'I'm being serious, Laz.'

'I. . . You haven't called me "Laz" for months.'

Steel sighed. 'Fuck's sake, you're hard work. You know that, don't you?'

For a minute the only noise in the little office was the gurgling rattle of the radiator. Logan shifted in his seat. 'I'm sorry.'

Another awkward pause.

Another sigh. 'Thought you were supposed to be getting yourself sorted out.'

'Yeah, well. . . Not going quite so well at the moment.' Fidget. 'What do you want to do about Polmont's post mortem?'

'Don't look at me – got a flight to sunny Puerto de la Aldea at eleven, need to pack my bikini.'

Now there was an image worth a thousand condoms.

'Can't believe you're still going, when—'

'Course I'm still bloody going. I'm no' giving up my last holiday of freedom just cos there's a murder on the go. Susan would sodding kill me.' She sniffed. 'Get DI Whatshisface from Fraserburgh to attend. Be a nice welcome to Aberdeen: seeing an alcoholic sparky getting hacked out of a concrete block. Meantime,' she thumped a hand down on Polmont's journals, 'take a squint through these, see if there's anything worth taking a punt on. And get someone to process all that stuff he nicked.'

'What about the book Danby took?'

She pursed her lips. 'You let me worry about that.'

Logan hauled himself out of the chair. 'Anything else?'

'Aye, try no' to fuck anything up, or anyone off, while I'm away. I can't be arsed breaking in a new DS.'

Logan deleted the last sentence and rewrote it again, before firing the whole thing off to the printer in the corner of the sergeants' cubbyhole. One formal letter of apology.

Someone said, 'Knock, knock?' and he looked up to see PC Butler standing in the doorway, holding a sheet of paper. 'Thought you'd be gone by now.'

Logan groaned. 'Not another bloody armed robbery. . .'

Biohazard Bob grinned. 'Sergeant McRae's feeling a bit down this evening, Vicki. Professional Standards gave him a rough seeing to. Without the benefit of foreplay or lubricant.'

'Up yours Bob.'

'No, up *yours*. That was the problem, remember?'

Butler held up the sheet. 'It's that e-fit you asked for.'

Logan took a look. Then groaned again. 'This is crap.'

'Yup.'

The computer identikit face was dominated by a big comedy beard and a pair of dark glasses. 'So all we need to do is arrest every member of ZZ Top and we'll be laughing.' He stuffed the e-fit in his in-tray and slumped back in his seat. 'Brilliant.'

'He wore gloves, a disguise, kept the door from locking when they tripped the silent alarm, and never even glanced at the CCTV camera once.'

Logan covered his face with his hands, mumbling through the fingers, 'But he grabs the crappest, shiniest baubles and doesn't even think to go for the cash register.'

Bob performed a little drum roll on his desk. 'You want to know what *I* think?'

'Not really.'

'Suit yourself.'

Logan let his hands drop and watched Bob gather up a handful of Unlawful Removal forms, stand, and make for the door. He stopped right on the threshold, turned back, scrunched up his eyes, raised a finger and said, 'Just one more thing. . .' in his best Columbo voice.

'What?'

But Bob just grinned, stepped outside and closed the door.

PC Butler turned back to Logan. 'So what do you want me to do about our armed robber?'

'Go round anyone we've done for resetting in the last five years, better do the pawn shops too. Whoever he is, he'll be trying to flog his takings. . .' Logan drifted to a halt as he saw the expression on Butler's face sour. 'Are you— Oh *Jesus*! Bob, you filthy bastard!'

'What's that, Sweetheart? No, you'll have to speak up.' Julie sticks a finger in her ear, face turned away from the steering wheel. 'Yeah, that's better. . . How's Tiggy and Milly?' She laughs. 'Did she?'

Tony sits in the passenger seat, trying not to eavesdrop as she asks after her tabby cat and Tibetan terrier. The Range Rover's illegally parked on a double yellow, but when Julie's driving stuff like that kinda gets forgotten about. Along with the speed limit and the number of obscene gestures you should make at other motorists.

He stares out of the window, watching the main entrance to the hotel. It's a fancy looking place, all carved granite and sticky-out bits.

Still no sign of Neil.

Tony searches through his pockets for a packet of chewy antacids, pops one in and grimaces his way through it. Bloody balti lamb.

Finally. . .

He nudges Julie and points across the road. Neil's marching

down the hotel steps and out onto the pavement. The big man looks left, then right, then left again – like a good little boy – then hurries across to the car and clambers in the back seat.

'Bloody freezing out there, like.' He shuffles forward. 'Turn the blowers up.'

'Yeah. . . No. I gotta go, OK? Bye, Darling.' And Julie hangs up. Doesn't turn around. 'What's the score on the doors?'

Neil grins. 'You were right: we *can* stake out a Jock cop shop and no bugger'll notice.'

She nods. 'Told you.'

'He's staying in room Three Twenty-Two.'

'You sure?'

'Followed him down the corridor, like. Watched him go into his room – it's a king-sized double, if it helps?'

Julie turns in her seat and smiles at him. 'You did good, Babe.'

'Checked out the back too. There's a loading dock we can jimmy open and a couple of CCTV cameras. But the cables run along the wall, so you can cut them without the daft sods seeing nowt.'

Tony pops another antacid. 'You want to take him tonight?'

She pauses, head on one side, chewing the inside of her cheek. 'Think we'd better call the boss first, don't you?'

Neil nods. 'Then grab something to eat?'

Tony burps and winces. 'Not bloody curry again.'

Then Neil asks the *Who Wants To Be A Millionaire* £500,000 question: 'What about Knox?'

'What about him?'

'Well . . . shouldn't we be doing something? Getting ready, like?'

'All in good time, Babe.' She draws a smiley face on the inside of her window with a fingertip. 'All in good time.'

19

Logan sat bolt upright on the couch, blinking, head reeling. The lights were all on, the TV grumbling away to itself in the corner. 'Urgh. . .'

Steve Polmont's journals were scattered across the lounge carpet; one open on the coffee table, the tatty pages marked with the occasional bright yellow Post-it note, where Logan had found something at least partially legible.

Blink. He checked the time on the DVD player. Quarter to midnight.

Yawn.

'Sam? You home?' Logan scrubbed his face with his hands. The message on the answering machine said she was pulling yet another green shift – saving up for a new tattoo.

And then the doorbell went again.

'Bloody hell, Sam. . .' He peeled himself upright, then lurched to the front door, shivering and feeling like crap. Hadn't even been drinking, just came home, microwaved some vegetarian lasagne, and sat down with Polmont's journals and a rerun of *Taggart*. 'There's bin a murrrrrrrrdurrrrrrrrrrr. . .'

Cold leached through Logan's socks as he padded down the stairs to the communal front door. The bell went again, an irritating dringing buzz. 'All right, all right.' He undid the latch. 'Why can you never remember your damn—'

Reuben.

Fuck.

The big man's face was a mass of bruises, radiating out from a nose covered in gauze and white bandage. His eyes were swollen, shrouded in blue and purple. The left one didn't have any white left, it was a sea of scarlet, with the iris floating in the middle. An angry olive in a bloody Mary. Butterfly stitches on his forehead.

Logan tried to slam the door shut, but Reuben had his foot jammed in the opening. It didn't budge.

Run. Turn around right now and run like hell up the stairs. Maybe he'd get into the flat before Reuben caught him and beat him to death.

Logan took a step backwards.

The big man held up a package. It was about the size of a laptop, only thicker, wrapped in cheery yellow paper tied up with a blue ribbon, the ends all curly and worked into a bow.

'Compliments of Mr Mowat.' Voice all bunged up.

Logan cleared his throat. 'Look, Reuben, I—'

'I have to apologize for my lack of respect yesterday. I was out of order.' Reuben stood stock still, delivering his message in a nasal monotone.

'It was a. . . Look, I'm sorry, OK? I just snapped. I didn't mean to—'

'Can I tell Mr Mowat you accept my apology?'

'Yes, of course. I shouldn't have—'

Something slammed into Logan's stomach. Pain tore through him, radiating out like a wave of fire. He opened his mouth, but all that came out was a rasping wheeze as his knees gave way and he fell to the hallway floor.

Jesus, *God* that hurt. . .

Reuben flexed a huge hand, open, then closed again. 'You're fucking lucky Mr Mowat likes you, McRae, or you and me'd be taking a wee trip out somewhere quiet, with a welding torch.'

He bent down, looming over Logan. 'Understand this, you're nothing more than a wee piece of shite to me. Mr Mowat's no' a well man. See if he dies? You and me are going to have another talk.'

Reuben tossed the rectangular package at Logan. A sharp edge clunked against his head, making hot stars flash across the dark sky.

'Enjoy your fucking present.'

'Logan? Why are you sitting here in the dark?' Click, and the kitchen light blossomed slowly to life, the energy efficient bulb flickering to a dull-white glow. Sam stood with one hand on the switch, eyebrows knitted together. 'Are you OK?'

Logan looked up from the table, clutching a bag of defrosting peas to the top of his head. One hand wrapped around his stomach. 'Not really.'

She peeled the bag of peas away from his head and peered at the skin. 'God, that's some bump!'

'Walked into a door.'

Samantha frowned. 'Have you been drinking?'

'Tea.' He pointed at the mug on the table, sitting next to Wee Hamish Mowat's present.

She pressed the bag back against his head. 'You wouldn't believe the day I've had. Like Muppet Central out there. . .' The fridge broke into a droning burr as she stood, peering in at the contents. 'We got any white wine left, or did you finish it?'

'I've been on orange juice and bloody lemonade all night, give me a break, OK?'

She turned. 'I just asked if there was any wine left.'

Pause.

'Sorry. I've. . . Not been the best of days.'

'Been a lot of those recently.' She clunked the fridge shut. 'You want some more tea?'

'Any chance of a hot water bottle?'

She filled the kettle, set it to boil, then disappeared from the room, coming back a couple of minutes later wearing her pink fluffy bathrobe and matching socks. Samantha thunked a roadkill-shaped Winnie The Pooh on the kitchen worktop, and unVelcroed his head. Unscrewed the plug and poured Pooh down the sink. Then filled him up from the steaming kettle.

'Here.'

Logan held it against his stomach with his free hand. Groaned.

She stared at him. 'Have you got your period, or something?'

No answer.

There was a rattle of spoons and mugs. Then she sat down on the other side of the table and handed over a fresh tea. 'Here.'

'Thanks.'

Pause. 'Didn't know you played chess.'

The set was made of wood – beech and mahogany – all laid out on a matching board. One of the pieces had a little cardboard tag tied around its neck, spidery copperplate marking out the words, 'DETECTIVE SERGEANT LOGAN McRAE'.

She picked the piece off the board – a horse's head, carved in pale wood. 'So you're Batman now?'

'That would be the *Dark* Knight.'

'OK, I'll bite. What the hell is going on with you?'

'I'm turning into a cliché.' He tried for a laugh, but it came out sounding forced and painful.

Silence.

'Logan? Look at me, Logan.'

He pulled his eyes up from the tabletop. She placed the white knight back on the board. 'You know. . . It's OK to feel a bit down every now and then, but . . . well, maybe you should think about getting some help?'

Logan went back to staring at the coffee rings. 'I've been seeing someone for about three months.'

There was an awkward pause. 'I. . .' A sniff. Then her voice went hard, brittle, 'I see. Is she *pretty*?'

'What? No, it's Goulding. You know: the criminal psychologist? Once a week, getting my head shrunk.'

'Oh . . . right. Yeah, of course.' She was blushing. 'What does he say?'

'I need to lay off the booze. Cut down on the cigarettes. Not be such a miserable bastard. Stop antagonizing my colleagues and superiors. Give up sitting in the dark, brooding.'

'Not going that well then.' Samantha picked up her tea and walked around behind him. Wrapped her free arm around his chest, her breasts pressing into the back of his head.

Logan took a deep breath. 'You know it's not like the world's a better place when I'm drunk. It's still shite. It's just . . . a little easier to cope with.'

'Am I part of the problem?' Voice barely above a whisper.

This time the laugh was slightly more genuine. Logan dumped the bag of peas on the table and gripped her arm. 'You're the only decent thing I've got going for me.'

'Your hand's bloody freezing.' She bent and kissed him on the top of his head, where the chess set had bounced off his skull. 'You silly bugger.'

20

Logan stood out on the rear podium car park, round the back of Force Headquarters, in the lee of a police van, smoking a sneaky cigarette and trying to stay out of the battering sleet. It swirled and whorled in unexpected directions, slapping against windscreens and exposed skin like tiny frozen hands.

But he stood there anyway, wearing a borrowed police cap, pulling carcinogens down into his scarred lungs on a freezing Sunday morning.

Ah, you couldn't beat the first fag of the day.

A handful of other smokers were huddled together by the back doors – everyone who'd hurried out after the morning briefing to catch that desperately needed top-up of nicotine – all standing with their backs to the wind, trying to survive the long bleak winter.

Sod this.

He took one last sook on his cigarette, dropped it into a little mound of slush and watched it hiss out and die. Then hurried back inside.

Biohazard Bob caught him on the way back up to the CID room. 'Any sign of that new DI from Fraserburgh yet?'

'Nope and he's got a PM to attend at half nine too. Going

164

to give him another twenty minutes, then try the station.'
What was the point of Logan turning up at seven if there
was still no sign of the bugger an hour later?

'Well, you know what these Blue Toon folk are like. If it's
not fish or screwing their sister, they've no idea what day it
is.' Bob leant in close, and gave Logan a whiff of peppermint
chewing gum. 'You sure you don't want my startling insight
into your jewellery heist sledgehammer guy?'

Logan backed off a step. 'Is this another lead up to you
farting and running away?'

Bob grinned. 'Good was it? Been holding that one in for
ages, fermenting it just for you.'

Another step backwards. Checking there was a clear line
of emergency exit. 'Well?'

'A sledgehammer's not exactly your weapon of choice for
a jewellery job, is it? No, for that you want a shotgun: shock
and awe. And. . .' He held up a finger – Logan had no intention of pulling it. 'If you haven't got a shotgun, you go for the
biggest kitchen knife you can hide up your jumper. What you
don't do is go out to your shed and saw a sledgehammer in
half.'

'And that's your startling insight? Our boy's got a shed?'

'No, you corrugated numpty. Using a sledgehammer like
that's pretty . . . unique. He's obviously never done over a
jewellers before, but maybe he's worked his way up from
other things?' Bob shrugged. 'Just an idea.'

'Oh. . .' It was obvious when you thought about it. 'Thanks,
Bob.'

'You're very welcome, young Master McRae.' Pause. Grin.
'And with that, I must leave you.'

The smell hit three seconds later.

Logan sat behind DI Steel's desk, with his feet up on the
handover notes, phone clamped to his ear, twisting his finger

through the spirals in the chord. 'Yeah, Detective Inspector Harvey. . . No, "Harvey". Hotel – Alpha – Romeo – Victor. . . Yeah, *Harvey*, that's him.'

There was a pause as the duty constable in the Fraserburgh control room transferred Logan's call through to their small CID department, where Logan had to go through the whole phonetic spelling thing again. Then someone called DI Chapman came on the line. *'You want to know where he is?'*

'He's supposed to be here in Aberdeen this morning. He's filling in for Detective Inspector Steel.'

'Intensive care, that's where he is. Last night's drug operation . . . suffered unforeseen complications.'

Which meant it was a complete balls-up. 'He going to be OK?'

'He was stabbed three times: what do you think?'

Logan almost smiled. 'Been there, it's not as much fun as everyone imagines.'

'I see. . .' And the next time Chapman spoke it didn't sound as if he was trying to drag a pineapple out of his own rectum. *'They've put him into one of those medically induced comas. We won't know any more till it's safe to bring him round.'*

'I'm sorry to hear it. So . . . are you sending us anyone else?'

'You are *kidding, aren't you? We've got one officer in a coma, three seriously injured, and the bastards got away with over half a million in uncut heroin. Everyone we've got's on this.'*

Which was understandable. 'Well . . . good luck.'

Logan stuck Steel's phone back in the cradle and swore for a bit. Brilliant. No replacement DI meant he'd be lumbered with one of the numerous tosspots around here. Like Beardy Beattie, or that idiot McPherson. Run a murder enquiry? He wouldn't trust them to run for a bus.

He tipped the inspector's seat back and scowled at the ceiling. . .

Unless he didn't tell anyone? Kid on that this DI Harvey had turned up as planned and was now running things. Long as no one actually had to *meet* with him, it'd be OK, wouldn't it? It was only for two weeks. DI Harvey, where 'DI' stood for Definitely Invisible.

'And then,' he told the ceiling tiles, 'hilarity would ensue.'

Bugger it. He was going to have to tell DCI Finnie.

Logan dragged himself out of the chair, along the corridor, knocked on Finnie's door, then waited.

'Enter!'

The Chief Inspector's office was about twice the size of Steel's, with a bank of filing cabinets, a huge whiteboard, a couch, two comfy chairs, a big beech desk, a large computer screen, and a frog-faced git.

'Ah, McRae, to what do I owe the *dubious* pleasure? Perhaps you're lost? The Professional Standards office is upstairs. You're spending so much time up there, I'm thinking of transferring you to their department, then you can give yourself a bollocking every morning and save everyone else a load of time. How does that sound?'

Wanker.

'Very funny, sir. I've just chased up Fraserburgh CID. DI Harvey was stabbed last night and they can't spare anyone else. To stand in for Steel?'

'Yes, thank you, *Sergeant*, I am *quite* aware what DI Harvey was coming down here to do.' Finnie sucked at his teeth for a minute, staring at Logan. As if he was thinking about eating him. 'Tell me, Logan, has DI Steel had a word with you?'

Logan kept his face dead still. 'About what, sir?'

'Your attitude, Sergeant.'

'Yes, sir.'

Finnie leaned forward. 'And?'

'We had a full and frank exchange of views.'

'You know, last year I wouldn't have hesitated to hand all her cases over to you and make you up to acting inspector. But now. . .?'

Logan could feel the heat rising in his cheeks. 'It. . . I. . .' He shut his mouth again, before it got him into any more trouble.

'I've seen people resurrect their careers from worse than this, Logan. Not *much* worse, but it is possible.'

'Thank you, sir.'

Finnie nodded. Those wide rubbery lips pressed tight together. Watching him.

'Er, is there something—'

'You can assist DSI Danby this morning, while I decide what to do about DI Steel's caseload.'

'But they're doing Steve Polmont's post mortem at—'

'Mr Polmont will survive without you, Sergeant. Now run along.'

Logan tried not to groan. He really did. 'Yes, sir.'

'And Sergeant, please remember that Danby outranks both of us. *Try* not to do anything *too* stupid.'

Logan parked the pool car outside Knox's granny's house, then pointed at the scabby old Transit van parked down the road with a half-hearted collection of orange plastic cones surrounding a couple of rusty road signs. The Aberdeen City Council crest sat on the side – two leopards holding a shield with three wee sandcastles on it – the sticker cracked and peeling, showing the burgundy paint underneath. 'That's the surveillance team.'

Wind battered down the road, whipping the trees and bushes, buffeting the pool car, slamming great icy gobbets of sleet against the windscreen. Quarter to ten on a Sunday morning and the streetlights were still on, their dim orange glow wobbling back and forth in the gusts.

Danby frowned. 'Better wait till the weather lets up a bit, then we can. . .' He trailed off, staring at Logan. 'What?'

'This is Aberdeen. Trust me, it's only going to get worse.'

The DSI sighed, unclipped his seatbelt, counted to three, then opened the door and stepped out into the howling sleet. Logan took a deep breath and followed him, plipping the pool car's locks as he hurried down the pavement after the limping Danby.

They banged on the council van's grubby back door, then hauled it open and clambered in without waiting for an answer.

'Shut the bloody door!' A red-nosed plainclothes PC was huddled in a mountain of coats and scarves – gloves on his hands, woolly hat on his head.

His partner was fighting with the lid of a tartan thermos.

It wasn't much warmer in here than it was outside.

Logan wiped the melting sleet from his face. 'Anything happening?'

'Sod all.'

The one in all the coats and scarves stuck up his hand. 'I got frostbite.'

'Your leg fell asleep, it's not the same thing.' PC Thermos gave the top one last twist and the smell of instant coffee drifted out into the van's rusty interior.

At one point the ancient council van must have been lined with metal shelving, now only the uprights remained, still bolted to the bare walls. The floor was a rust-streaked landscape of bumps, dents, old Burger King wrappers and Coke cans. A portable TV and video recorder sat on top of a stainless steel box, a thick black cable connected to a set of big batteries in the corner, another stretching up the van's wall and across to a video camera mounted in the air ventil-ation unit on the roof. Everything held in place with masses of silver duct tape.

Seating was courtesy of a set of green plastic chairs that looked as if they'd been stolen from someone's patio.

PC Thermos waggled his tartan container. 'Coffee?'

Danby settled himself down on one of the plastic chairs, stretched his right leg out and rubbed at a spot on his calf, grimacing. 'Long as it's hot.'

Logan peered at the little TV – getting a bleary view of Knox's front garden. 'So what's the plan for today then?'

PC Frostbite shrugged. 'Maybe a barbecue later on, if the weather picks up a bit. Game of tennis on the lawn. Perchance some skinny-dipping in the Don.' He took a slurp from his coffee. 'We haven't quite decided yet, have we Sandy?'

Thermos filled a plastic cup for DSI Danby. 'Apparently Knox wants to go see his sainted granny's final resting place. Sacro's going to drive him, we'll give them a thirty-second head start, then follow.'

Danby nodded. 'What about the rest of the surveillance team?'

Thermos looked at Frostbite, then Logan, then back to Danby. Eyebrows squinched together, top lip curled. 'Erm . . . we're it.'

There was a pause. 'Are you seriously telling me that the best Grampian Police can manage for a *level one surveillance* is two constables in a crappy old van?'

'Well, it's not like we have to keep it low-key, is it? He knows we're watching him. We don't need to do the whole line-of-sight-target-handover routine.'

Danby closed his eyes and massaged his big, pink forehead. 'When's he going out?'

PC Frostbite checked his watch. 'About half an hour? Want a biscuit while you wait?'

Fucking Aberdeen. Not even snowing properly yet, and it's already colder than a witch's titties. Tony shifts in his seat, wriggles even deeper into his jacket and wishes he'd brought some decent gloves with him. Not just the latex ones that don't leave any fingerprints. 'Think I saw a polar bear over there, hiding behind a wheelie bin.'

Julie just smiles at him. She's got Frank Sinatra on the Range Rover's stereo. Old-fashioned shite warbled by some Mafia stooge. Whatever happened to proper music, eh? Bit of Coldplay, or Travis, or James Blunt: something with a decent tune.

But it keeps her happy, so they put up with it.

Neil turns round in the driver's seat. 'Yeah, but look on the bright side.' He points through the windscreen at where Danby and some local plod from CID are clambering out of a maroon piece-of-shit Transit van. 'Now we know where the surveillance is on Knox's place. One council van and two cameras covering the front. Long as we go in round the back, no bugger'll see a thing.'

Tony has to admit that he has a point.

Danby hobbles across the road and through the gate to a shagged-out two-storey with rain-streaked walls and a garden Tarzan would have felt at home in. Yeah, if he'd had a fucking parka on. Wear a loincloth in that and it wouldn't just be the brass monkeys missing something, know what I mean?

'So,' Tony rubs his hands together, 'we going in tonight?'

Julie shakes her head, boop-de-booping along with that Sinatra crap.

Neil groans. 'Tell me we don't have to spend *another* night in this freezing shithole?'

'Sorry, Darling.' Julie stops singing, but she's still keeping time with a finger on the dashboard. 'The boss says we wait till Monday. He's got to get everything in place for when we show up with Danby. Don't want it turning into another Birmingham, do we, Babe?'

Tony shivers, and for once it's got nothing to do with the crappy weather. 'Fuck that.'

'Exactly.' She smiles. 'Now why don't we go drop off our little present, then we'll see if we can't find a Starbucks, OK?'

Neil puts the big Range Rover into gear, and pulls away from the kerb.

Sitting in the back, Tony watches Knox's house disappear into the sleet. Two more days and they'll be back in Newcastle, and DSI Danby will wish he was never bloody born.

The lounge was actually warm for a change. All that praying Knox had done was finally paying off: God had brought the three-bar electric fire back from the dead.

Unfortunately it just made the stink of mildew even stronger.

Knox had the armchair by the fire, clutching his plastic bag to his chest – fiddling with one of the handles, making irritating scratchy crinkly noises.

Danby took up most of the couch, Mandy from Sacro had the other armchair, and Logan stood back against the wall, watching them all. No one said a word.

The sound of flushing came from upstairs and a minute later, Mandy's partner, Harry, appeared in the doorway, looking a lot paler and a bit thinner than he had yesterday. 'Sorry about that.' He hauled at his trousers. 'We all set to go?'

Knox turned and stared at him for a moment. 'I'm gonna go in the car with Graeme and his new mate.'

Harry looked at Mandy. 'Is that. . .?'

'Well. . .' Mandy stood. 'I mean, if it's OK with Sergeant McRae?'

'Erm, yeah. Why not. We're going that way anyway.'

Danby didn't say a word.

Logan hurried out into the sleet, opened the rear passenger door and snibbed on the child lock, before ushering Knox into the car. Then scurried round and climbed in the other side. Danby got behind the wheel.

Logan leaned forward. 'Are you sure you don't want me to drive, sir? I mean, I know the town, and the force insurance policy doesn't—'

'I'm perfectly capable of driving a car, Sergeant. And I do know how to work a sat-nav.'

Knox turned and smiled at Logan as Danby took them to the end of the road and out into the sparse Sunday morning traffic. 'Graeme doesn't want to sit next to us. Barely said a word on the plane on the way up, like.' Knox reached across and tapped Danby on the shoulder. 'That not right, Graeme?'

The superintendent ignored him.

Knox shrugged. 'Don't know what *you've* got to sulk about, I'm the one spent seven years in prison with a bunch of perverts – don't see us complaining.'

Still nothing.

Knox hugged his carrier bag. 'See, I don't bear a grudge, cos I know it's what I needed to make us a better person. Learned a lot in prison, like. About the nature of man; good and evil; the haves and have nots. That kind of stuff.' He rested his forehead against the window. 'Shared a cell for while with this bloke . . . let's call him "Charley". Charley turned his back on God when he was eight years old. Used to be a choir boy, know what I mean? Priest got a bit carried away with the whole sacrament thing – "eat this for it is my flesh". Only he was talking about his knob.'

Danby threw the car round the corner onto Rosehill Drive. The sky was almost black, hurling sleet down on the grey city. Traffic on the other side of the street sent up little geysers of spray as they jolted from one pothole to the next.

'Charley was doing a sixteen stretch. He liked to break into people's houses at night and tie them up. Beat the shit out of the wife, then make her watch while he forced the

173

husband to suck his dick. "Do it, or I'll fuckin' slit the bitch's throat. . ." Thought it was only fair, like.'

Logan glanced back over his shoulder. The ancient council van was three cars back, struggling to keep up with Danby's driving.

Beside him, the weaselly little man gave the carrier bag a squeeze. 'Said it didn't always go according to plan, though. One time the bloke won't go down on him; man's on his knees, hands tied behind his back, but he won't do it. And Charley's screaming at him, and the wife's crying, and he cuts her. Not much, just enough to show the husband he's not screwing around, like. And the bloke opens his mouth, and Charley sticks his cock in, and the guy tries to bite it off.'

Knox rocked back and forth in his seat, shaking with laughter. 'He's going at it like a bloody mad terrier, shaking his head, sinking his teeth right in. . . Brilliant. Charley got his cock out and showed us – like a half chewed sausage it was. Had to have about twenty stitches. Ah. . .' He wiped a hand under his pointy noise. 'So funny.'

Logan looked at him. 'What happened to the husband and wife?'

Knox sniffed. 'Killed them, didn't he? Whole family – think he said they had a couple kids too. Course, Charley's running round with blood pouring out his bitten cock, getting his DNA everywhere, like. Had to burn the house down in the end. Got away with it too.'

Silence.

'All because that priest made him turn his back on God. Fascinating bloke, like, you wouldn't believe how much Charley knew about picking locks, bypassing alarm systems, getting rid of evidence. . .' Knox gave Logan a wink. 'Course, might've made the whole thing up, you know? For all I know he got too frisky with someone's Jack Russell and didn't want anyone to think he was a pervert.'

Danby snapped on the radio, then poked at the buttons until something orchestral thumped out of the speakers. North Anderson Drive was usually quiet at this time on a Sunday morning, but one lane had been blocked off to allow orange traffic cones to breed. There was no sign of anyone actually working, but it was enough to force the traffic to crawl all the way from Middlefield Road to the Haudagain roundabout. The other side of the Don was barely visible through the sleet; the whole scene rendered in shades of grey, punctuated by angry red taillights.

'Nothing like being at home, is it, Graeme?' Knox wiped a hand across the window next to him, clearing a space in the fog. 'Do you still see Billy Adams's wife?'

Danby stared straight ahead, following the stream of flickering brake lights.

'Think he ever found out? Think that's why he topped himself?'

The superintendent's voice was a dark rumble. 'Leave it, Richard. Know what I'm saying?'

'Just wondering. Trip to a graveyard makes you think about things like that, doesn't it? Death. Life. Betrayal.'

'I *said*, drop it!'

Knox shrugged, then went back to staring out of the window.

21

Logan stuffed his hands deeper into his pockets. 'He's going to catch his death.'

Danby shifted his weight, and grimaced. 'What a shame *that* would be.'

They were standing in the lee of a small mausoleum, about thirty yards from where Knox was kneeling, head bent in prayer, in front of a weathered headstone, carrier bag clutched to his chest. A gust of wind brought in another flurry of sleet, shivering the skeletal trees dotted between the graves.

The Sacro team had positioned themselves a respectful distance from Knox and his devotions – trying to control a writhing umbrella that looked determined to make a break for freedom.

Logan watched Danby rubbing his leg again. 'You OK?'

'When it's really cold the metalwork in my leg contracts. Nips a bit.'

Grove Cemetery perched on a steep slope overlooking the River Don, a huge Tesco supermarket, the Grampian Country Chickens factory, and a sewage treatment plant. Today Logan could barely see the lights twinkling on the other side of the river – the view swallowed up by the low clouds and driving sleet.

A train grumbled past on the line at the top of the grave-yard, windows full of miserable faces on their way north.

Logan craned his neck looking through the trees at the bottom of the hill, towards the wee park where Samantha still kept her Portakabin-style static caravan. Not that she spent much time there any more.

Danby turned his head and spat, the wind whipping it away before it could spatter someone's headstone. 'Soon as we're back at the station, call Frankland Prison: I want the name of everyone Knox shared a cell with. We're looking for someone done for housebreaking and rape. Then cross-check for unsolved murders where a house was burnt to destroy the evidence – two or more victims. The bastard might've got away with it up till now, but that's about to change, know what I'm saying?'

Logan nodded. 'Was already on my to-do list.'

'Good.'

Knox still hadn't moved.

Danby hunched his shoulders, pulling his upturned collar closer to his ears. 'Should've brought a bloody hat.' The top of his bald head was getting pinker and pinker in the driving sleet. 'Or stayed in the car.'

The DSI turned and glowered downhill at the car park, where the scabby maroon council Transit van sat between the CID pool car and a massive black Range Rover. The sur-veillance team would be sitting with the engine running, heaters on full, sharing a tartan thermos of hot coffee.

Bastards.

Logan cleared his throat. 'Why's Knox so obsessed with DI Billy Adams?'

Danby kept his eyes on the ex-council van. 'DI?'

'I did some digging.'

Sniff. The superintendent sent another gobbet of spit flying. 'Did you now.'

The only sound was the wind, slamming into the exposed cemetery, the creak of the bare trees, the distant rumble of traffic on Auchmill Road.

Ah well, it'd been worth a go.

Danby sighed. 'Billy was a friend, known him since we were both in uniform. Never really wanted promotion, said he liked it at the sharp end. Spent three months infiltrating Michael "Mental Mikey" Maitland's operation.' The big man gave a small, unhappy laugh. 'Far as Mikey's crew were concerned, Billy was a cop on the take: ready to do favours for a reasonable price. But he was really following the money.'

'So why's Knox being such a—'

'*Organized* crime. Clue's in the name, know what I'm saying? They don't make millions out of drug running and hide it under the mattress anymore: they've got lawyers, accountants, trust funds, offshore holding companies.'

Logan frowned. 'But what's that—'

'If you'll bloody shut up for a minute, you'll find out.'

Silence.

'We only started looking into Knox for the Brucklay rape and abduction because Billy tipped us off. There were rumours Mikey's principal accountant had "unusual tastes".'

Logan opened his mouth. Shut it again. Then turned to stare at the weaselly little man kneeling in front of the gravestone. 'Knox worked for the mob?'

'Graduated with a BA in accounting and finance from Northumbria University. He was their main money man. That's why he got away with raping old men for so long; a visit from Mental Mikey's boys tends to encourage amnesia in victims and witnesses.'

'But . . . no self-respecting criminal's going to put up with

178

that, they'd carve "nonce" in his forehead and string him up by the goolies.'

Danby laughed, a deep rumbly sound that boomed out over the graveyard. Knox didn't even look up.

'Sergeant, think about it. That weedy strip of piss over there is the only person Mikey *knows* won't roll over on him if something goes wrong. Knox'll always keep his trap shut about his employer's operation, because if he breathes a word, Mikey can tie him to at least half a dozen rapes. And prison's a dangerous place when your ex-employer's a vicious bastard with connections.'

Over by the grave, the man in question reached out a hand and caressed his granny's headstone.

Logan finally got it. 'And let me guess: there's no way the CPS is going to turn a blind eye to Knox abducting and violently raping someone's grandad, not even to get info on a mob operation. So he can't cut a deal.'

'Exactly. Long as Knox doesn't go mad, keeps the rapes down to a couple a year, it's manageable, know what I'm saying? Look at premier league football, never did them any harm, did it?' Danby rubbed at his calf. 'When we arrested Knox for the William Brucklay rape, Mikey got him the best lawyer; made sure Knox's mum went to a good care home. And Knox kept his mouth shut. Seven years he was inside, never said a single word about Mental Mikey's empire.'

Danby shivered as another gust of sleet battered across the graveyard. 'Think I'll wait in the car.'

Logan glanced over at Knox – still praying. 'That's why you're up here, isn't it? You think he'll talk to you.'

'That nasty piece of shite knows everything there is to know about Mental Mikey's operation. Crack him and you could tear the whole thing apart, know what I'm saying?'

The DSI turned his back and limped towards the exit.

Logan shouted after him, 'So . . . why does he keep winding you up about Billy Adams, then?'

Danby didn't even turn around.

'Because he's a sex offender. Manipulating people is what they do.'

Logan picked his way between the graves, lurching as the wind strafed the cemetery with slivers of ice, joining the team from Sacro.

Mandy had her whole body hunched up, stamping her feet, huddling under the bucking umbrella her partner was holding. 'We're not going to have to do this every Sunday, are we? I can't feel my toes any more.'

Harry wiped a sleeve across the underside of his nose. 'Could be worse. At least we're out of that mould-ridden filthy— Fuck!'

The umbrella whipped inside out: a satellite dish on a stick. Harry tried to force it back into shape while the wind hammered them.

Mandy grabbed Logan's sleeve and nodded at a life-sized statue of an angel, perched atop a big square plinth on the other side of the path.

'Erm . . . I . . .'

'It's OK, Sergeant, I'm not going to molest you.' She led him over into the relative shelter of the angel's wings. 'Wanted to have a word with you about our boy over there.' Mandy nodded in the direction of the praying Knox.

'Still creeping you out?'

She shuffled round, using Logan as an additional wind-break. 'I think he's in touch with someone, passing messages. Got no proof though, and I can't exactly spin his pad, can I?'

Logan must have looked as confused as he felt, because she sighed and said, 'Spin his pad: search his cell?'

'Mobile phone?'

She chewed at the inside of her cheek. 'Probably. I'm

guessing he'd want to keep it close, so . . . maybe that plastic bag he takes everywhere like a sodding security blanket?'

'Trouble is, we can't really do anything about it, even if he has. There's nothing about owning a mobile phone in his prevention order.'

'No, but his SOPO says he can't make contact with other people on the Sex Offenders' Register. And if he's got a mobile, we can't tell if he is or not.'

They watched Knox pray for a moment.

Mandy nodded. 'Be a shame if he violated his order and had to be banged up again for a couple of years, wouldn't it?'

'Terrible shame.'

'Could be planning anything. . .'

The smile slipped from Logan's face. Given Danby's story about Mental Mikey Maitland that wasn't exactly good news. 'Excuse me a minute.' He marched over to where Knox was kneeling.

The silly sod had to be frozen – sleet crusted across his shoulders and back, hair dripping wet, one hand clutching that carrier bag to his chest, the other on the lichen-speckled gravestone. 'HERE LIE THE MORTAL REMAINS OF JOSEPH ALBERT MURRAY, BELOVED HUSBAND AND DEVOTED GRANDFATHER. ALSO EUPHEMIA ABERCROMBIE-MURRAY, DUTIFUL WIFE.'

'Richard, I'm going to need to see what's in the bag.'

Knox looked up, nose dripping, lips a pale shade of purple, eyes rimmed with red. 'It's private.'

'I have to make sure you're not violating your prevention order.'

He closed his eyes, worrying the plastic bag round and round. 'Don't want it to get wet.'

Logan stuck out his hand. '*Now*, Richard.'

Knox bit his lip. Clutched the bag tighter. 'Promise you'll be careful?'

'Just give me the bloody bag.'

The little man did what he was told.

Logan pulled the handles apart and peered into the grubby, creased plastic. It was a book – a tatty bible, the blue fabric jacket scuffed and fraying.

'Was Granny Murray's: left it me in her will. Thought she was taking the piss at the time.' Knox smiled, a lopsided thing made of sharp, squint teeth. 'Had a lot of opportunity to read it in me cell though, know what I mean?'

Logan reached into the bag and opened the book, flicking through the pages. Some were held in with ancient amber Sellotape, others were smudged, passages highlighted in fading yellow, underlined in biro, tiny notes scribbled in the margins.

He closed the bible again. Stupid idea – why would Knox carry an illicit phone about with him? But it was too late to back down now. 'I'm going to have to ask you to empty your pockets.'

'At me granny's graveside?' The little man hung his head, then stood and held his arms out. 'Go on then.'

Logan kept it quick: a once through Knox's pockets then a pat down of arms, legs and torso. He passed the carrier bag back. 'Sorry. Thought you had a phone. . .'

Knox shrugged, clutching his plastic-wrapped bible to his chest again. 'Just doing your job, like.'

'Right, well. . . Let us know when you're ready to head home.'

The cold feels good, you know? Like being a kid again, on his holidays, sitting on the living room floor, listening to Granny Murray telling stories about the old days. Grandad Joe asleep in the other chair, a copy of the *Press and Journal* draped across his chest, snoring quietly to himself. Mouth a gaping cavern of pink.

They took all his teeth away when he was doing his national service in Cyprus, like. Went out with a full head of hair and all his own teeth, came back a slaphead with a set of falsies. He takes them out after dinner and leaves them on the table by the ashtray. Smokes rollies that smell of herbs and spices.

His mam's gone out for the evening, same as she does nearly every night since Richard's da ran out on them. Trading wife and kid for some girl works down the chipper in North Shields. Can't trust Geordie harlots – that's what Granny Murray says – God turn His face against their sinful hearts. Then she spits in the fire, that little spatter of yellowy-white hissing against the glowing electric bars. Never up high enough to warm the room, like: just enough to let Grandad Joe sleep with that cavernous mouth of his hanging open.

Pink and glistening.

Richard sneaks a glance at his keepers – the man and woman from Sacro, huddled together under a broken brolly, the nosey sergeant shivering beside a big carved angel.

It's a much fancier memorial than the simple granite slab Granny Murray picked out for her and Grandad Joe; she never was one for flash. The only decoration's a bunch of porcelain roses, sealed away in a glass dome. Only the glass has cracked and the whole thing's full of dirty water, the faded pink blossoms tainted with grey mould and trapped dirt.

Appropriate really.

He reaches around the back of the fake floral tribute, fingers drifting carefully through the matted yellow grass – don't want to find some junkie's needle the hard way, know what I mean? And then he finds it. A little rectangular box, about half the size of a toothpaste tube, hidden away in a little plastic bag.

Doesn't take much to palm it while he tidies the grave.

Richard pulls a few weeds, then fakes a sneeze, slipping the box into his pocket while he drags out a handkerchief.

Blows.

He levers himself upright, and crosses himself – testicles, spectacles, wallet, and watch – then bends and kisses the headstone. It tastes of pepper and gritty ice. But it smells of freedom.

Logan sat at his desk in the sergeants' cubbyhole, hands wrapped around a hot mug of coffee. Probably got pneumonia after this morning's little outing. Standing about like a pillock in the sleet, while Knox prayed at his granny's grave.

Logan wiped his nose with a pilfered packet of handy-wipes.

It hadn't taken long to find a contact number for HM Prison Frankland in Durham, but getting a list of everyone who'd ever shared a cell with Richard Creepy Bastard Knox had been more of a problem. Logan had finally managed to persuade someone to go digging through seven years' worth of prison records. They'd promised to call him back, soon as they had time to look into it.

So Logan went searching through the PNC for any unsolved murders where the house had been burned. Without a specific timeframe to narrow the search the results would be virtually useless, but it would give him somewhere to start when Frankland Prison got back to him.

He dragged another tissue out of the pack and made snottery noises into it.

'Urgh, could you *please* stop sniffing for five minutes?'

Logan twirled his seat around, until he was looking at the room's only other occupant. Detective Sergeant Doreen Taylor wrinkled her nose and stared back at him. 'Honestly, Logan, you're like a small child.'

Well, if he was like a small child, she was like someone's plump auntie: blue jeans, grey cardigan, shoulder-length bob.

'Didn't see you stuck out in the sodding sleet all morning, did I?'

'Don't be petulant. Here. . .' She dug into her handbag and came out with a packet of Lockets. 'And for goodness sake, try—'

The door bashed open and Biohazard Bob skittered to a halt on the carpet tiles. He poked a finger in Logan's direction. 'You! Run! Run now!'

'What are you—'

Bob grabbed Logan by the shoulders and hauled him out of the chair, snatched the jacket off the rack by the door and thrust it into his hands. 'Trust me. Get your arse in gear and find somewhere else to be. *Now!*'

Logan shuffled sideways. 'Have you been at the cauliflower cheese again?'

'Go!'

Frown. Logan pulled on his jacket. 'OK, OK. But this better not be a wind up, or. . .'

He drifted to a halt as someone bellowed, 'Where the *sodding hell* is he?'

DI Steel.

Logan stared at Bob. 'But she's supposed to be—'

Bob shoved him towards the door. 'Will you take a bloody telling?'

He staggered out into the CID room, took one look at the door leading back to the main part of FHQ – where all the DIs had their offices, and where the shouting was coming from – and legged it in the opposite direction instead, barrelling through into the bare concrete stairwell.

From here he could see through the window into the CHIS handlers' room, segregated from everyone else by a keypad door and double glazing. They were all getting out of their seats, moving towards the tiny side window that looked out on the main CID area. Staring at something.

Logan took the stairs two at a time, no idea what he'd done wrong.

Whatever it was, he wanted to be as far away from DI Steel as possible before he found out.

22

'You're late.' Isobel's eyes narrowed above her white elasticated mask.

Logan adjusted his safety goggles. 'Blame Finnie – I had to go babysit a huge Geordie DSI and his pet pervert. Found anything yet?'

The makeshift mortuary was a huge drive-in fridge, part of an old cash-and-carry on an industrial estate in the Bridge of Don, commandeered to act as Isobel's secondary crime scene. It was the only place big enough for the forklift truck they'd needed to move the concrete slab containing Steve Polmont's remains.

All the fridge's usual contents – the boxes of fruits, vegetables, fresh meat, and milk – had been stacked against the walls, clearing a space in the centre about the size of Logan's flat.

The IB had constructed a makeshift sterile room from clear plastic sheeting, the pieces held together with strips of duct tape. A portable X-ray machine was over by the back wall, a frame beside it displaying ghostly snapshots of a skeleton curled on its side. Four heavy-duty arc lights, one in each corner, illuminated the interior and its collection of white suited technicians like something out of the *X-Files*. An Aberdonian alien autopsy.

Polmont's slab of concrete rested on a platform wrapped in blue plastic, keeping the remains at table-top height. The electrician's right hand and left leg sticking up out of the pitted grey surface.

The room's ancient refrigeration units hummed, making the air crackle with cold.

One of the white oversuits waved at him. 'Sergeant McRae! Dr Frampton, we met at the scene?'

Her assistant waved too, balancing a collection of evidence bags in the crook of his arms. They were filled with something lumpy and brown, giving them a colostomy look. 'Wassup?'

Dr Frampton patted one of the bags. 'We've just finished retrieving the soil from the block, should get something back to you mid-week. Let you know its secrets.'

Logan looked at Isobel, then back again. 'OK. . . Thanks.'

The soil scientist gave him a little bow, then turned and slipped out of the enclosure, Igor the Dude hot on her heels.

Isobel held up a hand. 'Mr Haffenden?'

Someone dressed head-to-toe in SOC white shuffled over, a black toolbox held tight to his chest. He fiddled with the elastic hood encircling his masked face. Coughed. Cleared his throat. 'Actually, my friends call me Ian so—'

'Don't be shy, Mr Haffenden.'

With all the soil and mud gone, more of the body was on show. About a quarter of Steve Polmont stuck out of the concrete, the left leg from the knee down, the right arm from the elbow, a hip, a bit of shoulder, and the side of his face. Lividity had stained the flesh dark purple – except where Polmont's skin had been pressed against Dr Frampton's precious soil. There it was a pale waxy-yellow, patterned by the dirt and rocks.

Haffenden shifted his feet.

Isobel placed her hand on his shoulder and guided him towards the remains. 'As soon as you're ready.'

The little man looked up at her. 'It's just . . . *normally* archaeology doesn't have quite so much. . .' Back to the body again. 'You see, usually it's just fossils and bones.'

She tilted her head to one side, staring at him.

Logan stepped forward. 'Just pretend it's one of those peat bog people. The ones that are all preserved by the tannin and whatever?'

'Yes . . . right. Peat bog.' Haffenden placed his toolbox on the edge of the concrete slab and pulled out a set of tiny chisels. 'A very hard peat bog. . .'

The plastic enclosure rippled with white light: the IB photographer's flash recording everything as the nervous archaeologist chipped at the concrete around the body. Loosening it off.

He'd partitioned the slab into a grid of three-inch squares, piling the waste concrete from each section into separate evidence bags, the whole exercise meticulously documented on video and digital cameras.

After half an hour Haffenden seemed a lot more confident, following the lines of the shoulders and head, chipping around the ends of the hair. The more he exposed, the worse the smell got.

The archaeologist put his chisels down. 'I've got the head free.'

Logan followed Isobel over to the slab.

Polmont's head lay back at an awkward angle, the whole thing oddly shaped – slightly flattened. The side that had been embedded in concrete was puckered and blackened, flecks of grey still stuck to the cracked skin, a trickle of yellow-green liquid seeping from his nose.

'Ack. . .' Logan cupped a hand over his facemask, the

189

fabric damp with absorbed condensation. 'Thought he was supposed to be preserved by the cold.'

Isobel leaned forward and gently cupped Polmont's distorted cheek, turning the head until it was staring straight at them. The nose had been broken, one ear torn, the open mouth a solid grey mass – not excavated yet – but it was definitely Steve Polmont.

She felt her way around the back of the head. 'Some concretes are exothermic – they generate heat as they set. A mass the size and thickness of the foundations probably stayed warm for days. He's basically been cooked on one side and deep-chilled on the other. . . His head's been deformed by the weight of the concrete. I won't know if the damage to the skull was post or ante mortem until I open him up.'

Isobel ran a gloved finger down the body's twisted neck. Just above the clavicle there was a circle of black puncture wounds. 'Bite mark.'

Isobel frowned at the exposed arm, the dark brown discolouration on the sleeve. Then unbuttoned the cuff and rolled the fabric back to expose another bite.

'Of course, I've had to lose some of the hair.' The archaeologist pointed at the strands still embedded in the wall of the block. 'And the outer clothing's going to be a challenge.' He shrugged at Logan. 'The concrete's seeped through the weave of the material, then set solid. Should make the actual body easier to remove though, like getting a moth out of a cocoon.'

Haffenden picked up his little chisel again. 'You know, this isn't nearly as bad as I thought it was going to be. It's really kind of fascinating when you think about it.'

Good to know someone was enjoying themselves.

Half an hour later they were gathered around the body again. Haffenden had moved on to the torso, excavating the left shoulder and upper arm.

'Problem came when I hit the first one, took a bit of doing to get them chiselled out without damaging any.' He pointed at the shoulder, where ten or twelve metal spikes protruded from Polmont's jacket, the fabric stained dark brown.

Isobel held one of the X-rays up for comparison. 'Excellent job.' She leaned in, touching the end of one spine with her gloved finger. 'Definitely nails.' She laid a ruler along the arm and waited for the photographer to finish, before slicing the sleeve open with a scalpel, then did the same with the jumper and checked shirt underneath. The arm had that familiar mouldy cooked look, but where the nails went in the skin was darker.

She prodded at the base of one metal spike. 'Signs of bruising . . . these were inserted before death. And do you see where some have obviously been removed?' Pointing at a blackened hole in Polmont's arm.

Logan nodded. 'He was tortured.'

Isobel called for a set of pliers and eased one of the nails free, then held it up like a tiny Excalibur. 'Four-inch wire nail, probably from a nail gun. Going by the diameter it's probably the same thing that made the holes in the palm.'

Behind them, someone said, 'Maybe he was crucified?'

Logan froze. Sodding hell – Steel.

He turned and there she was, standing less than a foot away, staring at him over her mask. A large figure in an SOC suit pushed through the flaps of the makeshift mortuary, limping slightly. That would be Danby. The big Geordie took up position at the head of the slab.

Steel grabbed Logan's arm. 'Sergeant McRae, can I have a wee word? Outside?'

'I thought you were on holiday?'

'*Now.*'

Outside, the cash-and-carry car park was almost deserted, just the little cluster of IB vehicles, Logan's manky brown

Fiat, a pool car, and a fat man loading crates of tins into a mobile burger van – shoulders hunched against the sleet.

Steel ripped her mask off. 'Tell me, Sergeant, was it too much to hope you bunch of dicks could get along without me for two sodding weeks?' Her face had an unnatural orange-brown tint to it, like she'd been smearing Marmite into her skin.

'I didn't—'

'WAS IT?' The inspector turned her back and marched over to a row of oversized shopping trolleys and kicked one. 'Susan's spitting fucking nails. Crying. Shouting. Making my life a bloody misery because we're *supposed* to be in Puerto de la Aldea drinking non-alcoholic san-fucking-gria and shagging like sea otters!'

Logan took a step back. 'Then why—'

'But where am I? Here: in fucking Aber-fucking-deen because *you* had to go crying to bloody Finnie!' She gave the trolley another kick, then turned on him.

'But—'

'Couldn't cover for that prick Harvey from Fraserburgh CID for another sodding hour, could you? We were in the airport: forty minutes more and we'd've been on the fucking plane!' Steel dug a bundle of paper from her pocket and hurled it at him. Passports, e-tickets, and boarding passes bounced off his SOC suit, fluttering down to the sleet-puddled tarmac.

He watched a duty free receipt flutter away on a gust of wind. 'Fuck you.'

She froze, eyes bugging. 'How dare—'

'I didn't stab the bastard, did I? You gave me all that shit yesterday about not being a team player and soon as I follow the rules, you throw a hissy fit?'

'You can't—'

'What was I supposed to do: kid-on he'd turned up?'

Getting louder, shouting in her face. 'And what about you? You could've told Finnie to get stuffed, but you didn't, did you? No, you came trotting back here like a good little girl.'

'I didn't—'

'So don't blame me because Susan's pissed off. You had your chance and you screwed it up.'

She stood there, scowling at him. 'I had a sodding bikini wax.'

Logan threw his hands in the air. 'Then go on bloody holiday! Tomorrow: go to the airport and turn your phone *off*. Tell Finnie to screw himself. Sod off to Puerto del Whereverthefuck and stop getting on my tits!'

The word 'tits' echoed around the car park. The big man stopped in the middle of loading a box of burger buns to stare at them.

DI Steel slumped back against the cash-and-carry wall and hauled at the crotch of her trousers. 'How am I supposed to tell Finnie to go screw himself if my phone's turned off?'

Logan picked up the soggy bits of paper. 'So . . . Susan's really pissed off?'

'Oh Jesus, like you wouldn't believe.' Steel sagged even further. 'Last chance we had to go on holiday too: leave it any longer and the airlines get all wanky about pregnant women flying. Scared she'll give birth in cattle class, and they'll have to give the sprog free flights for life.'

'Thought that was an urban myth.'

He wiped the gritty ice from a burgundy passport, then handed everything back.

Steel sniffed. 'You know, we've no' had sex in months. *Months.* Beginning to forget which bit goes where. . . Thought pregnant women were meant to get all horny.' She scowled at Logan, then smacked him on the arm. 'And soon as she pops your sprog, it's another six months of celibacy! Could you no' have kept it in your bloody pants?'

'Ow! For your information, you *begged* me to get Susan up the stick. Remember? "Oh Logan, please can we have some more sperm? Oh please? Just one more try? *This* time it'll work. I promise. I'll love you forever?" Remember that?'

She shrugged and peered out at the dreich afternoon. 'Aye, well if your bloody sailors had been any good they would have taken the first time.'

Mr Burger-Van loaded three cases of Diet Coke, then slammed the van's doors shut, abandoned his trolley in the middle of the car park, and drove off.

'Lazy bugger.' Steel had another dig at her parts. 'You any idea how much it hurts to get a full Brazilian?'

'What's Danby doing here?'

'Only did it cos Susan thinks it's sexy. . .' Scratch, rummage, fiddle.

'Will you stop doing that!'

'Itchy.' She shivered. 'Bloody freezing too.'

'He just seems to be taking a lot of interest in Polmont. First the journals, now the PM. . .?'

Steel pulled out a packet of cigarettes, offered one to Logan, then lit them both. 'The Ice Queen find anything we can pin on someone yet?'

'He was tortured with a nail gun, then buried alive.'

'Poor bugger. . . Anything else?'

'Bite marks on his arms and neck. Look like dog.'

The inspector dug her hands deep into her armpits. 'So we're looking for a big violent bastard with a huge dog, and access to the building site. Think, think, think.'

Logan nodded. 'I chased up the lookout request on Andrew Connelly – nothing yet. Lothian and Borders are keeping an eye open, just in case he really *has* gone off to see his mum.'

'Warrant?'

'PF says we don't have enough for an arrest. If they can get DNA off the body that matches Connelly or his dog—'

'Whatever happened to the good old days, when you could just kick someone's door in and beat a confession out of them?' She smoked in silence for a minute. 'What about those journals?'

'Still working on them.'

'Right.' She ground her cigarette out against the cash-and-carry wall. 'I'm taking over here. You go through that stuff we got from Polmont's flat.'

Steel turned and hobbled back towards the door.

'But—'

'Team player, remember? And do something about your jewellery heist. I'm no' running a holiday camp here.'

The door clunked shut behind her, leaving Logan alone in the car park.

Bloody typical.

23

'This all of it?' Logan stood on his tiptoes and peered at the row of boxes arranged on the metal shelving.

'Next one down too. And the one under that. And we got some more over there.' The sergeant in charge of the Water Lane evidence store turned and pointed at another rack over by a stack of archive files. 'That's everything they brought in from Polmont's flat.'

The store was a converted Victorian warehouse, a pile of filthy granite hidden away down a narrow alleyway off Mearns Street, just wide enough to get an unmarked Transit van down, if you were careful. Quiet and anonymous. The building's high windows were nearly opaque with dirt, and barred on the inside.

The room was partitioned up with adjustable shelving units, turned into a maze with the heavy metal cage for drugs and confiscated money lurking at its heart. The shelving groaned under the weight of seized goods and lost property, the wooden floorboards gouged and scuffed. Strip lighting hung from the bare rafters, buzzing and flickering, making Logan's breath glow white in the cold air.

'OK. . . This lot been processed yet?' Trying not to sound too hopeful.

The sergeant laughed, a surprisingly high-pitched sound for someone who looked so much like an axe murderer. 'You're kidding right? What am I, your mum?'

Logan groaned. There had to be two or three hundred items on the shelves, all of which needed to be catalogued, verified, and checked against the stolen property register. Bloody DI Steel – this was going to take him forever.

Sergeant Axe-Murderer patted him on the back and grinned. 'Look on the bright side, at least it's sodding freezing in here.'

'You can bugger off now, Clive.'

'Don't mention it.' Clive gave him one last pat, then wandered off, hands in his pockets, whistling. Git.

Logan pulled the first box from the shelf and dumped it on the floor. It was full of Sony MP3 Walkmans in their original packaging. He dug them out one by one, opening the cases to make sure they contained what they said they did, then wrote everything down in his notebook. Knowing that he'd have to type it all up when he got back to FHQ.

The next box was full of watches, the one after that: digital cameras. Logan sat back on his haunches and stared at the stacks of stuff still sitting waiting for him.

Bugger this.

He dug out his mobile and went hunting through the contacts, then hit the button. It was Sunday, so he'd have to leave a message, but if anyone asked he could honestly say he was doing something.

But a real person answered the phone: *'Trading Standards, can I help you?'*

'Dildo? It's Logan. What are you doing in the office?'

'Fucking overtime. Got a backlog like you wouldn't believe.'

'I need a favour from the Shop Cops.'

'Oh aye. . .?' Pause. 'Still owe me a pint from last time, remember?'

Logan looked up at Polmont's collection. 'I think we've found a stash of counterfeit goods.' Not entirely true, but it *could* be. And that made it Trading Standards' responsibility.

There was a groan. 'Do me a favour and lose it again. We're up to our ears in the bloody stuff as it is.'

'My heart bleeds. We've got the lot down at the Water Lane store, get your bum over here and work your magic.'

He was silent for a moment. 'This you trying to get me to do your bloody paperwork again?'

'Dildo, I'm hurt.'

'Yeah, and you didn't answer the question.' Sigh. 'What have you got?'

Logan smiled. 'MP3 players, hair straighteners, video games, bunch of other stuff. All boxed.'

'Sod. . . OK, OK, I'll come over. But it's going to have to be Monday: got a bunch of Weights and Measures reports to write up, and I'm bloody well going home tonight before my kids are asleep.'

They set a time and Logan hung up. Then stood and stuck two fingers up at the contents of Steve Polmont's flat, now officially someone else's problem. Who said he couldn't be a team player?

Logan parked outside the fourth address on his list and checked the caller display on his phone, just as it rang through to voicemail: Colin Miller – the *Aberdeen Examiner*'s star reporter. Logan gave it a minute, then checked his messages. Four from Steel threatening to castrate him; one from Samantha asking if he fancied taking her out to dinner for a change; one from Beattie – had he done anything about that meeting yet?

Logan frowned. What bloody meeting?

And then it was Colin, asking to be called back.

Logan hit reply and three rings later the reporter's Glasgow burr rattled his eardrums.

'*Laz, my man, how they dangling?*' He didn't bother waiting for a reply. '*Great. Listen, I'm free the night, fancy hittin' the town? Grab a bite to eat and some beers?*'

'Can't tonight, got a date with a tattooed lady.'

'*Aw, come oan! You got any idea what I had to do to get a free pass? Couple of pints, bit of banter, just like the old days.*'

Logan creaked open the car door.

A security light cracked on, bathing the gravel parking area with harsh white light. Twenty past four and the sun was taking its hat off, packing its bags, and sodding off home, leaving the countryside washed in dull pink and cold blue.

'I'm kinda off the booze for a bit.'

'*You're kidding me!*'

'Antibiotics.' As good a lie as any.

'*Shite. . .*'

There were no streetlights out here in the sticks. It was a cluster of converted farm buildings between Dyce and the Bridge of Don. Not all of them had been finished, and an old steading sat off to one side, the roof a ribcage of pale pine joists with a tatty-edged chunk of blue plastic sheeting draped over half of it.

At least the wind and sleet had died down. Still bloody freezing though.

'*Then we'll grab a curry. You can have a Lambrini, or what-ever it is you teetotal homosexuals drink these days.*'

'Colin—'

'*We can moan about work – got this new bloke in charge of the news desk, carrot-top bastard thinks I'm "too sensationalist". Wanker. You can bang on about that tit Beattie, or your lezzer boss.*' Pause. '*Bet that wee shite Richard Knox is a nightmare to deal with. . .?*'

Logan slammed the car door. Somewhere in the distance a dog barked. 'Subtle, Colin, *real* subtle.'

'What? I just—'

'I'm not giving you info on an ongoing investigation, you know that. Curry and a pint my arse.'

There was silence for a moment, and when Colin spoke again Logan could hear the grin in his voice. *'Can't blame a guy for trying, right? Tell you what, you tell me all about Knox, and I'll let you in on Monday's headline.'*

'Bye Colin.' Logan hung up. Cheeky bugger.

He pulled out the list he'd downloaded from the Police National Computer – people convicted of robberies involving sledgehammers – and read the summary for number four. Damian Atkinson, AKA: Daniel Francis, AKA: Danny Saunders, AKA: Donny Ferrier. Done for burglary, demanding money with menaces, aggravated assault. And most importantly, for holding up a series of all-night petrol stations with a sledgehammer.

Only two houses in the little development had lights on. The first turned out to be a drunken middle-aged man with a beard and a beer belly. No, he didn't know any Damian Atkinson, or a Daniel Francis, but Danny Saunders lived over there. He pointed a wobbly finger at a mouldy caravan parked alongside the unfinished farm building.

'Doin' it. . . Doin' it up hisssself. Yeah?'

Very industrious.

Logan crunched his way across the gravel driveway to the steading. Random construction materials were heaped up on the grass outside: pallets of bricks, boxes of slates, piles of timber. Logan stuck his head through the open door, but it was dark in there. Just the sound of something dripping and the fusty smell of dust and mouse droppings. A pile of tools lurking in the shadows.

Danny Saunders's caravan wasn't a big Portakabin-style one like Samantha's, it was a small two-wheeled model. The kind that always slowed traffic to a funereal crawl on the summer roads, dragged behind a Volvo estate full of unhappy children.

The thing was streaked with dirty green mould, the roof almost black. At some point it had been given a coat of beige paint, but it was blistered and peeling, showing off the rust underneath.

Muted light shone from somewhere in the caravan, so Logan picked his way across the long damp grass and peered in through the side window. It was surprisingly clean inside, the bed stowed away to make room for a Formica table and two bench seats.

A man sat at the table, making notes on a thick pile of paperwork, with his back to the window. Hair thinning a bit at the back, stripy grey jumper, a fading blue DIY tattoo on the back of one hand.

Somewhere, a radio was playing – the end of a Paul Weller track drifting into a traffic update featuring the disastrous roadworks on the Haudagain roundabout.

'You want tea, Danny, love?' Female, young-ish.

The man glanced deeper into the caravan. 'Oh aye, ta. You know, we're still aboot twa grand short for gettin' the roof finished.' Definitely a local lad.

'Well . . . we'll just have to give him another call, won't we?'

'Do we have to? Can we no'—'

'We've been over this, Danny. Let's not argue.'

Logan inched his way over to the door. An upturned milk crate sat just outside, acting as a step. Logan kicked it out of the way, then knocked. Then pulled out his pepper-spray, just in case.

A face appeared at the window, but Logan flattened himself against the grime-streaked aluminium body, keeping out of sight, and knocked again.

Danny: 'Can't see anybody. . .'

Woman: 'If it's that pisshead Banks again, tell him to sod off, we're busy.'

Danny: 'You know he can hear you, don't you?'

Woman: 'Just answer the door.'

There was a clunk and the door swung outwards. 'Ray, dees a favour and...' Danny – thirty-two-ish, handlebar moustache and soul-patch, cheery cheeks, and spiky hair. He frowned. 'Can I help you?'

Logan smiled up at him. 'Damian Atkinson? AKA: Danny Saunders, AKA: Daniel—'

The caravan door slammed shut. Danny shouted, 'Fuck! It's the cops!' then the door battered open again. He charged out, his foot going for where the milk crate step *should* have been.

Oops.

He went sprawling, face first into the cold wet grass.

Thunk.

'Aya, bastard...'

That was the thing about people like Danny, AKA: Daniel, AKA: Damian, AKA Donny – the more aliases they had, the thicker they were. Really successful crooks never needed more than one name, because they never got caught.

Danny struggled up till he was sitting on his bum, framed in the pale rectangle of light from the caravan's open door, clutching his left wrist to his chest. Dark-red blood oozed into his moustache from a lopsided nose.

'Come on then.' Logan pulled out his handcuffs. 'On your feet.'

'You broke my wrist...'

'I never even touched you.' Logan took a step forwards. 'Now you can either get up and be handcuffed, or—'

Loud noise, ringing in his ears. Circles of yellow and black. The pain hit just before the ground did – harsh and throbbing at the back of his head. And then he was lying on the ground, something sharp and jagged clawing at his cheek.

Someone shouting, 'Run, Danny! Run!'

Fuck...

Logan struggled to his knees, the world whooshing in his ears, head pounding, scalp stinging, stomach churning. Not going to be sick, not going to be . . . yes he was. All over the grass and his own left hand. A hot splash of bitter, sour-smelling yuck.

'I said, *run*!'

'But he'll—'

'I'll take care of him. . .'

Oh shit. That didn't sound good.

He looked up. She couldn't have been much older than eighteen, bleached blonde hair showing an inch of brown at the roots, big red 'Should-Have-Gone-To-Specsavers' glasses, huge pregnant belly, chunky face, teeth bared, a heavy cast-iron frying pan clutched in both hands. She raised it over her head and brought it crashing down onto Logan's head.

Or she would have if he hadn't ducked. It slammed into his right arm instead, pain shooting up from his bruised elbow.

'I'm a bloody police officer!'

'Leave us the fuck alone!'

She grunted and dragged the frying pan round for another go. Logan scrabbled backwards through the wet grass, but she followed him. Swung. Missed.

Her left foot came down in the warm puddle of sick, and her leg shot out from under her, sending her crashing down on her backside. 'Urgh! There's puke everywhere!'

Logan staggered to his feet, lurched to the side, wobbled a bit.

Pepper-spray, where was the bloody pepper-spray?

He tried to steady himself, one hand on the manky caravan.

Where the hell was the god-damned bastarding—

There. Lying in the puddle of vomit.

Logan bent down and grabbed it. The world did a somersault, then the hokey-cokey. He staggered back, clutching the damp, black canister in his hand.

She was getting to her feet, face creased up, teeth bared, swearing. . .

Logan was sick all over her.

There was a pause, and then she started screaming. 'Agggh! It's in my fucking mouth!'

He fumbled with the cap on the little black canister. Damn thing wouldn't come off. . . But it didn't look as if he'd be needing it any more. She'd dropped the frying pan, now she was bracing herself against the caravan, spitting and gagging. Then spattering the filthy paintwork with whatever it was she'd had for lunch.

Logan put a hand to the back of his head, waves of pain rippling out from his battered elbow as he bent his arm. His fingertips came away dark and sticky. 'You,' he turned to the vomiting woman, 'are fucking nicked.'

He took a step, then froze as Danny came hurtling around the side of the steading clutching a sledgehammer in his one good hand.

'Bastard!' Danny swung the thing at Logan's head. Missed. The sledgehammer crashed into the caravan wall, tearing straight through the aluminium, buckling the doorframe.

Logan scrambled away as Danny tried to haul the sledge-hammer's thick steel head out of the hole he'd made.

Pepper-spray. Why couldn't he get the lid off the bloody pepper-spray? What the hell was the point of even *having* pepper-spray if you couldn't get the sodding lid off?

There was a squeal of metal – Danny had finally managed to rip the sledgehammer free.

Time to go.

Logan stumbled to an unsteady run, making for the car. Getting the hell away from that bloody hammer.

It whistled past his left shoulder and Danny swore as it clunked into something.

'Aya, fuckin' Jesus. . .' Pause. *Fuck.* Hissed breath. 'Ow. . . My FUCKIN' FOOT!'

Logan kept going.

The next swing clattered into the steading wall, sending hot yellow sparks flying.

'Stand fuckin' still. . . Ow, ow, ow. . .'

The security light blared out across the cold gravel as Logan struggled around the corner. He made it as far as his crappy brown Fiat, then turned to see Danny limping after him, grunting through gritted teeth every time his left foot touched the ground, breath streaming out behind him in a white cloud.

Logan struggled with the cap again. Bastarding thing still wouldn't budge.

He stuck it between his teeth and twisted – the plastic tasted bitter and biley.

'Aaaaaaaagh!' Danny dragged the sledgehammer up and round, swinging one-handed, putting all his weight behind it.

Logan flinched back and the hammer caught the edge of his coat, slamming it through the passenger window in a hard crash of fractured glass. Little cubes of shining diamond sprayed out across the vinyl seats.

He spat the canister's lid out and pointed the pepper-spray right between Danny's eyes. 'Drop it!'

'Fit did you dee to Stacy, you bast—'

Logan pressed the trigger.

There was a brief moment of stunned silence, then Danny started screaming, fell to the gravel driveway, both hands over his face, legs kicking out in random directions. Leaving the sledgehammer sticking out of Logan's passenger window like a jaunty wooden erection.

They sat at the caravan table, Logan on one side, Danny Saunders slumped on the other. The windows were all fogged up from the kettle being boiled, emptied, filled, and boiled again, the steam permeating the small space, even thought there was a brand-new hole in the wall and the door wouldn't close properly any more.

The cloying, bitter stench of sick hung thick in the muggy air.

'You feeling any better?' The woman – Stacy – peeled the soggy tea towel off Danny's face. His skin was almost scarlet, eyes scrunched shut, tears dribbling down his cheeks, snot oozing out of his nose. He raised a hand to his eyes.

Logan grabbed his sleeve. 'Told you not to rub it. You'll only make it worse.'

'Hurts. . .'

Got to love pepper-spray.

Stacy scowled. One side of her hair was sticking out in random directions, little things stuck in the blonde mess. Whatever perfume she used, it wasn't up to hiding *Eau de Vomi*. 'Look what you've done.'

Logan scowled back, keeping the bag of frozen peas pressed against the back of his skull. 'You tried to bash my head in with a frying pan, and he tried to take it off with a bloody sledgehammer. Remember?'

She turned and stomped back to the fridge, pulled a carton of whole fat milk out, and sploshed some into the tea towel. 'It was an accident.'

'How? *Exactly?*'

Silence.

'Gave you the peas, didn't I?' She put the milk back in the fridge, then draped the wet towel over Danny's face again. 'You sure this'll help?'

'Positive.'

Stacy wrinkled her nose, pulling a chunk of regurgitated something from her hair. 'Urgh. . .' The kettle whistled to the boil. She took it off the gas and poured it straight into a steaming bucket, then checked the temperature with her little finger. 'I wanted a caravan with a shower, but *no*, that would've been too *expensive*. . .'

She peeled off her jumper then the T-shirt underneath,

206

revealing a none-too-sensible bra and her stretch-mark-rippled pregnant bulge. She sniffed at the stained T-shirt, grimaced, then dumped it in the corner with the spattered jumper. Logan didn't watch her washing her puke-matted hair in the bucket.

He leaned across the tabletop and lifted the edge of the milky tea towel. 'Feeling any better?'

'It burns. . .'

'It's pepper-spray, it's meant to burn.' Logan let the towel slap back against the angry skin. 'You're a silly bastard, Danny, you know that, don't you?'

The man on the other side of the table coughed. His voice was all wheezy, slightly muffled by the tea towel. 'Thought you were here about that. . .' He drifted into silence.

Logan pulled out his notebook. 'Where were you at nine fifteen yesterday morning?'

Stacy took her head out of the bucket, shampoo froth clinging like candyfloss. 'Don't you tell him anything. Didn't read you your rights, did he?'

'But—'

'But *nothing*, Danny.' She raised her chin and stared at Logan. 'Why you want to know?'

'Just answer the question: Saturday morning, quarter past nine.'

Silence.

Danny coughed again. 'We were—'

'Danny Saunders, don't you dare!'

'Fit dis it matter? We werenae up tae anything, were we?'

'That's not the point.'

'We were doon the Oldmachar Church, OK?'

Logan laughed. 'Yeah, right.'

'Aye we were!' Danny sat upright, and the cloth fell off his face, splatting onto the Formica tabletop in a little eruption of warm milk. It was working, he was actually able to open his eyes a crack, just enough to glare at Logan. 'You ask the minister, we were there bang on ten till aboot eleven.'

Logan looked around the cramped caravan with its sledgehammer hole in the wall. '*You* went to church?'

'You can gie the minister a call if you dinna believe me.'

'I don't.' He reached into his coat pocket and. . . Fuck. Fucking . . . fuck. He came out with a handful of broken plastic and circuit board shrapnel. All that was left of his phone – caught between Danny's hammer and the car window. 'Oh that's just. . .' He thumped it down on the tabletop. 'That was you and your bloody sledgehammer!'

'It's only a phone. You broke my wrist!'

Logan took a deep breath, tried really hard not to lunge across the table and punch Danny in the throat, then stuck out his hand. 'Give me your mobile.'

Stacy: 'We don't have to do any—'

'GIVE ME YOUR BLOODY MOBILE PHONE, or so help me. . .' He closed his eyes, gritted his teeth. 'Please, may I borrow your phone?'

Danny handed over a cheap-looking handset. Logan called the Control room. 'I want a number for whoever the minister is at Oldmachar Church, Bridge of Don. . . Yeah, I'll wait.'

Danny picked the milky tea towel off the tabletop and flopped it back across his face. 'Reverend Williams. He's helpin' us get the wain baptised, you know, when he pops oot?'

Logan dialled the number Control gave him, then sat there, staring at the shattered remains of his phone. He'd only just learned how to programme the damn thing and now he'd have to buy a new one. And would they let him claim it back on expenses? Would they—

'. . .Hello? Is anyone there? Hello?'

'Can I speak to the minister?'

'That'd be me. Fit can I dee for you?'

Logan glanced up at Danny's towel-covered face. 'What's your name?'

'*If we're being formal, it's Reverend Williams, if not, you can call me Charley.*'

'This is Detective Sergeant Logan McRae: Grampian Police. I need to know if you met with a Danny Saunders and his. . .' he looked at the shiny bauble covered with soap on Stacy's ring finger, 'fiancée any time in the last week?'

There was a pause. '*Can I ask fit this is aboot?*'

'Trying to establish their whereabouts.'

'*Oh aye, and why's that?*'

Danny leant forwards, face still making yoghurt underneath the cloth. 'It's a-right, Charley, you can tell him.'

So the minister did. Logan told him someone would be round to take a formal statement, thanked him for his time and hung up. Then swore.

Danny held out his hand for the phone. 'See: told you. We wis doon the church.'

Today just . . . fucking *wonderful*.

'So you don't know anything about the jewellers that got knocked over on Crown Street, yesterday?'

Stacy patted her swollen belly. 'Danny doesn't do that kind of thing any more, he's got responsibilities now.'

'We wis taking care of my wee loon's spiritual upbringing. Nowhere near Henderson's.'

Logan smiled. 'I never said anything about Henderson's.'

Stacy squirted more shampoo into her hand. 'Nice try, *Inspector Rebus*, but it's been on the radio all day.'

Bugger.

24

Bloody snow.

Logan sat on the upturned milk crate outside the steamed-up caravan and watched the first tiny flakes drifting down from a dark black sky.

He shivered and took another drag on his cigarette, then hissed the smoke out through his teeth. The bag of frozen peas was starting to go all soggy and limp. Logan knew how it felt. He pulled it away from his aching head and probed the lump underneath with his fingertips. Winced. Put the bag back.

All he'd wanted was one little success to prove everyone wrong. Was that really too much to ask for? Just one measly case closed, out of the dozens littering the whiteboard in the CID office. And all he'd ended up with was a bash over the head, a broken car window, and a smashed mobile phone.

He pulled the cigarette from his mouth and stared at the glowing orange tip. No point in putting it off any longer. Logan pinged the butt away into the darkness. 'Right. . .'

'Made you a tea.'

He looked up to see Stacy standing over him, clutching a steaming mug. She'd changed into a baggy hooded top that didn't reek of vomit. She held the mug out. 'I didn't spit in it, if that's what you're thinking.'

What the hell.

'Thanks.' Logan took an experimental sip. Hot. Milk, three sugars. 'How's he doing?'

Stacy wrapped her arms around herself. Shuffled her feet. Looked off into the middle distance. 'Sorry about belting you one.'

'Me too.' Logan hauled himself up, handed her the bag of defrosting peas, then pulled out his handcuffs. 'Time to go.'

Stacy's mouth fell open. 'But. . . We. . . I thought we'd—'

'You assaulted a police officer with a frying pan. He did it with a sledgehammer. We've been over this.'

'That's not fair!'

'Stacy. . .' Logan stopped. 'What's your full name?'

'Get stuffed.'

'Fine, we'll add "giving false details" to the list of charges.'

'You can't do that!'

'Listen, Stacy, right now I'm looking at a buggered phone, a broken car window, and a fucking big lump on the back of my head, OK? You're under arrest.'

She threw a finger at the ragged-edged hole by the caravan door. 'What about our bloody wall?'

'Your boyfriend did it, not me.'

She stomped her foot. 'But I'm *pregnant*!'

'I didn't do that either.'

Stacy glared at him for a moment, then dropped her eyes again. 'We. . . Maybe we could come to some sort of under-standing?' Twirling her fingers through the ends of her damp hair. 'You know, as we didn't have anything to do with that jewellers got knocked over?'

'Soon as Danny knew I was CID he tried to do a runner,

211

and you tried to cave my head in.' Logan took another mouthful of hot sweet tea. 'Doesn't matter if you raided Henderson's or not, you've been up to something: we'll find out what down the station. Now, I want your full name and address.'

'It was. . .' She coughed. The snow was getting heavier, beginning to settle on her bleached hair. 'We had to borrow some money for the roof on the steading. The people . . . well, they're not regulated by the FSA, if you know what I mean?'

'I'll get your last name when we process you anyway. Might as well save the extra six months on your sentence.'

'Danny's a bit behind on his payments, OK? These guys don't come round and repossess your telly, they repossess your kneecaps.'

Logan looked at Stacy. Standing there in the snow, with the security light behind her, she had a glowing halo of little sparkly flecks, like an angel who'd forgotten to use a condom. 'Names.'

'OK, OK. Jesus. . . Stacy Gardner. You happy now?' She folded her arms over her swollen belly, muttering, 'Fascist Nazi bastard.'

'*No*, the people you borrowed money off: what – were – their – names?'

'Oh. . . Right. I . . . ahem . . . don't really know.'

'Fine.' Logan stood. 'Stacy Gardner, I'm arresting you for assaulting a police officer—'

'I don't know, OK? Danny sorted it all out.'

After being outside in the snow, the caravan was cosy and steamy, the gas heater hissing away to itself. Logan tried to shut the door behind him, struggling to get it into the buckled frame. Danny was hunched over the little kitchen sink, face down in the soapy water.

212

Stacy pulled off her thick-rimmed glasses and wiped them on the hem of her hoodie. Then slapped her fiancé on the back. 'Danny, tell him about the blokes you got the money off.'

He rose from the basin, dripping wet, his red face covered with soapy bubbles. His eyes were still scrunched up, all pink and swollen, but he did a swift scan around the room before saying anything. 'You ken whit these guys are like, I can't—'

She hit him again. 'Do you *want* to see me in prison, is that what you want?'

'But they'll—'

'Your pregnant girlfriend, in handcuffs?'

'Stacy, love, we—'

'Sharing a cell with some junkie lesbian scumbag?'

'But—'

'God, I *hate* you!' She turned her back and stomped over to the hole in the wall, making the whole caravan rock on its windy-down legs.

'Come on, Pooks, don't be like that. . .'

Her shoulders came up. 'Don't you "Pooks" me.'

Danny turned his swollen squint on Logan. 'I dinna know their names. Got introduced by a friend of a friend.'

Logan held up the handcuffs again. 'No deal.'

'Honest, I dinna remember, it's—'

'How's the face?' Logan stepped forward and peered at the bright-pink skin. 'Looks sore.'

Shrug. 'Soapy water's helping, but it—'

Logan reached out, placed the back of his thumbnail against Danny's cheek, then raked it downwards.

'What the hell was that. . .?' Danny's swollen eyes bugged, he gasped, then went, 'AAAAAAAAAAGH!' Clutching his hand over the new scarlet line down his face. Deep breath. 'AAAAAAAAAAGH!'

He plunged his head back into the sink, sending soap suds

213

spattering up the walls, across the working surface, and out onto the carpet. Gurgling and glubbing.

Stacy turned, sniffed, then thumped herself down on the bench by the table. 'Serves you right.'

'Burns, doesn't it?' Logan settled back against the wall. 'That's why you're not supposed to rub – it opens up the capillaries and lets the capsicum oil in. Disco inferno.'

Danny surfaced, dragged in a deep breath, then dived in again.

Logan grabbed him by the scruff of the neck and hauled him out. 'Who loaned you the money?'

'My face. . .'

'You're a Christian, right Danny? Feel like turning the other cheek?' Logan held his thumb up again.

'NO! No. . . I'll. . . It was these two new blokes with posh accents, Angus Black put us on till them, they was in the snug at Dodgy Pete's—'

'Names, Danny, Mr Thumb's getting itchy again.'

'Gallagher and Yates, that's all I know, I didn't get first names, please it—'

Logan let go and he splooshed into the sink again, sending another mini tidal wave crashing to the carpet.

Stacy folded her arms under her swollen breasts. 'And if you think I'm cleaning that up, Danny Saunders, you've got another think coming!'

Logan looked around for something to dry his hands on, but all the tea towels smelled of yoghurt. 'He'd better be telling the truth, or I'll be back for the pair of you, understand?'

Stacy just stuck her nose in the air.

Logan let himself out.

He hauled the car up onto the pavement behind a dented blue skip overflowing with battered kitchen cabinets, swathes of plaster, and a stained mattress. A streetlight washed the road in sulphur-yellow light. Like God had peed on everything.

The back of Logan's head stung if he touched it, and throbbed when he didn't. It felt as if there was a rat gnawing on the back of his eyeballs with sharp little teeth.

He clambered out into the cold, dark night. No point locking the car. A: there was nothing there worth stealing, not even the car. B: the passenger-side window was missing. C: it was a piece of crap, ancient, brown Fiat, and if anyone *was* stupid enough to nick it, they'd be doing him a favour.

Fat snowflakes drifted down in a slow-motion ballet. When they touched the tarmac they disappeared into off-brown sludge, but it wouldn't be long before they started to lie and the whole city ground to a standstill.

He turned up his collar and lurched up the street through the snow.

Bucksburn was one of those strange little self-contained areas of Aberdeen, stranded out on the north-east corner of the city, on the end of Auchmill Road. The kind of place people from Blackburn, Kemnay, and Inverurie drove through on their way to a long delay at the Haudagain roundabout.

This side of the dual carriageway was lined with little shops, most of them closed for the evening. The lights flickered off in a newsagents as he passed, the owner rattling down the security grill over the window. A few doors down, the smell of garlic, frying onions and sesame oil wafted out from a Chinese takeaway. Logan's emptied stomach growled.

A little alleyway led between two of the shops. He lifted the catch on a wrought iron gate and stepped into orange-tainted gloom, feet squelching through puddles of slush. A light was fixed to the wall above his head, but it couldn't seem to muster much beyond a faint glow.

He skirted a cluster of wheelie bins, past a featureless

metal door with reggae music thumping out from somewhere inside, and turned the corner.

The pub sitting at the end of the alleyway wasn't called Dodgy Pete's. Not officially anyway. The sign above the chipped red door said 'THE BURNING BUCK', complete with a demonic *Monarch of the Glen* illustration.

Logan pushed through into the muggy interior.

At least it wasn't one of those places where everyone stopped talking and turned to stare when someone new entered. No one in Dodgy Pete's cared.

It was a traditional, old-fashioned Scottish pub: cracked vinyl seats; a dart board; a puggy machine in the corner, flickering away to itself; a cigarette machine with an 'OUT OF ORDER' sign Sellotaped to it; a short wooden bar; and a smell of stale beer and damp dog.

Logan levered himself up onto a barstool. 'Quiet tonight, Pete?'

The barman looked up from the copy of *Private Eye* he was reading. Grunted. His chest-length white beard was flecked with little grey streaks of cigarette ash, the hair around his wide mouth stained a dirty yellow. Large nose with red veins capering around the tip, a shock of unruly white hair. Half-moon spectacles. He looked like Santa Claus after a particularly nasty divorce.

'Usual?' He was already reaching for the Stella tap.

Logan licked his lips.

Prove it. Go a week without getting hammered every night.

The DIs are fed up with you complaining all the time and stinking of booze.

Maybe you're angry with her because you think she's right.

Damn.

'Make it a fresh orange and lemonade. Pint.'

Pete raised a snowy eyebrow. 'Oh . . . you're on *duty*.' He shuffled off to get the drink.

Logan turned his back to the bar, scanning the low room. A couple of old men were slumped over a game of dominos by the fire, a young woman in a Royal Bank of Scotland uniform was getting herself outside a pint of Guinness and a packet of prawn cocktail while a bloke in a soggy hoodie tried to chat her up. No sign of Danny Saunders's friend.

'Angus Black about?'

Pete squirted lemonade from the gun into a pint glass. 'What you reckon to Scotland's chances in Antigua then? Daz says three nil, but you know what he's like.'

'I need to have a word.'

'Three nil. Pffff. Daz wouldn't know his cock from a bicycle pump if he didn't keep yanking the damn thing.'

'What about two posh-sounding blokes: Gallagher and Yates? Supposed to be new in town?'

'Caught him having a tug in the ladies' bog last week.'

Logan swung back round to the bar. 'Come on Pete, I just want to talk to Angus. Nothing serious, just a quick word.'

The big man stuck the glass in front of Logan, foam dripping down the side. 'I mean, Daz is OK, you know, for a registered sex offender, but. . .' He shrugged.

'Got anything for a headache?'

Pete stuck his hand under the bartop and came out with a small blue packet, placed it next to the glass.

Logan reached for his wallet, but Pete gave him a broad smile.

'Nah, on the house, *Officer*.'

And in the mirror behind the bar, Logan saw a man framed in the open doorway to the gents freeze – eyes wide – then disappear back into the toilets. Angus Black.

Logan took a sip, then knocked back a couple of Pete's paracetamol. 'Bog windows still got bars on them?'

Another shrug.

Logan picked up a beer mat and stuck it on top of his pint glass. Then turned and wandered across the sticky linoleum to the sign marked 'Bucks'. Stopped for a moment outside. Then pushed the door open.

25

The toilet door creaked open on a dark room.

Blink. Bzzzzzzzz. Blink.

The fluorescent lamp never got past the start-up phase, sending out little flashes of dim light.

Bzzzzzzzz. Blink. Blink. Bzzzzzzzz.

A short, stainless steel trough ran along one wall, the tiles beneath them shiny with poor targeting. Two graffiti-scrawled cubicles, one with the door missing. Toilet seat was gone too, and there was no way you'd want to expose your bare bum to whatever lurked in the bowl.

The drip, drip, drip of water in the cistern above the urinal made a dark heartbeat in the gloom.

Blink. Bzzzzzzzz. Blink.

Logan stepped into the eye-biting nip of old urine and let the door swing shut behind him. 'Jesus, Pete, when did you last *clean* this place. . .?'

Drip. Drip. Drip.

Bzzzzzzzz. Blink. Bzzzzzzzz.

It was like standing in the middle of a horror movie.

'Come on, Angus, I know you're in here.'

Pale orange light oozed in through dirty windows, slowly

bringing the shapes back into focus. The door to the second cubicle was closed. Not wanting to touch anything, Logan raised his foot and gave it a shove.

Locked.

Blink. Bzzzzzzzz. Blink. Blink.

'Daz?' He tapped the graffiti-covered chipboard with the toe of his shoe. 'That better not be you in there having a wank. . .'

Silence.

Logan pulled back his foot and gave the door a kick, springing the lock. The boom reverberated around the narrow, stinking room. Someone gave a little yelp.

Whoever it was, they'd managed to get their top half out of the narrow window above the toilet, one foot on the cistern, the other waving about in the air, backside wiggling, rucksack stuck in the small opening.

'Angus?'

The thrashing stopped. Then started again, feet swinging about madly.

Logan crossed his arms and only just stopped himself from settling against the cubicle wall. 'It's OK, take your time.'

The legs went limp. Then started up again.

'Should have taken the backpack off *before* you tried to sneak out the window.'

A muffled, 'Fuck. . .' One last kick, then everything sagged. 'I'm stuck.'

'Really?'

'Er. . . How about we cut a deal?'

'Sorry Angus, it's against Grampian Police policy to negotiate with people's backsides. What's in the rucksack?'

Pause. 'Stuff?'

'You put Danny Saunders in touch with two loan sharks.'

'Er. . . I. . . I'm getting snowed on.'

'Pair of blokes called Gallagher and Yates.'

220

Another bout of wriggling. 'I'm catching my death out here!'

'Good. Now tell me about Gallagher and Yates.'

'This is police brutality. . . Can I at least come in out the snow?'

'No. Talk.'

'Fucking CID.' Sigh. 'They're new boys, OK? Pair of big bastards up from Edinburgh looking for *investment opportunities*. You know?'

'Who do they work for?'

'I. . . Look, I'm losing all sensation in my arms here.'

'Come on, Angus: are these guys freelance, or part of someone's crew?'

'I don't—'

'Where can I find them?'

Silence.

Fine. Be like that.

Logan grabbed both of Angus's ankles and pulled.

'FUCK!' He came clattering back into the cubicle, hands grabbing at the window frame. A skinny wee man with a face that was all nose and no chin. His legs scrabbled, but Logan wouldn't let go.

'Where do I find them, Angus?'

'Aaagh, I'm—' And then he fell, bashing his face on the top of the cistern. One hand hauling the toilet roll dispenser off the wall.

Logan let go of Angus's legs and the man tumbled to the cubicle floor, groaning and swearing.

'Aw . . . *fuck*, my head!' Pause. Swear. Moan. 'Urgh, it's all damp down here!'

Logan hauled the rucksack off him, before it got covered in whatever was all over the floor. 'You want to stay here, rolling about in it, or you want to go back to the bar?'

* * *

They took their drinks into the snug, a tiny room at the back of the bar, just big enough for two bench seats, a small table, and some dark-red wallpaper. It was like sitting in a blood clot.

Angus sniffed at his jacket sleeve, grimaced, then scoofed down a mouthful of dark brown beer. 'Covered in pish. . .' The left side of his forehead was already swelling up, a thin smear of blood oozing out onto his pale face.

Logan squeezed into the seat opposite and handed him a damp bar towel with a couple of ice cubes folded in the middle. 'Try this.'

Angus dabbed at his smelly sleeve.

'It's for your head, you idiot.'

'Oh. . .' He pressed it against his lump. Winced. Squinted. Took another mouthful of beer. 'I should sue.'

'For what? You were breaking and entering.'

'I wasn't *entering*, I was exiting. Since when was breaking and exiting a—'

'Why don't we take a wee peek in your rucksack?' Logan flipped open the plastic toggles, then upended the contents on the little table. About a dozen iPod Nanos, still in their boxes; perfume gift sets from Dior and Gucci; a couple of fancy-packaged hair straighteners.

'I got receipts for all that, honest.'

There was something wedged in the bottom of the rucksack. Logan gave the whole thing a shake, and a small padded envelope – about the size of a paperback book – thunked onto the pile of merchandise.

Angus groaned. 'I've no idea how that got there.'

'Sure you don't.' Logan flipped the envelope over: it was from Amazon.co.uk, addressed to 'Mr Thomas Black.'

'Maybe. . .' Cough. 'It. . . You like music? Cos I got more iPods than I really need for Christmas, and you could—'

'Don't be an idiot.' Logan winkled the flap open and

upended the envelope. A handful of little white packages fell out, held together with sticky tape, closely followed by twenties, tens, and fives, all done up in drug-dealer-bundles. He reached into his jacket pocket, pulled out a pair of blue nitrile gloves and snapped one on. Picked up one of the packets. 'Angus, Angus, Angus. Is this what I think it is?'

'It. . . I. . .' He shifted in his seat, licked his lips. 'Don't suppose you'd take cash instead?'

Angus Black was chatty enough on the way back to FHQ, and while the nice Police Custody and Security Officer photographed, fingerprinted, and DNA-sampled him. And while they made themselves comfortable in interview room two with mugs of tea and stale digestive biscuits. But as soon as Logan switched on the audio and video recorders – silence.

Logan struggled on for half an hour, before giving up and terminating the interview. And as soon as the tapes were off, Angus started talking again. Typical.

He shrugged. 'Exercising my human rights not to in-criminate myself, aren't I?'

'So come on then,' Logan led the way down to the cell block, Angus Black in the middle, PC Butler bringing up the rear – carrying the contents of Angus's rucksack in half a dozen evidence bags – as they clomped down the stairs, 'where did you get the gear? Wee Hamish?'

'Off the record?'

'Off the record.'

Angus made humming noises for a bit. 'Same place I sorted out Danny's loan. . . You meet that bint of his? Face like the back end of a wellington boot, how the daft sod managed to get *that* up the stick is anyone's guess. Bag over her head and do her from behind?'

Butler gave him a shove. 'Chauvinist pig.'

Angus staggered down the last couple of steps. 'Hey, no pushing! Know what you buggers are like for people "falling down stairs". Tell you—'

'She's a human being, not a sex object.'

'Bloody right she isn't. I wouldn't poke her with—'

Logan stepped between them. 'Enough, OK? These loan-sharks-slash-drug-dealers, where can I find them?'

Angus laughed. 'No chance. You want that kinda info, it's gonna cost. I'm not grassing those bastards up for free, they'll sodding kill me. Don't fancy ending *my* days as a big pile of dogshite.'

They handed him over to the PCSO who'd processed him in the first place, signed him into custody again, then headed back upstairs. Butler set off at a brisk pace, Logan struggling to keep up. He was huffing and puffing after a couple of flights, and by the time they reached the third floor, he was bent double, wheezing.

Butler patted him on the back. 'You OK, Sarge?'

'Just need a minute.'

Need to lose some weight. Get some exercise. Cut down on the fags. Lie down and die. . .

He coughed for a bit, every hack making his head pound. Finally he straightened up, held out his hands for the evidence bags, and told Butler to go see if they'd done a preliminary report on Steve Polmont's post mortem yet.

As soon as she was gone, Logan pushed through the double doors into the hallowed ground of the Identification Bureau. Or the Scenes Examination Branch. Or whatever the hell it was the Scottish Police Services Authority were calling them these days. It was a long corridor with a scuffed green terrazzo floor; lots of corkboards covered in posters, memos, and holiday postcards; and a collection of wooden doors leading off into each sub-department.

Logan made straight for the little lab, knocked on the door, then stuck his head in.

The FHQ lab wasn't much bigger than a large kitchen, lined with worktops, chunks of machinery, and a couple of upright fridges. The room was in partial darkness, a single anglepoise lamp shining down on a set of golf clubs. The metal shafts glinted as an IB tech swabbed the striking face of a nine iron with a cotton bud, headphones clamped over their ears. Bum twitching in time to the music.

Logan crept in and gave it a pinch.

'WhatthefuckinghellRennie!' Samantha span around, left hand flashing out. Logan danced backwards and the slap went wide.

'Woah!'

She blushed. 'Oh. . . Thought you were someone else.' Her scarlet hair was stuffed into a baseball cap, the piercings in her ears, nose, and lip glinting in the light from the glowing tabletop. She had a smiley-face badge pinned to her *My Chemical Romance* T-shirt.

Logan stiffened. 'Rennie comes in here and grabs your arse?'

Little bastard.

'So, where you taking me for dinner?' She wrinkled her nose. 'What's that horrible smell?'

'I'll bloody kill him.'

She patted Logan on the cheek with a latex glove, talking in a flat, deadpan voice, 'Oh yeah, you're so manly and butch. Uh-huh, it really turns me on. Etcetera.' She dropped her hand. 'Told him I'd kick his knackers up round his nipples if he does it again.'

'Why's he grabbing your arse at all?'

'Don't be so jealous.' She turned back to the light box. 'He does it then runs away giggling like a schoolgirl. Don't think you've got anything to worry about.'

He was still a little bastard.

Tiny wrinkles appeared between her eyebrows, then she leaned in and sniffed again. 'It's you! Why do you smell of sick?'

Logan hefted the evidence bags onto the table. 'Any chance. . .?'

Samantha groaned. 'Might have known. And there was me thinking you'd come to carry me off to a nice romantic restaurant.'

'I didn't mean—'

'What is it anyway?' She pointed at the clear plastic evidence bag – the one full of Angus's little white parcels. 'Heroin?'

'Hopefully.'

'Ooooo, these are nice. . .' She picked up one of the boxed hair straighteners. 'Hundred quid in Boots. Make a good Valentine's Day present for a loved one, don't you think? You know, if you wanted to let them know you weren't a tight-arsed skinflint with no prospect of ever getting his leg over again.'

'Subtle.'

She poked at the other bags. 'You want the iPods and perfume tested too?'

'Might as well.'

She frowned at the bag with the money in it, snapped on a fresh pair of gloves, and pulled out one of the bundles. Unfolding the origami shape till it was a stack of battered-looking twenty-pound notes. 'Jesus, these things are everywhere.'

Logan leant against the central unit. 'You wouldn't *believe* the kind of day I've—'

'Got to admire the workmanship.' She flicked on the light box and held a note against the glowing surface. The metallic strip showed up like a malignant shadow on an X-ray.

226

'Clydesdale-Bank-issue Robert the Bruce twenty, circa 1994. Still in circulation.' She opened a drawer, took out a jeweller's glass and squinted through the magnifying lens at the note. 'Real money, you've got about eighty, eighty-five different inks, all printed one after another. These are CMYK. Resolution's amazing though. . .'

Logan picked one of the notes out of the bundle. 'Looks OK to me.'

She straightened up. 'Paper's too white. They don't make the original stock any more, and it wasn't available for public sale anyway. Whoever's making them's faked up the watermark pretty well, but the trouble is making them look old enough. So they stick them in a cold tumble drier with a bunch of tea towels, or socks, or something, and squirt in some stewed tea every now and then. Softens them up and makes them all sepia. Good enough to fool the punters.'

She delved into the bag and took out another bundle. 'They're doing fives now too! How cool is that?'

Logan smiled, pulled up the bill of her baseball cap, and kissed her on the forehead. 'If I'd known counterfeit cash got you this excited, I'd have brought some home ages ago.'

She pushed him away, smiling. 'Cheeky. Give me a couple minutes to finish up.' Samantha pointed at the nine iron. 'DS Taylor got herself a murder. Wife paid a couple of blokes to teach her cheating husband a lesson with his own golf clubs. They kinda got carried away. . .'

'Lucky old Doreen.'

'You know, maybe we should skip the restaurant – grab a curry, go home, and climb into a nice hot bath. Get all soapy. . .' She stepped in close, chest-to-chest, and kissed him, running her hands through his hair.

Logan flinched back – hot shards stabbing out across the back of his head. 'Ow!'

'Not still sore, is it?' She grabbed him, turned him around, then Logan could feel her fingers working their way across his scalp. 'What the hell did you do to yourself? Got *another* lump like a pickled egg back here. You collecting them?'

'Like I said: it's been a bad day.' He forced a smile. 'Now tell me again about getting all soapy.'

26

'C'mon, Sparks, just a wee one, eh?' She flutters her eyelashes, big thick black things like mouldy caterpillars. 'Please?'

Sparks turns his back, gives her the hard shoulder . . . or is that only on motorways? Fucked if he knows. Shouldn't be parking on the hard shoulder: no, no, no. Dangerous. Saw this bloke on that CCTV camera show getting his piece of shit Mondeo squashed by an eighteen-wheeler. Fuck kind of car is called 'Mondeo' anyway? What: some marketing cunt couldn't come up with a better name than—

'Sparks? Come on, it's fuckin' freezin' out here.'

Big Eleanor's right for a change – it *is* fucking freezing. Big bastard flakes of snow, coming down like . . . dandruff or something.

She sidles up, gives him a smile with that bullet-hole mouth of hers. 'Give us a cuddle. . .'

She snakes her arms around him, big chunky things, like a fucking anaconda. 'Ooh, you're all warm.' She lays a padded cheek against his neck, a cold pillow of flesh, nuzzling in deeper.

Sparks is always warm, got one of them internal thermostat

things, like central heating, always up full crank. Roasty toasty, fever fun.

'Come on, Sparks, just a wee wrapper, yeah? Do you a favour for it?' Big Eleanor's hand drifts down his back and into his trousers. She wraps her cold fingers round one bony arse cheek and squeezes. Runs a wet tongue up his throat, scritching through the stubble.

Sparks wriggles free. 'Fucksake, leave us alone, you horny fat cow.'

She steps back, bottom lip out, wobbling in the piss-yellow light like an epileptic slug. Big Eleanor sniffs. 'Don't be like that, Sparks, I'm only wantin' a wee—'

'No.'

She sticks her hand down the front of his trousers, rummaging about till she's got hold of his cock. Squeezes. Steps in close again. 'Just one wrap, couple of rocks, just to keep the cold—'

'WILL YOU FUCK OFF?' He shoves and she stumbles back, goes sprawling. Lies there with her wee black skirt up round her thighs, spotty, shaved minge on show.

Sparks wipes a string of spit off his chin. 'Doing business here.'

Big Eleanor gets to her feet, pulls her skirt back into place, stamps her strappy high-heel down on the pavement and gives him the finger. 'WANKER!' She storms off, slipping and sliding on the snowy pavement.

Silly cow.

Like he's going to do her a freebie? Fat chance.

And he's no' a wanker. No' got time for wanking, got a beautiful girlfriend to keep him company.

He licks his lips.

She's whispering from his jacket pocket. Telling him she wants it. Love him *long* time.

He shifts in his little spotlight. Looks up and down the street. Clears his throat.

Never touch the merchandise: never. No' like Shaky Jake, silly cunt. Lot of good it does you when you're on your back in intensive care with fucking gravel for ankle bones. Mr Mowat's people don't like sales staff with sticky fingers.

Sparks checks his watch: eight fifty-three and fourteen seconds. Fifteen seconds. Sixteen seconds. Looks up, makes sure he's standing right under the streetlight, gotta be keen to be seen. Eighteen. Nineteen. Time is money, yeah, but money's no' time, is it: otherwise all them rich cunts would buy more of it and never have to die.

Fucking profound that is.

Sparks twitches, jitters, keeping time to the beat no one else can hear. OK, so he likes a wee smoke every now and then, the odd pipe, a wee syringe or two, but who doesn't? No' his fault, is it? Nah, Mum was an alky, wasn't she? And Dad was a junkie. That's genetics. Gee-net-tick. Tock. Tick-tock. Tick-tock.

Stand still you daft bastard and *concentrate*.

Force the twitches to stop. Stand dead-still under the street-light.

A car goes past. A seagull screeches.

More silence.

Fucking cold when you're standing still.

The car does a three-pointer at the end of the road, then heads back towards him. Big black fucker. Headlights for eyes. Staring. Making all them snowflakes shine.

Sparks's knee twitches.

The big car stops by the kerb right in front of him and the window slides down. Woman looks out: blonde, no' bad looking. If Sparks wasn't spoken for, he'd probably do her, you know? But his girlfriend's a jealous bitch. . .

Blondie says, 'Looking for someone.' Sounds posh, doesn't she: like something off the telly. English. Nothing wrong with that, long as she's got the cash.

'Yeah? Who?' Sparks tells his knee to stand the fuck still, but it's off on its own, taking no prisoners.

'Charlie about?'

'Might be. Who's asking?'

She reaches into her jacket pocket and pulls out a couple of notes. Holds them up and peers at them. 'Charles Darwin and . . . Sir Edward Elgar.'

Sparks curls his top lip. 'Fuck's that supposed to mean?'

'Thirty quid.'

Nod. Yeah, that's more like it. He does a quick calculation in his head, totting up the number of wrappers and the change from thirty. Always shite at arithmetic at school, you know? Much better now, yeah, like Carol Fucking Vorderman with the old arithmetic, fractions, and shite like that. Teachers want to make kids better at maths? Learn them how to do a decent drug deal: Wee Jonnie has a sixth of an ounce, and Sarah wants an eighth – how stoned will she be, and how much change does she get from twenty and a handjob?

Blondie's looking at him like he's supposed to know the answer to some fucking question he wasn't even listing to.

Sparks spits a chunky lump of yellow into the snow at his feet. 'Thirty gets you two.'

Not really: thirty gets you three, it'll be two for Blondie and one for Sparks. Market economy. Thatcher and Blair's fuck-you Britain.

The door cracks open and Blondie steps out into the snow. Holds up Elgar and Darwin. 'How do I know it's any good?'

He sniffs, spits again. 'Calling us a lying cunt?'

Blondie looks back over her shoulder. '*Am* I calling him a lying cunt?'

Car's back door opens and fucking Elvis steps out. 'Looks like a lying cunt to me.' Elvis with a Geordie accent. Wye-aye man, am all shook oop, like. Big bastard though.

Sparks takes a step back, but Blondie's already there. Right behind him. Bump.

He gives a wee squeal, flinching like a spaz. Calm the *fuck* down and take charge. Sparks clears his throat, turns round and gives her the evil. Asserts his authority. 'Thirty gets you two.'

Blondie nods, reaches into her pocket and comes out with a pair of leather gloves. Doesn't want to touch the merchandise, doesn't want to get her English bitch hands dirty.

While she's doing it, Sparks sneaks a good hard stare at her tits. Not bad.

Elvis taps him on the shoulder, but Sparks ignores him, keeps his eyes on the perky prize. Licks his lips. Thinks about his girlfriend snaking her way through his bloodstream, bringing the good times with her.

Something hard bumps into his back, just above the waist of his trousers. And then the pain, stabbing out from his right kidney. Waves of jagged ice, throbbing fire. 'Fuck. . .' Knees give way. But a thick arm whips round his throat, *squeezing*.

Sparks's dirty fingernails scrabble at the leather sleeve.

Blondie draws back her fist and slams it into his belly.

Breath splutters out of Sparks's mouth. Then she does it again.

His stomach muscles scream. It's like being sick a thousand times, all in one go.

Sparks tries to say something. Threat. Plead. Prayer. Doesn't matter, *something*. His feet skitter on the slippery pavement, then Elvis's arm loosens off and Sparks drags in a broken-glass breath.

'Ayafucker. . .'

Blondie pats him on the cheek. 'Who'd you get your stuff from, Sweaty?'

Sparks's eyes flash left and right. No one. Not a fucking

233

soul. Where's the bloody plod when you actually needed the cunts?

'I don't. . .' His voice comes out all hoarse and squeaky. 'I'm no' sweaty, I've got a thermostat thing and—'

This time her fist snaps his head back, fire and pepper exploding in his nose. Knives digging into his face.

'Fucksake. . . Bleeding all over me jacket!'

And then Sparks is on the ground. Coughing, spluttering, blood making Ribena-stains in the white snow. Jesus, that hurts. . .

Something sharp cracks into his ribs. A boot. Then another one. They're going to kill him. The fuckers are going to kick him to death on some shitty street down the docks. Every breath is like glass, slashing across his lungs.

'Sweaty,' says Blondie, panting. 'Sweaty Sock: Jock. Honestly, how ignorant are you?'

And then her boot cracks into his ribs again.

Tony watches Julie kick the living shit out of the stick-thin junkie. Doesn't know when to leave well alone, that one.

He's not moving any more. Not on his own, only when Julie slams her foot into his ribs. A twitch. Reflex.

She bends double, hands on knees, back rising and falling, breath whoomphing out in big steamy clouds. She points at the body on the pavement. 'Check his . . . check his pockets. . .' Puff, pant, puff, pant.

Neil frisks the guy. 'Eight wrappers, couple ounces of blow, and about. . .' He rifles his fingers through a small bundle of notes. 'Hundred, hundred and twenty quid?'

Julie sticks her hand out. 'Give me a wrapper.'

She stands up straight, unfolds the little tinfoil package, peers at the contents, then marches over and thrusts it through the open car window. 'Tony?'

Sigh.

234

He takes the wrapper. Looks like it could be anything: flour, icing sugar, rat poison. Tony licks the end of his pinkie, sticks it in the powder, then sticks it in his gob and rubs the stuff along his gums.

'Fucksake. . .'

It fizzes up, bitter and frothy. Tony spits out the driver's window, leaving a seagull-stain that bubbles and drips down the black paintwork. Howchs, spits again. He's got that familiar teeth-numbing buzz, but it's barely there.

Another gob spatters into the snowy tarmac. 'Fucking bicarbonate. . .'

Julie sticks the boot in a couple more times.

'You water down this shit yourself, or did it come pre-fucked?'

The junkie doesn't – *can't* – say anything, so Julie tries to break a few more ribs with those cowboy boots of hers.

Thump.

Thump.

'Last chance, Sweaty.'

But Tony's stopped listening. He's got that old familiar feeling. Might start with froth and spitting, but it ends up like a warm hand cupped round your balls. Probably won't last long, it's been cut so much, so Tony checks Julie and Neil are still busy with Junkie-Boy, before scarfing the last of the wrapper.

He licks the tinfoil clean. Doesn't mind that it froths up on his tongue. Just gets it into the bloodstream all the quicker, doesn't it?

Tony settles back in his seat, grips the steering wheel. Belches. Lets it all wash over him, as Julie and Neil get to work on the guy's arms and legs.

Well, every job has its perks.

27

DI Steel slouched through the door to her office, carrying a cup of coffee in one hand and a bacon buttie in the other, tomato sauce making a jaunty little goatee on her chin. She froze, staring at the weedy, pointy-nosed bloke digging away at her window lock with a Swiss Army Knife.

'What the sodding hell do you think you're doing?'

Angus Black looked up and shrugged. 'Breaking and exiting.' The side of his face was a swollen, angry bruise where he'd bounced off the toilet cistern in Dodgy Pete's.

Logan leant back against the filing cabinet. 'Call it an early Valentine's present.'

Angus gave one last grunt, and the window sprang open, letting in a rush of cold air. Snow drifted down in the space between the buildings, big fat flakes that clung to the brickwork and piled up on the window ledge. Five to seven on a dark and freezing Monday morning, and for once Logan actually felt human. No hangover. No feeling queasy. His head didn't even hurt. Well, as long as nothing touched either of the lumps. Maybe laying off the booze wasn't such a bad idea after all.

Angus creaked the window open and closed a couple of times. 'Told you. Now, we had a deal. . .?'

Logan produced a packet of Benson and Hedges.

'Ace.' Angus helped himself to one, then frisked through his pockets. 'Got a light?'

'Oh no you bloody don't!' Steel dumped her coffee on the desk and snatched the packet off Logan. 'If anyone's having the first fag in this office, it's me.'

She lipped one out of the pack, pulled a Zippo from her pocket and sparked it up. The sweet tang of raw petrol was drowned out by the curling smoke. The inspector sighed, eased herself gently into her office chair, and stuck her feet on the desk. 'Ahhhhhhhhh, Bisto.' She slumped there, with the cigarette sticking out the corner of her mouth. 'Laz, make sure the door's locked, yeah?'

Angus shuffled his feet. 'Come on, I'm *gasping* here. He promised. . .'

Steel took a long drag, aimed smoke at the ceiling tiles, then tossed the pack over. 'Knock yourself out.'

'Ta. . .' He fired one up, making post-coital noises. 'Long night in a cell when you've got no smokes.'

'Shouldn't be a nasty wee drug-dealing turd-burglar then, should you?'

Logan locked the door. 'Tell the inspector what you told me.'

Angus blew a lazy stream of smoke out into the snow. 'What's it worth?'

Steel frowned at Logan. 'What's what worth?'

'Mr Black here wants paid to tell us where he got his drugs from.'

'Get bent, we're no'—'

'I'm saying sod all otherwise. These bastards'll kill me if they find out – you gotta make it worth the risk.'

Logan pulled out his notebook and flipped back a couple of pages. 'Dog shit.'

Angus shook his head. 'No it isn't, you haven't seen them, they're fucking *huge*.'

'No, you idiot – "dog shit". You said you didn't want to end your days as a big pile of dog shit.'

'Oh . . . right. Yeah, their boss's got this massive Rottweiler. Thing'd have your hand off like *that.*' He snapped his fingers, sending a tumble of ash to the carpet. 'So it's cash up front, or no deal.'

Steel waved a hand at Logan. 'How much we pick him up with?'

'About a grand's worth of heroin.'

'Wasn't mine – I was just holding it for a friend.'

'Aye, right.' Steel took a bite of her buttie. 'McNab's on the bench today, Angus, how many times has he done you for dealing? Word is he's looking to set an example. Only way you're going to see the sun again in the next seven years is if you dob in your suppliers.'

'Old ones are the best ones, eh Inspector? What's next: going to terrify us with poofter cellmate stories?' Angus grinned. 'Done my time before, can do it again. At least I'll still be alive when I get out.'

The phone on Steel's desk started ringing. She peered at the little LCD display. 'No one important.' She hit the disconnect button. 'Start talking, Angus.'

'Not till I see some cash.'

Steel took her wallet out and slapped two tenners down on her desktop. 'Twenty quid, take it or leave it.'

'*Twenty quid?* You're taking the piss, right?'

Logan shifted against the filing cabinet. The smell of Steel's bacon buttie was making him feel hungry and nauseous, all at the same time. It was getting cold in here too, all the heat disappearing out of the open window, along with the cigarette smoke.

He let them haggle for a bit, then pulled a clear evidence pouch from his pocket and gave it a shoogle. 'Three hundred pounds.'

'What?' Angus curled his lip. 'Three thousand, *maybe*.'

'That's how much you had on you when I picked you up: three hundred pounds in counterfeit notes.'

He stood there with his mouth hanging open. It wasn't a good look. 'Counterfeit. . .? I sold my bloody car to buy that stuff! Four and a bit *grand* that crap cost me.'

'So where's the rest of it?'

Pause. 'Rest of what?'

'You had a thousand pounds' worth of heroin in the rucksack, where's the other three?'

The phone started ringing again. Steel raised an eyebrow. 'Little Miss Popular today.' She hit disconnect again, settled back in her seat and stuck the smouldering cigarette between her teeth. 'Laz, get a search warrant. We're going to do Angus a favour and tidy his house before he gets out.'

'Erm. . . Maybe we could come to some sort of understanding? You like iPods, right?'

Logan clapped a hand down on Angus's shoulder. 'Not your day, is it?'

'You try to do a bit of business, and what happens? Everyone screws—'

A thump at the office door. Then the handle jiggled up and down a bit. Someone outside called, 'Steel? Inspector? Are you in there?' DCI Finnie.

Steel sprang upright in her seat. 'Arse!' She flicked her cigarette through the open window, grabbed a file off her desk and started fanning like mad. Angus obviously wasn't as daft as he looked. He followed her lead, hurling his fag out into the snow, then, while she was busy clearing the air, grabbed the remains of her buttie and crammed it into his mouth.

'Inspector?'

She ripped open a pack of extra strong mints and crunched one down, then waved at Logan. 'Door, door, door!'

239

Logan unsnibbed the lock, just in time to catch Finnie turning away. 'Sir?'

The head of CID stared past Logan into the room. 'I hope you weren't indulging in some sort of orgy, Inspector.'

'Ha-ha, very funny, sir.' She made a show of rearranging a stack of paper on her desk. 'Just having a quiet word with Mr Black here. He fancies the glamorous life of a paid informant.'

Finnie sniffed. 'I would have thought you had other, more *pressing* matters to attend to today.'

Steel shifted in her seat. Looked from Finnie to Logan and back again. 'Oh aye?'

'"Oh aye" indeed.' He pulled a folded newspaper from under his arm and slapped it against Logan's chest. 'Do the honours, Sergeant.'

Logan unruffled the front page. It was a copy of that morning's *Aberdeen Examiner* with a photo of Richard Knox on page one – not the old stock photo every other paper was using, but a new one, of Knox kneeling in front of his granny's grave. 'Oh no. . .' The headline screamed: 'SEX-BEAST LIVES IN ABERDEEN STREET SHOCK.'

'Exactly.' Finnie pulled on a thin smile. 'Perhaps you'd like to read it out for the inspector.'

'Ah . . . er . . . "When the residents of a quiet Aberdeen street went to sleep on Wednesday night, little did they realize that they'd be getting a new neighbour the next morning. But now the *Aberdeen Examiner* can exclusively reveal that notorious sex beast Richard Knox is living at Thirty-Five Cairnview Terrace, in Cornhill". . .'

Steel closed her eyes and swore.

Finnie nodded. 'Now the first thing I'd be asking myself, *Inspector*, is where the media got their information from – considering the whole operation's been on a need-to-know basis. Supposedly under *your* supervision.'

240

'Arsing cock-biscuits. . .'

'And the second question I'd be asking is, what's going on at Thirty-Five Cairnview Terrace right now? What do you think: ticker-tape parade? Bake sale? Auditions for the *X Factor*?'

Steel scrabbled out of her chair. 'Laz, get Angus back in the cells, then find us a car: blues and twos. And a couple of Uniform!' She grabbed her coat and threw it on. 'Why did no bugger tell me about this?'

'I've been trying to call you for the last five minutes.'

She didn't even blush. 'Must be something up with the phones.' She paused, then stared at Logan. 'Well don't just stand there, get moving!'

Logan sat in the back with DI Steel, holding his breath and the grab handle above the door every time PC Butler threw the patrol car into another corner. The council gritters must have been out in force overnight, but every now and then the whole car lurched sideways as it flashed across a ridge of dirty slush. Blue lights strobing, freezing snowflakes in mid-fall. The electronic hee-haw of the siren clearing a path through the early-morning traffic.

Steel poked at the newspaper, jabbing her finger into Richard Knox's face. 'How the hell did they find out where he's staying?' She thrust the newspaper into Logan's lap. 'Call him.'

Logan looked down at the photo. 'What, Knox?'

'No: that greasy wee journalist mate of yours, Colin Buggering Miller. I want to know who told him where Knox was, and I want whoever it was buggered with a traffic cone!'

PC Guthrie turned around in the passenger seat. 'I suppose as it's pointy, they'd have time to get used to—'

'Are you looking for a slap?'

Guthrie faced front again.

Logan stuck his hand in his pocket, looking for his

phone, and finding a handful of circuit board shrapnel instead. 'Bloody hell. . .' He had to borrow Steel's mobile to dial Colin's number.

The Glaswegian's voice was barely audible over the siren. Logan stuck his finger in his ear and tried again. 'I said, who told you where Knox was staying?'

'. . .freezin', man. Stop . . . tea or somethin' . . .'

'Colin?'

'. . .before . . . in . . .'

'Hello?' Logan slapped a hand over the mouthpiece. 'Switch off that bloody siren!'

PC Guthrie did. Now there was just the roar of the engine.

'Hello?'

'Hello? You still there?'

'Who told you?'

'About Knox? Privileged sources, journalistic integrity, etc. So you going to stop past a bakers or what?'

'Don't pull that privileged source crap with me: do you have any idea the kind of shit-storm you've started?'

'Story was in the public interest, Laz. People got a right to know if a rapist moves in next door.'

'There'll be bloody riots!'

'Shoulda thought about that before you dumped him on the poor people of Cornhill, shouldn't you?'

'I didn't dump. . .' Logan ran a hand across his forehead, gritted his teeth. 'Where are you?'

'Outside Knox's house, freezin' my nads off, where do you think? And when you go past the bakers get a couple of teas and a wee steak pie or two.' There was some muffled conversation. 'Yeah, and Sandy wants a macaroni pie, or sausage roll.'

'I'm not going to a bloody bakers!'

'Might tell you where I got the info. . .?'

Logan told Butler to stop at the next bakery she saw.

* * *

'Took your time.' Colin Miller swivelled round in his seat as Logan clambered into the back of the ancient beige Volkswagen and slammed the door. The engine was running, so at least it was warm inside.

The bald man in the driver's seat turned and frowned. 'Watch the car, yeah?'

Colin smiled. He was immaculately turned out in brand new designer jeans and a leather jacket that probably cost more than Logan's Fiat. A muscle-bound action figure with a faint whiff of cologne. 'Laz, this is Sandy. Don't let the crappy manners fool you, he's a photographic wunderkind. Aren't you Sandy?'

'Sodding thing's falling apart as it is. You any idea how much it cost to get it through its MOT?'

'Then buy a decent bloody car for a change.' Colin held out his black leather-gloved hands. Some of the finger joints didn't bend, making them look like deformed claws. 'So . . . tea?'

Logan dug into the white plastic bag and produced two wax-paper cups with plastic lids. 'Milk, no sugar.' Handed them over, then dug out a pair of paper bags, partially transparent with grease.

'Good man, yersel!' Colin peeked into the paper bags, then passed one to the driver. 'Your lucky day, Sandy: macaroni pie *and* a sausage roll. Say thank you to the nice police officer.'

Sandy grunted and took a bite of his sausage roll. Flakes of pastry tumbled down the front of his baggy green jumper.

Colin gave him one of the teas. 'Go make yourself scarce for a couple minutes.'

Sandy stopped chewing, looked out at the street with his mouth hanging open. 'It's snowing.'

Cairnview Terrace was a winter wonderland. Big fat flakes drifted down from a gunmetal sky, flaring as they passed through the streetlights' glow, blanketing everything. Pre-dawn light painted the street in shades of blue, making it look even colder.

The photographer's Volkswagen was parked directly in front of Knox's house, the patrol car two doors down, behind a blue Volvo estate with 'BBC SCOTLAND' down the side, across the road from a Transit Van bearing the SKY NEWS logo, exhaust fumes clouding out into the cold morning.

No signs of a lynch mob waving pitchforks and burning torches. Maybe they were having a long lie?

Colin reached over from the passenger's side and fumbled with the driver's door handle. Popped it open. 'Take your tea for a walk; enjoy the taste of your pie in the great outdoors; bum a fag from the Sky lot.'

Sandy grumbled for a bit. Stuffed his sausage roll in his mouth, grabbed his greasy paper bag and his tea, them clambered out into the early morning and slammed the door even harder than Logan had. But at least he'd left the engine running.

Colin watched Sandy stomp away into the snow, then helped himself to a steak pie. Talking with his mouth full. 'So what you doin' about Knox, now his cover's blown, and that?'

'Yeah, and who blew it?' Logan went back into the plastic bag for a milky coffee and a cheese and onion pasty. 'Who told you?'

'Suppose you'll have to move him. Might be an idea to let him put his side of the story first, you know?'

'Colin, my boss is sitting in that patrol car over there, thinking up new ways to make my life a living hell, because I talked her into stopping off to get you breakfast. Now who told you where Knox was staying?'

'And how is Madame Wrinkles the Lesbo Lothario?'

'Colin!'

'No one told me.' Colin took another bite of pie, the hot meaty smell oozing out into the Volkswagen's interior. 'See, the thing about bein' an investigative journalist is you go out and *investigate*. Should try it some time, be amazed what you can turn up, but.'

Smug git.

Logan creaked the plastic lid off his coffee. 'How about I tell Isobel where you *really* were two weeks ago? When she thought you were in Dundee interviewing the idiot who got hypothermia trying to steal that statue of Desperate Dan?'

Colin stared at him. 'You wouldn't.'

'Got till I finish my pasty, then I'm calling her.'

'You are such a. . .' Scowl. 'OK, OK: when I was down in Newcastle I spoke to a neighbour, who put me onto his old English teacher. Creepy auld wifie with too many cats and a face like a skelpt arse. She says every single one of Knox's "What I did on holiday" essays was about him comin' up to Aberdeen and stayin' with his granny and grandad, while his mum went aff on the pull.'

Colin took another bite of pie, taking care not to get any gravy on his gloves. 'Offered to sell me one of the essays, you believe that? Soon as they charged Knox with raping that old man she went and dug everythin' she could out of the school records. Knew it would be worth somethin' some day.'

He shook his head, took a sip of tea. 'Report cards, notes from his mum, complaints from the gym teacher. . . Tell you, makes you proud of the education system, doesn't it? First thing she thinks of is how much cash she can rake in.'

'And?'

'Gonnae be in tomorrow's *Examiner*: "Portrait of the monster as a small boy", kinda deal. Four-page spread.'

'No, you idiot, how did you get the address?'

'School kept next-of-kin details on file. Mrs Euphemia

Abercrombie-Murray was down as a second point of contact, in case they couldn't get hold of Knox's mum.'

At least that meant Finnie could call off his witch hunt.

Logan looked out through the falling snow. Lights were on in Knox's house, everyone probably woken hours ago by Colin and his grumpy photographer. That was one good thing about the weather: no journalist was daft enough to camp out on the doorstep.

'Anything else I should know?'

'Well—'

The driver's door creaked open and Sandy stuck his head in, snow clinging to the shoulders of his blue parka and the fringe of hair around of his head. 'God it's freezing out—'

'No' yet, eh, Sandy?'

'Oh for. . .' He threw his arms wide. 'It's my bloody car!'

'Five minutes, mate.'

'You know what: it's my bloody petrol too.' He yanked the key out of the ignition, then slammed the door again and marched off, hauling the parka's fur-trimmed hood over his bald patch.

Colin dropped his voice to a whisper, 'Ever heard of someone called Michael "Mental Mikey" Maitland?'

'Newcastle mobster. If you're going to tell me Knox was working for him, save your breath. I know.'

The reporter seemed to deflate a bit. 'Oh.'

'Anything else?'

'You know he died Friday night?'

Pause. 'So?'

The smile was back on Colin's face. 'Welcome to Wednesday's exclusive: Knox was Mental Mikey's accountant, right? Not someone you'd trust your grandad with, but cash: genius. Word is Mikey got Knox to squirrel away a bit of rainy-day money.'

'How much?'

'*Millions*. Two weeks ago Mikey has himself a wee "cardiac incident" and they wheech him into hospital for observation. He has three more, then a bloody huge one on Friday. Mental Mikey, Terror of Tyneside finally passes away in the wee small hours, surrounded by his nearest and dearest.'

'Who all now want to get their hands on Mikey's nest egg.'

Colin tapped the side of his head with a stiff, leathered finger. 'Aye, but our boy Knox is the only one knows where it is and how to get at it.'

Logan watched a robin bob and hop across Knox's front garden, leaving little CND footprints. 'The lying bastard. . .'

'Eh?'

'Nothing.' He clunked open the back door. 'Anything else comes up – and I mean anything at all – give me a call.'

Colin shrugged. 'Aye, and what's in it for me?'

'Dundee, Desperate Dan: truth. Remember?'

Logan climbed out into the snow, shutting the door on the reporter's reply.

28

It was almost as cold inside Richard Knox's house as it was outside, the windows spidered with tendrils of frost. So everyone gathered in the kitchen, listening to the kettle rumbling its way back to the boil again.

Everyone except Richard Knox: he was through in the lounge, kneeling in front of the three-bar electric fire, praying.

Logan nodded towards the door. 'How's he doing?'

Mandy from Sacro pulled a face. 'Not happy. When that Weegie short-arse hammered on the door this morning Knox went off on one. Smashed the rest of the ornaments and broke all the furniture.'

Harry, her partner, stifled a yawn. 'Only thing he didn't do was lie down and beat his fists on the floor.'

Steel hauled herself to her feet. 'Good. Maybe he'll get so upset he'll sod off somewhere else.' She clunked her mug on the tabletop. 'Anyone wants me, I'm outside having a fag.'

Guthrie worked his way through the cupboards as Steel shouldered the back door and stomped out into the over-grown garden. 'Any biscuits?'

'Already?' Butler shook her head. 'You just had three pies.'

'Got a fast metabolism.'

'Got a bloody tapeworm, more like. . .' She trailed off into silence.

Someone was hammering on the front door. Then the letterbox clattered open and a voice shouted in through the gap, 'MR KNOX? RICHARD? WHAT WOULD YOU SAY TO THE FAMILIES OF YOUR VICTIMS?'

'Christ, not again.' Guthrie looked at Butler. 'Whose turn is it?'

'I did the last two.'

'Sod.' Guthrie grabbed his peaked cap off the kitchen work-surface and jammed it on his head, then marched down the corridor.

'RICHARD? DON'T YOU DESERVE THE CHANCE TO TELL YOUR SIDE OF THE STORY?'

Logan watched Guthrie haul open the front door – the woman squatting on the other side almost fell on her bum. It took Guthrie nearly two minutes to get rid of her, with a lot of arguing, complaints about freedom of the press, two attempts at bribery, and a veiled threat that Guthrie hadn't heard the last of this.

She stormed off down the snow-covered garden path, a photographer in tow.

Guthrie closed the front door again. 'Bloody *Daily Mail*.'

Something thumped against the wood and he sagged. Swore. Then put his hat back on again and wrenched the door open. A second snowball thumped against the wall beside him, sending out a flurry of white.

Logan could just make out the *Daily Mail* reporter ducking down behind Sandy the grumpy photographer's beige Volkswagen.

Guthrie shouted: 'Hoy! You!' then hurried down the path after her.

Logan closed the door.

*   *   *

Richard Knox crossed himself, stood, then wiped a hand across his eyes. The room was even gloomier than usual, curtains drawn, the only light coming from the three-bar electric fire: its middle coil giving off a weak orange glow, the other two dead and dark.

Logan stood on the threshold, looking into the lounge. There wasn't a single ornament left in one piece, the faded wallpaper pockmarked with the residue of ceramic explosions. The standard lamp lay tipped into the corner, its wooden upright snapped in the middle, brown wires poking out. Broken television on its back. Coffee table on its side, missing two legs. The overturned sofa missing an arm.

The only thing he hadn't touched was his three-bar votive flame.

Logan hauled one of the armchairs back onto its legs, shoogled it in front of the fire and sat. 'Like what you've done with the place.'

Knox didn't look around, his voice small and snivelly. 'How did they find us?'

'Your old English teacher sold your school records.'

'She always was a bitch, like.' He rubbed his eyes again. 'You ever stop and think, "maybe God doesn't love us any more"? That he's doing all this to punish us?'

Knox turned and wandered over to the closed curtains. 'It's a test, though, isn't it? All this? A test of me faith.'

'We have to move you somewhere else.'

'Like prison.' Knox smiled, his face creasing up on one side. 'It was a test of me faith, and when I passed, God rewarded us. Got the prison shrink help us come to terms with me childhood. Stuff that was confusing us, *subconsciously* and that.'

Logan sat forward. 'You know, there's a psychologist in Aberdeen who wants to help you as well.'

'Like after Grandad Joe died in his sleep. Me mam was

250

downstairs in the kitchen, arguing with Granny Murray – can't remember what about, but there was lots of crying. . . And there was us upstairs, alone in the room with Grandad Joe.' Knox reached out and stroked the faded velvet curtains. 'He looked like butter, like he was made out of it, you know? All yellow and greasy, but when I touched his skin it was dry. Dry and cold. I was nine.'

'His name's Doctor Goulding. I can set up an appointment for today, if you like?'

'His teeth was sitting in a whisky glass beside the bed, and he's lying there, mouth not quite shut, you know? Like he's about to say something? So I pulls his mouth open, all the way, and runs me finger round the inside. His skin was cold, but inside he was still warm. . .' Knox trailed off into silence, one finger tracing a circle on the dried-blood curtain. The smell of mould getting stronger.

Logan cleared his throat. 'Maybe we should just—'

'In the beginning God created the heaven and the earth.'

'Richard, we're going to need to get you out of here.'

'And the earth was without form, and void; and darkness was upon the face of the deep.'

'Look, we've got a contingency plan for—'

'And the Spirit of God moved upon the face of the waters.' Knox stopped drawing his circle and grabbed the curtains with both hands.

'Richard, this is important. I need you to—'

'And God said, "Let there be light"!' He threw the curtains open and Aberdeen did its best to rise to the occasion. Dawn had finally breached the horizon, colouring the snowbound garden with gold and amber.

Knox turned and smiled at Logan. 'And there was light.'

And then there really was – blinding white light, shining straight in through the bay window. Logan covered his eyes with a hand, peering out.

Someone shouted, 'There he is!'

An outside broadcast van sat on the other side of a lopsided holly bush, TV spotlights trained on the house. A bank of cameras. A group of people, placards jabbing into the cold morning air: 'KNOX OUT!', 'ABERDEEN DOESN'T WANT GEORDIE RAPISTS!!!', 'PERVART GO HOME!'

'Bloody hell.' Logan creaked out of the armchair. 'Richard, close the curtains!'

The weaselly little man just stood there, staring out at the people staring back at him.

'Richard!' Logan pushed past him, hauled the dusty red curtains shut.

Darkness.

Then the chanting started. '*Knox, Knox, Knox: Out! Out! Out!*'

'But . . . it's me *home*. They. . .'

'Go. Pack your stuff.' Logan grabbed him by the sleeve. 'We have to—'

'DON'T TOUCH US!' Knox scrabbled backwards, hands working at his chest like angry spiders. 'Don't touch. You're not allowed to touch!'

'I'm sorry, OK? Calm down.' Logan held his hands out. 'No one's going to hurt you.'

'*Knox, Knox, Knox: Out! Out! Out!*'

'Make them stop!'

'It's OK, you're safe. They can't—'

A loud crash ripped through the musty room, the curtains billowing, the shatter of falling glass, shards spilling out across the carpet.

'*Knox, Knox, Knox: Out! Out! Out!*'

The lounge door clattered open: Mandy from Sacro. 'What the hell was that?'

Another crash and the curtains humped out again. More glass. A fist-sized lump of rock rolled out into the gloom.

Logan backed away, looked at her. 'Get him out of here.'

'Come on, Richard, it's not safe.'

'Don't touch us!'

'I'm not going to touch you—'

'*Knox, Knox, Knox: Out! Out! Out!*'

Through the lounge door, Logan could see Butler and Guthrie running for the front door, extendible batons at the ready.

More glass, another rock.

'*Knox, Knox, Knox: Out! Out! Out!*'

Logan stood at the upstairs window, looking down at the crowds. They'd grown thicker over the last hour, now the whole street was packed with angry faces, staring up at the house, shouting.

'Knox, Knox, Knox: Out! Out! Out!'

Had to be two, maybe three hundred people out there, chanting in the snow, breath steaming into the cold morning air. Waving their placards. Being outraged for the cameras.

And there were a *lot* of cameras: newspapers and TV channels basking in the collective hatred of a community at war with one creepy little man.

At least reinforcements had arrived. Two uniformed officers shivered at the front gate, while a reporter with a *Channel 4 News* umbrella did a piece to camera with them in the background. BBC Scotland had done exactly the same thing ten minutes earlier, probably catching the last live slot on *Breakfast News*.

A pair of large police vans had parked at the edge of the crowd, one of them slowly filling up with people arrested for public order offences.

The snickt of metal sounded behind him, and Logan turned to see DI Steel sparking up a cigarette. She wiggled the pack at him.

'Thought Knox didn't want us smoking in the house?'

She settled onto the room's single bed. 'Screw him.'

It was obviously a boy's bedroom: dusty Airfix model kits of Spitfires, Hurricanes, and other assorted warplanes, sitting on top of a tatty chest of drawers. A football poster on the wall, so faded that the Newcastle United team were a collection of ghosts. Blue wallpaper. A *Thundercats* duvet and pillow set spotted with mildew.

Logan took a cigarette and lit it, then hauled the sash window open, the swollen wood squealing.

'Knox, Knox, Knox: Out! Out! Out!'

Steel plumped up one of the pillows and settled back. 'Think they'd get bored after a while, wouldn't you? Same thing, over and over.'

'Every oddball, weirdo, and tosspot in town is going to descend on this place.'

'Yup.' She blew a smoke ring at the ceiling.

'There's something else.' Logan told her about Collin Miller's little revelation. 'So with Mental Mikey dead. . .'

Steel didn't even blink. 'I know. Danby told me. Why do you think Knox wanted to move up here: our balmy climate and café culture? Nah, knew Mikey was on the way out, needed to be . . .' She waved her hand in a circle, the cigarette leaving a trail in the air. '. . .somewhere all those ambitious wee radges couldn't get their hands on him. With Mikey dead he's no' protected any more.'

'Oh.' So much for that. Logan turned back to the window, watching the snow settle on the crowd.

'You get anything out of Polmont's journals?'

'Still working on it.' He'd taken them home again last night and forgot all about them after Samantha came through wearing nothing but her tattoos, stripy hold-ups and a pair of knee-high kinky boots. 'Why's Danby so interested?'

'Who says he's interested?'

'Do we have to go through this *again*?'

'Can you imagine lying here every Friday night listening to your granny and grandad humping like horny gerbils?'

'Fine, keep it secret, like I bloody care.' He flicked ash out of the window. 'How are we going to get Knox out of here?'

'Wonder if she was a moaner, a screamer? Or did she just lie there like a sack of tatties?'

'Road's packed. Maybe we can get him out over the back wall?'

'Looking at her photo, I bet she was a screamer. "Oh, Grandad Joe, you're so big!"' Steel lowered her voice for: '"Who's the grandaddy?" "Oh, *you* are! Yes! Yes! Yes—"'

'Do you have to do that?'

Shrug. 'Got to take pleasure in the simple things, Laz. Otherwise, what have you got?' She stuck the cigarette between her teeth and had a scratch at her crotch.

'Better go see if they've got him packed up yet.'

Knox was curled up on his granny's tatty quilt in the master bedroom, the handles of his plastic bag sticking out like rabbit ears.

'Come on, Richard, you're going to have to help.' Mandy from Sacro stuck her hands on her hips, still clutching a white T-shirt. A battered leather suitcase sat open on the foot of the bed, with a little pile of clothes in it.

'I'm not going.'

Logan knocked on the door frame. 'How we doing?'

Mandy glowered at him. 'How do you think?'

'I'm not going. This is me house. You can't make us leave.'

She gritted her teeth, stared at the ceiling for a moment, then marched out, thrusting the T-shirt into Logan's hands. '*You* deal with him.'

'I'm not leaving.'

Logan rolled the T-shirt into a ball and lobbed it into the open suitcase. Five points. 'Not open for debate.'

Knox wouldn't look at him. 'You can't make us.'

'Want to bet?' The curtains were closed in the bedroom. Logan opened them. So much for trying to smuggle Knox out over the back wall and through the neighbour's garden. There were photographers up stepladders on all three sides, zoom lenses trained on the house. Silly sods. It had to be minus-four out there.

It looked as if the paparazzi in the garden opposite had broken their vigil at one point to build a small, vaguely obscene snowman.

It didn't take long before someone spotted Logan at the window, and flashes started flickering. He closed the curtains again.

'On your feet, we're leaving.'

'Told you, I'm not going anywhere.' Knox stuck his forehead on his knees. 'Why does no one listen to us?'

'Right, Richard Knox, I'm arresting you for—'

'You can't do that!'

'There's a mob out there, and they've already attacked the house once. By staying here you're inflaming the situation – that means I can do you for causing a breach of the peace.'

'But—'

Logan took out his handcuffs. 'Look on it as a test from God.'

Silence. Then Knox rolled off the bed and yanked open a drawer in an ancient dresser. Various old clothes went into the suitcase: shirts, socks, Y-fronts.

Logan watched him pack. 'So, you're on the run from the mob then?'

The little man stopped in the middle of packing a string vest. 'Who told you that?'

'All those years Mental Mikey took care of you, and now

he's dead. Every crook in Tyneside must be after a slice of his nest egg.'

Knox shrugged, then fetched an antique grey suit from the wardrobe, laying it carefully into the suitcase. 'God takes us all in the end, like.'

'You know, if I was sitting on some gangster's millions—'

'That's what they're saying about us, is it? I've got Michael Maitland's cash?' Half a dozen sombre ties followed the suit into the case.

'Don't you?'

'Nearly forgot. . .' He disappeared through the bedroom door. There was the sound of someone rifling through a medicine cabinet, then Knox was back with a dusty bottle of Old Spice. He wrapped it in a pair of Y-fronts and placed it carefully next to the suit. Then shut the lid.

Steel popped her head around the door, mobile clamped to her ear. She stuck it against her chest. 'Ricky the Rapist ready to go?'

Logan nodded and she raised the phone to her ear again.

'Yeah. . . Yeah, he's ready.' Then she was gone, clumping down the stairs.

Knox looked around the shabby room. Sighed. 'I was happy here, long time ago.'

'You want a blanket?'

'What?'

'Over your head when we take you out the front. Do you want a blanket?'

'Oh. . .' He ran a hand across the faded, cat-scratched bedspread, the one his grandparents used to hump under every Friday night. Knox pulled it off the bed and draped it around his shoulders, then collected his bible in its tatty plastic bag. 'Ready.'

29

Dear God, there's hundreds of them. A wall of angry jock bastards, all waving placards and chanting: 'Knox, Knox, Knox: Out! Out! Out!' Like he's some sort of animal, like. . .

Richard ducks back behind a policeman. Takes a deep breath. Pulls the bedspread over his head. Now everything smells of dust and mildew, with the faintest memory of Granny Murray's night cream.

Someone says, 'You ready?'

'Knox, Knox, Knox: Out! Out! Out!'

Richard nods. Clutches the carrier bag tighter to his chest.

'There's more officers just outside the door, OK? We're going to be all around you.'

'I'm ready. . .' His voice sounds high and scared, even to him.

Never been hated by this many people all in one place. Yeah, there was a crowd outside the court when he got sent down, like, but they was all outside. He was in a police van. Tinted windows. Safe. Not like now. . .

'Knox, Knox, Knox: Out! Out! Out!'

'OK, let's get going.' That sounds like the bloke, Sergeant McThingy, the one who wants to know about Michael Maitland's rainy-day money. Probably wants a cut – typical bloody copper.

A hand in the small of Richard's back pushes him forward.

'Don't touch us!'

He stumbles out the door, bedspread over his head, watching the world change beneath his feet. Top step. Garden path, the snow trampled to grey mush.

'Knox, Knox, Knox: Out! Out! Out!'

And then they see him. They have to, because the chanting becomes screaming. Insults, threats. The police hurry him forward, closing in on all sides. *Touching him.*

Don't freak out. Please don't freak out. Stay calm.

'FUCKING WANKER!'

'YOU SHOULD HANG!'

'PERVERT BASTARD!'

The police get closer as the garden path comes to an end beneath Richard's feet. Squeezing through the gate.

The jostling gets worse, shouts louder.

'KNOX, YOU'RE DEAD! YOU HEAR ME? DEAD!'

'WE DON'T WANT YOUR KIND HERE!'

Richard keeps his eyes on his shoes. 'Our Father who art in heaven, hallowed be Thy name. . .'

A shove and he nearly falls.

'RAPING SCUM!'

'GO BACK WHERE YOU CAME FROM!'

Lurching forwards, tears streaming down his face in the darkness. Oh God. . .

Something bangs against the top of his head. A policeman swears.

'You! I saw that!'

'HOPE YOU FUCKING DIE!'

'KNOX! KNOX! KNOX! OUT! OUT! OUT!'

More shoving, pushing – Richard stumbles and falls against the policeman in front of him, ends up on his knees in the slush.

Why can't they leave him alone? He just wants to—

Rough hands on his elbows, hauling him back to his feet, hurrying him onwards.

'BASTARD!'

'KNOX! KNOX! KNOX! OUT! OUT! OUT!'

And then a metal clunk and he's dragged into the back of a police van. Richard steps on the trailing edge of the bedspread and ends up on his hands and knees, pain lancing through his palms. Then daylight floods over him as the quilt snags on the metal floor.

'KNOX! KNOX! KNOX! OUT! OUT! OUT!'

Richard turns and looks out across a sea of hate, crashing against the police cordon. People jabbing their placards at him, men and women, faces pink and screwed up, teeth bared.

Someone spits, a thick glob of yellowy-white that flies through the falling snow and spatters against Richard's chest.

'THEY SHOULD STRING YOU UP!'

And then the van door thumps shut and everything is darkness again.

Someone says, 'Thank fuck *that's* over. . .'

And then the van starts to rock. People slamming their hands against the sides.

'BASTARD!'

'KNOX! KNOX! KNOX! OUT! OUT! OUT!'

It's not over. It'll *never* be over.

'A complete disaster!' DSI Danby stabbed his thumb on the remote, freezing the picture on the boardroom TV as someone slammed their placard down on Richard Knox's bedspread-covered head: 'DETH TO ALL RAPIST!'

The emergency MAPPA meeting wasn't really going that well. They'd gathered in the boardroom at FHQ – Steel, Logan, DI Ingram from the Offender Management Unit, some hairy woman from the council, a Sacro supervisor, and DCI Finnie. Everyone trying to make sure they didn't get blamed for anything.

Danby thumped the TV remote down on the boardroom table, and turned to glower out of the window at the snow slanting horizontally across Broad Street. 'You couldn't even keep his location secret for four days!'

Steel leaned over and whispered in Logan's ear, 'You want to tell him, or should I?'

Logan pretended he hadn't heard.

DI Ingram ran a hand across his little military moustache. 'I don't think that's entirely fair. . . The Offender Management Unit has done its best—'

'Its best?' Finnie frowned. 'Well, that's all right then, isn't it? I must have *imagined* there was a riot outside Knox's house this morning because his *address was in the bloody papers*!'

Danby poked the polished tabletop with a finger. 'I want a full enquiry. I want to know which one of your lot went running to the media, first chance they got!'

Steel settled back in her seat, left hand scritching away beneath the desk. 'Actually, Sergeant McRae has some information on that, don't you Laz?'

'Er . . . yes. We know who leaked Knox's location to the press.'

'Who? I want them up on charges, you know what I'm saying? I want them bloody crucified!'

'The leak didn't come from Aberdeen, it came from Newcastle. Knox's old English teacher sold his school records to the papers. His granny's address was in there.'

Danby backed off a step. 'Ah. . . I see.' He cleared his throat. 'Right, well . . . contingency plan then.'

And that was it, no apology, no nothing.

DI Ingram went over the plan again, the alternative address they had in waiting, just in case things went horribly wrong.

261

He was droning on about cost models when the board-room door creaked open and a rumpled corduroy man slumped in, dumped a little leather rucksack on the table and collapsed into one of the vacant chairs. He took off his glasses and rubbed at his eyes. 'Sorry I'm late. Any chance of a coffee?'

'Ah, how nice of Social Work to *grace* us with their presence.' Finnie checked his watch. 'We started *twenty minutes* ago!'

The newcomer polished his glasses on the edge of a hanky. 'Good for you. I started twenty-four *hours* ago. One of my clients got the crap kicked out of him down the docks last night, and I've been trying to get things sorted out ever since.'

Danby's face twitched. 'I'd have thought Richard Knox would get your undivided attention, know what I'm saying?'

'Yeah, that's a great idea, I'll just tell my thirty other clients they don't matter any more. That how they do things in Newcastle, is it?' He dug into his corduroy jacket and came out with a piece of paper. 'Desk sergeant gave me a message for a Sergeant McRoy?'

'McRae.' Logan held out his hand. The note was barely legible – which meant Sergeant Eric Mitchell was manning the desk – 'There's A Tim Mair Here To See You + Overtime: WTF?!?' and then a doodle of a skull and crossbones.

Steel leant over and squinted at the note, then put her lips against Logan's ear. 'I hope Social Work Boy's no' propositioning you for hairy bum sex in the toilets.'

'Someone's here about Polmont's stash of electrical equipment.'

'Well, don't just sit there – bugger off and. . .' Everyone was staring at her. Steel smiled. 'I was just consulting with my colleague about the viability of Knox staying on in Grampian. Everyone knows he's here, they'll be on the lookout for him. He's a target. Move him somewhere else and he might live to see his next birthday.'

DI Ingram cleared his throat. 'Actually, there's a lot of merit in the inspector's suggestion—'

'Course there is.' She thumped Logan on the back. 'Now, Sergeant, why don't you run along and see if you can't get a nice constable to whip us all up a wee cup of tea?'

Dildo, AKA: Tim Mair, was leaning on the reception desk downstairs, helping himself to Sergeant Mitchell's bag of Revels. The bag's owner had the kind of moustache that would have made walruses jealous, and it twitched as Logan tried to join in.

'Hoy! Who said you could have one?' Mitchell snatched the bag away. 'Been trying to get you all sodding morning. Turn your bloody phone on!'

Dildo grinned, pulling his black goatee out of shape. 'You tell him, Eric.'

Logan dug into his jacket pocket and let a handful of plastic shrapnel tumble onto the reception desk. 'If you can figure out how, be my guest.'

'Fair enough.'

'Oh, and Steel wants someone to make a load of teas for the MAPPA meeting.'

Sergeant Mitchell's moustache bristled. 'Well don't look at me!'

'Just get some PC to do it.' Logan turned to leave. 'Oh, and make sure whoever it is spits in DSI Danby's mug.'

'Right.' Dildo wiped the steam from his John Lennon glasses. 'Let's see these dodgy goods you found.'

Logan pointed through the glass front wall, at the swirling snow. 'They're at the Water Lane store.'

'Oh for Christ sake . . . could you not have brought them up?'

'No room. We can take your car if you like?'

'Left it at the office.'

'OK.' Logan swept the bits of phone back into his pocket. 'We'll go in mine.'

'Piece of shite. . .' Dildo hauled at the passenger door release. 'Have you got the child locks on or something?' The black plastic bag duct-taped over the missing window bucked and shuddered in the wind, the engine running on for a whole three seconds after Logan pulled the keys out of the ignition before it finally gave up and died.

'Don't be such a girl – got you here, didn't it?'

'Only just, would've been quicker bloody walking.' It had taken them over twenty minutes to drive the quarter mile from the station, crawling through the snow and snarled up traffic.

'Yeah, if you want to die of frostbite.' Logan climbed out into the narrow lane. White flakes swirled around the car, battering against the rusty paintwork as Water Lane funnelled the wind into a teeth-chattering gale. He hurried round and hauled open Dildo's door from the outside. 'Well, don't just sit there!'

They bustled through the keypad-locked door, into the little corridor on the other side. Stomping their feet to get rid of the snow. They signed in with a red-nosed, sniffly constable, and headed through to the evidence store.

If anything, it was even colder than it had been yesterday, their breath trailing behind them as Logan led the way through the minotaur's maze of metal shelving. 'Over here.'

Dildo took his glasses off, wiped them dry on a cloth, and put them back on again. 'Where?'

Logan waved a hand, indicating the eight shelves packed with the stuff they'd taken out of Polmont's flat.

'Oh buggering hell! All of it?'

'Yup.'

Dildo hauled a box out and thumped it down on the

scuffed floorboards. 'Got to be twenty below in here, and this'll take sodding *ages*.'

'You get cracking and I'll go see what I can do.'

By the time Logan returned, trundling a battered oil-filled radiator in front of him, the man from Trading Standards was surrounded by iPhones. He held one up to the light and sniffed. 'Definitely fake.'

Logan peered at it. 'Looks OK to me.' He uncoiled an extension lead and plugged the radiator in. 'Should help a bit.'

'Watch.' Dildo pressed something and the screen came to life, revealing a display that looked nothing like it did on the TV adverts. 'They make them by the bucket-load in China, ship them over hidden in containers. You know how much this costs to make? Peanuts. . . Well, prawn crackers anyway.' He pointed at the radiator. 'That thing working yet?'

'Give it a minute.'

Logan picked up one of the iPhone boxes. It had all the documentation and everything. 'So they're crap then?'

'Depends on your definition of crap. You can make phone calls, and you can run a couple of applications, play MP3s, but that's about it.'

He stuffed it back in the box. 'Hair straighteners are fake too. *And* the portable DVD players.' Dildo grabbed a cardboard box marked up with the Grant's Vodka logo, clinked it down on the floor, and hauled the flaps open. Then took out a clear glass bottle and handed it over. 'What do you see?'

Logan shrugged. The bottle was cold, deep-chilled in the fridge-like warehouse. 'Vodka?'

'Try again.'

Logan turned it over. '*Cheap* vodka?'

'God, it's like teaching a monkey to yodel. . .' Dildo prodded the red-and-silver label. '*Now* do you see anything?'

'You, being a dick?'

'Read the sodding label!'

Logan did. According to the bottle it was Grant's Vodka, seventy centilitres, thirty-seven-and-a-half-percent. Produced and bottled in Great Britain, Glen Catrine Distilers, Catrine, Ayrshire, Scotland. 'So?'

'How do you normally spell "Distillers"?'

'D-I-S-T-I-L-L. . . Oh.' Logan stared at the label again.

Dildo grinned. 'Do you think a genuine distillery might *actually* be able to spell the word "Distillers"?'

'It's counterfeit.'

Dildo took the bottle back. 'There's two or three bottling plants for this stuff somewhere down the south of England. Trading Standards have been after them for years – shut one down and two months later another one springs up.' He stuck the bottle back in the box.

'Who the hell makes fake Grant's Vodka? It sells for, what: eight quid a bottle? If you're going to counterfeit something, counterfeit the expensive stuff.'

'Mate, I've seen faked Tetley tea bags, Surf washing powder, Heinz baked beans.' Dildo held his hands against the radiator's peeling paint. 'Boots were selling fake Colgate in 2008. *Toothpaste.* Someone managed to slip it into the wholesalers and they didn't notice for nearly a fortnight. I mean, nobody got hurt, it was still toothpaste, but it sure as hell wasn't Colgate. Trust me: if you can sell it for a profit, someone, somewhere, is counterfeiting it.'

Logan stood there for a minute, staring at the boxes and boxes from Polmont's flat. Then down at the pile of hair straighteners, still in their original – fake – packaging. They were the kind that made a good Valentine's Day present for a loved one, if you wanted to let them know you weren't a tight-arsed skinflint. . .

'Dildo?'

'I don't think this thing's working.' He slapped the radiator.

'Fancy a cup of tea?'

Logan lowered the two mugs carefully down on top of a case of not-Grant's Vodka. Then pulled out the evidence bags he'd wedged under his arms.

Dildo pulled a face. 'What, did you fly to India and pick the tea leaves yourself? I'm freezing here.'

'Don't moan. Couldn't find the milk.' Which was a lie. What he'd had difficulty locating were the items confiscated from Angus Black when he'd been picked up. The IB had signed them back into evidence after checking for fingerprints and PC Sniffles had promptly filed them in the wrong place.

Logan stuck the evidence bags on one of the shelves. 'Did you get anything out of our friend the used car salesman, by the way?'

Blank look. 'Remind me?'

'Kevin Middleton, got a dealership out by Kirkton of Skene?'

'Oh, yeah: Sicknote paid him a visit yesterday. Impounded one cut-and-shut, a pair of "unsafe for road use", and three clocked four-by-fours. Result.'

'Speaking of results. . .' Logan held up the evidence bag with the hair straighteners in it. 'These look fake to you too?'

Dildo groaned. 'Have I not got *enough* to do with all this stuff?'

'Humour me.'

'Tea.' He helped himself to a mug, wrapping his gloved hands around it, shrouding his face in steam. Getting condensation in his goatee beard. 'Open the box and check the grub screws on the handle. If they're hexagonal heads, the thing's real.'

Logan did, getting Amido black fingerprint powder all over his hands. 'Phillips screwdriver.'

'Fake.'

They went through the same process with the rest of Angus Black's merchandise – Dildo drinking his tea and straddling the radiator, calling out instructions and occasionally asking to see something. Everything was counterfeit.

'Perfect.' Logan smiled and downed the rest of his lukewarm tea. 'I've got to get back to the station, you be OK here?'

'In the cold? On my own? You ungrateful sod.'

'And you won't need a lift back, will you? I mean, you'll have to get the Shop Cop van down here to cart all this stuff away when you're finished, right?'

Dildo stared at him. 'You're a rotten bastard, McRae, I ever tell you that?'

Logan scooped everything back into their respective evidence bags and hurried off. 'Thanks, Dildo.'

He weaved his way through the stacks of seized items with Dildo's parting shot echoing around him.

'A rotten bastard!'

Logan barged through the door and clunked it shut behind him, finding himself in a little airlock festooned with posters for local bands he'd never heard of, the doormat soggy with melted snow. He stomped his feet, adding to the mush, then pushed through into the pub proper.

The Tilted Wig was once the exclusive drinking hole of lawyers and their assistants from the Sheriff Court across the road, but ever since the High Court had taken over the old Clydesdale Bank building on the corner of Marischal Street and Union Street – next door – the clientele had become a little less exclusive. Now they let anyone in.

Logan brushed the snow off his shoulders and scanned

the faces. Just after twelve and one or two were making serious efforts to not see any more of the afternoon if they could possibly help it. Like Angus Black, sitting at a scuffed wooden table, basking in the glow of the one-armed bandit, a pint of heavy, and three empty shot glasses. He polished off a fourth and added it to the graveyard.

'It didn't go well then?' Logan settled into the chair opposite.

Angus looked up, closed his eyes, and swore. 'Have you not done enough damage?' He took a bite out of his pint, then went back to staring at the table.

'Nope.' Logan dumped the evidence bag with the iPod Nanos in front of him. 'Recognize these?'

'Trial's in six weeks. My brief says I'm looking at fourteen years. You believe that? For a little bit of H? Who's it hurting?' He went back to his pint. 'Like living in Nazi Germany.'

Logan poked the bag. 'You said you got these from your Edinburgh friends: Gallagher and Yates. They tell you they were all fake?'

Angus swore some more, then let his head sink to the table. 'Fucking hell. . . I need a drink.' He went up to the bar and came back with what looked like three double whiskies in the same glass. 'I'd get you one, but this is all your sodding fault.'

'They really screwed you, didn't they? Fake iPods, counterfeit money – irony is, if they'd given you fake heroin as well, you wouldn't be looking at a fourteen stretch. Well, not unless you tried to sell it.'

'Ha-bloody-ha.' He took a big swallow of whisky, shuddered, then followed it with a mouthful of beer. 'And I didn't get the cash from them, thank you very much.'

Logan shifted in his seat. 'You didn't?'

'That bastard who bought the car. Everyone's always out to bloody screw you. . .'

'The bloke who bought your car paid you in counterfeit

cash?' Logan picked up the bag of faux iPods, then put it down again, frowning. 'Wasn't a small place out by Westhill, was it? Middleton Family Motors?'

Angus sent more whisky south. 'None of your business.'

'It was, wasn't it?' Logan grinned. 'That's brilliant!'

'Were you always a complete—'

'You don't get it, do you? Middleton paid you in dodgy notes, and *that's* what you bought your drugs with. How chuffed are this Gallagher and Yates going to be when they find out your money's fake?'

There was a pause, then the colour drained from Angus Black's face. 'Fuck.' He stared at Logan, then banged his head off the table again. 'Fucking . . . *fuck*.'

'Want to have another think about turning them in, before they come looking for you?'

30

Logan stuffed Angus Black's statement back in his pocket as PC Butler pulled up outside Middleton Family Motors. The used car lot was just as crowded as last time, even after Trading Standards had confiscated half a dozen illegal vehicles.

Butler raised an eyebrow. 'You're not thinking of trading in that crappy car of yours for something here, are you, Sarge? Only this lot looks like a good sneeze and the wheels'll fall off.'

Logan climbed out. A layer of snow covered the bonnets, boots, and roofs, more thick white flecks drifting down from the gunmetal sky. It was cold enough to make his fingertips throb as he shuffled sideways between 'BARGAIN OF THE MONTH!!!' and 'LOW MILEAGE SUPER-SAVER!!!', heading towards the main entrance.

The sound of a radio. A tractor grumbling in the distance, getting closer. A whurrrrrring noise somewhere on the fore-court, hidden amongst the vehicles.

Logan paused. 'Hello? I'd like to buy a car.'

'With you in just a tick. . .' The voice was coming from behind a brown Toyota with a dented wing.

Logan inched his way through the cars, craning his neck to get a better look. A man in grubby blue overalls was squatting by the Toyota's back wheel, a portable air pump connected to the saggy tyre.

Logan pulled out his notebook and checked the details Angus had given him again. 'Looking for a Volkswagen Golf, GTI, green if you've got it.'

'You know, I think you're in luck. I've. . .' The man looked up and his voice trailed off. 'Fuck.' Middleton scrambled to his feet, eyes darting left and right, then he ran for it. Jinking between the jammed-in cars, making for the road.

Logan hurried sideways after him, then jerked to a sudden halt as his jacket pocket caught on a wing mirror. There was a tearing noise.

PC Butler was still over by the pool car, staring open mouthed.

'Don't just bloody stand there!'

She charged forward, then skidded, arms pinwheeling. Her head disappeared from view and the word 'Shite!' echoed out across the little car lot.

Logan yanked his pocket off the wing mirror and struggled on.

Middleton had made it to the road and a dull blue MX5 – just like DI Steel's, only older and with a huge 'ZOOM ZOOM 4 LESS!!!' cardboard star wedged between the dashboard and the rearview mirror.

He dug about in his trouser pocket, then clambered in behind the wheel. Threw the sales sign out into the street.

Logan vaulted the bonnet of a Ford Mondeo, heels scraping through the inch-deep layer of snow. He slithered down the other side just in time to hear Middleton cranking over the Mazda's engine.

It spluttered a couple of times, then roared into life.

Butler had her extendible baton out, limping towards the car.

Logan crunched through a ridge of dirt-brown snow, reaching for the driver's door, but the tyres screeched, and the MX5 lurched forwards.

The back end shimmied from side to side, the little rear-wheel-drive sports car struggling for grip on the icy road.

PC Butler froze, eyes wide, as the car fishtailed towards her. She dived onto the bonnet of a Volvo estate, lifting her legs high as the Mazda clipped the front bumper. Chips of coloured plastic went flying.

And then Middleton was past, accelerating around the corner, the back end kicking out again.

Logan ran out into the road. Swore.

Butler lay spread-eagled on the Volvo bonnet, breath turning the air above her white. 'Jesus. . .'

The sound of squealing brakes. Then, BANG.

A horn, blaring.

Logan hurried over to PC Butler and helped her to her feet. 'You OK?'

'God, that was close. . .'

He lurched around the corner – Butler limping along behind him – and froze. The little sports car was wedged in at forty-five degrees between the grass verge and a drystane dyke; front end crumpled; the folding soft-top torn off, exposing its soft chewy centre. A huge tractor idled in the middle of the road, massive, mud-covered wheels sitting on the sports car's missing roof.

The farmer clambered down from the cab, and stood, swearing at the deep scrape along the side of his tractor.

Middleton was slumped over the Mazda's steering wheel. Dark-red seeped out onto the white deflated sack of his burst airbag.

*　*　*

PC Butler looked up from the Airwave handset pinned to her shoulder. 'Control says the ambulance should be here in five or ten.'

Logan nodded and added milk to all three mugs of tea, then lumped four sugars into the one on the end. As was traditional.

Kevin Middleton pulled the dripping towel off his face. 'Told you, I don't *need* an ambulance.' The right side of his face was bright pink and swollen, and a tail of red-stained toilet paper stuck out of one nostril.

Logan handed him the hot, sweet tea. 'You want more snow in the towel?'

'I just want to go home.' He sipped. Grimaced. 'How much sugar did you put in this?'

'Tell me about Angus Black.'

There was a pause. 'Never heard of him.' Middleton pressed the towel gently back against his face.

'He's the one who sold you the green Golf GTI sitting on your junkyard forecourt.'

'So what? I buy lots of cars.'

Logan pulled out Angus Black's statement. 'He says you gave him six and a half grand for the car, in cash?'

'Might've done.'

'It was counterfeit, wasn't it?'

Middleton huddled over his tea. 'When's that ambulance getting here?'

'You went back to Douglas Walker's house, didn't you? You went back for more counterfeit money. What did you do, threaten him? Beat him up again?'

'Think I might have that internal bleeding. . .'

'Good.' Butler scowled at him. 'Nearly killed me with that bloody car.'

'Wasn't my fault: road was slippy.' He took another sip of tea. 'And I didn't have anything to do with any dodgy notes.'

'Then why'd you run?'

No answer.

Logan stood. 'Soon as you've been checked out by the hospital I'm doing you for reckless driving, resisting arrest, and attempted murder.'

Tea went everywhere, in a sticky beige spray. 'I didn't—'

'You drove straight at PC Butler. I saw you do it.'

'It was slippy!'

'You tried to run me over.'

Middleton slumped forwards in his seat. Shoulders rising and falling beneath the grubby boilersuit. 'OK, OK. So I went to see Walker a couple of times, gave the cheeky wee fuck a smack.'

'How much did he give you?'

Middleton shrugged. 'Twenty grand. Said that was all he could take without anyone noticing.'

'And where's the rest of it?'

The garage owner's eyes darted to the safe in the corner, then away again. 'Spent it.'

Sigh. 'Fine, I'll get a warrant.'

Middleton just stared at his shoes.

'It's for you.' PC Butler unfastened the Airwave handset and passed it over, keeping her other hand on the steering wheel as they followed the ambulance through the snow towards A&E. At least the blue flashing lights meant they were making decent time.

Logan turned the radio down, putting Whitney Houston out of everyone's misery. 'McRae.'

Detective Inspector Beardy Beattie's bunged up voice boomed through the little speaker. *'When's the meeting?'*

Logan looked at Butler, but she just shrugged.

'Meeting?'

'I've been trying to get you on your mobile all day, honestly it's—'

'What meeting?'

'You said you'd set something up with Trading Standards and HMRC. We're supposed to be cracking down on those counterfeit goods.'

'When did—'

'Saturday morning! You said you'd do it. You stood there and told me you would.'

Logan watched the ambulance squeeze between a massive four-by-four and a bendy bus. 'I'm kinda in the middle of something.'

'I don't believe this.' The sound of someone scratching their beard crackled out of the handset. *'No, you know what: I do. You don't give a toss about doing what you're told when it's me, do you? If it's Steel, or McPherson, oh then you're all over it, but you think you can ignore me because we used to work together, don't you?'*

Logan clamped his hand over the mouthpiece. 'How do I turn the volume down?'

Butler waved a finger at the Airwave handset. 'Button on the left.'

He pressed it until Beattie's rant wasn't hammering out of the speaker loud enough for everyone to hear.

'. . .long enough. I've been patient with you, because of . . . you know . . . but that's it. I'm making a formal complaint to the head of CID.'

'Gordon, have you *seen* the news today? The *Examiner* outed Knox, what am I supposed to do?'

There was a pause. Then, *'It's not "Gordon" any more. It's "Sir", "Guv", "Guv'nor", "Inspector", or "Boss". Meeting, today, Sergeant.'*

And then the bearded tosser hung up.

Logan turned up the radio again – getting the tail end of a news report about the protests outside Richard Knox's house.

'. . .made a number of arrests, say the Newcastle-born rapist will be moved to a secure, undisclosed, location. Do you have an opinion about the demonstration? Maybe you were there? Then why not give us a call on 01224. . .' Logan switched it off again.

Bloody Beattie. How was he supposed to get a meeting organized at that short notice? It was. . . He frowned – Butler was staring at him.

'Eyes on the road, Constable.'

She fluttered her eyelashes a couple of times. 'Trouble, Sarge?'

'Do you think?' He punched a mobile phone number into the Airwave handset. 'Dildo? It's Logan. I need another favour. . .'

Julie sits back in her seat and says, 'Fuck.'

The TV's on, but the sound's turned off – the BBC News Channel playing them crowd scenes outside Knox's house again.

Tony wanders over to the window of the room they've rented in the same hotel as that tit Danby. Place is nice enough, if you like tartan. He hauls up the net curtains, letting in the view: skeletal trees scratching at the grey sky, some sort of park sunken way below street level, a railway line, a dual carriageway, a bunch of granite buildings. . . Grey, grey, grey. Like no bugger ever invented colour.

Snowing again too.

'Well?' Neil's lying on the double bed, feet dangling over the edge so Julie doesn't shout at him for putting his shoes on the covers. 'What's the plan now, then?'

Tony sniffs. 'Need to find out where they're moving him to.'

Julie doesn't even look up. 'Sweetheart, where would we be without your lightning-sharp intelligence?'

'Only saying.'

And it's *razor* sharp, not lightning. But Tony's lightning-sharp enough to keep his mouth shut.

Neil yawns. 'We still going after Danby the night?'

'I'd love to, Babe, but Danby's useless without Knox.' She frowns at the TV. 'Supposed to pick them both up at the same time, can't do that if we don't know where Knox is.'

'Maybe he'll phone, like?'

Tony settles back on the windowsill. 'Might not get the chance. They'll be keeping him under the thumb till things calm down.'

'Doesn't stop us grabbing Danby, does it?'

Julie sighs. 'If we grab Danby first they'll know something's up. Knox'll be locked up tighter than a Scotsman's wallet.'

A vacuum cleaner rumbles down the corridor outside, someone whistling along to a pop tune Tony almost recognizes as it goes by. On the TV the local plod bundle a quilt-covered figure into the back of a police van.

Julie pulls on a scuffed tan cowboy boot, the drug dealer's blood all washed away. 'OK, new plan: if we don't hear from Knox, we just have to stick with Danby. Sooner or later he's going to lead us right to him. Bish, bash, and indeed: bosh.'

Tony sticks up his hand. 'Bags not first to trail Danby.'

Julie: 'Second.'

Too slow off the mark, all Neil can do is lie there looking out at the snow. 'Ah . . . fuck.'

31

Logan waved a thank you to the patrol car and struggled through the snow, up the slippery steps, across the front podium – brown with sand and salt – and in through the front doors of FHQ.

Big Gary was sitting behind the reception desk, his head propped up with one hand, a battered paperback lying on the desk in front of him.

'Any messages?'

The big man reached beneath the desk and thumped a pile of Post-its on the counter. Never even took his eyes off the page.

'Anything important?'

'I'm *reading*.'

Logan flipped through the stack of yellow stickies. 'Rennie, Rennie, Beattie, Rennie, Beattie. . .' These went in the 'when hell freezes over' pile – there was no way Logan was talking to DI Beardy Beattie until Dildo called back. And he'd still not forgiven Rennie for grabbing Samantha's bum.

Then there were a couple of burglary victims looking for an update; someone wanting to know why no one had found his missing Mercedes yet; a woman from the *Independent* wanting an interview about Knox: another complaint from Douglas Walker's idiot lawyer; and right at the bottom, one from DI Steel.

A summons to her office.

He stuck the Post-its back on the desk. 'Any idea what Steel's after?'

Big Gary sighed, his jowls inflating and deflating like a pair of ruptured space hoppers. He marked his page with a Curly Wurly wrapper, then slammed the book shut. 'Why can't you buggers leave me alone for five minutes?'

Logan stared at him. 'Sorry for interrupting your reading time, Gary. My apologies, mate, I thought you were manning the *sodding desk.*'

The sergeant narrowed his eyes. 'Meant to be on my break, but that useless tit Jordan's still in the bog.' He narrowed his eyes. 'Where's that PC I sent you off with?'

'Butler? Left her up at A&E watching a used-car dealer.'

'For how long?'

Shrug. 'Till the doctors give us the all clear to bang him up.'

'Oh for. . .' Big Gary pinched the bridge of his nose. '*How* am I supposed to manage resources if you buggers in CID treat Uniform as your own personal property?'

'You really are in a foul sodding mood today, aren't you? Not my fault Jordan's got the squits.'

The desk sergeant scowled, then made a big show of opening his book again. 'And you better get back to that wee shite Barrett.' Big Gary's voice jumped an octave and went all nasal, 'of McGilvery, Barrett, and McGilvery.' He cleared his throat. 'Says it's a disgrace his poor wee client's been kept in over the weekend waiting for his shot in front of the Sheriff.'

'Then his client shouldn't be circulating forged twenties, should he?' Logan rearranged all the Post-its back into a single stack. 'When's he up?'

Big Gary squinted at the charge book. 'Court One at two-fifty.'

Logan checked his watch. 'Just enough time to have another crack at him.'

Douglas Walker slumped over the interview room table, the fingers of one hand wrapping themselves through his unwashed, greasy hair. Twisting it into little curls, then letting them go again. The fibreglass cast on the other arm lay flat against the chipped Formica. He smelled of stale sweat, over-laid with something sour.

Logan glanced up at the camera bolted to the wall, watching the little red light winking. 'Come on, Douglas: you're up in front of Sheriff McNab in twenty minutes. Sure you don't want me to put in a good word for you?'

'Lawyer.'

It was the only thing he'd say: 'Lawyer.'

State your name for the tape. 'Lawyer.'

Do you know why you're here? 'Lawyer.'

Would you like a cup of tea? 'Lawyer.'

'Let me paint a little picture for you, Douglas. What's going to happen is that your idiot lawyer, Captain Baldy the Estate Agent, is going to stand up at ten to three and waffle for a bit about criminal law – which he knows sod all about – and then Sheriff McNab – who's an utter bastard – will ask how you plead.'

Douglas Walker just kept on playing with his hair.

'Your lawyer will make you plead "not guilty", even though we all know you *are*, and then McNab'll set bail.' Logan smiled. 'And that's where it gets interesting. If you can't make bail, you end up in Craiginches for six or seven weeks, till the trial date. If you *can*, you're out on the street for tea time; then the press harassment starts. They camp outside your house, take photos, talk to neighbours—'

Douglas's head snapped up.

'Think how proud your mum and dad are going to be when they get back from holiday!'

The young man fidgeted with the rim of his cast, tugging little bobbles out of the tube-bandage lining. 'They. . . They can't put my name in the papers. I'll sue!'

'For what?'

'I don't know. Defamation of character! Slander. Libel, whichever one it is. They can't—'

'Don't be stupid, Douglas. All they'll say is you've been charged with passing a large sum of counterfeit currency. Can't be libel when it's the truth.'

'No. . .' It came out low and quiet. 'They can't put my name in the papers. They *can't*!' He raked his fingers through his oily hair. Harder and harder. 'They can't. . .'

Logan sat back. 'Dear God, a member of Generation-Y who doesn't want his name in the papers. Don't you *crave* your fifteen minutes of fame, Douglas? Your chance to shine for all the other brain-dead *X Factor Celebrity Come Dancing on Ice MasterChef* junkies?'

Douglas curled up, until his forehead thunked against the table. 'They can't. . .' Voice small and trembling.

'You know what?' Logan scooted his chair forward. 'You're right to be scared, because your friend Kevin Middleton – the nice man who sold you that second-hand Honda Civic? We arrested him this afternoon. He says you've been supplying him with counterfeit money, not just the notes you tried to buy the car with. The Sheriff's not going to like that, is he? An extra twenty grand of dodgy cash on the streets, because of you.'

He buried his head in his arms. 'I'm fucked. . .'

'Yes, you are. And I'm the only person who can un-fuck you. Now where did you get the money from?'

*　　*　　*

'Yeah, if you could, thanks.' DI Beattie shifted his phone from one side to the other, and looked up at Logan standing in the office doorway. 'Can I call you back?'

He hung up and stared. 'I've been phoning you all day.'

'My mobile had a run-in with a sledgehammer. That meeting's set up for half past four, today – two from Trading Standards and one of the Revenue's top people.'

Beattie's face broke into a big, hairy smile. 'That's brilliant news.' He took a deep breath. 'Look, about earlier. . .' He paused, obviously waiting for Logan to jump in and say it wasn't a problem. Don't worry about it. Water under the bridge.

Well, sod him.

Logan let the silence stretch, enjoying it.

'I wanted you to know I didn't put in a formal complaint.'

And then he wasn't enjoying himself quite so much. Feeling like a bit of a child for making Beattie struggle for it.

'I hope this means we can work together now?'

'Yes. . . Guv.' Didn't matter if he was trying to act like a grown-up or not, there was still no way Logan was calling the beardy idiot 'Sir' or 'Boss'. That would be taking things too far.

'OK.' Nod. 'Good. . . Half four.' Beattie looked around his office. 'I don't think we'll all fit, but—'

'The Shop Cops have got a meeting room organized at St Nicholas House. All we've got to do is bring the biscuits.'

The smile became a grin. 'Excellent. Biscuits, yes. . .' He produced a fiver from his wallet and handed it over. 'You see to the biscuits and I'll get going on the PowerPoint presentation.'

Logan suppressed the urge to shudder. 'Yes, Guv.'

'And Logan. . .?'

'Yes, Guv?'

'Good work. Thanks.'

Logan actually took a step back. It'd been ages since a DI had bothered to say thank you for anything. Maybe Beattie wasn't such a tit after all?

Steel was in her office, two doors down, with her feet up on her desk, frowning at a pile of paperwork. Probably trying to work out who to palm it off on.

Logan knocked on the open door – please let someone else have to deal with whatever crap she had on her desk.

'Ah.' She looked up. 'Just the wee man I've been looking for.'

Bugger.

'Shut the door, and lock it.'

Logan did, while the inspector cracked open her office window, then pulled out her cigarettes and jiggled the pack at him.

'Trying to cut down.'

'Suit yourself.' She lit up, exhaling a happy cloud of smoke and sighing. 'So, what did our friend the art student have to say for himself?'

'Sod all. Doesn't want his name in the papers, doesn't want to cut a deal, doesn't want to go to prison.'

Sniff. 'Silly git.' Her left hand drifted down below the desk. 'Still, McNab'll stick him out on bail and we can have another poke in a couple of days. If we can be arsed.'

'Got some good news on Polmont though: all the stuff we got from his flat is knock-off – even the vodka's fake. And guess who had identical counterfeit goods on him?'

'Basil Brush?'

'Angus Black.' Logan placed Angus's statement in the middle of Steel's desk. 'Apparently he got the drugs *and* the gadgets from a pair of Edinburgh heavies called Gallagher and Yates.'

'Who typed this?' She held the statement out at arms' length. 'Can barely read a bloody thing.'

'I ran a PNC check – they're Malcolm McLennan's boys.'

'What about. . .' She pulled a face at him. 'Malcolm McLennan?'

'It's his name isn't it? Both have done time for drugs and extortion, and according to Angus Black their boss is a big bald guy with a huge dog.'

Steel tapped the report against her cheek. 'The elusive Mr Connelly?'

'Plus. . .' Logan pulled one of Polmont's battered journals out of the pile on Steel's desk and flicked through it to a page he'd marked with a yellow stickie. One of the sparky's more legible entries. '"New shipment coming in for G and Y. Maybe leave it alone this time – think they suspect." G and Y appear about every two weeks.'

'Do they now?' She grinned and scratched. 'Smells like corroboration to me.'

'And best of all, Angus gave us an address.'

'Warrant?'

'Couple of hours. McNab's on the bench till four, and Harper's in Lerwick for that fish farm murder.'

Steel blew a stream of smoke out into the snow. 'Get Uniform organized; soon as the warrant clears we'll go pay Malk the Knife's wee toerags a visit.'

'Can't.' Logan pulled his jacket shut and buttoned it. With the window open it was getting nippy in here. 'Got a meeting with Beattie, HMRC, and the Shop Cops at half four – supposed to be working out what to do about all the fake goods knocking about. . . I'd cancel it, but Beattie's got his heart set on showing off his PowerPoint skills and I'm trying to be nice to him. Like you said.'

Steel settled back in her chair, one hand foostering about under the desk. 'You've done well, young grasshopper.'

Two pats on the back in one day – throw in a bottle of wine and some energetic sex and this would be the best day he'd had in about. . . two years?

Might as well push his luck. Logan put his head on one side and stared at Steel.

She stopped scratching. 'What?'

'Why's Danby so interested in Polmont?'

Steel puckered up her face. 'No' going to let that one go, are you?'

'Nope.'

Silence.

'OK. Seeing as you've been such a good boy: Polmont's what we call a serial chiz. Before Aberdeen he was ratting on Malk the Knife in Edinburgh. Before Edinburgh—'

'He worked for Mental Mikey.'

Steel made guns with her fingers and shot Logan in the head. 'Bull's-eye.'

Which explained a lot. 'That's why Danby's got one of Polmont's journals.'

'Covers the time he was in Newcastle.' Steel finished her fag and pinged the butt out into the snow. 'Anything else while I'm feeling generous?'

'Where are they sticking Knox this time?'

'Strictly need to know.'

'What, and I don't—'

'Right now, Danby's arse is eating his panties: thinks the fewer people know where Knox is the better. And don't look at me like that, this is for your own good. Trust me, if I could get out of knowing where the raping wee shite was staying, I would. Sooner or later Knox is going to go back to his bad old ways – the less involved you are, the better.'

Logan settled into his office chair.

The little detective sergeants' cupboard was littered with

boxes of files, all radiating out from Doreen's desk. She was on the phone, haranguing the lab about how long it was going to take them to analyse all the samples she'd brought in, and how much of the CID budget it was going to cost.

Biohazard Bob helped himself to one of Logan's prawn cocktail crisps, crunching and talking at the same time. 'You'd think she'd been asked to solve the Great Train Robbery, wouldn't you?' He nudged one of the file boxes with a scuffed shoe. 'I mean, look at all this crap.' Sniff. 'And how come she gets all the classy cases? She gets "contract killing with expensive set of golf clubs", I get "junkie booted half to death". Where's the bloody justice in that?'

'Yeah, because you're *such* a classy guy.' Logan creaked the plastic lid off his extra large mochaccino. 'Any more word on Knox?'

Just because Steel was foretelling doom didn't mean he didn't still want to know.

'That Liverpool psychologist was with him for a couple of hours. Apparently he's worried our visiting rapist's on a –' Bob put on a big dramatic voice, '– "COUNTDOWN TO DISASTER!". I swear to God, he even said it like that. "COUNTDOWN TO DISASTER!"'

Doreen swivelled round in her chair and shushed them, then went back to her phone call. 'How can it take all week to analyse half a dozen blood spatters?'

Bob grinned. 'She's cute when she's pissed off, isn't she?'

'Goulding leave a report?'

'Nah, went back to his lair to write it up. Says we should keep an extra close eye on young Master Knox. Apparently all this stress is going to send him right back to his auld-mannie-raping ways. Should've hacked his bollocks off in Newcastle when they had the chance—'

'Here we go. . .'

'Look, I'm just saying OK? Everyone who ends up on the

287

Sex Offenders' Register should be castrated. You remember that bloke from Banchory we did for kiddie-fiddling? What did he do, soon as he got out?'

'Not listening, Bob.' Logan powered up his computer.

'Or that rapist who liked pregnant women. Remember him?'

'Anyone say what they're doing about security at Knox's new place?'

'Or what about the bloke who. . .' Frown. 'Oh, you know: in Duthie Park. What was it, "The Winter Gardens Wanker"?'

'*Security*, Bob. What are they doing?'

'Hmm? Oh, no idea. Ask Steel, that's her poison chalice full of turds.' The phone went and he snatched up the receiver. 'Big Bob's House of Sexual Deviancy, Big Bob speaking. . .'

Idiot.

Logan called up his email and waited for it to chug through the backlog on the server. Buried in the usual office-related dross was a message from an admin officer at HM Prison Frankland, with a spreadsheet attached of everyone who'd ever shared a cell with Richard Knox. The officer had even included a breakdown of what each of them had been convicted of. It wasn't exactly edifying reading.

Near the bottom of the list was one Oscar Renwick: he'd got seven years for breaking into a family home and 'forcing the husband to perform fellatio on him by means of threatening the wife with a serrated hunting knife'. Exactly the MO Knox had told them about on the drive out to see his granny's grave.

Logan opened up the list of murders he'd downloaded – where the victims had been burned to try and hide the evidence. First get rid of any that happened after Oscar Renwick was arrested. And Renwick was only twenty-four when he was sent down, which meant his raping career couldn't be more than, what, eleven, twelve years? So anything before that could go too. Which left about three dozen. Eliminate any where the victims weren't stabbed or slashed and Logan was down to eight.

Do a quick analysis on the victims – make sure there was an adult male *and* female killed. That left just six crime scenes: Brighton, Swansea, Darlington, Ballymena, Corby, and Fort William.

Logan settled back in his seat and smiled at the blinking cursor. Less than thirty-six hours in and he was already on the brink of solving a twenty-year-old murder from 230 miles away.

All he'd have to do was call up the files for the six cases, check to see where Knox's cellmate was on those days, and wait for the commendations to come rolling in.

Result.

He was putting in a request to South Wales Police when the door thumped open and DC Rennie lumbered into the room, carrying a plastic crate full of files. 'Golf club murder?'

Logan pointed at Doreen's collection. 'Anywhere over there.'

'Ta.' He dumped the crate on the carpet, then stood, rubbing his hands on his trousers. 'Thought you were supposed to be at some meeting Beattie's been banging on about?'

Logan frowned, then checked his watch. 16:35.

Shite. Completely lost track of time.

He jumped to his feet, stabbed the button to switch off his monitor, then grabbed the big square tin from the shelf by the 'UNSOLVED' whiteboard. 'Stealing the biscuits!' And charged out of the door.

32

Broad Street was like a wind tunnel. The snow not so much falling as hammering sideways. St Nicholas House loomed on the other side of the street, a fourteen-storey slab of concrete and glass, the upper floors hidden by the howling weather.

Cars and buses crept past, headlights on full, windscreen wipers thunking back and forth. Logan hurried across the road, ground his cigarette out in the little receptacle by the automatic door and shivered inside. Stomped his feet on the coconut matting, shook the snow off his coat and the tin of biscuits. Wiped the meltwater from his stinging face.

Five minutes later he was steaming quietly next to the radiator in reception, flicking through a copy of that morning's *Press and Journal*, when someone said, 'You're late.'

Logan held out the damp tin. 'Brought biscuits.'

Dildo sniffed. 'Not digestives are they?' He popped off the lid, 'Ooh, Jammie Dodgers. . .'

He handed Logan a visitor's pass. 'Your guv'nor's a randy old sod, by the way – been trying to chat up Susanna since she got here.'

'Please, tell me you're kidding.' Trust Beattie to find a way to make things even more awkward.

'I wish.'

Dildo turned on his heel and marched towards the stairs.

Logan didn't move. 'Any chance we can take the lifts for a change?'

'It's only four floors, you lazy bugger. Anyway, the lifts are playing Russian Roulette again. Anne's ended up in the basement twice today, doors wouldn't even open the second time.'

Four flights later, Logan was puffing and wheezing, lurching after Dildo as he pushed through a set of double doors into the dark heart of Trading Standards. Which was about sixteen desks arranged back-to-back in the near left corner, sectioned off from Bereavement Services by a wall of shoulder-height partitions in a grubby shade of burgundy.

The dirty salmon carpet was a crime scene map of dark spills, the ceiling tiles scarred where someone had moved a partition wall. St Nicholas House: proof that ugly wasn't just skin deep.

'Thought this was only supposed to be temporary?'

'Council, isn't it?' Dildo grabbed a notebook off the nearest desk – covered, like the rest, in product boxes, plastic bags, and paperwork. He pointed at the team. 'You know Anne, Sicknote, Clive, and Hughie?'

Logan gave them a wave.

Everyone waved back, except for the one on the phone – short-sleeved shirt, tie, baldy head – who held up a thumb. 'No, sir. . . Yes, I understand, but you've got to use lubricant. . .'

'We're in the Grief Counselling room – all I could get at short notice.'

'Yes. . . Yes, I'm sure it *was* very painful, sir, but it's not an allergic reaction, it's a friction burn. . .'

Logan followed Dildo through Bereavement Services to a little meeting room in the far corner of the building, with a projector bolted to the ceiling, and a pull-down screen taking up a large chunk of one wall.

Beattie was sitting at the table, fiddling with a laptop, a winter panorama of Aberdeen stretched out behind him. Rooftops, the back entrance to Markies, bits of Union Street, the defunct Christmas lights swaying in the wind, waiting for someone to take them down.

A familiar gravelly laugh made Logan freeze in the doorway. DI Steel. She was over by the window, talking to a tall blonde woman in jeans and a thick woollen jumper.

Logan opened his mouth, then closed it again.

Dildo gave him a shove, then closed the door behind them. 'DS McRae, this is Susanna Frayn from Her Majesty's Revenue and Customs.'

She stuck out a hand. 'Pleased to meet you.' One of those jolly-hockey-sticks English public school accents.

Steel grinned. 'Susanna was just telling me about her photography classes, weren't you, Susanna? So, do you do nudes?'

Over at the table, Beattie hit something and a PowerPoint slide appeared on the wall. 'Got it working!'

There was an audible groan from Steel, then everyone took their seats around the table: Steel next to the woman from HMRC, Logan next to Steel, Dildo next to Logan, leaving Beattie stranded on his own on the other side.

'OK, first item. . .' A blue-and-white PowerPoint slide appeared on the screen, the names of everyone present fading up, or sliding on with a different effect, as if they couldn't tell who was there just by looking around the room. The only name that didn't have a fancy effect was DI Steel's, as if she'd been added at the last minute.

Logan leant over and whispered at her, while Beattie pulled

up the next slide and read out the agenda. 'What are you *doing* here?'

'What, can I no' take an interest in ongoing cases?' Steel gazed at Susanna from Her Majesty's Revenue and Customs. 'Wonder if she'd be interested in a full-body-cavity search?'

'You're *married*.'

'Pfff. . . No harm in looking, is there? Sides, Laz, right now I'm that horny I'd even do *you*. Susan's still no. . .'

Beattie was staring at her.

'Don't you mind me, Gordon: just telling McRae here what a great job you'd done on your presentation. Very professional.'

'Oh, right. Thanks.' He actually puffed up a little. Then produced handful of biros and some packets of Post-it notes. 'Now, if we begin with the counterfeit merchandise, we need to assess what *kind* of goods are out there, and where they're coming from. Why don't we workshop a list of—'

'Actually,' Logan just stopped himself sticking up his hand, 'we have a lead that—'

Something hard slammed into his left shin. 'Ow! Who bloody—'

'What Sergeant McRae is trying to say,' Steel pulled on a smile, 'is that we're all committed to getting these hooky goods off the streets.'

The front of his leg was stinging.

Beattie nodded. 'Yes, exactly. Now, if you all want to take a pad and a pen, we'll each write down the kind of things we're seeing being counterfeited at the moment. . .'

Logan thumped Steel on the sleeve, hissing, 'What the hell was that for?'

'Gallagher and Yates are *mine*. I'm no' handing them over to that beardy buffoon.'

'Actually.' Susanna placed her biro on the table with a loud thunk. 'Perhaps we can move on to discussing what

293

we're *actually* going to do about it?' She flashed Beattie a red-lipped smile. 'Don't you think?'

'Ah, yes. . .' Beattie fumbled with his packs of Post-it notes, sending them skittering to the floor, pink rushing up his hairy cheeks. 'Erm. . . Right.' He licked his lips. 'Well, obviously I don't want to dictate what. . . when, erm, bringing various expertise to bear.' He made a floppy hand gesture, as if he was trying to whisk an invisible egg. 'Why we're all here, after all.'

Inspiring.

Dildo slid a folded piece of paper in front of Logan. 'YOU REALLY SODDING OWE ME FOR THIS!!!'

Logan cleared his throat. 'We arrested someone— Ow!'

Steel kicked him again. 'Someone who'd been sold a fake Rolex.' She turned a crocodile smile in Logan's direction. 'Didn't we, Laz?'

He moved his legs as far away as possible. 'Yes.'

Beattie wrote 'Rolex' on a lonely stickie. 'Well . . . the best thing from a policing point of view would be to catch someone in the act of selling the counterfeit merchandise on, and trail them back to their supplier.'

'Really?' Dildo sat back in his seat. 'That's amazing! We at Trading Standards have been puzzling long and hard about how to trace naughty fake goods. If *only* we'd asked the long arm of the law to—'

'All right, Timothy, I think we get the picture.' Susanna twiddled one of her pearl earrings. 'I'm more concerned with the movement of counterfeit twenty-pound notes than knock-off hair straighteners. Where have you got with that?'

Beattie harrumphed. 'Well, we did have a suspect in custody. . .' He drifted off, then stared at Logan.

Here we go again. 'Douglas Walker, eighteen. We arrested him for passing four and a half grand in dodgy twenties, but at least another twenty-three thousand's passed through his hands. Released on bail till,' Logan checked his watch, 'beginning of March, I think.'

Susanna nodded. 'Did he say where he got it from?'

'Like interviewing a wooden leg. He—'

'Wouldn't tell us anything about where he got the stuff.' Beattie nodded. 'He's obviously covering for someone.'

Steel snorted. 'Aye, or he's scared.'

'Erm . . . yes, well, we'll obviously have to follow that up.' Beattie wrote 'D WALKER' on another stickie. 'Now, can we—'

'And it's not just fake twenties any more, there's tens and fives as well.'

'I still don't think—'

'Tens and fives?' The lady from HMRC sat forward. 'We've not had any of those in yet.'

Beattie flushed again. 'Yes, but shouldn't we be—'

'Do you have any samples?'

Logan pointed in the vague direction of FHQ. 'IB's analysing them now. Rumour is they're local.'

'Interesting, interesting. . .' She went back to fiddling with her pearl earring.

Steel leaned over and whispered at Logan again. 'Think she's got a necklace to go with those, cos if no' I could give her one. Well, metaphorically speaking.'

Logan grimaced, he couldn't help it.

Beattie's meeting limped on until the stroke of five, then the DI shook everyone's hands, told them how productive it had been, thanked them for coming, then bumbled about, packing away his Post-its, biros, laptop, and cables.

Steel gave a yawn and a stretch. 'Did I miss anything?'

Soon as Beattie was packed up, they all followed Dildo back down the stairs to Reception and handed in their visitor's passes.

'OK.' Dildo clapped his hands. 'We'll be in touch about the—'

'Wait a minute. . .' Beattie thrust his laptop bag into Logan's hands. 'Forgot my jacket.' Then he turned around and hurried towards the lifts.

Logan watched him mashing the up button. 'Should we tell him?'

'Should we buggery.' Dildo stuffed his hands into his pockets. 'With any luck he'll get stuck in the basement all night and be eaten by the rats.'

They made for the front door. Outside, thick white flakes of snow drifted down from a dark-orange sky, shining as they passed within reach of the street lights, glowing red behind the cars and buses, settling on the shoulders of people tromping their way home.

'Right.' Susanna turned and shook Steel's hand. 'Anything comes up on the counterfeit notes, please let me know. I'll see if I can get someone from our end to look into Walker: you'd be surprised what a sudden tax inspection can turn up.'

Steel still hadn't let go of Susanna's hand. 'Why don't I walk you to your car? We can swap contact info. . .?'

Susanna pulled a wee collapsible umbrella from her bag and clacked it up, then picked her way daintily out into the snow, with the inspector close beside her. Three steps out of the door, the woman from HMRC slipped. Steel grabbed her. They both laughed. Then disappeared around the corner.

Dildo smiled. 'Got to admire her for trying, but Susanna's *way* out of her league.'

'Steel's *married*.'

'And no offence, but Beattie?'

'Tell me about it. Look, hold off on doing anything, OK? I might have some good news for you in a couple of. . .'

He trailed off as the lift doors pinged open and Beattie stepped out – still without his jacket – frowned, turned around twice, then stepped back into the lift and pressed a button.

'They made *that* a DI, but you're still a lowly sergeant.' Dildo put a hand on Logan's shoulder and gave it a squeeze. 'You must be so proud.'

33

Logan's manky little Fiat grumbled to a halt, the engine making Death Watch Beetle ticking noises as it cooled. The warrant hadn't been that difficult to arrange, but by the time they'd done the risk assessment and the briefing, and organized a firearms team, it was gone half seven.

Sitting in the passenger seat, Steel tapped two fingers against the black-plastic-bag window. 'This supposed to be stylish, is it?'

'You want to walk home?'

They'd parked on a little side road, north of Balmedie, where they'd have a decent view of proceedings. The address Angus Black had given them for Gallagher and Yates turned out to be a smallholding surrounded by miles of nothing. The cottage sat in the darkness, its windows glowing with amber light; a couple of tumbledown outbuildings lay off to one side, spilled granite blocks slowly disappearing under the falling snow; a large barn with a dark-red door. No sign of the unmarked van the eight-man firearms team had turned up in.

'Why can I no' see anything?' Steel shoogled closer to the windscreen, the hot orange glow of her cigarette reflected in the pitted glass.

Logan pointed at a pair of black shapes moving slowly along the line of a drystane dyke. 'There.'

Steel hauled out her Airwave handset and hit the button. 'What's taking so long?'

'It's bloody freezing out here.'

'Boo hoo. Just get your arses in gear. Haven't got all bloody night.'

Then there was a muttered, *'Jesus, she's a sodding nightmare.'*

'I heard that!'

And the connection went dead.

Logan cupped his hands and blew into them. 'Whatever happened to all that crap you told me about being a team player?'

'Meaning?'

'Meaning you turning up to Beattie's meeting and not letting me tell him about Gallagher and Yates.'

She stuck a cigarette between her teeth and lit it, blowing out a mouthful of smoke that oozed across the windscreen. 'Beattie's a moron.'

Unbelievable. 'How come when *I* say he's an idiot I've got an attitude problem, but when *you* say it—'

Steel smacked the back of her hand against his chest. 'Shhhhh!'

'No. It's one bloody rule for—'

She hit him again. 'Down there, you twit.' She pointed through the snow at the main road, where a large Transit van was turning onto the farm track, bouncing and rolling along the icy, rutted surface. Steel fumbled with the handset again. 'All teams, hold position. We've got visitors. . .'

'Sodding hell. I'm up to my tits in a snowdrift here.'

'I don't care if you're up to your tits in shark-infested tampons: keep your gob shut and your arse where it is!'

The big van jounced in through the gates, did a tortuous three-point-turn then reversed towards the door of the barn, brake lights flaring red through the falling snow and cloud of diesel exhaust.

Steel flicked ash into the footwell. 'What do you think: doing a midnight flit?'

The driver hopped down from the cab, then crunched his way over to the cottage, leaving the engine running.

Logan turned the key in the ignition and the Fiat whined and groaned into life.

'What the hell are you doing?'

'Being proactive. . .' He inched the car along the side road with the headlights off, navigating by the faint reflected glow of the snow. 'What's happening?'

'Driver's back out . . . got two mates with him . . . going round the back of the van. . .'

A whin bush grated along the side of the Fiat, scratching at Logan's window.

'They've opened the doors on the cattle barn . . . light's on. . . Shite, can't see anything – could you no' get the bloody window fixed properly?' She thumbed the button on the Airwave handset again. 'What's going on?'

'We're all getting hypothermia.'

'Donald, you make me come down there and I'll jam my boot right up—'

'Looks like they're unloading stuff from the back of the van.'

Logan had finally turned out onto the main road, the Fiat's front wheels skittering from side to side, scrabbling for purchase.

'Get into position.'

'Finally!'

Bloody brakes weren't working. Logan stomped his foot hard to the floor, and the car slithered to a halt, overshooting the end of the farm track. A bit of blind reversing, and the thing was pointing the right way again. He eased into the road.

'Fuck. . .' A ditch ran along one side, the verge invisible as the wind picked up, throwing snow against the windscreen.

'*Team One – good to go.*'

'*Team Four – aye, we're ready an' a'.*'

'*Team Three – in position.*'

'*Team Two – Bastard, just stepped in something. . .*'

'Right, listen up.' Steel took an inspirational sook on her fag. 'There will be no getting shot. There will be no shooting anyone else. Most importantly, there will be no extra sodding paperwork for me to do, understand?'

There was a replying chorus of, '*Yes, ma'am.*'

'Who are we no' at home to?'

'*Mr Fuck-Up!*'

'Right. Russell, they're all yours.'

Logan could hear the lead firearms officer giving his team instructions as the little Fiat juddered and snaked up the track. When he was roughly halfway to the cottage, Logan tapped the brakes again, grinding to a halt. He hauled on the handbrake. 'Roadblock.'

Steel shrugged. 'Good an idea as any.'

Probably unnecessary, but at least now they couldn't do a runner in the Transit van.

'*All teams, move in on my mark. And . . . mark!*'

The inspector wiped at the windscreen with her sleeve. 'Can you see anything?'

'No.' Just the halo of the van's headlights and the glow from the cottage. Everything else was swallowed by snow and darkness.

'*Police! Hands where I can see them!*'

'Susan asked if you want to be there.'

'Where?' Logan killed the engine.

'*I said, keep your bloody hands where I can see them!*'

'You know, when she. . . When the baby comes.'

301

In the dark of the car, Logan grimaced. 'Never really thought about it.'

'On the ground. On the ground now!'

'Well, it's technically your kid too, so if—'

'SHITE!'

A bright flash, followed by a hard pop.

'Live fire! Officer down!'

Three answering flashes, and then the Transit van shot forward, headlights sweeping towards the farm track.

'Laz. . .?'

Logan fumbled with his seatbelt. 'Out!' He snapped on the hazard lights, hauled open the door and scrambled out into the snow. The van was picking up speed, barrelling down the road towards them.

Oh, crap. No way that was going to stop.

He lunged for the drystane dyke, pulling himself up the slippery stones. The top course gave way and Logan tumbled down the other side into a bank of freezing white, boulders thumping down all around him.

BANG! The sound of shattering glass. The squeal of tortured metal.

Swearing.

Logan hauled himself upright, hands and face stinging with the cold, and peered over the wall. The Fiat was at least six feet back from where he'd abandoned it, wedged across the track – the back end in the ditch, one headlight smashed, front bumper hanging off, the bonnet crumpled into a sneer of metal. The Transit van looked as if nothing had happened.

Behind the steering wheel, the van's driver blinked and shook his head. A lumpy man with rough features and Lemmy-from-Motorhead stubble.

'You dick!' Logan stumbled across the scattered wall stones, through the snow, and round to the driver's door. 'That was my car!' He hauled the door open and dragged the man out into the snow.

Resisting the urge to kick him in the goolies, Logan produced his warrant card and rammed it in Lemmy's face. 'POLICE!' Then flipped him over onto his front and cuffed his hands behind his back. 'You're nicked.'

Lemmy just lay there and groaned.

That'll teach him not to wear a seatbelt. . . Logan jumped to his feet. Steel – where the hell was Steel? He hurried over to the car. She wasn't in the passenger seat. She wasn't in the ditch ether.

Then he heard the swearing again.

'Inspector?' Logan waded through the snow in the ditch and peered over the wall into the field beyond. Steel was lying flat on her back with the cigarette sticking straight up out of her mouth, smoke trailing away into the sky. 'Inspector? You OK?'

She didn't get up, just raised a hand. 'Either I'm having one of them sympathetic pregnancies and my water's just broke, or I've peed myself a little.'

Steel slumped back against the barn wall and ran a hand over her face. 'He going to be OK?'

'He's a lucky sod – shotgun wasn't close enough, so the vest took most of it. Got some pellets in his arms and chin, but other than that, yeah.' Which was more than could be said for Norman Yates.

'The other one?'

'Depends how quickly the ambulance gets here. Did you see the state of my bloody car?'

'What did I tell them? No getting shot, no shooting anyone. Why does no *bastard* ever listen?' She kicked one of the many boxes littering the barn, but instead of the thing sailing off into the shelves that lined the rough stone walls, her foot thumped through the cardboard, leaving her stuck. 'Arse. . .'

'Not like they had any choice, is it? They identified themselves; he opened fire; they took him out.'

'Get this bloody thing off me!' She hopped on one foot. 'And what sort of moron takes a shotgun to a firearms team anyway?'

Logan hauled the box off, then took a look around the barn: shelves on all four walls, stacked with cartons and containers; pallets on the floor, keeping more stuff off the compacted dirt. There was a whole section devoted to Grant's Vodka. He tore a case open, pulled out a bottle and read the label. 'Counterfeit.'

'Bollocks.'

Logan handed it over. 'See anything suspicious?'

Frown. 'That's no' how you spell "Distillers".'

'Oh. . .' She'd got there a lot faster than he had. 'I'm guessing most of this is dodgy, if not all of it.'

'Yes, well done Sherlock, I think I might have worked that one out on my own.' She cracked open another box. 'Fancy some knock-off Calvin Klein's Obsession?'

'No.'

Steel stuck the carton back in the box. 'Well, one thing's for certain, Malk the Knife's no' going to be too pleased with Mr Gallagher when he finds out he's lost a whole shipment of dodgy goods. Poor baby.' She grinned. 'Want to go rub it in?'

Outside the barn a crumpled trail of boxed hair tongs, digital radios, and other assorted goods stretched away to the open back doors of the abandoned Transit van. As if Hansel and Gretel had been shoplifting.

Logan followed Steel through the snow to the little cottage. The whole place smelled of curry and the bitter-sweet sweaty tang of cannabis.

Gallagher was in the lounge, handcuffed and sitting in a

wooden dining chair at gunpoint – three grim-faced constables all aiming at various portions of his anatomy. He was a chunky lump of muscle with a spade-shaped head, tattoos poking out from the neck of his dark-brown fleece, one eye swollen and already starting to turn purple. 'I want a fucking lawyer.' His voice had a surprisingly high-pitched Fife lilt.

'And I want Helen Mirren to slather me in chocolate and eat me like a Curly Wurly, doesn't mean it's going to happen.' Steel slumped into the couch. 'Who you working for?'

'I'm saying nothing.'

'We know anyway, just want to hear you say it.' She pulled out her cigarettes and offered the packet around to everyone except Gallagher. 'Think Malk the Knife's going to be happy with your wee performance tonight?'

'Police brutality. You fuckers killed that bloke.'

So much for honour among counterfeiters and drug dealers.

'"That bloke"?' Logan crossed over to the wood-burning stove, glowing merrily in the fireplace. 'No way to speak about your friend Norman Yates, is it? According to Lothian and Borders the pair of you have been joined at the hip since you did over that Post Office in Leith.'

Steel nodded. 'Very romantic.'

Sniff. 'Never seen him before in my life.'

Steam was starting to rise off of Logan's trousers. 'Where's Andrew Connelly? Big bald bloke with a huge dog? Supposed to be your boss?'

Gallagher stared at him with one blue eye. 'I only stopped here to ask directions. Never seen any of these guys before in—'

'Your life, aye, we get it.' Steel stood. 'This mercenary wee shite's no' going to tell us anything. Get his arse back to the station.'

*   *   *

It took four burly police officers, their van, a tow rope, and a lot of swearing to get Logan's battered Fiat out of the ditch. It thumped down on the snowy track, and the front bumper fell off, the bonnet flapping open and closed like the car was laughing at him.

'Fucking hell. . .' Logan stared at the buckled mess.

The lead firearms officer patted him on the shoulder, grinning. 'It was a mercy killing.'

'Bugger off, Russell.'

Russell waved at the rest of his team. 'We'll drag it back to the farm, you can give it a decent burial later.'

Logan hauled open the driver's door and threw the dented bumper into the back, then stood there, looking down at the keys, still dangling from the ignition. He reached in and gave them a twist.

The Fiat's starter motor made whining, gurning noises.

'God, you're hopeful, aren't you?' Russell blew into his hands. 'Come on, give it up. Ambulance needs—'

The engine spluttered, then gave a painful growl.

'Bloody hell.' The firearms officer stepped back, and threw his arms in the air, spotlit by the Fiat's one remaining headlight. 'IT'S ALIVE! ALIVE!'

Logan stared at him. 'You're a dick, you know that, Russell, don't you?'

34

Logan pushed through the flat's front door, into the scent of garlic, herbs and cheese. He banged the snow off his feet, took off his shoes, and padded through into the lounge. His head was pounding – they'd had to tie the resurrected Fiat's bonnet down with hairy string and nearly a whole roll of silver duct tape, driving it back to town in the rattling growl of a broken exhaust. 'God what a day. . .'

Samantha looked up from the couch, then away again. She was wearing her pink fluffy robe, red-and-black stripy socks sticking out of the end. Her nose was deep pink, eyes too. 'What happened to you?'

'Raid out by Balmedie – someone got shot.'

'I waited for you.'

'Did you?' He peeled off his jacket. 'Were we going. . .' He stopped.

Samantha sniffed. 'I can't do this any more.'

Pause. 'Do what?'

'This.' She waved a hand, staring at the blank TV screen. 'Playing the tart. Being the good little woman. Never rocking the boat.'

'Playing the—'

'Do you have any idea how difficult this is? Watching you destroy yourself. Trying not to say anything. Living with your constant—'

'Where the hell's this coming from?' Logan dumped his jacket on the back of the couch.

'When was the last time you came home and said something positive? About anything?'

'Someone rammed my car with a Transit van! What am I supposed to say, "everything's fucking peachy"?'

She wiped her sleeve across her face. 'I can't. . .' Stood. Turned to march out of the room.

Logan grabbed her. 'What happened?'

She wouldn't look at him. 'I can't be your security blanket any more. It's too much.'

'I don't *need* a security—'

'Just stop it.' Samantha placed two hands on his chest and shoved him away. She stormed out, slamming the door behind her.

'Oh for fuck's. . . Samantha!' Logan followed her through to the bedroom. She was stuffing clothes in a holdall.

'Can we at least talk about it?'

'What's to talk about?' She rammed a pair of black leather pants in the bag, voice clipped and angry. 'You're going to be a *father*. You'll have a family. What the hell do you need me for?'

'What do I need. . .? I don't love Steel, or Susan. OK? I love you. I don't want—'

'Then why is it always me? Why do *I* always have to be the one who suggests sex? Why do you never *want* me?'

'I do! I'm just. . . Bloody hell.' The phone was ringing, a handset warbling away on top of the bedside cabinet. 'I'm trying to—'

She pushed past, back out into the hall.

'Samantha, it's not. . .' Through into the lounge again. 'Will you stand still for two minutes?'

She grabbed a handful of CDs from the pile by the TV. 'When you figure out what you want you can call me.'

'I want *you*!'

The ringing stopped and the answering machine picked up: Logan telling whoever it was to leave a message.

DI Steel's voice growled out of the speakers. *'Laz?'*

'I'm sorry, OK? I'm just . . . everything's screwed up and I don't. . .'

'Laz, I know you're there – pick up the bloody phone!'

He reached for her. 'Why didn't you say something?'

'Don't make me send someone round!'

Samantha wiped her eyes again. 'You're supposed to *know*.'

'Laz?'

'I didn't. I'm sorry.' This time, when he held her, she didn't push him away. 'Stay, OK?'

'Laz, I'm serious!'

Samantha sighed. Looked away. 'Go on then. Answer it.'

'Screw her, it's—'

'You know what the old bag's like – she'll just keep ringing and ringing till you do.'

Logan snatched the phone out of its cradle. 'Are there no other bloody police officers in Aberdeen you can annoy?'

'Get your arse back to the station. Someone's set fire to Knox's house.'

There was something strangely comforting about watching a house burning in the middle of a snowstorm. Choking black smoke curled up to meet the low clouds: the sharp smell of bubbling plastics, the soft edge of charring wood. Up close, the snow had melted away, beaten back by the blistering heat, but that didn't stop more from whipping down from the February night sky.

Logan sidled up next to DI Steel. Her face was all pink and shiny and she'd put on a thick, padded parka, the front unzipped and pulled wide while she sipped at a polystyrene cup of something brown. 'Hope you brought some marsh-mallows.'

'Fire Chief says it'd be out already if it wasn't for the wind. At least they've managed to stop it spreading.'

A pair of huge white fire engines blocked the street, their flickering lights sparkling through the snow, thick jets of water raining down on the burning building.

'Got any fags? I'm gasping.'

Logan handed her the packet.

'Ta. Neighbour called it in about nine, seems our con-scientious media bastards stood and filmed the place burning; never thought to actually get on the blower and call nine-nine-nine.'

'There's a shock.' Logan turned on his heel, looking past the blue-and-white 'POLICE' tape cordoning off the front garden, to the forest of TV cameras and zoom lenses on the other side. 'Think they got whoever did it on film?'

'God, that's *brilliant*!' She slapped a hand against her fore-head. 'Why do you think I dragged you all the way out here, to sing songs round the camp-fire?'

'Thanks. Couldn't have got Uniform to do it, could you? *No*, had to drag me out in the middle of the night. Just because you're not getting any—'

'Don't whinge. Think I want to be here? Should be back at the nick interrogating the wee sods we arrested. Gallagher's no' saying anything, but the van driver was beginning to. . .' She frowned. Then smiled. 'You were at it, weren't you? You and the gorgeous goth! Come on then: blow by blow.'

At it? The way things were going he'd be lucky if she was still there when he finally got home.

310

Steel pursed her lips. 'Bet she goes like a bloody steam-engine.'

Logan glared at her, then turned around and marched off towards the ranks of cameras, the inspector's words ringing out behind him: 'And see if you can't scrounge up some more tea!'

Half an hour later he was hunched over in the BBC Scotland Outside Broadcast Unit – which was a fancy way of saying 'Transit Van Stuffed With Weird Bits Of Equipment'. A generator grumbled away somewhere behind a bank of knobs, switches, and flickering lights, just loud enough to be annoying.

'I'd love to, but it's editorial policy.' The bearded bloke in the polar fleece, blew his nose into a damp hanky; never taking his eyes off the screen in front of him, where a rosy-cheeked reporter was doing a piece to camera, the snow whirling down around her head. '. . .*sense of anger in Aberdeen tonight. We spoke to some of Richard Knox's neighbours. . .'*

'We're talking about an arson here.'

The man twisted a dial on his little editing desk. 'Mate, if it was up to me I would. . .'

Logan sighed. 'But?'

'The BBC *has* to be seen to be impartial, otherwise no bugger's ever going to trust us again. I'm not allowed to give you any footage without a warrant.'

Which was the same reply he'd got from every other sod camped outside the cordon of 'POLICE' tape.

'Can you at least *show* me it?'

Mr Beard puckered up. 'Give us a second, OK?' Then he leant forward, clicked a button, and spoke into a little microphone. 'That was great Janet, now can we try it again? And make sure you mention the campaign to have him deported.'

The woman on screen scowled. *'You can't deport someone*

311

from Aberdeen to Newcastle, it doesn't make any sense! And it's flipping freezing *out here.'*

'So say "repatriate", "forcefully relocate", or "hound out". Something. Then you can come in, have a cup of tea, and get ready for the next bulletin: we're live at twelve past.' He let go of the button. 'Bloody prima donnas.'

He spun around in his seat, ducking to avoid a dented anglepoise lamp. 'Going to be on *News at Ten* anyway, so I suppose I can give you a preview. . .'

He flicked a switch on the back wall of instruments and a small screen, mounted above what looked like an eight-track recorder, came alive with static.

'Headphones.' He pointed at a scabby pair hanging from a bent coat hanger looped through the equipment rack, the cable plugged in next to the screen.

A quick rattle across a dirty keyboard, and the female reporter appeared again. Behind her Knox's house was ablaze, sheets of orange and yellow billowing out of the lounge window, red sparks mingling with the falling snow, the upper windows glowing with flickering light.

'This morning notorious rapist, Richard Knox, was escorted from his family home by police—' The picture cut to familiar footage of the crowd surging outside the house. *'—after angry scenes. Local residents, and people from as far away as Cheshire, descended on a quiet Aberdeen street when a North East newspaper revealed that Knox was living in the city's Cornhill district.'*

Cut to a puffy-faced man with a strawberry birthmark across one cheek. *'No' right is it? Why should we be lumbered with Newcastle's perverts?'*

Then a woman with her hair scraped back in a Torry face lift. *'Revolting, so it is! It's an utter disgrace!'*

A teenager with more acne than skin, nose like a sharpened pencil. *'Nasty gay—'* Loud bleep. *'—shouldnae ever been allowed out o' prison.'*

Back to the reporter. *'But events escalated this evening, as tensions, already running high, exploded into violence.'*

Another cut: night, snowing. The crowd had thinned down to the hard-core, frozen few. Then someone emerged from off camera, a lit petrol bomb in their hand. It sizzled across the screen, leaving a trail of glowing white, and the camera swung around to watch it explode against the granite wall of Knox's house. The flash was bright enough to overload the camera for a moment, and then it was back in focus, just in time to catch the second bomb being thrown. It burst on the sill of the broken lounge window – sending burning petrol all over the curtains.

'With Knox moved to an undisclosed location, the police are appealing for calm, but it seems unlikely that local anger will be defused so easily.' Another shot of the reporter, staring straight at the camera. *'This is Janet Milton, BBC News, Aberdeen.'*

The screen went blank.

Logan pulled up one side of his headphones. 'How do I rewind?'

'Big black knob to your right.'

The Transit's side door slid open and there was the reporter. She froze, one foot up on the van's floor, thick flakes of white specking her shoulders and hair; nose and ears a deep shade of pink. Her forehead creased. 'Where am I supposed to sit?'

Logan turned his back on her, twisting the big black knob till she appeared on screen again.

'Come *on*, Gavin, this is ridiculous.'

'Shut the door, eh, Janet? Freezing me nuts off here.'

'You're freezing yours off? What about *mine*?'

'There's a thermos in the cab. . .'

Logan stuck the headphones back on and set the report running again. Shutting out the argument.

'But events escalated this evening, as tensions, already running high, exploded into violence.'

The first petrol bomb was too quick – the cameraman didn't catch much more than the rough shape of someone wrapped up in a padded jacket hurling the bottle. But the second time he'd got the camera around in time to catch the thrower centre frame.

Logan hit pause.

It was either a very effeminate man, or a slightly butch woman. Difficult to tell with all the padding. They had a black-and-white bobble hat pulled down over their ears, wisps of dark hair sticking out of the bottom. Eyes screwed up, nose crinkled. A checkered scarf covered the lower half of their face, and they were wearing what looked like a blue North Face jacket – the logo just visible on the left chest – with matching gloves.

So that probably meant no prints on the bottle.

Logan frowned, then took off the headphones and hung them back on the improvised hook. 'Do you have any other shots of who threw the petrol bomb?'

'You're bloody impossible, Gavin! How am I supposed to work under these conditions?' The reporter stormed out and slammed the side door shut.

Gavin rubbed his hands across his face. 'No idea. Maybe in the crowd shots?'

'Any chance you could—'

'Mate, I've got a live bulletin on in ten, a. . .' He lowered his voice, 'A reporter with PMT who won't deliver her bloody lines properly, a dodgy sound desk, and about three thousand other things I've got to do before we hand over to the London studio. What do you think?'

Logan sighed. 'OK, OK. I'll get a warrant.'

The man nodded. 'Good idea. Now, if you don't mind. . .?'

Logan stood off to the side, watching the woman from BBC Scotland doing her live broadcast for the *News at Ten*. 'It's too early to tell yet, Simon, but Grampian Police issued the following statement this afternoon. . .'

Behind her, Knox's house was a blackened shell, steam and thin ribbons of greasy smoke rising from the blackened windows while the Fire Brigade rolled their hoses up.

A fake English accent sounded at Logan's shoulder. ''Allo, 'allo, what's all this then?'

He didn't even have to check. 'Evening Colin.'

The wee reporter rubbed his leather-gloved hands together, the rigid finger joints sticking out at odd angles. 'Brass monkeys, but.'

'Isobel give you a late pass, did she?'

'Why, fancy a pint later?'

'Can't: on the wagon.'

'Fuck me, must be serious.' Colin blew into his cupped, gloved hands, wreathing them in a white cloud. 'Any off-the-record statements you'd like to make for your old mate?'

Logan frowned for a minute. 'Yeah. Can you say: "sources close to the investigation think the media are a bunch of sketchy bastards for standing about filming Knox's house burning down when they should have been calling the Fire Brigade"?'

'Ah. . .' Colin bit his top lip and stared at his shuffling feet. 'It was. . . Well, you always think someone else must've. . . Ahem.'

'Yeah, I'll bet you do.'

Logan hunched his shoulders. Now the fire was out, winter was reclaiming the street.

'You still got Grumpy the Photographer with you?'

'Driving us mental with his moanin'. You'd think he'd be happy to get a nice juicy story like this, wouldn't you? Got to be better than coverin' some crappy cow auction at Thainstone.'

Logan glanced back along the street to where DI Steel was slumped in the passenger seat of a pool car, cigarette smoke drifting out into the frigid night.

'How'd you like to help the police with their enquiries?'

35

The photographer's battered Volkswagen was parked under a streetlight, three doors down from the smouldering remains of Knox's house. Probably moved to keep its delicate rusty bodywork safe from the riot Colin's article had caused. The car's owner was out in the middle of the road, the hood of his parka zipped all the way up, hiding his bald head, a huge camera pressed to the fur-trimmed porthole. Capturing the Fire Brigade's retreat.

Colin made a loud-hailer with his mangled hands. 'Hoy, Sandy, you nearly done?'

The man stayed where he was, taking another shot of a massive white fire engine grumbling and hissing its way out through the police cordon, the flash freezing the snow in midair.

Colin pulled a face. 'God forbid we should interrupt his muse. HOY, BALDY!'

Sandy lowered his camera and turned, scowling away in the depths of his coat. 'Can we fuck off home now?'

'You downloaded everythin' to the laptop yet?'

Shrug. ''Cept this lot. Why?'

'Car keys.' Colin held out a hand.

'Bastard. . .' Sandy rummaged in his pocket, then dropped them into Colin's black-leather palm. 'I'm never getting home, am I?'

Colin grinned. 'I've seen your wife, you should be thankin' me. Now away you go back to your wee photos.'

They climbed into the back of the car, while Sandy stomped off towards the burnt-out house, swearing.

'No pleasing some people.' Colin pointed. 'Laptop should be under the seat in front of you.'

So were a bunch of empty crisp packets, and a couple of crumpled Coke cans . . . Logan's fingers brushed against a flat rectangle of neoprene. He dragged it out and handed it over.

Colin powered the thing up. 'Right, let's see if the wee jobby's actually put them in the right. . . Buggering. . .' His crooked fingers fumbled with the mousepad. 'Fine, sod you.' He hauled his right glove off. The pinkie stopped at the second joint, the finger next to it at the first, the puckered ends shiny and hard looking. He tried again, and the cursor wheeched through the menu structure. 'Here we go.'

The screen filled with the mob gathered outside Knox's house, pinched faces, mouths caught open, screaming abuse, placards waving. It was a good photo, very atmospheric. Sandy might have been a miserable sod, but he knew what he was doing with a camera.

Logan scanned the crowd, looking for a black and white bobble hat. 'Next.'

Colin hit the key and they were looking at the same shot a fraction of a second later. And again. Then another photo of the crowd. The house. A sequence of Knox throwing the curtains wide, then his eyes bulging, then Logan lumbering up in stop motion to drag them shut again. The window shattering. More shots of the crowd.

Logan sat back in his seat. 'Crap. This is going to take *forever*.'

'How's he taking it?'

Standing in the hall, Mandy shrugged. 'Think he misses his electric fire.'

Knox was in the lounge, kneeling in front of the window. Praying. He'd switched off the lights, but a faint yellow glow seeped in from outside, accompanied by the distant hum of traffic on the North Deeside road.

It was a nice little flat, the kind of place they liked to feature on those makeover shows, where the before always looked a hell of a lot better than the after.

Three bedrooms, a galley kitchen, flat-screen telly, and central heating. Bliss.

Harry shifted from foot to foot. 'You want a cup of tea, or something? I'm making anyway, it's no problem?'

'Coffee: black, two sugars.'

Nod. 'Nice to be warm again, isn't it? After that bloody great fridge of a place.'

'The stink of mildew and mould.'

Harry grinned. 'Those mushrooms growing under the kitchen sink.'

'All gone up in flames.'

Silence.

'You know.' Harry worried at a loose button on his shirt. 'Would've thought he'd be a bit more . . . upset. Family home, and all that.'

Mandy stepped back and closed the lounge door. If Knox wanted to sneak off through the lounge window – good luck to him. The flat was on the fourth floor, so the fall would probably break his neck. Save everyone a lot of time and trouble.

She followed Harry through to the kitchen, and watched

319

him fill and boil the kettle. 'I'm still not happy about the security.'

'Yeah, well.' He shrugged. 'They'll get the CCTV installed outside tomorrow. We can manage for one night, right? You want a biscuit?'

'What if there's an auld mannie living next door?'

'Rocky or Caramel Wafer?'

'Got any HobNobs?'

Harry handed over the biscuit tin. 'Even if he gets all horny, he can't *do* anything about it. Not with you and me here, and that pair from the Perv Patrol sitting out. . .' Harry cleared his throat, then pulled on a smile. 'Richard, you want a cuppa?'

Knox was standing in the doorway, wiping his sleeve across his eyes. 'Me mam was born in that house.'

'Mandy's got chocolate bikkies. . .?'

The weedy little man took a deep shuddering breath, then helped himself to an orange Penguin. 'Kind of a relief, like. In a way. . .' He peeled back the wrapper. 'Was tying us to the past, wasn't it? All them ghosts holding us back. . . Yeah. Maybe it's for the best.'

'That's the spirit.' Harry spooned bitter-smelling brown granules into three mugs, then sloshed boiling water over the top. 'Onwards and upwards, eh?'

'You know,' Knox opened the fridge and peered inside, ''stead of takeaway tomorrow I could whip us up a prawn curry if someone nips down the shops? Feels like I haven't had a home-cooked meal in months.'

Mandy nudged the fridge door shut again. 'Maybe later. Need to get stuff organized.'

Knox stared at the vinyl floor for a moment, his cheeks flushing a deep rose pink. Shrug. 'If you like.'

Harry put a hand on his shoulder. 'We're getting another visit from Babs and Paul tomorrow, I'll ask them to swing by Asda on the way: get the prawns and stuff. I like a nice curry, don't you, Mandy?' He stared at her, making his eyes go wide. Like she was supposed to feel guilty about denying Knox his little *MasterChef* moment.

Sometimes Harry could be a bit of a tit.

He nodded, like they'd all agreed it was a *great* idea. 'Right, you let me know what you need, and I'll phone Babs.'

Knox smiled. It made his face even pointier, like a shaved rat. Then he scribbled down a long list of ingredients and handed it over. 'Might as well do it properly like. Not the same if it all comes out of a jar.'

'Sounds good – back in a tick.'

Knox waited till the kitchen door clunked shut. 'You don't like us, do you?'

Mandy shrugged. 'Why do you think that?'

'The way you look at us. Like I'm still inside: a rule forty-three. Dirty fucker, who likes to rape old men.'

'I just want everyone to be safe.'

'That's not me any more. God reached out to us in prison. I was standing there, watching this bloke Rupert bleed to death on the landing, and I was thinking, maybe he's got the right idea, you know? They gave him eight years, cos his home computer was full of photos: little boys getting shagged off the internet. Took a safety razor, snapped it open, and hacked through his veins from elbow to wrist. Couldn't take the shame and the guilt any more. . .'

Knox's eyes were focussed somewhere between the vinyl floor and his knees. Biting his bottom lip.

'Maybe your mate had the right idea.'

'And that's when I heard His voice. "Richard," He says, "Richard you're one of Me creatures, and I love all Me creatures. Doesn't matter what you've done in the past, like, you've got a bit of Us in you. Put you on this earth to do Me work, didn't I? Can't go throwing it all away like this idiot."'

'Thought God spoke all "thee" and "thou", like in the bible.'

Knox looked up, staring straight at her with those rodenty little eyes. 'It's all God's work, isn't it? Everything we do serves His purpose.'

'Even raping old men?'

'War, Famine, Pestilence, Death. He made all them things. Ethnic cleansing, suicide bombers, drought, global warming, AIDS, swine flu, tidal waves, earthquakes. . . If you took everyone who died in the last hundred years, and stacked all the bodies up, it'd reach from here to the moon, four and a half times.' A small smile. 'Not given to us to understand His plans, is it?'

Mandy didn't know who was creepier, Richard Knox or his god.

Julie sits on the end of the hotel bed, feet tucked up under her, watching the telly. It's Sky's twenty-four-hour news thing, some plastic-haired bloke being all serious about the situation in Afghanistan.

Tony takes another swig from his mug, the sharp edge of cheap brandy, turning into instant warmth and sweetness. Think Julie would notice if he helped himself to another wrapper of fizzy coke? Probably. Then there'll be some serious fucking fireworks.

Have to make do with supermarket brandy.

Neil clumps in through the front door, cradling a couple of big brown paper bags from KFC round the corner. The smell of deep-fried chicken wafts out into the cramped room. 'Bloody freezing. . .' He dumps the bags on the bed and wriggles out of his coat.

Julie looks up. 'Sweetheart, you're getting snow all over the carpet.'

'Like Santa's bloody grotto out there.'

She stretches out a foot and wriggles a pink-and-green-polka-dot sock. 'Not wearing any shoes, Darling.'

Neil freezes. Scoops up his coat and hurries into the bathroom. Comes back with a bunch of towels and dumps them on the wet carpet. 'Sorry.'

Tony holds his breath, waiting for it to kick off, but Julie just shrugs and goes back to the telly.

Neil opens one of the bags and peers inside. 'Who wanted corn on the cob?'

Julie holds up her hand and Neil passes her dinner over. 'Thanks, Babe.'

Tony gets a Boneless Banquet For One, with a side of beans. Or the 'Fat Bastard Special' as Neil calls it. Cheeky bugger – he can talk, like.

Neil pulls out a little wax-paper bag full of thin rustling chips and crams a handful into his gob. 'Mmmnngfff, mmmn-nfffif, fffm mmmnnnt?'

'Yeah, Knox phoned about half an hour ago. Her nibs took the call.'

Julie holds up a hand. 'Shhhh!'

That report about Knox's house burning down is on again. Kicks off with someone silhouetted against the flames, chucking a petrol bomb. Placards. Angry faces. Fire engines. Then some local plod bigwig giving a statement about how Grampian Police don't like vigilantes.

Tony sucks the grease off his fingers and takes a swig of the Diet Coke that came with his meal, then tops it up with a good glug of that cheap brandy.

Neil holds out his Sprite. 'Go on then, give us a splash, like.'

'You're designated driver.'

'Aw, come on, that's not—'

'Sweethearts, I'm not going to ask you again.'

Silence.

323

They sit and eat, Tony flicking through Julie's file on Danby with greasy fingers. Looking for an edge. Thinking about the little plastic baggie of wrappers in her handbag.

The piece on Knox goes back to the studio: a photo of him up in the background while some tree-hugging corduroy types get all worked up about why he was there, why he couldn't be left alone, why it was costing so much. . . Blah. Blah. Blah.

And then the weather.

Neil blows his nose on a napkin, getting the Colonel's face all covered in bogies. 'What now?'

Julie clicks the TV doofer, and the screen fades to black. 'Finish up, then we're heading out.' She stands, making for the bathroom, picking her way around the soggy towels on the carpet. 'I'm driving.'

Tony tries not to shudder, then tops up his Coke again. What the hell – he pours a generous measure of cheap brandy into Neil's Sprite as well. Solidarity.

If Julie's driving they'll both need it.

36

Colin jabbed his stumpy ring finger at the screen. 'Hello darlin'. . .'

The woman in the photo had shoulder-length brown curly hair, fierce green eyes, and a ski-jump nose, her face contorted in a snarl. Steam curled from her open lips in the snowy afternoon. She was clutching a placard in her thick blue gloves: 'RAPING SCUM OUT!!!' with a photocopy of Knox's face underneath. Logan scribbled down the filename displayed at the bottom of the screen. 'Right, now we're looking for her friend.'

Colin blew into his naked hand. 'Friend?'

'You try lighting a petrol bomb wearing padded gloves. How do you get the lighter to spark?'

'Aye, well, maybe she—'

'What, took the gloves off, set the wick, lit it, then put her gloves back on to chuck the thing?'

The reporter stared at him. 'You'd be surprised what you get used to when you have to wear gloves all the time.'

Sigh. 'Yes: it was all my fault and I'm sorry. Happy?'

'I'm just—'

'Every damn time. . .' Logan reached over and poked

the laptop's 'next' button a couple of times, flicking through the photographs. 'Anyway, she chucked *two* petrol bombs, there wasn't time to get her gloves off and on between them.' He flicked through to the end of the sequence, then back again.

Someone was standing next to Miss Black-and-White-Bobble-Hat in every single photograph. A young-ish man with the same curly brown hair; the same green eyes; the same snub nose; the same expression on his face.

Lynch mob, a game all the family can play.

Colin leaned forward, staring at the faces. Then gave a low whistle.

'What?'

He pointed at the screen.

'And?'

'Do you lot no' do *any* research?' He tapped the young man right between the eyes. 'That's Ian Leadbetter. See his grandad? Supposed to be one of Knox's earlier victims. What the hell was it. . .' Colin screwed up one side of his face. 'Seventy-six-year-old, Parkinson's, went missin' from a park. Cops found him six hours later on a patch of waste ground, bashed and bruised. Wouldn't talk about it. Wouldn't take a rape kit.'

Another poke. 'The kids' parents were all for keepin' it quiet, but wee Ian here's been shootin' his mouth off to anyone who'll listen. Wants Knox strung up for what he did to his grandad.'

'Any proof?'

'Says the old man saw Knox's picture in the paper when he was released a couple years ago and wouldn't come out of his room for a week. Got blootered a month later and told Ian all about it.'

'He could still make a formal complaint.'

Colin shrugged. 'Bit difficult when you're sittin' in a wee

brass urn on the mantelpiece. Pneumonia, three months ago.'

Good point.

'Can you email me a copy of the photos?'

'Do you one better. . .' Colin dug about in his jacket with his stumpy-fingered hand, and produced a little blue USB stick with 'THE ABERDEEN EXAMINER, SERVING THE NORTH EAST SINCE 1856' printed on the side.

Snoring rattled the windows of the CID pool car. Steel was slumped back in the passenger seat, a dead cigarette butt dangling from her open mouth, stuck to her lower lip – a slug-trail of ash tumbling away down the front of her padded jacket.

Logan tried the door handle.

Locked.

The street was almost deserted: the media hadn't hung around after the fire engines had gone. A burning house was news. A burnt-out shell was *old* news. One by one they'd drifted off till all that was left was Sandy the photographer's antique Volkswagen, and DI Steel's pool car.

Logan tried the door again, just in case it had magically unlocked itself in the last ninety seconds.

It hadn't.

He knocked on the passenger window. Steel jerked upright in her seat, blinking, the cigarette butt still stuck to her bottom lip.

Logan knocked again.

The inspector wiped a hand across her mouth, sending the butt tumbling into her lap, then frowned at him.

'Come on, it's bloody freezing out here!'

She leaned over and opened the driver's door. Logan scrambled in behind the wheel and turned the engine over, then cranked up the heat – treadling the accelerator, trying to get it to warm up faster.

'Was having this really . . . *weird* dream about Gloria Hunniford, and she was wearing this huge black cloak, and carrying a scythe. . .'

Logan held up the little USB drive Colin had given him. 'Got the arsonist and her accomplice on film.'

'And she had this massive red strap-on, and she wanted—'

'You still got that Airwave handset on you?'

Steel blinked again. Then shuddered. 'How long does it take to get hypothermia?'

'Mobile phone'll do.'

Steel passed over her little Nokia, and Logan punched in the number for Control, then waited for someone to pick up at the other end.

'Yeah, I need you to run a PNC check on one Ian Leadbetter, Newcastle, late teens/early twenties. While you're there, see if he's got a sister, or a female cousin.'

'Hud oan a mintie. . .'

He pinned the phone between his shoulder and his ear, flipped his notepad open, and pulled the lid off his biro with his teeth. 'Uh-huh. . .' Scribbling down the details as Control gave him everything the Police National Computer had on Ian and Wendy Leadbetter.

'Right, I need you to get a lookout request on both of them.'

'Fit for?'

'Arson – Richard Knox's house.'

'Oh aye? You sure we shouldnae gie them a medal instead?'

'Just get them picked up.' He snapped the phone shut and handed it back.

'Got any fags?'

'All out.' He clicked on the headlights and pulled away from the kerb, the Vauxhall's wheels crunching through the snow.

'In that case, you can drop us off at home on your way back to the station.'

Logan groaned. 'It's nearly eleven! I'm not going back to the—'

'You've got to sign the pool car back in, you idiot. And while you're at it, check on the search teams. I want to know what else is lurking in Gallagher and Yates' Grotto O'Fun.'

'But—'

'And tell Big Gary I said to put us both down till midnight on the overtime. Got a kid on the way, after all.'

Night-time CID were all gathered around the middle set of desks in the office, drinking tins of Irn-Bru and sharing two coffee-table-sized pizzas, the smell of garlic, tomato and spicy sausage hanging in the air – Detective Inspector Bell handing out the food and telling stories of the good old days.

Logan turned down a slice, and slumped over to the DSs' cubbyhole. Someone had stuck up a sheet of A4 on the wall, with 'THE WEE HOOSE' printed on it. The door was locked.

'Oh for fuck's. . .' He closed his eyes, screwed up his face. Then placed a hand against the wood.

Know what: who cared? Steel would just have to wait for her update. It wasn't as if she could do anything about it till the morning anyway. And at least this way he'd be home before midnight – hopefully to find Samantha still at the flat.

Logan turned on his heel, and the door clunked open behind him.

Crap.

He turned back and pushed through into the little room.

Doreen's desk was as immaculate as ever, Mark's was covered with dusty cardboard boxes from the archives, but

Biohazard Bob's was a disaster area. He was sitting with his back to the door, ruffling a sheaf of paper into some kind of order.

Logan paused. 'You weren't in here playing with yourself, were you, Bob?'

The DS cleared his throat. Didn't look around. 'Just getting caught up on some paperwork.'

'With the door locked?'

Shrug. He ran a hand across his face. 'What you doing here? Thought your shift ended six hours ago.'

'You and me both.' Logan collapsed into his office chair, jabbed a finger at the computer's power button. 'Ding-Dong's got pizza out there if you fancy it?'

Another shrug. 'Not hungry.'

Silence. Just the whirr and bleep of the machine coming online.

'You OK, Bob?'

Pause.

'Yeah. Fine. Never better.'

'OK. . .' Logan logged into the crime management system and called up the Police Search Advisor's contact details, then dug out the Airwave handset from under a pile of junk in his top drawer and punched in her warrant number.

'Aye, just finishing up now – got a couple kilos of heroin in the back of the cottage, and twa bin-bags of ecstasy.'

'What about the IB?'

'Done a wee whilie ago. Now they're awa' building a snowman.'

All right for some. Logan thanked her and hung up, then called the hospital for an update on Norman Yates. Still critical, but stabilizing. Which wasn't bad for someone who'd been shot three times.

Logan cobbled together a quick incident report on the fire at Knox's house, and how they'd identified Ian and Wendy Leadbetter, then sent it off to the printer. While it was chuntering away to itself he called up his emails and checked to see if anything interesting had come in.

Couple of memos. A new directive about Stop And Search procedures. Something from DC Rennie inviting him to a stag night in Amsterdam at the end of the month. One from a DI in Northumbria Police, saying they'd been to see Knox's cellmate, Oscar Renwick, in Frankland Prison about the four house-fire murders Logan had identified. Renwick had been up for probation in three weeks, but with this on the go, it looked as if he'd be waiting at least another sixteen years before he set foot in the real world again. And the DI would be writing to Aberdeen's Chief Constable to tell him how it wouldn't have been possible without Logan's help.

Logan grinned: result.

Then there were a couple from someone offering to 'EMBIGGEN YOURE TROUSER BEAST AND THE WOMENS WILL QUEUING UP!'

And right at the bottom, an email from Beattie, CC'd to Dildo and the woman from HMRC, saying how pleased he was they'd made so much progress at the meeting that afternoon. So the rats in the basement hadn't eaten him alive. Shame. . .

Logan closed his eyes. 'Bugger.' He'd forgotten to call Dildo about Gallagher and Yates. Too late now. He scribbled himself a note and stuck it on his monitor, then powered the computer down and grabbed the sheets of paper from the printer. He stopped with one hand on the door knob. 'You *sure* you're OK, Bob?'

'What are you, my mum now?' Bob turned around for the first time, eyes red-rimmed and swollen. A forced smile. 'Go on, sod off home. Give that redhead IB tech of yours a good seeing to from me.'

Logan didn't answer that.

*　　*　　*

He pushed into the flat and flicked on the hall light. Silence. The whole place was in darkness. 'Sod. . .' He peered into the bedroom, closed his eyes, sighed, then shut the door, gently. Samantha was still there. She hadn't abandoned him for her static caravan.

At least that was something.

He dumped his coat on the hook and wandered into the kitchen. Stared at the contents of the fridge for a while, before helping himself to a tin of Irn-Bru. Opening it on the way through to the lounge.

Maybe watch a little telly to help him unwind.

The curtains were drawn, the only light coming from the LEDs on the TV and PlayStation, and the blinking one on the answering machine.

Logan closed his eyes and groaned.

Probably Steel. Or even worse – his mother. He took a scoof of vaguely fruity fizzy juice and hit the button.

'MESSAGE ONE: *Hello, Logan, it's Hamish. I—*'

'Fuck!' A mouthful of sticky Irn-Bru sprayed out over the sideboard.

Logan scrabbled for the volume control, turning it down in case Samantha woke up and heard Aberdeen's biggest crime lord leaving a message ON HIS BLOODY ANSWERING MACHINE.

He squatted down and hit play again.

'MESSAGE ONE: *Hello, Logan, it's Hamish. I notice you've not done anything with your money yet.*'

Oh *fuck*. What the hell was Wee Hamish Mowat thinking?

'*It's important for the local economy that we all do our bit, don't you think? Don't leave it too long, eh? Oh, and do let me know if you need any more.*'

Beeeeeeep.

'END OF MESSAGES.'

He flipped open the cover and hauled the little cassette

out. What if someone found out? What if Samantha picked up his messages? How the FUCK was he supposed to explain it?

He dug his fingernails into the cassette, tugging out the tape and unreeling the whole thing until there was a spaghetti mess of shiny brown-black ribbon curled across the sticky sideboard. Then dropped the plastic case and stomped on it.

Still not enough. The IB could just wind it back onto another cassette.

Logan scooped the lot up and carried it through to the kitchen, dumped it into the empty sink, then went rummaging through the cupboards for the methylated spirit and drenched the lot.

Better be on the safe side. . .

He tore a dozen pages out of that morning's *Press and Journal* and mixed them through the slippery mess, before throwing the window open and dragging out his lighter.

Whooomp: the stainless steel sink filled with purple-blue flame, the newspaper crackling as the tape melted and shrank. Until there was nothing left but curls of ash, a lump of brittle plastic slag, and a gnawing coldness in the depths of Logan's stomach.

37

Our Father who art in heaven.

Just six words, like, but they're true. Richard Knox places a hand against the doorway, stands there quietly, looking into the bathroom. Three o'clock in the morning, and all the lights in the flat are off. Except for this one.

Richard's da's in heaven – had himself a bit of an accident, didn't he? With a length of metal pipe over the back of the head. On his knees in a vacant warehouse, blood pouring from his shattered mouth, making gurgling noises. Sobbing. Trying to kid on he was really sorry, you know? Like he didn't mean to run out on Richard and his mam. That it wasn't his fault.

Mandy from Sacro's on her knees too. Gripping onto the toilet bowl. Heaving and retching. Bile spattering from her open mouth. Not caring she's getting sick on her hair.

'Are you all right?'

She waves a hand, without looking up. 'I'm fine. . . I just. . . I. . . Oh shite—' She heaves again, spine humping as the sound echoes back from the toilet bowl.

It's a crappy modern flat, in a crappy modern development, walls and carpets the same colour as prison porridge.

334

Mandy groans, then gives the toilet another mouthful.

Richard's eyes drift down to the rolling pin in his hand. It's no lead pipe, but it'll work just as well. Only Christian to put someone out of their misery, like. . .

There's a fine mist of red on his face. Tiny red dots.

His arm aches. Wrist throbbing.

Richard pushes open the door to the third bedroom. Harry's there, lying curled up under the covers, face all pale and glistening. The room stinks of sour sweat.

Richard flicks on the light.

Harry gives a little moan in protest and sticks a hand over his eyes. Poor lamb. All helpless and defenceless. Richard could do whatever he wanted, and no one could stop him.

Been a long time.

There's clothes spread all over the floor: jeans, jumper, shirt, towels. . . Hasn't even been here twenty-four hours, like, and already the place is a tip.

'Please . . . you need to call . . . call a doctor. . .' Voice all slurred and blurry.

Richard licks his lips, they taste of copper pennies.

Course Harry's a bit young, isn't he? Bit podgy. Not quite Richard's type. Still. . .

Been a long, *long* time.

He steps inside. 'Hey Harry, not feeling so well?'

Harry forces a smile. 'Something didn't . . . didn't agree with . . . with me.'

Richard smiles back. 'It's called Flunitrazepam, you know? Rohypnol? Takes everyone different, like. Your mate Mandy's in the bathroom spewing her ring. Sometimes happens if you take it with alcohol – think she's a secret drinker?'

He closes the door. Not that Mandy's going to interrupt them, just . . . well, modesty and that.

'Rohyp. . .?'

'AKA: the date rape drug.'

Richard steps towards the bed, unfastening his belt. Then the secret mobile phone he's not supposed to have bleeps. Got a new text message. All it says is: 'DOWNSTAIRS.'

He checks his watch. Twenty minutes early.

Richard shuffles to the front window and peers out at the street, four stories below. There's a big black car sitting in the car park at the back of the flats, its hot exhaust pluming out into the cold night air.

'Sorry Harry. Love to stay and get better acquainted, like, but me lift's here.'

Twenty minutes. . .

Maybe they'll wait?

38

'Fuck.' This was no way to start a Tuesday morning. Half past eight and the day was already ruined. Logan puffed back up the eight flights of stairs to the fourth floor, then stood at the top, wheezing and dizzy. *Got* to cut back on the fags.

He straightened up and shambled through the door into the corridor.

Knox's new flat was part of a huge, ugly development – a long winding terrace that looked more like municipal buildings from the 1970s than modern housing. A developer's dream: build them cheap, pile them high, and charge a fortune.

There were six flats on the fourth floor, all leading off the main corridor. Alpha Three Nine were second on the scene, so they'd been given the task of going door-to-door, stopping people from getting to work. That and blocking off the elevator with 'POLICE' tape.

DI Steel was slouched against the wall outside Knox's new flat, having a scratch.

Logan waved the plastic packages he'd dug out of the pool car's boot at her. 'Smurf time.'

She stuck her hand out. 'Give.'

They struggled into the white paper oversuits, Logan hopping about like an idiot. Bloody shoes never went down the legs properly, did they? He fought his arms into the sleeves, hauled the hood into place, and zipped the thing up, from groin to chin, then slipped the blue plastic booties on. The elasticated facemask went on over his nose and mouth, he pulled on a pair of purple nitrile gloves, and finished off by sticking a second pair over the top of those.

DI Steel hauled her own zip up and stood there: booted and suited, masked and gloved, just like he was. She sniffed. 'It's what all the best-dressed people are wearing this season.'

Logan knocked on the door.

PC Irvine from the Offender Management Unit opened it, wearing the same protective clothing. She made them sign in before she'd even let them over the threshold.

Steel picked her way into the hall and Logan followed, avoiding a dark smudge on the oatmeal-coloured carpet in case it was evidence. 'Any word on the ambulance?'

'Should've been here five minutes ago.' Irvine pointed a shaky hand at the bathroom. 'She's in there.'

Logan peered through the open door. Mandy from Sacro lay on the bathroom floor, her curly brown hair matted to her head with something dark and sticky. A pool of red on the linoleum beneath her. Spatters up the cream tiles, a misting of pink on the underside of the hand basin. 'Bloody hell. . .'

Someone had arranged her in the recovery position. And if Logan stared hard, he could just make out her chest rising and falling.

Irvine nodded. 'Paul and me got here about quarter past eight to run through the matrix again. No answer when we knocked, so we gave it a couple of minutes, tried phoning. Nothing. Paul used the spare key.'

Steel cleared her throat. 'Where's the other one?'

'Second bedroom from the end.' She glanced down the hall. 'Can't believe we bought prawns for him.'

The room was small, a double bed crammed in against the wall, an upturned bedside cabinet, a wicker chair lying cracked and bashed next to it. The eye-nipping, throat-catching, bitter reek of vomit and urine.

'Oh, Jesus. . .'

Harry, the other Sacro volunteer, was tied facedown on the bed, a stack of pillows under his groin propping his backside up in the air. Naked. Blood caking the sheets around his ruined face, his back covered in scarlet welts, bite marks, cigarette burns.

Steel blinked. Voice muffled by the mask. 'Is he. . .?'

'He's alive.'

The inspector turned and smacked PC Irvine on the chest. 'Then why the bloody hell haven't you untied him! Fuck is *wrong* with you?'

'But we don't have a camera, and the crime scene—'

'FUCK THE CRIME SCENE!' Steel stormed into the room, grabbed the T-shirt tying Harry's right ankle to the bedpost and hauled.

'Inspector, I really don't think this is a good—'

'He's been raped, you bloody idiot!' Steel yanked on the T-shirt again. 'Laz, into the kitchen: get me a pair of scissors, knife, something.'

'But—'

'NOW!'

Logan ran through the house, plastic booties slipping on the vinyl floor. He rummaged through the drawers, grabbed a pair of kitchen scissors and a box of freezer bags. Then hurried back to the bedroom.

Steel was kneeling on the floor next to the bed. 'What's his name?'

'Er. . .' Constable Irvine glanced at Logan and back again. 'Harry. Harry Weaver. He used to be a—'

'Harry? Can you hear me, Harry?'

Logan stopped at the foot of the bed. 'Anyone got a camera on their mobile?'

'Yeah, but it's not—'

'Harry? It's going to be OK.'

'Better than no photos at all, right?'

Irvine unzipped the front of her oversuit and reached inside, coming out with some sort of fancy touch-screen thing, then zipped herself up again. 'Right. . .'

She stepped up and held the phone out, pressed something and it went *Click*, a little burst of flash. Another click, another flash.

'Does it do video?'

She nodded. 'You can upload to Facebook and—'

'Just video the bloody scene.'

'Harry? Come on, Harry, you're safe now.'

'Oh. . . Right.'

Logan pointed at the T-shirt with his scissors. 'Close up.'

Irvine did what she was told, then Logan carefully cut through the shirt where it looped around Harry's ankle. 'Other leg.'

'Harry? Come on, speak to me, Harry!'

'Wrists. . .'

Finally the naked man was free.

There was a muffled groan.

'Harry? Can you hear me? You're safe now.'

His eyes were swollen shut, the skin around them purple and deformed, his nose crooked, the lower half of his face smeared with dark-red clots.

'He's got something in his mouth. . .' PC Irvine stuck her phone in his face, till Steel batted her away, leaving scarlet smears on her white oversuit.

The inspector cupped one hand around Harry's forehead, supporting it while she pulled a matted lump of black from his mouth. Logan popped open one of the freezer bags.

'What are you playing at?'

'Didn't have any evidence ones with me.'

She dropped the gag in, then jerked back from the bed, as Harry retched – blood and bile spattering out across the stained sheets.

'Fuck.'

Someone knocked on the front door. 'Hello? Anyone in?'

Logan stepped out into the hall. A pair of sweaty paramedics were puffing and panting in the corridor outside. One wiped a hand across his forehead and scowled. 'You the funny bastard taped off the lifts?'

'Erm. . .'

'Any idea how much one of these bloody stretcher bed things weighs?'

'Well . . . could've been worse, I suppose.' DS Mark MacDonald swivelled his chair back and forth a couple of times. 'I mean, they're both still alive, right?'

The Wee Hoose was quiet, just Mark and Logan in the little walled-off area, with the door shut, muting the sounds from the busy CID office. Phones going, people bustling about trying to look busy, the occasional bout of shouting. The predictable aftermath of something going seriously wrong.

Mark nodded at the room outside. 'Media briefing at eleven. You going?'

'Not if I can help it.' Logan took the whiteboard eraser and scrubbed off the counterfeit goods investigation. One less thing to worry about.

'Don't blame you. Finished that big fraud case yesterday, so Finnie's got me down for "Information Support".' Mark took another sip at his coffee. 'I bloody *hate* media briefings, like feeding time at the zoo. . . And all the animals are bastards.'

Logan went back to his desk and checked his email again. Success: the big IB lab on Nelson Street had rushed through the DNA from the bite marks on Harry Weaver's back and thighs. Their report was full of the usual disclaimers and bet-hedging, but right at the bottom was the bit Logan wanted: the DNA was a ninety-nine-point-nine-eight percent match for Richard Knox. Not only that, the bite pattern was iden-tical to the teeth marks they had on file from William Brucklay, Knox's Newcastle victim.

Not exactly unexpected news, but everything that tied Knox to the attack helped.

The rest of the forensic evidence was still being examined – fibres in the bedroom, the soil from a partial footprint in the hallway, something that looked like tears on the back of the victim's thighs.

Logan turned back to Mark. 'You talked to Bob recently?'

'Biohazard?' The DS shuddered. 'Not since he had that curried mackerel. Jesus, we should get danger money.'

'You think he's OK?'

Frown. 'What's he done?'

Logan shrugged. 'It's probably nothing. . .' He swivelled back to his computer. A pile of statements took up most of his desk – the firearms team accounting for what had happened last night and why they'd felt it necessary to shoot Norman Yates three times in the chest. Logan had checked – they all matched, but not in a way that screamed 'cover up!' Yates had shot a police officer – it was his own stupid fault.

The statements went into an internal mail envelope, along with his own report, and marked for the attention of DI Steel. With the statements out of the way, there was a rare clear patch on Logan's desk. The Post-it note about phoning

Dildo first thing sat right in the middle of it, staring up at him. Must have fallen off his monitor. Damn.

Logan picked up the phone and dialled Dildo's extension at Trading Standards, flicking through the rest of his emails as it rang.

The worst was from Professional Standards: Douglas Walker's estate-agent lawyer had made another official complaint. Apparently his client had been 'subjected to undue harassment and unwarrantedly heavy-handed interrogation techniques'. Would Logan care to comment?

Yes. Two words: 'get' and 'fucked'.

It wasn't even as if they'd made a special case of the art student. Just interviewed him once on Friday, stuck him in the cells for the weekend, then had a final crack at him before he went up before the Sheriff on Monday. How the hell was that, 'undue harassment'?

'*Tim Mair, how can I—*'

'Dildo, it's Logan. We—'

'*Did you get my email?*'

'Er. . .' He skimmed through the next few – and there it was, from Dildo's official email address, sent about an hour ago and completely ignored. 'Yeah, got it right here. . .'

'*What do you think?*'

It was some sort of proposal for two-man teams to stake out various dodgy pubs in Aberdeen, looking for people selling counterfeit goods. 'Yes, very good. Very . . . thorough.'

'*Cool. We can start with—*'

'Actually, Tim, I've been meaning to call you.'

Silence. '*Did you just call me "Tim"?*' Dildo swore. '*Come on, what have you done?*'

'No, it's—'

'*You've bloody done something, haven't you? What is it? What the hell have you lumbered me with this time?*'

'Nothing like that: we arrested a couple of guys late last

343

night. . .' He filled Dildo in on the details, leaving out the fact that they'd known about Gallagher and Yates all day. 'So, you see, we don't need to do the undercover thing. It's all taken care of.'

There was a groan. *'You mean I attended that sodding awful meeting with Beardy the Boy Cretin for nothing?'*

'Well . . . sort of, but—'

'You knew all the time, didn't you? I had to pull in bloody huge favours to get Susanna there, and all the time, you knew!'

'It wasn't. . . Look, the stuff's in a barn out by Balmedie.'

He gave Dildo the address to go pick it all up, then the Trading Standards officer hung up, but not until after some choice swearwords.

Bugger. That was going to take more than a tin of biscuits to sort out.

He was writing up his notes from Knox's flat when the door thumped open and DCI Finnie stalked into the room, bringing with him the sound of phones ringing and general pandemonium.

'Ah, McRae.' The head of CID pulled a newspaper from a manila folder and thumped it down on Logan's desk. The banner headline, 'Rapist "Victim's" Family Strike Back' stretched across the front page, above a photo of Wendy Leadbetter hurling the second petrol bomb into Knox's house. 'Would you care to tell my *why* the *Aberdeen Examiner* knows who the arsonists are before we do?'

'Actually, sir, we've had a lookout request on Ian and Wendy Leadbetter since late last night. In fact, it was Mr Miller who helped me identify them. I filed a report and—'

'Oh really? Well, why didn't you say so? That's just spiffing. Can't see why *anyone* would have a problem with *that*. And tell me, Sergeant McRae, you didn't think to put some sort of embargo on the details?'

'I. . .' No, he hadn't. Logan cleared his throat. 'Well, perhaps this will help us pick them up? If people see them in the . . . paper.'

Mark made a big show of going back to his burglary forms.

'And while we're on the subject of "the paper".' Finnie flipped through the pages, until he came to a full page spread: 'Counterfeit Cash Threatens Local Economy'.

Logan looked up at the DCI. 'Well, it's not—'

'Tell me, Sergeant McRae, how *clever* are Grampian Police going to look when it gets out that the only suspect we had was released on bail yesterday, and we *still* don't have a clue where this stuff is coming from? Hmm? Think the local media are going to run a two-page spread on how great we are? Or will they tell everyone we're a bunch of incompetent amateurs?'

'But it's—'

'Oh, and I see from the crime board,' he pointed at the whiteboard with all the DSs' names on it, and their list of open cases, 'that the counterfeit cash job is one of *yours*.'

'I've been—'

'Where are we with the investigation?'

Logan glanced round at Mark, but he had his head down over his keyboard. No help there.

'It's been deprioritized.'

'Deprioritized?' Pause. 'I see. And what about all the other cases you're currently not solving, have *they* been "deprioritized" too? Have you "deprioritized" the armed robbery at Henderson's Jewellers? Because I think it might be kind of *fun* if you actually managed to solve that one, don't you?'

And then he made Logan go through each of the cases on the board under his name.

Jewellery heist: no progress.

Counterfeit money: no progress.

Stolen cars: no progress.

Cemetery flasher: no progress.

OAP burglaries: no progress. . .

The list went on, and on, but the result was always the same: no progress.

'I see.' Finnie pursed his wide, rubbery lips. 'And if you were me, Sergeant, what would *you* do?'

Logan's chin came up. 'I'd maybe wonder why one of my team was being given so many cases to work on. I'd ask how he was supposed to get anything done with a work-load that big. Sir.'

Finnie nodded. 'Hmm. . . And yet you've still found time to help Northumbria Police with one of their unsolved crimes from twenty years ago?'

Bloody hell. Only Finnie could make solving the murder of an entire family sound like a bad thing.

'Perhaps, *Sergeant*, you'd find it a little easier to deal with your own caseload if you weren't so busy helping others with *theirs*. Do you think?' The DCI poked the newspaper again. 'You're supposed to be a detective sergeant. Get out there and *detect something*!' And then Finnie was gone, slamming the door behind him.

Logan collapsed into his seat. 'Christ. . .'

Mark sniffed. 'Don't mind Finnie. His arse is knitting buttons because Knox is missing. Give it a couple of weeks and it'll all blow over.' The DS shook his head. 'Why didn't you tell him about all the dodgy goods you seized last night?'

'Didn't get the chance.' Every time he'd tried, Finnie had moved on to the next stalled case.

'Word to the wise – *never* take a case off the board till Finnie's there to see you do it.'

Logan made a few calls – chasing up the investigations Finnie had moaned about – then sodded off to the canteen for a cup of coffee and a sticky bun.

Biohazard Bob had taken a table by the window, gazing out at the grey lump of the mortuary on the other side of the rear podium car park.

Logan settled in beside him. 'Please tell me that's not beans on toast. . .'

Bob shrugged and shovelled in another mouthful. 'Why should I be the only bastard suffering?'

There was a pause. 'OK, I'll bite.'

'You're looking at the lucky recipient of *another* junkie drug dealer with the shite kicked out of him. They found the poor sod about one this morning – nearly died of hypothermia. Which brings us to my next moment of joy.' He scooped up more beans and chewed as if they were poisonous. 'You remember Big Willie, the tramp used to hang about on George Street, occasionally getting his knob out for the tourists? Turned up behind the recycling bins at Sainsbury's, stiff as a board. Got his post mortem in twenty minutes.'

'Yeah?' Logan took a sip of coffee. 'Well, *I* just got my arse handed to me by Finnie for solving a twenty-year-old murder in Newcastle.'

Bob picked up his milky tea and held it out. 'I hereby call to order, the inaugural meeting of the World's a Bag of Shite Club.'

They clinked mugs and drank.

Bob cleared his throat. 'I think . . . Deborah's having an affair.'

Silence.

'You sure?'

'She's out all the time, she's never interested in sex. . . Won't even get undressed if I'm in the room.' He ran a hand across the bald patch at the back of his head. 'Then there's the secret phone calls. Cryptic messages on the machine.'

'Well . . . maybe. . .' Logan blew a breath at the ceiling. Searching. 'Maybe you should talk to her?'

A short, bitter laugh. 'What if she says "yes"? I can't—'

'God, you're a happy looking pair of monkeys.'

Logan looked up to see Samantha standing over him, carrying a tray of wax-paper cups and tinfoil parcels. She slid the tray onto the table, then plonked herself down in the seat opposite.

Today's outfit was black jeans, black boots, and a black hoodie top over a Ragamuffin T-shirt, her scarlet hair sticking out at improbable angles. Her smile looked forced, the cheerful voice a little strained. As if she was trying too hard. 'So come on, what's up? Did naughty Mrs Steel touch you two and make you feel dirty?'

Bob patted her hand. 'Sammy, my dear, if you *ever* get tired of this pudding-faced loser, I'll happily abandon the wife and kids for you. OK, so I'm not the prettiest, but I make up for it with an unfeasibly large dick and ear-breathing techniques.'

'I'll keep that in mind.' She stole a scoof of Logan's coffee. 'Urgh, that's cold. Listen, I got the results back on that second batch of forged notes you dropped off. Fingerprints aren't up to much, but if you can get me a printing press I can match the ink.'

'If I ever come up with a suspect I'll let you know.'

Samantha sat back. 'Boy, you do have a dose of the dark-and-moodies, don't you?'

'Been one of those days. . .' Mistake.

When was the last time you came home and said something positive?

He cleared his throat. 'Well, it's . . . you know.' He tried a smile. 'This Knox thing's just getting to me a bit.'

Bob held out his tea again. 'Welcome to the World's a Bag of Shite Club.'

348

'No thanks, I'm what you'd call a happy-go-lucky kind of goth.' She stood and picked up her tray again.

'If it makes you feel any better, I hear on the grapevine that our home-grown counterfeit twenties are being spotted as far away as Carlisle. Who says local business can't make a difference?'

Great, so now Cumbria Constabulary would be moaning to Aberdeen's Chief Constable, who'd pass it on, till it dolloped onto Logan's head in a great steaming pile. Hurrah.

'God. . . Now you look even worse.' A frown creased her forehead, making the piercing in her eyebrow sparkle. 'Listen, Knox escaping: it wasn't your fault.'

'Doesn't help Harry Weaver, though, does it? Poor bastard was tied to the bed, beaten and raped.'

'No he wasn't.'

'I was there, I *saw* him. Covered in burns and bites and—'

'No, I mean he wasn't raped. They did the tests up at the hospital and it came back negative. No semen, no lubricant, no anal bruising. Looks like your boy Knox couldn't get it up. Probably explains why he went to town on the burning and biting.'

Bob held up a finger. 'Maybe it's because Harry Weaver wasn't old enough? Knox likes oldies, yes?'

Samantha reached out, grabbed Bob's finger, and pulled. 'Got to go.' Then ran away, giggling.

Logan shrank back as the smell of rotten eggs wafted out from under the table. 'Bob! You dirty—'

The canteen doors banged open. DI Beattie stormed in, paused for a second, then bellowed, 'MCRAE! MY OFFICE! NOW!'

39

Finnie was already in there, sitting in one of the visitor's chairs, thumbing away at his BlackBerry as Logan stepped into Beattie's office, still carrying his mug of coffee.

The bearded DI stomped round behind the desk and sat, glowering. 'Well?'

Logan stared back at him. 'Well what?'

'Sergeant McRae.' Finnie slipped his little email/phone thing back in its leather case. 'Tell me, did I *imagine* it, or did we not have a talk about being a team player?'

'No, you got Steel to do it.'

The head of CID raised an eyebrow and pursed those thick rubbery lips. 'I see. . . Tell me, Sergeant, do you have some sort of alternative definition of the term "Team Player?" In the *wonderful* world of Logan McRae, does it mean something entirely different? Hmm?'

Logan folded his arms. 'What's he told you?'

'Don't you dare!' Beattie thumped a fist on the desktop. 'The counterfeit goods were *my* case, and you damn well knew it. I spent a lot of time and effort putting that meeting together yesterday, and what do I find when I come in this morning? You arrested someone last night – you had a suspect the whole time and didn't even bother telling me!'

'Is that *it*? You didn't arrange a bloody thing yesterday, I had to set it all up.'

'That's not—'

'All you did was turn up with that awful PowerPoint presentation and make an idiot of yourself!'

Beattie went pink, trembled, then turned to Finnie. 'You see what I have to put up with?'

'Oh, grow up.'

The DI jumped to his feet. 'Don't you tell me to grow up! *I* am your superior officer, and it's about time you bloody learned that!'

Finnie steepled his fingers and tapped them against his chin. '*Well*, Sergeant?'

'No. You know what? I'm sick and tired of being a chew-toy in this sodding department. You want to know why I didn't tell you about Gallagher and Yates? Ask Steel, she was down as SIO last night – go bust *her* hump for a change!'

There was silence.

Beattie: 'I *demand* that Sergeant McRae—'

Finnie: 'That's hardly—'

Logan: 'Blow it out your—'

'Hoy!' Steel stood in the doorway, mobile phone clamped to her chest. 'Keep it down, some of us are trying to work here.' She nodded at Finnie. 'Morning, Guv, nice tie: didn't know the circus was in town. You'll no' mind if I borrow McRae here, will you? Need him for the Knox media briefing.'

'But. . . With. . .' Spittle fell into Beattie's beard. 'This is *exactly* what I'm talking—'

'I'll leave you to it.' She grabbed Logan by the sleeve and hauled him out of the office, closing the door behind them.

*   *   *

'. . .always have to be such a pain in the arse?' Logan feathered the brakes, turning the CID pool car into the entrance to Cairnview Terrace. The road was like glass – all that water the Fire Brigade pumped into the place had frozen overnight, covering the tarmac in a thick layer of ice.

'Give it a rest, eh? Doing my head in.' Sitting in the passenger seat, Steel stared out of the window. 'Are detective sergeants this bad down in Newcastle?'

'Always.' Danby's deep, bass rumble filled the car from the back. 'What about the CCTV cameras?'

'Don't ask. Bloody things were meant to be installed before Knox moved in. "Technical difficulties" my fruit-flavoured arsehole. Idiots in the surveillance van weren't much better – thing was parked the wrong way round. Knox probably walked right past them, and they never even blinked. Should've heard the bollocking they got; thought one of them was going to cry.'

The song on the radio ended, and the DJ announced that the news was coming right up, after these messages.

Danby drummed his fingers on the back of Logan's seat. 'Search teams?'

'Somewhere between sod and bugger all. Got lookout requests on the go with every force in the UK, emailed posters to every port, airport and bus terminal. . .' Steel shrugged. 'I'm no' holding my breath, though. If our wee raping tossbag's sitting on X-million quid's worth of gangster's money he'll be away on a fake passport to the Costa del Pervert by now.'

Logan sniffed. 'That or he's holed up somewhere torturing someone's grandfather. . .'

'God, you're a wee ray of sunshine today, aren't you?'

Logan just grunted, trying to keep the car from mounting the pavement as it slithered to a halt outside the burnt shell of Knox's house.

'Ooh, here we go.' Steel reached out and turned up the radio.

'. . .angry scenes. Grampian Police issued this statement.'

DCI Finnie's voice crackled out. '*Richard Knox is considered* extremely *dangerous. If anyone sees him, they should call nine-nine-nine immediately, do not, under* any *circumstances approach him, or try to apprehend him yourself.*'

There was an explosion of questions, all shouted at once:

'*Chief Inspector! Why did Grampian Police allow him to escape?*'

'*What are you doing to recapture Knox?*'

'*Are the public at risk?*'

'*Is it true he raped one of the team supervising him?*'

A cut, then Finnie was back, '*. . .want to assure you that we're doing everything we can to bring Richard Knox back into custody as quickly as possible.*'

Then the radio moved on to a piece about all the traffic accidents caused by the snow.

'Bloody media.' Steel stabbed the off button. 'How come they use everything Finnie said? Where the hell was *my* bit?'

At least she'd had a bit – all Logan had done was stand at the back, like a spare fart.

The car rocked as Danby popped the back door and clambered out, then picked his way carefully towards what was left of Knox's house.

Logan killed the engine. 'You've got to speak to Finnie about Beattie.'

'Screw the pair of them.' She dug out a packet of cigarettes and offered Logan one.

'It's all right for *you*, I'm the one getting hauled up for doing what you sodding told me!'

'OK, OK, I'll talk to him. Honestly: moan, bitch, whinge.' She opened her door, put one foot on the road, gave a little squeak, and ended up flat on her back. 'Buggering turd-burglars. . .'

Logan clambered out, inched around to the other side of the car, and hauled her to her feet. 'Serves you right.'

'Don't push it.' Her cigarette was bent like a dog's leg. She spat it out onto the ice. 'Should be off tanning my white bits on some sun-drenched beach, not looking after ungrateful bastard detective sergeants.'

'You want me to let go again?'

'Do it and I'll kill you. . .'

They crab walked to the kerb, then shuffled their way across the slippery pavement and in through the front gate. Knox's house was barely recognizable. The roof had gone, the walls were blackened and stained, windows missing, chunks of charred timber sticking up from the rubble, everything topped with a layer of snow.

Danby was standing in the hallway, hands in his pockets, breath steaming out around his big pink head.

Steel lit another cigarette, hissing the smoke out between her teeth. 'Still don't see what this is supposed to accomplish.'

'Walking the ground.' Danby held out a hand, as if blessing the fire scene. 'No point going back to the flat he disappeared from: wasn't even there twenty-four hours. This is where his roots are, know what I'm saying?'

Logan stepped across the threshold into what used to be the lounge. Blackened chunks and lumps, a scattering of slates from the roof. Humped shapes that could have been the remains of the sofa, or bits of collapsed ceiling – it was impossible to tell. The place stank of melted plastic and bitter charcoal. 'Don't think his roots exist any more. They've all burned.'

There was a deep sigh. 'That's what I'm worried about. The only place he's got left now is his mother's old house in Newcastle. Don't think we really want him back. At least when we knew where the filthy little bastard was we could keep an eye on him, but now. . .'

Logan nudged a twisted metal shape with the toe of his shoe. Took a moment to realize it was the three-bar electric fire Knox prayed to every day.

'Pfffff. . . Sod this: it's too cold to be buggering about outside.' Steel jammed her hands in her armpits. 'You two can commune with the spirit of Pocahontas all you like – I'm going back to the car.'

Logan looked up and watched Danby haul a section of metal pipe from the rubble and start poking.

On his own in a strange city, surrounded by ruins.

The car door clunked shut, leaving them alone.

'Why are you *really* here?'

Danby didn't turn around. 'Told you – Knox has info on Mental Mikey's operation.'

'You hate him, and he hates you. Why would he tell you anything?'

'He'll be heading south.' The metal pole poked into a mound of something that disintegrated. 'We need to start pulling in the local perverts, see if he contacted any of them for help, know what I'm saying? I'll get my team to do the same in Newcastle.'

Logan just stared at him.

Silence.

Another sigh. 'Billy Adams was my friend, and that . . . and Knox killed him.'

'Thought Knox was in prison when Adams killed himself.'

'Nah, he didn't stick the gun in Billy's mouth, or pull the trigger, but he might as well have done. See I got Knox on the forensic evidence from William Brucklay, but how do you think I knew to look at him in the first place?'

Logan frowned. 'You said Adams heard rumours Mental Mikey's accountant was into—'

'I knew because he raped Billy. Must've found out he wasn't really on the take – or Billy slipped up somewhere – but Knox had him in that basement for three days. I saw him after he escaped, bruised to hell, back all covered with bite marks and cigarette burns.' Danby let the metal pole clatter to the ground. 'Wouldn't talk about it, wouldn't press charges, wouldn't even let me tell anyone. And three months after we put Knox away for what he did to William Brucklay, Billy drove off into the middle of nowhere with a shotgun. . .'

The DSI kicked a lump of charcoaled wood down the hall. '*That's* why I'm here. So that bastard Knox can't get away with it again.'

The old man screams, high pitched and angry. 'Aya, fucking poof bastard!'

Richard Knox bites him again – on the buttocks, hard enough to break the skin, tears rolling down his face. Then he does it again.

Doesn't have any choice, does he? Like with that prat Harry from Sacro: doesn't *want* to do it, but has to.

Cos this is the path God has chosen for him.

'AAAAAAAGH. . .!'

The room's cold, a crappy little bedroom in a crappy little house out in the countryside, surrounded by sheep and snow. It's got puffy patterned wallpaper – painted a rancid-butter yellow – and a double bed with one of them tartan blankets on top, scratchy beneath Richard's naked skin.

Maybe it's the old man's house. Maybe he was just visiting. Doesn't really matter, does it?

'AAAAAAAGH. . . *Fuck* that *hurts*!'

It's a test. Has to be: another test from God.

Richard stifles a sob, face pressed against the old man's thigh, and bites down hard.

40

'Any luck?'

Steel didn't look up from the paperwork heaped on her desk. 'Bugger all.'

Fair enough.

Logan added another couple of sheets to the pile. 'I got them to pull all the security camera footage for any business within half a mile of the Sacro flat, like Danby wanted. No sign of Knox.'

Steel was a dead jellyfish in her chair, staring at the ceiling tiles, limbs hanging loose. 'Finnie's going mental, the newspapers and TV are milking it like a pregnant hoor, peasants are revolting, and we've still got sod all clue where Knox is.'

'You speak to Finnie and Beattie yet?'

'Susan won't talk to me, my career's a used sodding tampon, I've got itchy bits, and I'm out of fags.' Scowl. 'If there is a God, He's a rotten bastard.'

Logan dug out a packet of Silk Cut and chucked it onto the desk. 'I'm cutting down.'

She just flopped there. 'Why am I even bothering?'

'Gallagher's up in front of the Sheriff at half three, want to have another go at him? Or the van driver?'

'Never makes any bloody difference, does it?' She winkled out one of Logan's cigarettes and opened her office window. 'Where's Danby?'

Logan stared at her. 'Are you going to speak to Finnie and Beattie, or not?'

'I'll talk to them. Jesus: nag, nag, nag. You're worse than bloody Susan.'

'Do you want to get me fired?'

'I *said* I'll talk to them!' She reached into a drawer, then threw something across the desk to him. A mobile phone. 'Not that you deserve it.'

It was one of those touch-screen jobs, all new and shiny. It must have cost a fortune. Logan felt his face flush. 'Thanks.'

'Nicked it from the lost-and-found. Get your mate the van driver in an interview room and I'll go see Lord Volderfinnie.'

The sim card was about the only bit of Logan's mobile still in one piece. He popped the back off his new – slightly stolen – phone, slipped it in, and turned the thing on. There was a small pause, then the dings and bleeps started. 'You Have 57 New Messages'.

Logan switched it off again. Sod that.

He headed downstairs instead, signed the van driver out of custody and stuck him in interview room number two. The one with the broken radiator, that stank of cheesy feet.

Arnie Urquhart cupped his hands to his mouth and blew. He had 'Hate' tattooed between both sets of knuckles, a blue swallow on the side of his neck, a spider's web on his wrist, and eyes that darted left and right every time anyone in the room moved.

Logan sat on the other side of the interview room table, the audio and video tapes all set up and ready to go as soon as DI Steel arrived. PC Butler was on looming duty, just over Urquhart's shoulder.

The van driver licked his lips. 'Always this cold in here?'

Logan stared at him. 'Did I say you could speak?'

Urquhart shrank back in his seat. 'Sorry.'

So much for the hard man act.

He was right though, the little room was freezing.

Logan thumped an evidence bag down on the tabletop. There were two rectangular packages inside, both about the size of a house brick, wrapped in light-brown packing tape. One was slit open, showing the hard-packed powder within. 'Uncut heroin. About six hundred and fifty thousand quid's worth.'

Urquhart squirmed. 'It's—'

'Did that sound like a question to you?'

He pressed his lips together. Looked down at his tattooed hands. Shrugged.

'This stuff came from Fraserburgh, didn't it? Saturday night.'

Urquhart fidgeted.

'You can answer that.'

'It. . . I don't. . .'

'A DI was stabbed, Arnie. That's attempted murder, and you're an accomplice.'

He flinched, as if he'd been slapped. 'But. . .'

Logan suppressed a smile. Now all they needed was Steel to get her finger out and—

The door opened. Speak of the devil. The inspector stood just outside the room, lips pressed into a thin, downturned line. 'Stick him back in his cell.'

Logan got to his feet. 'Mr Urquhart was just about to—'

'I don't care. Our wee art student friend with the counterfeit twenties: his mum and dad just got back from Corfu, found him in his bedroom. Gin and sleeping tablets.'

41

'He was in here.' The PC opened the door.

The familiar smells of turpentine, oil paint, and bitter vomit curled around Logan as he followed Steel into the room. The house was silent, just the *tick-tock* of a clock somewhere on the floor below.

The constable flicked on the light, turning the window into a mirror.

Douglas Walker's bedroom looked much the same as it had the last time Logan was there: the same half-sketched painting on the easel, the same unmade single bed, the same flat-pack wardrobe, the same little computer desk and cheap swivel chair.

The only difference was the puddle of sick on the floor, next to an empty litre bottle of Plymouth gin and a little white packet from a chemists. Logan snapped on a pair of gloves, squatted down, picked up the empty packet and read the label. 'Temazepam.'

Steel wrinkled her nose. 'Can we no' open a window or something?'

Logan levered up the edge of the mattress, peering between it and the bed frame. Nothing.

The inspector's voice came from over by the wardrobe. 'If you're looking for porn, I can bring some in tomorrow. You like Dutch gay hardcore, right?'

'Looking for counterfeit money, *actually*. If he was getting more cash in for Middleton it'll be around here somewhere.' He let the mattress fall back and Steel sat on the end.

She glanced around the room. 'He leave a note?'

The constable shrugged. 'Dunno, didn't want to disturb anything.'

'Bet he left a poem. Artistic types always leave bloody poetry.'

Logan went through the chest of drawers, wardrobe, computer desk, the toolbox full of oil paints and charcoals, but there was no sign of any notes – suicide or counterfeit. 'Nothing.'

'Wanted to keep it mysterious.'

Logan stared at her. 'It's not funny.'

She shrugged. 'If he'd actually managed to do himself in, *then* it wouldn't be funny, but he didn't, did he? Cocked it up. That's bloody students for you: they'll no' put the effort in.'

The constable shifted his feet. 'He's in a coma.'

Logan knelt on the floor, taking care to avoid the puddle of sick. Nothing under the bed either.

'Don't see what the problem is.' Steel leant back and had a scratch. 'I mean, you want to kill yourself – up to you isn't it? Long as you don't do it driving the wrong way up the motorway, it's nobody's business but. . .' She stopped fiddling with herself and scowled at Logan. 'What?'

'He was terrified they were going to put his name in the papers.'

'Didn't want mummy and daddy dearest to know.'

'Or,' Logan stood, taking another look around the room, 'maybe he thought whoever he got the cash from would come after him? Might be some clue in the suicide note, if we can find it.'

'He's no' bloody dead. Want to know why he did it? Get your arse up the hospital and ask him.'

Logan dragged a big, black leather portfolio out from between the wardrobe and the single bed, dumped it down on the mattress beside Steel, and unzipped it. It was basically a huge ring binder: large sheets of black paper in clear plastic sleeves, held together with six shiny steel clips. Some photos, some prints, some originals. All pretty good.

Steel flipped through the pages. 'Got any nudes?'

There was a little pocket at the front with some leaflets for local galleries stuffed into it, and a fancy-looking CV with abstract black-and-white photos mixed in. Very arty.

'Course, you know why he did it, don't you?'

Logan looked up. 'What, Walker?'

'No, *Finnie*. Sent us out here cos he's pissed off about Knox going missing – spreading the misery. Petulant tit.' She looked up at the constable. 'Anything else? Any missing kitties we should be getting out of trees? Stolen gnomes? Stuff like that?'

The PC's cheeks went pink. 'It's not my fault. I just—'

'Come on Laz.' She levered herself off the bed. 'I hereby declare this a waste of CID resources. Our plucky boys in uniform can save the day for a change. We've got a van driver to interview before they let the bugger go.'

The Airwave handset clipped to the constable's shoulder started making bleepy noises. He fumbled it round to his mouth and squeezed the button. 'One-Zero One-Twenty, over?'

A broad Aberdonian accent crackled out of the little speaker. *'That you Lachlan?'*

'Roger that Control. Over.'

'You still got DS McRae there?'

'Aye. . . I mean, affirmative. Do you want—'

362

'Tell the loon to switch his bloody phone on: there's bin anither of his wee jewellery heists. Mackenzie and Kerr, that place on Huntly Street, next to the naughty knicker shop.'

Logan hauled out his notebook, flipped it open and scribbled down the jewellery shop's details. 'Does he know if—'

'See if you're going to the naughty knicker shop—' DI Steel jabbed her elbow in Logan's ribs.

'Shite!' Logan flinched. The notebook tumbled from his fingers, splatting down in the puddle of sick.

Steel blew out her cheeks. 'Clumsy.'

'It wasn't clumsy, it was you!' He looked down at the vomit-sodden book. No way he was picking that up. Logan grabbed one of Douglas Walker's fancy CVs, writing 'Mackenzie & Kerr – Huntly St' on the back of it. 'Ask them how much he got away with.'

The constable relayed Logan's question.

'Aboot two hunnerd thou, give or take a couply watches.'

A much better haul than last time.

'And you're *sure* it's the same person?'

The constable hadn't even opened his mouth before the voice of Control crackled back, 'Aye, I'm sure. Yer mannie had a sawn-off sledgehammer and a wee bairn with him.' There was a pause. 'And DI Beattie's looking for you. Something about a flasher?'

As if Logan didn't have enough to worry about.

He flipped open an evidence bag, turned it inside out, then used it as a pooper-scooper to pluck his notebook from the rancid mush. He sealed it closed, the sodden pages feeling cold and slimy through the plastic. 'Tell him he'll have to take it up with DI Steel.'

'Turn yer bloody phone on and tell him yoursel!'

It took over forty minutes to get into the centre of town – a little snow and everyone forgot how to drive, pootling along at ten miles an hour and *still* managing to crash into things.

Logan parked the pool car just down from the jewellery shop.

Huntly Street was a little cobbled road, setting off from Union Street at a jaunty angle. The granite hulk of St Mary's Cathedral loomed on the other side of the road, a mass of sharp edges and shadow, washed in yellowy streetlight. Thick flakes of white drifted down from the dark-orange sky.

Mackenzie and Kerr – Jewellers by Appointment to Princess Anne, according to the understated sign above the shattered window – was sealed off behind a cordon of blue-and-white 'POLICE' tape, a filthy patrol car sitting right outside it.

Logan stepped out into the bitterly cold evening, then stood there, waiting for DI Steel to finish staring at the display of basques, suspenders, and shiny leather kinky boots in the window of the shop next door.

She hitched up her trousers. 'You need me, I'll be in there trying on something naughty.'

Logan picked his way across the slippery cobbles, ducked under the cordon and peered in through Mackenzie and Kerr's shattered shop window. All the display cabinets lay smashed and empty on the floor, the counter little more than a broken wooden frame. The burgundy carpet was awash with glass, chains of gold and silver trodden into the deep pile.

He pulled on yet another pair of gloves, hauled the buckled front door open, and stepped inside.

It smelt vaguely of wee. And dust. And air freshener.

A handful of rings and bracelets lay scattered on the glass-strewn velvet of the counter.

A face poked through from a door at the back of the room. 'Sarge?' PC Guthrie grinned, his cheeks straining like an overgrown, shaved hamster's. He chewed, swallowed then pointed over his shoulder. 'Got the kettle on if you want a brew?'

Guthrie led the way into a little kitchen, just big enough for a small fridge, kettle, microwave, and breadbin; a half-sized sink and draining board; a tiny table complete with carrot cake; and two wooden chairs. Both occupied by grey-haired women – one in a pink twinset and pearls combo, the other wearing enough tweed to upholster a medium-sized hippopotamus. Which was appropriate.

PC Guthrie did the introductions. 'Ladies, this is Detective Sergeant McRae. Sarge, this is Nora Mackenzie and Peggy Ramsay, the owners. They were here when it happened.'

The tweed hippo pressed a hand to her considerable chest. 'It was horrible! He went mad, didn't he Nora?'

Twinset-and-Pearls nodded, setting the sag of skin beneath her chin wobbling. 'Smashed everything—'

'Everything.'

'Kept screaming it wasn't his fault—'

'On and on. I was terrified, wasn't I Nora?'

'Look at the state of the place, it's all ruined!'

Logan held up his hands. 'Did either of you get a good look at him?'

'I mean, you read about these things in the papers, but you never think they'll happen to you, do you?'

'Terrible.' Nora Mackenzie fingered the pearls around her throat. 'He was a big man, broad shouldered, and he had a thing. . .' She waved a hand in front of her face. 'Didn't he Peggy?'

'Glasses and a big pink nose. And one of those bristly moustaches.'

'And a mole, on his cheek.'

'Oh yes, a mole. And a wee toddler in a pushchair.' Peggy picked at the slice of carrot cake in front of her. 'Poor little mite. What's she going to think, growing up with a father like that?'

'It's a disgrace so it is.'

Logan looked at Guthrie. 'You checked with CCTV yet?'

The constable nodded. 'They're running the footage back at HQ.'

Nora tugged at her pearls. 'You will catch him, won't you?'

Logan pointed through the door at the bombsite shop. 'You've got a security camera?'

Peggy raised her not inconsiderable frame and lumbered over to a little telly and video recorder, mounted on a bracket in the corner. 'My nephew James put it in last year.' She pressed a couple of buttons and the machine whirred for nearly a minute. Then clunked. Then started to play.

The shop interior appeared on the TV: Peggy rearranging something in a glass-fronted display cabinet. The picture was jerky, probably shooting one frame every two seconds, meaning a single tape would last the whole day. The time stamp at the bottom of the screen said '15:28:36'.

'I'll fast forward.' She fiddled with the recorder and everything lurched into super-speed. Nora's grey-haired head appeared behind the counter, swooshing back and forth. A young man came in, bought something, left. More footage of nothing happening. 'There!'

The picture slowed to normal speed. A large man wearing a baseball cap had just stepped in from the snowy street, hauling a pushchair after him. Logan watched him bend to talk to the child strapped in the chair, pull something from beneath the blanket and casually stick it between the closing door and the frame. Exactly the same MO as last time.

Nora and Peggy descended on the little child, smiling and making goo-goo faces.

The man glanced around the shop while they were busy

and the security camera got a perfect shot of his face: big nose, big glasses, big moustache. He was wearing one of those Groucho Marx kits – the only thing missing was the cigar.

Logan tapped the screen. 'You didn't think he looked a bit odd?'

Nora shrugged. 'Well, they do these days, don't they? When my children were wee you gave them a box of plasticine, told them not to eat it, and stuck them in the back garden while you got on with the housework. These days it's all television, and happy meals, and keeping them entertained the whole time.'

On screen, Nora turned away from the pushchair, frowned, then picked up the floppy-eared bunny the man had dropped between the door and the frame, and handed it back to the toddler with a smile.

Peggy waddled over to the counter, where the man was peering into the display case. All nice and friendly.

Then the sawn-off sledgehammer came out. Peggy backed off, mouth open, hands in the air. Glass went everywhere. Groucho's gloved hand scooped rings and watches and chains into an Adidas holdall.

'He told me to open the till or he'd break Nora's legs.'

On screen, the woman in twinset and pearls crouched down behind the pushchair, hands over her ears. Peggy stop-motion marched to the till and pinged out the cash drawer, flinching back against the wall as he stuffed everything into his bag.

'Of course.' She raised the uppermost of her chins. 'I tripped the silent alarm.'

Bag full, the man hurried for the exit, grabbed the door handle and pulled. Nothing happened. He tugged and yanked, then turned and shouted something at the large woman behind the counter.

Back in real life Nora shivered. 'His language was *appalling*, and in front of a wee girl too!'

The sledgehammer battered against the door: once, twice, three times, turning the clear glass into a sagging web of fractures. But it still wouldn't open. He scrambled into the window display and swung the hammer again. The whole thing shattered, exploding outward in a shower of glittering cubes. Then the man hopped back down on the carpet, and manhandled the pushchair out of the window and onto the street.

Peggy lumbered around the counter and stared out through the shop front, then Nora stood and swept the much bigger woman up into a hug. Kissed her on the cheek. Then Peggy kissed her back on the lips, and they stood that way for at least a minute, locked together at the mouth, hands in each other's hair, while the time stamp at the bottom of the screen flickered past.

Logan cleared his throat and looked away.

The shop door groaned open and clunked shut, the sound of someone walking over broken glass. 'Dear Lord it's *cold. . .*' A red-nosed, red-eared PC Butler appeared in the kitchen doorway. Thick flakes of snow clung to her fluorescent-yellow high-vis 'POLICE' vest, and the black jacket underneath.

'Hello, Sarge.' She stomped her feet, and rubbed her hands. 'Any chance of a cuppa?'

Nora filled the kettle from the tap over the tiny sink, and its steamy rumble soon had Butler standing over it, warming her hands over the spout. 'Been up and down the street: no witnesses.'

Logan nodded. 'Right, Guthrie you stay here: watch the shop till someone comes and boards up that window. Get them to do the door too. Ladies, you'll need to come down to the station. We'll get you to do an e-fit of the robber, make a formal statement, that kind of thing. Nothing to worry about.'

Peggy stood, her expansive bosom straining the stitches of all that tweed. 'Oh I'm not worried. You give me five minutes alone with the animal who did this and I'll give *him* something to worry about!'

She probably would too.

Logan told Butler to drive the ladies back to the station, then dug out his new phone and dialled the CCTV room at FHQ.

'*Fit like' i day?*'

'Inspector Pearce about, Chris?'

'*Hud oan. . .*'

And then the woman in charge of every closed circuit television camera in Aberdeen was on the line, her voice all muffled. '*Who's this?*'

'DS McRae, ma'am. How are you getting on with the footage for the Mackenzie and Kerr jewellery heist?'

'*Mmmmph, mmfff mnpmmph nmppph.*'

Logan frowned at the phone. 'Hello?'

'*Sorry, coconut cake. Hang on. . .*' Pause. '*You want the good news, or the bad news?*'

'Surprise me.'

'*We've got a man fighting a pushchair into a red Fiat Panda on Summer Street, three minutes after the silent alarm was tripped. Got a perfect shot of the registration.*'

'That's great! Can we run a PNC—'

'*Bad news is the car was registered stolen at half nine this morning.*'

Logan put his hand over the mouthpiece and swore.

'*You still there?*'

'Yeah, just having a think.'

'*While you're thinking.*' Her voice went all cake-muffled again, '*a little word to the wise: DI Beattie's been combing the station for you. I've had him down here twice in the last hour asking if we've seen you on any of the monitors.'*

'Bugger.' Logan chewed the inside of his cheek for a moment. 'Who was the car registered to? I mean, someone's going to have to tell him his car's been used in an armed robbery, aren't they?'

'I'll get Control to send a couple of Uniform, soon as anyone's free.'

'Er . . . no. I think as SIO I should really speak to him myself. Get an . . . erm . . . you know, details.' Cough. 'Or something.'

42

Alan Gardner's living room was uncomfortably warm, a wall-mounted flame-effect fire blazing away beneath a mantelpiece laden with photo frames. More pictures hung on the wall: a happy family sharing holidays and birthdays.

Alan shifted in his creaky armchair and stared at the fire. 'Might as well have it up full blast, bloody electric's getting disconnected tomorrow. . .' What little hair he had left was white and tufty, most of it concentrated in two feral eyebrows, the rest holding on for dear life behind his ears. He sighed, looking out at the spartan living room, reflected in the black mirror of the bay window. No television. No sofa. No bookcases.

There wasn't anywhere for Logan to sit.

He reached for his notebook, top lip curling as his fingers touched the evidence bag he'd stuck it in – locking in all that vomity goodness. It was all cold. . . 'Can you remember where you parked your car, Mr Gardner?'

The man shrugged, then worried at a hole in his thread-bare green jumper. 'My wife died last year. March. Kidney failure. We were on holiday in Kenya. . .'

Logan looked above the mantelpiece, finding a happy

blonde lady with her balding husband, the pair of them grinning like idiots in the basket of a balloon, pale yellow grass far below. 'I'm sorry.'

'At least it was quick.' He shifted again, making the chair creak. 'Quick and painful. Doctors said there was nothing they could do. Hit Stacy really hard, losing her mum like that, never getting to say goodbye. . .'

Silence.

'About the car, Mr Gardner?'

'What? Oh . . . yes. It was parked round the corner. Couldn't get it out front because that idiot next door always leaves his sodding car outside my house. Rubbing it in, because he's got a brand-new Audi estate, and I'm driving a third-hand Fiat Panda.' Gardner tugged at a bushy eyebrow. 'Surprised he doesn't park his wife out there too.'

Logan scribbled the details down on the sheet of paper he'd liberated from Douglas Walker's bedroom.

Have to pick up a new notebook when he got back to the station, one that didn't reek of art student vomit.

He checked his watch. Nearly quarter past six. Beattie would be long gone – back home to put curlers in his beard, or whatever the hell it was he did when he wasn't making Logan's life miserable at work.

'Right, well, I suppose I should be heading. . .'

Gardner hauled himself out of his chair and walked Logan to the front door. 'Are you a family man, Sergeant?'

Logan pursed his lips. 'It's kind of complicated.'

Gardener nodded, his eyes watery, rimmed with pink. Bit his bottom lip. 'Never gets any easier, does it?' He rubbed his hand across his face. 'I'm sorry, it's. . . It's been a tough couple of months.'

Logan laid a hand on his arm. 'If we find your car I'll let you know.'

'Can I get a crime number for the insurance?'

'I'll get someone to phone it through. . .' Logan trailed off. The hallway had a set of stairs leading up to the first floor. 'Did you hear—'

There it was again: a soft gurgling noise.

Logan looked back at Gardner, then took a step towards the stairs.

'Well. . .' Gardner unsnibbed the front door. 'Anyway, thanks for coming – I know you must be very busy.'

Upstairs, the gurgling stopped and the crying started, quickly building to anguished howls.

Gardner smiled, a single bead of sweat trickling down his pink neck. 'I . . . must have left the TV on in the bedroom.'

Logan put his hand on the balustrade. The old man flinched.

'If I search this place am I going to find a pushchair, a sawn-off sledgehammer, and a bag full of stolen jewellery?'

'I don't. . . Erm. . .'

'Your car wasn't stolen, was it?'

Gardner just sagged.

The upstairs bedroom seemed to be the only place in the whole house with any furniture. It had bright yellow walls, a pile of soft toys, a sparkly mobile, and a big wooden cot. A little girl, dressed in a tiny princess/fairy costume, was imprisoned inside, holding onto the bars.

Alan Gardner sat on the floor, clutching a floppy-eared toy bunny identical to the one on the security camera footage. 'It's under the crib.'

Logan squatted down and dragged out a black-and-red Adidas holdall. He dumped it on the pink carpet – it was full of watches, chains, rings, brooches, and bracelets, gleaming in the light of a Bob the Builder bedside lamp. A big wodge of cash stuffed in the side pocket.

'What happened to the first lot, from Henderson's?'

'Sent it off to one of those cash-for-gold places you see on the telly. Haven't even got the cheque back yet.'

'Alan Gardner, I'm arresting you on suspicion of—'

'I didn't have any choice.' He kept his eyes fixed on the bunny rabbit.

'Where's the sledgehammer?'

'She's my daughter, what was I supposed to do? Let him hurt her?'

Logan turned and looked at the fairy princess in the cot. 'Who'd want to hurt a little girl?'

'Not Nicole, her mum: Stacy, my daughter.' Gardner creaked himself upright and handed the rabbit into Nicole's sticky little fingers. 'When Laura died, Stacy . . . Stacy got involved with the wrong kind of people. Started taking drugs, drunk all the time, she just couldn't cope.'

Gardner reached down and ruffled his granddaughter's hair. 'So now I look after Nicole. She's my little tattieheid, aren't you?' The girl grinned, still chewing on the bunny's floppy ear.

And now Logan was supposed to feel all sorry for him? 'You robbed two jewellery shops, threatened the assistants with a sledgehammer.'

Gardner looked up, eyes pink and damp. 'What was I supposed to do? Stacy ran up a lot of debts: drugs. There's a man who's going to . . . cut her if she doesn't pay it all back. Break her legs. Worse. . . The interest is crippling.' He reached down and picked the fairy princess from her cot, holding her tight. 'I sold everything, cashed in my life insurance, pension, sold my car, put the house on the market. . . She's my little girl, what was I supposed to do?'

Damn.

'How about call the police?'

'He said if I went to the police they'd never find her body.'

374

Logan closed his eyes, ran a hand across his forehead. Swore.

'What's his name?'

'I. . . I don't know. I never spoke to him.'

'But you said—'

'He always made Stacy phone.'

They stood there in the gaily coloured bedroom, Logan swearing, Gardner crying, Nicole making nonsensical gibbery-sing-song noises.

Custody was busy – shouts and threats coming from the lower corridor of cells, where the female prisoners were normally kept. Logan hefted the sawn-off sledgehammer onto the desk, along with the Adidas holdall, both stuffed into oversize evidence bags.

'Two exhibits to sign in, and one prisoner.'

The custody sergeant nodded, reached below the level of the desk, pulled out a clipboard, and clacked it down next to Logan's evidence bags. Sergeant Downie's skin was so pale it fluoresced slightly in the overhead light, his hooded eyes moving restlessly across his twilight domain. The poster boy for generations of exuberant inbreeding.

He raised an eyebrow, giving Logan's prisoner the long, hard stare.

Gardner was standing on the bare concrete with his head down, fairy princess granddaughter clutched to his chest, her podgy legs and little pink shoes dangling against his belly.

'So,' Sergeant Downie pulled the cap off a chewed blue biro and smiled with tombstone teeth, 'which one am I checking in: the bald bloke, or the wee girl with the fairy wings?'

'Very funny.' Logan signed the custody form at the bottom. 'Mr Gardner's going to be helping us with those jewellery heists.'

'I see.' The sergeant took the clipboard back and started ticking boxes. 'And would Mr Gardner like a wake-up call, newspaper, breakfast in bed?'

'Don't be a dick, Jeff.'

Twitch. 'Fair enough.'

'You got any PCSOs knocking about? I need someone to look after the kid till social services get here.'

Sergeant Downie laughed. 'You're kidding, right? I've got half a female rugby team downstairs screaming blue bloody murder. Must be that time of the month. Speaking of which.' He leant forward and lowered his voice to a whisper. 'Think Steel's on the blob too. Been stomping about like someone's smeared her tampons with Deep Heat. Beware of the lesbian!'

Logan's phone was ringing again.

The Wee Hoose had been relatively quiet – unlike the main CID office – giving him a chance to type up Alan Gardner's confession before heading off home.

He peered at the phone's display, making sure it wasn't that idiot Beattie, before picking up. 'McRae.'

DSI Danby's huge bass voice boomed out of the earpiece. *'Any news on Knox?'*

Logan snatched the phone away from his ear. 'Bloody hell. . .' He trailed off. DS Doreen Taylor was staring at him, her eyes bugged out, mouth an angry line. She pointed at the little fairy princess sitting on her desk, legs dangling over the edge. Nicole's wings were getting crumpled, and the chocolate biscuit they'd used as a bribe to stop her crying was slowly making its way all over her face.

Doreen jabbed her finger at him, her voice a sharp whisper, 'Language!'

Logan grimaced. 'Sorry.' He swivelled his chair around until he had his back to them both, then turned the volume down on the phone. 'Sorry, sir, had to close the door. They're still swamped with sightings of Knox.' The last part was true at least, the phones hadn't stopped ringing in CID all day.

'How many worth chasing up?'

'Backshift are still checking, but you know what it's like. A big case like this brings out all the loonies.' Logan clicked on his email and skimmed through till he got to the message from the hospital. 'Harry Weaver from Sacro woke up an hour ago – DS MacDonald interviewed him, but he can't remember anything. Tox report says he was full of Rohypnol.'

'The woman?'

'Too early to tell.'

There was a pause. *'Been on to my team. No one in Tyneside's heard from Knox since he left, but there's a lot of folk wanting their hands on Mental Mikey's nest egg. Better tell your people to keep their eyes open for Newcastle gangsters, know what I'm saying?'*

Logan groaned. 'Christ, that's all we—'

A pad of pink Post-it notes clattered off his monitor.

Doreen had her finger out again. 'Language!'

'Oops. . .' Logan went back to the phone, thanked Danby, and hung up. Newcastle gangsters: as if things weren't complicated enough.

The handset had barely touched the cradle before it was ringing again. 'Oh for fff . . .' He shut his mouth before Doreen could throw anything else. 'McRae?'

Samantha: *'I was. . . Are you doing another late night? I mean it's OK if you are, I just wanted to . . . you know.'*

Logan checked the time on the computer – 19:40 – nearly three hours after the end of his shift. 'Drowning in paperwork: caught the guy doing over the jewellery shops.'

'Oh. . . Well, never mind.'

He took a deep breath. 'Actually, I'm just about done. How about I pick up a Chinese on the way home and. . . *Sod* it, I can't. I've got an unattended minor here. Have to keep an eye on her till social services turn up.' Logan closed his eyes and banged his head softly against his keyboard.

'*It's not important.*'

Of course it was, he could hear it in Samantha's voice.

Doreen cleared her throat. 'I can look after her.'

Logan raised his head. There was a long line of gibberish stretching across his screen.

Doreen ran a hand through the little girl's pale-yellow hair. 'Nicole can help me prepare case papers for the golf club murder, can't you Nicole?'

The fairy princess stuck her thumb in her chocolaty mouth and sooked. To be honest, she'd probably be more help than most of CID.

'*Hello? You still there?*'

Logan made more keyboard gibberish. 'I'm on my way.'

43

Logan picked his way down Marischal Street, a plastic bag from a nice little Chinese carryout on King Street swinging from one hand. The council hadn't bothered to grit this bit and the pavement was a treacherous mixture of snow and ice. Which would've been bad enough, but the road made a steep descent from Union Street all the way down to the docks, turning the whole thing into a toboggan run.

The wind wasn't helping any either, hammering icy nails into his face, making his skin throb and ache with cold.

He slithered to a halt outside the building's front door and fumbled in his pocket for the keys. Could barely see the lock in the gloom. . . He shifted sideways, letting the streetlight's yellow glow fall on the scarred wood.

The key skittered around the lock, before finally going in. And then the light disappeared.

'God's sake. . .' Bulb had probably blown again. The sea-gulls liked to eat the rubber sealant, letting the water in, because they were rotten evil bastarding things. . .

Not seagulls. The light hadn't gone out, it'd been eclipsed by a huge shadow.

'Been waiting fucking ages for you.'

Oh shit. Reuben.

Logan spun around, feet slipping on the ice, staggered, bounced off the damp granite wall and fell on his backside.

Pain jagged across the base of his spine.

The plastic bag made a dull thud as it bounced off the pavement beside him, egg foo yung and prawn crackers going everywhere.

Ow. . .

He looked up to find Wee Hamish Mowat's right-hand man standing over him, that scarred fat face twisted into a grin. 'Classic. Didn't even have to lay a finger on you.' In the dim light, the bruises were almost black, the plaster across the bridge of Reuben's nose a pale grey strip against the swollen skin.

The big man reached inside his thick padded jacket and Logan flinched. Gun? Knife?

Reuben sighed. 'Moron.' He pulled out an envelope and threw it in Logan's face.

It bounced, and fell into his lap.

'Open it.'

Logan peeled back the self-adhesive flap. More money. 'I can't—'

'Mr Mowat says if you want any more, you go see this man.' He pulled out a sticky note and slapped it onto Logan's forehead. Then stood there, grinning as the snow battered down all around them.

Logan pulled the note from his head and scowled at it – 'JAMES CLAY' and an address in the Bridge of Don.

One of Reuben's massive hands clamped down on the top of Logan's head. 'See you around.' He shoved, sending Logan sprawling on his back.

Logan tensed, waiting for the kicking to start. But it didn't. Instead he heard a car door slam, then the tractor-rattle of a diesel engine starting up. A car driving slowly away.

He sat up, watching the dented BMW pause at the bottom of the road, then turn right onto Trinity Quay and disappear into the night.

'What happened to you?' Samantha looked up from her spot on the sofa, electric fire blazing, a cup of tea steaming away on the coffee table, some sort of costume drama on the telly, and a book open in her lap.

Logan dumped the plastic bag next to her mug, then struggled out of his jacket. 'Going to have to share the chow mein.'

The seat of his trousers was soaked through and his left hand throbbed – the palm scraped and stinging. He sucked at it, then scowled at the little beads of red that seeped through the skin.

'You OK?'

'Fell on my arse.' Logan took off his trousers and hung them over the radiator.

'I'll get the plates.' She disappeared, calling through from the kitchen. 'You've got a message on the machine, by the way.'

Oh God, please not another one from Wee Hamish Mowat. . .

He pulled the envelope full of cash out of his jacket pocket and stuffed the crumpled sticky note in with the tens and twenties. There had to be over a grand in there, maybe two.

'Logan? You want chopsticks?'

'Yeah, thanks. . .' He pressed the button on the answering machine, standing there in his socks, shirt and damp pants as DI Steel's voice crackled out of the little speakers.

'You rotten bastard, I had to walk back to the station!'

Bugger. She'd still have been in the naughty knicker shop

when he'd headed off to tell Alan Gardner his car had been used in a jewellery robbery.

'*Was bloody soaked through by the time I got back; had to interview that bastard van driver dripping wet. If I die of pneumonia, you're sodding for it!*' There was more, none of it flattering or polite. Logan hit delete.

'You all right?'

'Yeah . . . just cold and tired.' He didn't look around.

He could hear her walk into the room, the clatter of plates on the coffee table, then the warmth of Samantha's body against his back, her arms wrapping around him, her breath hot on his neck. It was nice. Intimate. Maybe they'd be all right after all.

'God, you *are* freezing, aren't you?'

Logan gave a little shudder and slipped the envelope up the sleeve of his shirt. 'Baltic out there.'

'Right.' She stepped back, pulled up his shirt-tails and slapped him on his grey Markies pants.

'Ow!'

'Get your cold bum in the shower, we can always stick the noodles in the microwave.'

The bathroom filled with steam, the shower hissing and gurgling into the white plastic bathtub, the blower grumbling hot air from the dusty unit mounted on the wall. Logan locked the door and settled onto the toilet lid, pulled Reuben's envelope from his sleeve, and counted the contents. Two thousand, four hundred and sixty pounds, all in used notes. Less than last time, but then Logan hadn't actually done anything to deserve it. . . Unless you counted elbowing Reuben in the face.

He smoothed out the crumpled Post-it note – the name and address of the man to speak to if he wanted more cash from the DIY self-service bribery buffet.

Nearly six thousand pounds, when you added in the envelope hidden away in the back of the airing cupboard. Not that much in the great scheme of things. Not compared with being a corrupt bastard.

44

Bloody jocks are useless.

Detective Superintendent Graeme Danby sits on the end of the bed wearing the white fluffy bathrobe that came with his tartan hotel room. Remote in one hand, mobile phone clamped between his ear and shoulder so he can have a good scratch at his sack.

'Don't really know, Val, love. All depends on how long it takes to sort things out up here, you know what I'm saying?'

Eleven o'clock. There's a film starting on Sky, but he can't concentrate for more than five minutes. So he skims through the channels, always ending up with SKY NEWS and their coverage of Richard Knox's escape.

Hysterical – in both senses of the word.

Graeme slumps back on the bed, dressing gown falling open. Not like there's anyone there to complain, is there?

'And I managed to find this lovely blue bikini.' Her voice goes up and down, in that sexy Fife accent of hers that always gets more pronounced on the phone. *'It's going to be so nice to be* warm *again.'*

Graeme flicks through the channels: sports, music, documentary about Hitler, American sitcom . . . then back to the news.

'You won't need the top though; don't want white bits, do you?'

He can hear the smile in her voice. *'You're a bad man, Graeme Danby.'*

There's a knock at the door. Graeme groans.

'What?'

'Hold on. . .'

He stands, ties the robe shut and shuffles into the complementary towelling slippers.

'When are you coming home?'

Graeme marches over to the door and undoes the latch. 'Told you: when I'm finished here.'

Another knock. 'Mr Danby? Hospitality management, you have a problem with your shower?'

'But the flights are booked for—'

'Val, it's not a problem, you know what I'm saying?' He opens the door. 'I can always meet you out there, and—'

His head snaps back. Graeme stumbles, pain bursting inside his nose. 'Fucking. . .' Everything tastes of blood. Another thump, hard in his chest, knocking all the air from his lungs.

Detective Superintendent Danby staggers against the bed.

Thump – a stabbing ache in his kidneys.

He grits his teeth and throws a punch, eyes watering too much to aim, just going on instinct.

Misses.

Something hard cracks into the back of his head. The world goes white and crackly, then the carpet rushes up to meet him, slamming into his cheek.

His phone skitters away under the bed, Val's voice tinny and far away as she makes plans for their trip to New Zealand. His early retirement. Their happy life together.

A boot cracks into his ribs. 'Get up you fat bastard.' A Newcastle accent. Oh Jesus, no. . . Not now. Not when he was so close!

Graeme gets his right arm underneath him and pushes himself to his knees. 'Fucking bastards. . .' The words won't come out right, his face isn't working.

He struggles to his feet, rocking back and forth on his heels. The room swirls around him. Blink. He wipes a huge fist across his blurry eyes. 'Bloody kill. . .'

A shape swims into focus. Woman. Short. Blonde hair cut in a shoulder-length bob. Jacket, jeans, cowboy boots. A werewolf smile. 'DSI Danby, so nice to see you again. How's the wife and kids?'

He staggers back a step. 'You. . .?'

She looks to the side. 'Neil?'

Something slams into Graeme's head.

Darkness.

They carry him down the service stairs at the back of the building. Can't use the lifts, cos of the security cameras.

Neil grunts, arms wrapped around Danby's torso. 'Christ, he weighs a ton.'

Doesn't look too great either: his face is all covered in blood, there's a big lump on the back of his shiny head, and the bruises are already starting to darken.

They pause on the next landing, catching their breath.

Danby's white bathrobe is all stained red down the front. Flopping open.

Tony frowns. 'Urgh. . .'

'What?'

'Can see his cock.'

'Then don't bloody look.'

Julie's waiting for them at the bottom of the stairs, where there's a little car park and some industrial-sized wheelie bins. Tony peers out the door at the falling snow.

'Cameras?'

'Don't sweat it, Babe: all taken care of.' She frowns. 'Why's he got his knob out? Did you guys get all amorous halfway down the stairs?'

Neil grimaces. 'No offence, but this bastard's heavy.'

'Okeydoke.' She leads the way to the generic white van they stole earlier, the number plates fudged a bit with black electrical tape. Well, you'd have to be a right mentalist to use your own car, wouldn't you? Some nosey bastard or CCTV camera always sees something.

Julie pops open the back doors and they tumble Danby inside, hands fastened behind his back with thick black cable-ties, legs strapped together at the ankle, duct tape gag over that big hairy gob of his.

She ducks into the passenger seat and comes back with something tartan – a pillowcase from their room. She slips it over Danby's battered head, then fastens another cable-tie around his neck, just below his chin.

Tony shifts his feet. 'Are you sure that's—'

'Don't worry, Darling, he's not going to choke.' She smiles. 'You can ride in the back to make sure, if you like?'

Tony looks at the scarred, rusty metal floor of the van, then at the front seats. 'Actually, I think—'

'You can ride in the *back*.' Julie's not smiling any more.

Tony clears his throat. Stares at the ground for a moment. Then clambers up into the cold metal interior and pulls the doors shut behind him.

Julie and Neil get in the front.

The van slips out of the car park, windscreen wipers clunking back and forth.

OK, so it's uncomfortable and cold in the back, but it's nothing compared to what's waiting for Danby, is it?

Always gotta look on the bright side. . .

Moonlight casts a cold white bar across the bed, shining though the gap between the curtains, turning the scratchy tartan blanket monochrome beneath his naked elbows. Hands together. Head bowed in prayer.

Our Father who art in heaven,

He can hear the old man swearing in the other room. Has to hurt, all that violence – the whipping, the biting, the punches.

Hallowed be Thy name,

A tear plops onto the blanket, swallowed by the darkness.

Can't do this any more.

Don't want to do this any more.

Thy will be done,

That's the razorblade in the forbidden apple, isn't it?

Richard stands, wipes his palm across his wet cheeks. His hand aches, the knuckles swollen and cracked, covered in bruises. Cradling it against his chest, he picks his way through the gloom to the window and stands there with the blade of moonlight slicing down his naked body. The skin so pale it looks dead.

Thy kingdom come,

He peers out through the gap in the curtains. There's a car sitting in the snowy driveway, a new-looking people carrier. Richard doesn't know if it belongs to the old man or not.

On Earth as it is in Heaven. . .

Doesn't really matter, does it? Too risky to take it – people would know. The police've got them cameras now that photograph your number plate and run it against some sort of database.

Richard leans forward and breathes on the glass, turning it white, then draws on it with a finger: making a circle with a cross in the middle. It's not a crucifix unless it's got Jesus on it, you know? His Granny Murray would have tanned his backside for drawing graven images like, so it's just a cross.

Empty.

Waiting for its sacrificial offering.

Crying condensation tears.

Moonlight makes it glow . . . and then the clouds sweep back in, and the moon's gone, leaving the world to the shadows. Icy snow rattles the window.

Richard shivers, his pale, naked skin covered with goose pimples.

Let there be darkness.

45

DI Steel slumped back against the corridor wall, knocking a watercolour of Old Aberdeen squint against the burgundy wallpaper. 'If you were a chubby Geordie bastard, where would you run off to?'

Logan peered around the doorframe into the hotel room. Three IB techs, all Smurfed up in SOC-white, were going over the room with fingerprint powder, cotton swabs, and sticky tape. There was a stain of cherry-red on the oatmeal carpet, by the end of the bed.

'Did you get anything useful out of Urquhart? The van driver?'

She narrowed her eyes. 'I've still no' forgiven you for making me walk back in the bloody snow, you know that, don't you?'

'I said I'm sorry.'

'So you should be.' Sniff. 'For some reason the silly sod thought he was looking at attempted murder, nearly peed himself to cut a deal. He's giving us the whole smuggling operation from—'

'Inspector?' One of the IB techs, on their hands and knees at the side of the bed, dropped until their chest was resting on the carpet, one arm reaching into the space between the bed and the floor, round arse wiggling as they dug about. Logan recognized the view – Samantha. 'Think I've found something. . .'

She beckoned one of the other techs over, a bloke with a huge digital camera slung around his neck. He lay down next to her, and took a couple of shots. Then Samantha pulled a small silver mobile phone out from under the bed.

She flipped it open in her purple-gloved hand and pressed a couple of buttons. 'Last call was made at five to eleven last night, from "home": think it's a Newcastle number. Lasted twenty minutes.'

Steel stuck her hand out. 'Give.'

From the front, Samantha didn't look much like herself, everything hidden by that baggy white suit, the hood covering her bright red hair, wearing a facemask and safety goggles. She hesitated for a moment, slipped the phone into an evidence bag, wrote the time, date, location, and other details into the appropriate boxes printed on the outside, then handed it to another tech with a clipboard. Who made some more notes.

Steel puffed out her cheeks. 'Today would be nice!'

The Crime Scene Manager didn't even look up. 'Sounds like someone got out the wrong side of bed this—'

'Pete, I'm warning you – my holiday's been cancelled, my wife's no' speaking to me, and I've got itchy bits – don't screw me about!'

'Evidentiary procedures exist for a reason, Inspector.' He went back to making notes.

Logan looked up and down the hall. 'Have you checked the tapes from the lobby and the lifts? I noticed the security cameras when—'

Steel smacked him one. 'Course I bloody checked. Nothing.

Must've taken the service lift, or the back stairs. Got IB looking for trace as we speak. I *have* done this kind of thing before, you know?'

Logan wandered off to the end of the corridor, opened the door marked 'EMERGENCY EXIT' and stared down the service stairs – bare concrete steps, plain walls. Sod carrying someone like Danby down that lot, be just asking for a hernia.

Someone cleared their throat behind him, and Logan sighed. 'What now?'

'Just wanted to say hello. . .'

Samantha. She had her SOC hood thrown back, exposing a wildfire eruption of scarlet hair, her facemask dangling on the elastic, just beneath her chin.

He pulled on a smile, leaned in and kissed her. 'Hello.'

Logan nodded back towards the room. 'Any ideas?'

'Rough guess? It's an abduction. If they wanted him dead, there'd be a big pink corpse in there. . .' She ran a hand through her hair. 'You see the papers today?'

'What, "Tyneside Sex-Beast Strikes Again"?'

Richard Knox had attacked an old man living in Cove, just south of the city, and the *Aberdeen Examiner* somehow managed to secure a huge exclusive. Finnie hadn't exactly been pleased. Especially when it turned out that Danby had gone missing too.

'Actually. . .' A little wrinkle appeared between Samantha's neatly plucked eyebrows. 'You know what? It'll wait.' She leaned in and planted a soft kiss on his lips.

'Now I'm really starting to worry.'

She looked away. 'They found that kid's suicide note: the art student. He'd posted it on Facebook. Got a two-page spread in the *Examiner*, printed the whole thing. Said he couldn't live with the constant police harassment.'

Logan stared at her. 'What bloody harassment? I interviewed him *twice*!'

She backed off, hands up. 'Hey, I'm only telling you what was in the note.'

'Little *bastard*. How could he say that?' Logan buried his face in his hands. 'You know what this means, don't you? Parents make a formal complaint and I get hauled up in front of Professional Sodding Standards again.'

Which explained why Big Gary wouldn't look him in the eye when he'd signed in at the station this morning.

Steel came lumbering up the corridor. 'Called the number: Danby's wife. She spoke to him last night, hung up after the line went quiet for a while. Says he falls asleep in front of the telly a lot.' Steel looked Samantha up and down. 'Hey, Red.'

'Inspector.'

Silence.

'So, tell me.' Steel smiled. 'Collar and cuffs: they match?'

'. . .I need to get back to the scene.' Samantha marched back towards Danby's hotel room, her cheeks bright pink.

Logan closed the stairwell door. 'Did you have to do that?'

'Love-life's in the crapper, remember? Got to get my jollies where I can.' She made for the lifts, dragging Logan behind her. 'Come on, we've got an auld mannie to visit.'

Sunlight struggled through the blinds into the over-warm room. Unlike the rest of the hospital, the victim support suite had plush carpets, a soft sofa with stain-free cushions, a coffee table with gaily-coloured coasters and up-to-date magazines. And a camera sitting in the corner on a tripod, the red light glowing to show it was recording.

An old man crouched in a floral-print armchair, his clawed fingers picking at the seam of his trousers. His face was a mess of green and purple bruises, a bite mark clear on the wrinkled skin of his left wrist. Even so, the doctors said he'd got off lightly compared to Harry from Sacro. Small mercies.

His voice was barely a whisper. *'Want to go home.'*

'I know, Jimmy, I know. We just need to ask you a few more questions. . .' The Family Liaison officer shifted on the sofa. *'Can you describe the man who attacked you?'*

'Don't want to be here. Want to go home.'

Sitting in the little observation room next door, Logan watched DI Steel reach forward and take one of Jimmy's hands. *'It's OK, Jimmy, we'll take you home soon. We just want to make sure we catch whoever hurt you.'*

Her voice came from a small speaker bolted to the wall on the dark side of the two-way mirror.

Logan settled back in his plastic chair and picked up the copy of that morning's *Aberdeen Examiner*, abandoned on the little desk where the DVD recorder and TV screen sat. The front page headline screamed, 'TYNESIDE SEX-BEAST STRIKES AGAIN – RICHARD KNOX ON RAPE RAMPAGE IN THE NORTH EAST' above a photo of Jimmy Evans's bruised face. Christ knew how Colin Miller managed to get his hands on the victim before the police.

According to the paper, Jimmy Evans was a retired shipbuilder from Sunderland, who'd moved to the north-east of Scotland after the death of his wife. An unremarkable man who'd lived an unremarkable life, right up until yesterday afternoon. He'd come home and discovered someone breaking into his garage, tried to be a have-a-go hero, and ended up with Richard Knox.

There was a lurid account of the attack, and then a little tagline saying, 'COMMENT ON PAGE 6'.

Sod the commentary, Logan flipped through the rumpled newsprint, looking for Douglas Walker's suicide note. He found it on pages nine and ten, printed like a screen-grab, complete with the first few replies and comments from the art student's Facebook friends.

Steel had been right, a chunk of it *was* in poetry. According to the accompanying article, Walker was a naive young man who'd got caught up in things he didn't understand and been persecuted by the police because of it.

The note claimed he'd been interviewed all weekend, never allowed to sleep, pressured to make a confession. And the harassment had kept up once he'd been released on bail. Never ending. Poking and prodding. Until Douglas Walker just couldn't take it any more.

He was sorry.

Lying tosser.

Twice. Logan had interviewed him twice. And *never* at home.

Through in the victim support lounge Steel and the FLO were still trying to tease information out of Knox's latest victim.

Logan pulled out his phone, grimacing as his fingers touched the evidence bag with his puke-stained notebook in it. He pulled that out too and dumped it on the desk.

Should really throw the thing out. But it had Douglas Walker's statement in it, his handing over of the holdall full of counterfeit notes, and his agreement to come into the station voluntarily. All the stuff Professional Standards would need to see.

He picked up his new mobile and called Colin Miller.

'Laz, foos yer doos, my sheepshaggin' friend?'

'Where did you get the exclusive?'

'What, no witty repartee?' Sigh. *'Which one? Got three in the paper the day: Sex Scandal Rocks Local School, Drug Dealers' Vigilante Fears, or Tyneside Sex-Beast—'*

'That one: how did you get hold of Jimmy Evans before we did?'

'The auld mannie? His son emailed me.'

Logan flipped back to the paper's front page. Colin's *Aberdeen Examiner* email address was printed under his by-line. 'Email?'

'*Member of the BlackBerry generation, Laz. Online twenty-four-seven. Found out just in time to get it in: hold the front page, the whole works. Brilliant, so it was.*' Pause. '*So . . . what do you think? Knox has to be escalatin', right? First his Sacro handler and now the old boy. Two in two days.*'

'I'm not giving you a quote, Colin.'

'*Aw, come on, man. I'll make it, "sources close to the investigation" if you like?*'

Logan put the paper back on the tabletop. 'Tell me about Jimmy Evans and I'll think about it.'

'*The son's up visitin' from Sunderland with his wife – they come back from some party, and there's the old man in the back garden, wanderin' in the snow, wearing nothing but his jim-jams. They bundle him into the car and drive him straight to A&E. Son emails me from the waiting room, cos he'd seen my stuff in the papers.*'

'They didn't search the house?'

'*Laz, if your dad was workin' on a dose of hypothermia with his face all battered, would you?*'

46

'I'm not your enemy, Logan.' The Chief Inspector took a sip of tea, peering at him over the rim of the mug.

'All I'm saying is I should be out there, searching the house.'

'Oh, I'm sure DI Steel can manage without you for an hour or so.' Chief Inspector Young – filling in while Professional Standards' arch bastard Superintendent Napier was off at a conference somewhere – smiled. He had broad shoulders; short hair greying at the temples; big meaty fists, the knuckles criss-crossed with scar tissue; and small, dark eyes, surrounded by starburst wrinkles. The kind of man you'd want standing in front of you on crowd control, or forcing entry into a drug dealer's flat.

The Professional Standards Unit wasn't exactly Logan's favourite part of Force Headquarters, which was a shame, considering how often he had to visit. Young shared his office with another chief inspector, who'd excused himself as soon as Logan arrived – giving them a bit of privacy for the bit where Chief Inspector Young bent Logan over the desk and, as Biohazard Bob so gleefully put it, proceeded without the aid of lubricant.

Young nodded at the photocopied complaint sitting in the middle of the desk. 'And you never visited Douglas Walker at his home?'

Logan stared at him. 'I only interviewed Walker *twice*. Both times, right here. With all due respect, sir, this is bollocks.'

'You do know I can just check the custody log?'

'Good – check it.'

Young glanced down at his notes. 'His lawyer claims this was part of an "orchestrated campaign of harassment" that started when you dragged Walker into the station under false pretences.'

'Not this again. . .' Logan dragged the bagged notebook from his pocket and peeled it open. The bitter-sharp scent of bile crept out into the room.

Chief Inspector Young recoiled slightly in his seat. 'What is that *smell*?'

'It . . . kind of fell in some sick.' The pages were all stuck together on one side, so Logan stole the silver letter opener from the room's other desk and started flicking them apart, setting a little avalanche of pale yellow flakes free.

> **Sunday 31ˢᵗ January:**
> *Attended caravan in steading development. Questioned Danny Saunders and fiancée Stacy Gardner in relation to armed robbery at Henderson's Jewellers . . .*

'Sergeant I really don't think that's necessary. We—'

'Hold on. . .' He snicked a few more sheets loose.

> **Saturday 30ᵗʰ January:**
> *Attended incident at Richard Knox's house – Knox agitated and destroying his possessions. No charges made.*

A couple more and he had the declaration Walker had signed: the one saying he was coming into the station voluntarily.

'Look. All done by the book.' Logan held the notebook out.

Young backed away from the desk slightly. 'Any chance you can put that back in its bag?'

Logan did, then swept the little pile of yellow flakes left behind into the bin. 'I showed Walker's lawyer everything at the time. He's just chancing his arm.'

The chief inspector sat back in his leather chair, eyes creased, mouth working silently on something. 'You know, DCI Finnie has asked if we would consider taking you on secondment to Professional Standards.'

Logan stared back. And he'd thought the frog-faced bastard had been joking. 'Did he?'

'You look horrified.'

'Thank you, sir.'

'. . .and he said Finnie wants to palm me off on the rubber-heelers!' Logan shifted his shoulder, keeping the phone clamped to his ear as he washed the flakes of dried sick off his hands. The smell was getting worse as they rehydrated.

DI Steel made wet chomping noises in his ear for a moment. *IB found some decent prints on the window and the bedpost, if we're lucky they'll match.*

'Why the hell would *anyone* want to join Professional Bloody Standards!'

'Chase up the lab, OK? I want a definite on the bite marks and saliva by close of play.'

'First thing I'd do is investigate that sarcastic bastard Finnie.'

'Are you even listening?'

'What? Yeah: bite marks and saliva. Anything else?'

'Victim's house is on the south-east corner of Cove, down its own

*wee driveway. Nothing behind it but fields and the North Sea. I
want a fingertip search: hundred metre radius.'*

Logan frowned. 'Does this whole thing sound . . . *off* to
you?'

'And tell them to do it properly this time, no fuck-ups.'

'Knox drugs his Sacro handlers, beats the crap out of them,
gets past the surveillance team. . . Then stops off on the way
down the road so he can torture and rape an old man in
Cove? Like it's a service station and he fancies a burger?'
Logan hauled the plug out of the sink, letting the water
gurgle away. 'Do you think he's the one who snatched
Danby?'

He could hear her chewing again. *'Want to say yes, but. . .
How's a weedy wee shite like that get the jump on someone like
Danby, never mind carry him down the stairs?'*

'So he had help. Would explain where he got the Rohypnol
from. Half the heavies in Tyneside are after Mental Mikey's
millions, maybe this is Knox's price? He wants revenge on
the guy who put him away, and help to disappear?'

'Aye, maybe. . .' Pause. *'Listen, get onto Northumbria Police, I
want to know what Danby's been working on, just in case it's no'
got anything to do with our wee rapist chum. And while you're
doing the rounds: chase up Lothian and Borders. Andrew Connelly
must've shown his baldy head somewhere by now. Just cos everything's going to shite, doesn't mean I'm letting that big bald bastard
get away with what he did to Steve Polmont.'*

Biohazard Bob was hunched over a pile of paperwork in the
Wee Hoose. He looked up as Logan entered, then went back
to his forms. 'Shut the bloody door.'

Clunk. The noise of phones and harassed constables died
down.

Logan settled into his chair and called Northumbria
Police. Ten minutes later he had reference numbers for

every case Danby had worked in the last eighteen months, and a promise that the relevant files would be with him soon as possible. Then he was put through to a Detective Inspector Walsh.

'*You the one told us about Oscar Renwick? Used to share a cell with Richard Knox in Frankland Prison?*' The Newcastle accent was clipped and angry.

Logan frowned at the receiver. 'Yes?'

'*You got any idea how many man-hours we wasted looking into that?*'

'Wasted? But he was—'

'*He was nowhere near any of them house fires. None. Had cast-iron alibis, you know what I mean?*'

Logan opened the spreadsheet of Knox's cellmates from Frankland Prison. 'But Knox said Renwick told him—'

'*Knox's a sex offender, remember? They manipulate, that's what they do.*'

'But—'

'*Knox managed to smuggle a mobile phone into his cell, and Renwick sold him out to one of the prison officers. Knox knew Renwick was going to be up for parole soon, so he told you a happy little fairytale about murdered families. Bang: big investigation and no parole for Renwick. Knox was using you to get his own back, and you fell for it!*'

'But I didn't know—'

'*And now I've got me guv'nor breathing down me neck for all the overtime I've blown on this, Sergeant. Thanks. Thanks a bloody heap.*'

'But. . .'

He was talking to a dead line. The DI had hung up.

Logan leant forward, banged his head on the desk, and swore for a bit.

'You ever think about the job?'

Logan sat up. 'What?'

401

'The job.' Bob was facing the wall, but he was speaking to Logan. 'What the point is?'

'Every sodding day.'

Bob nodded. 'It's like the whole bloody city's on fire, and all we can do is piss on the bit in front of us.' He thumped his pen down on the desk. 'I'm fucking sick of getting my pubes scorched off.'

Logan laughed, but Bob wasn't even smiling.

'You talked to Deborah, didn't you.'

'I arrested someone yesterday. Every time his eleven-year-old daughter got a bad mark on her homework he'd tie her to the hot water pipes in the basement and crank the central heating up full. Arms and legs, covered with these huge weeping blisters. His own *daughter*.' Bob's shoulders sagged. 'Fuck's wrong with people?'

'You want to swap horror stories? Because I've got some good ones.'

'I talked to Deborah last night. Stood there and demanded to know what was going on. The secret phone calls, the weird messages, the whole lot. You know why she won't get undressed if I'm in the room? Why she won't let me *fucking* touch her?' He picked up a box file and hurled it across the room. Then sat there staring at the paperwork, fluttering to the carpet.

'Shit. I'm sorry, Bob.'

'She's been seeing a specialist: breast cancer.' He slumped back in his seat and stared at the ceiling tiles. 'Found a lump six months ago. She was scared to tell me in case I left her. . . Can you believe that?'

It went quiet again. And then Bob's phone rang. He sighed, rubbed his face, then picked up. 'Bob's House of Bouncy Boobies, Bob speaking. . .'

It was like watching someone pretending to be Bio-hazard Bob Marshall. The crude humour, the language, the mannerisms were all there, but there was no life to the performance.

Logan picked up his own phone and set up Steel's fingertip search. Then told the media office to get posters with Knox's face up in all the petrol stations from Aberdeen to London. It was a long shot, but if he had a car, he'd have to stop and fill it up somewhere.

Then Logan downloaded everything he could from the Police National Computer relating to Danby's case numbers, and sent the lot off to the printer in the corner. He bundled everything into a manila folder, and grabbed his coat.

Logan stood there for a moment, then put his hand on Bob's shoulder and gave it a squeeze.

Still on the phone, Bob just nodded.

Logan closed the door behind him.

He headed down to the front desk. Big Gary was on, sucking his teeth and reading his book again, hunched over it like a fat gargoyle.

Logan knocked on the worktop. 'Any chance of a pool car?'

'No. Those idiots in night-time CID have written off four of them since Monday. And there's a waiting list for the rest.'

'Oh, come on, Gary, I only need it for—'

'Did you get my message?'

'What message?'

Big Gary marked his place in the book with a 'DRINK-DRIVE-DIE!' leaflet and slammed it shut. 'Every bloody time.' He hauled out a sticky note and slapped it on the desktop. 'You're not getting on the waiting list till you've seen to your prisoners.'

'I don't have any prisoners: Gardner should have been up before the Sheriff by now.' Logan snatched the note off the desk. 'For God's sake Gary, I specifically asked for an early slot for him so he can get his granddaughter back from Social Services!'

'Mr Gardner was on at nine fifteen, and you're *welcome*. I'm talking about the couple you had a lookout request for.'

Blank look.

Gary sighed, straining the buttons on his white shirt. 'Leadbetter: Wendy and Ian. The brother and sister who torched Knox's granny's place?'

'Oh, *that* Wendy and Ian Leadbetter. Can't someone else—'

'No.'

'But Steel needs me out in Cove.'

'Better hope you get a confession quick then, hadn't you?'

Logan stomped down to the custody area. The place was quiet for a change, just the faint burble of an Airwave handset announcing the comings and goings of Aberdeen's boys in black and fluorescent yellow. A Police Custody and Security Officer was eating a yoghurt in the office that opened out onto the concrete corridor of the cell block.

She froze as he knocked, the spoon halfway between the yoghurt pot and her mouth, then stood.

Logan waved her back into her seat. 'Don't let me stop you.'

She shrugged and spooned in another mouthful. 'You making a deposit or a withdrawal?'

'Wendy and Ian Leadbetter?'

The PCSO rolled her eyes. 'Only been here half an hour, and they're already a pain in the arse.'

Logan flipped through the short stack of unfiled custody forms on the desk, spotting a couple of familiar names amongst them. 'You hear about the bloke Biohazard Bob brought in last week?'

Her face darkened. 'The one tortured his own daughter?

Oh yeah, I remember him fine. Never met anyone more in need of falling down the stairs a couple of times.' She dumped her spoon on the desk, then upended the yoghurt pot over her mouth, tapping the bottom and slurping.

Logan waited for her to resurface. 'Any chance of a squint at the custody log?'

'Paper or electronic?'

'Whichever's easier.'

'Knock yourself out.' She hauled a thick ring binder from a shelf and thumped it down next to him. 'You want me to get the Leadbetters into an interview room?'

'I've got Butler waiting in number four, we'll start with the sister.'

'Right, back in a tick.'

Logan opened the custody log, working back in time, skimming through the drunks and drug addicts, the burglaries and random violence. His own name appeared at twenty past seven, Tuesday evening – checking Alan Gardner in for armed robbery.

Then there was the usual mix of daily Aberdeen life: a mugging; six cases of shoplifting; two women done for kicking the living hell out of a Romanian bloke selling the *Big Issue* outside Boots. . .

Biohazard's 'Father of the Year' had been signed into custody on Monday afternoon, so with any luck the bastard got Sheriff McNab, and was right now being forced to pleasure some fat fucker in Craiginches.

Serve him right.

Logan went further back. His own name popped up again at quarter to two on Monday afternoon, handing Douglas Walker back into custody after a fifteen-minute interview. Fair enough.

He skipped through the next few pages: domestic violence, drunk driving, assault, another assault, more shoplifting, unlawful removal. . . And there he was again, checking Douglas Walker out of custody at quarter to ten on the Monday morning.

Logan frowned. Eight pages later and he was checking Walker out at half eight on Sunday evening. Then again at six twenty-two. And four. Ten in the morning. Saturday was just as bad: 17:43, 16:22, 14:12, 12:50. Always against his name.

He stared at the bottom of the last form. It *looked* like his signature, but there was no way he'd actually signed it.

'Right, the sister's in four with Butler.' The PCSO marched back into the room. 'Did you know that cheeky sod DS MacDonald tried to grab my—'

'This is bollocks!' Logan held the custody log up. Then slammed it back on the desk. 'I was nowhere near Douglas Walker on Saturday, or Sunday!'

She pursed her lips. 'OK. . .'

'Who's been screwing with the log?'

She backed off a step. 'Why would anyone screw with the custody log?'

'Look at it!' He thrust the heavy ring binder at her. 'I interviewed Douglas Walker twice. This thing has me doing it eleven bloody times!'

The PCSO picked her way carefully around the edge of the room, making for her desk. Keeping as much distance between them as possible. 'Maybe you should—'

'Check the computer.'

She smiled, but it didn't go anywhere near her eyes. 'Yes. I can do that. Right now. Checking the computer. . .'

Logan thumped the custody log back on the desk. 'That's *not* my signature!'

For the next two minutes the only sound was the rattle-clack of fingers on keyboard, then the PCSO cleared her throat. 'Ah. . . You know, your prisoner's been sitting in the interview room for a while now, and maybe—'

'What does it say?'

Silence.

'DI Beattie's down as the attending officer.'

47

The PCSO had fallen behind after the first two flights of stairs, but Logan wasn't waiting for her to catch up.

He stormed down the corridor to DI Beattie's office and barged through the door. It bounced off a filing cabinet with a loud clang and started to swing shut. Logan marched in.

Beattie was sitting behind his desk, eyes wide, phone clamped to his ear. 'What. . .?'

Logan slammed the custody log down on the desktop, hard enough to send a mug of tea spiralling to the new carpet. 'What the hell did you do?'

Beattie shrank back. 'I'm on the phone!'

'You're going to be on your arse in a minute!'

The PCSO's voice came from the open door behind him: 'I told you he'd taken it.'

Then a man: 'Sergeant McRae, would you care to explain yourself?'

Logan didn't need to look around, he knew it was Chief Inspector Young from Professional Standards, which meant he was probably already screwed.

'Beattie faked the custody log.'

The DI's chin came up. 'I don't know what you're—'

'Here!' Logan yanked the ring binder open, whipping through the pages until he got to the first forged custody record – the one that said he'd interviewed the art student at quarter to nine on Monday morning. 'Douglas Walker, checked out of custody at oh-nine-forty-five Monday by DS McRae.'

Chief Inspector Young appeared at Logan's shoulder. 'And how does that—'

'At nine forty-five I was making sure Richard Knox got through the lynch mob outside his house in one piece. You can check with DI Steel, and half a dozen PCs. It was on the bloody telly!' He flipped back a few pages. 'Twenty past six, Sunday night: I was arresting Angus Black for possession in Blackburn. *This* says I was interviewing Walker again. But the computer log says it was Beattie!'

The DI lumbered to his feet. 'Sergeant, how *dare* you suggest—'

Logan slammed his hand down on the open ring binder. 'What, you couldn't figure out how to fiddle the electronic version? Bit more difficult than faking a signature, was it?'

Beattie looked at CI Young. 'Chief Inspector, I want to make a formal complaint about DS McRae's behaviour. You're a witness, right? You and. . .' He pointed at the PCSO. 'You. He threatened me, and—'

'I'll do more than bloody *threaten* you!'

He lunged, but Young was faster, wrapping one of those huge scarred hands around Logan's arm. 'I think we should all calm down, don't you?'

'He tried to attack me! You saw him!'

Logan had another go, but Young's grip was solid.

And then everyone froze as DCI Finnie appeared in the doorway. 'Tell me gentlemen, am I running a CID department, or a *playground* for badly behaved children?'

Silence.

Logan tore his arm out of Young's grip. Pointed at Beattie. 'Tell him what you did.'

'DS McRae is being abusive and threatening—'

'You lying bastard!'

Young had to restrain him again.

Beattie backed away. 'I want him brought up on charges, and—'

'THAT'S ENOUGH!' Finnie's voice made the paintings rattle on the walls. 'You will *both* behave like professional police officers, or I'll suspend the pair of you!' He checked his watch. 'Chief Inspector Young, would you be so *kind* as to escort DS McRae back to your office for a small chat about appropriate workplace behaviour?' He turned to face Logan and Beattie. 'And I'll expect both of you in my office at five this evening when we shall discuss your conduct. Do you understand?'

Logan stiffened. 'Sir.'

'Sir, it's not my fault, he barged in and—'

'Do you *understand*, Inspector Beattie?'

The beardy idiot deflated a bit. 'Yes, sir.'

'We've got a rapist on the loose, and a missing detective superintendent. I *suggest* you redirect your energies to getting out there and bloody well finding them!'

Then the head of CID turned a thin smile on the PCSO. 'And Marie, I *hate* to be a stick in the mud, but the custody log is not supposed to leave the custody area.'

Pink crept up from the white collar of her shirt. 'But—'

'Don't let it happen again.'

'We didn't do nothing.' Wendy Leadbetter folded her arms across her chest. The white Tyvec SOC suit they'd given her to wear, while her own clothes were being examined, made rustling noises as she shifted in her seat. Up close she looked older than he'd been expecting, her face hard and cold, scowl lines already beginning to etch themselves around her eyes and mouth.

'I am now showing Ms Leadbetter exhibits three, four, five, and six.' Logan laid the photos out on the interview-room table, starting with the figure throwing the petrol bomb, then moving on to the reference shots of Wendy and her brother Ian in the crowd outside Knox's home.

She shrugged. 'Could be anybody. Got their face covered, like.'

'We found traces of petrol on your jacket, your gloves, your jeans, and your shoes Wendy. See, petrol's funny that way, it's like glue: sticks to everything.'

'Maybe I was filling up me car? Had a bit of an accident. Ever think of that?'

Logan packed the photos away again. 'Fine. Lie. See if I give a toss.' He stood. 'We've got you on camera, we've got witnesses, we've got forensics, and we've got motive. You want to play the hardnut? Go right ahead, see how much it helps when you're banged up for eight years.'

He glanced over Wendy Leadbetter's shoulder to where PC Butler was leaning against the wall. 'Get her out of here. We'll do her brother for conspiracy, then we can all sod off to the pub.'

Butler stepped forward. 'Up.'

She didn't move. 'Ian wasn't involved in nothing.'

'Yeah, right. He's an innocent little lamb with. . .' Logan flicked through the file. 'Look at that: eighteen counts of criminal damage, six public order offences, and four warnings for sending threatening letters.' He looked at Butler again. 'Cells.'

'I said, on your feet.'

'Who says Ian had anything to do with it? Knox didn't just rape *our* grandad, did he? Loads of families up for doing him a bit of harm.'

411

'Yeah, well, you're the only ones in Aberdeen, so—'

'Shows how much *you* know.' She rapped her knuckles on the chipped Formica. 'Seen at least two others outside Knox's house. Could've been any of them, like.'

'You really expect me to believe. . .' Logan trailed to a halt. Then pulled out the photos and laid them out on the tabletop again – along with all the others he'd printed off – until there was just a big sea of angry faces staring up into the interview room. 'Prove it.'

Leadbetter sniffed. Then leaned forward and stared, her hard green eyes sweeping back and forth. 'Him.' Her finger jabbed a pale-skinned older man in a leather jacket, red Man U scarf around his neck, mouth open shouting something. 'Lowe, or Lovie, something like that. Knox raped his dad.' Thirty seconds later she'd picked out another one: a heavy-set woman snarling beneath a 'DIE – KNOX – SCUM!' placard. 'No idea what she's called.'

Logan waited, but she couldn't pick out anyone else.

Wendy Leadbetter scowled at him. 'Our grandad was a good man, and that sick bastard tortured and raped him. You let Knox go, and now he's out there, doing it to other families.' She finally got to her feet. 'They should've killed him in prison. More than he fucking deserves.'

And she was probably right.

While Butler was sticking Leadbetter back into custody, Logan apologized to Marie, the PCSO. Sorry for nicking her custody log. Sorry for getting her in trouble with Finnie. But mostly he was sorry for not breaking DI Beattie's nose.

Butler was waiting for Logan outside the cells, running a hand through her short spiky blonde hair. 'You want me to go get the brother now?'

Logan shook his head. 'One mental family member at a time is enough for me. We need to go and. . .' Logan frowned.

412

He pulled out the plastic bag with his crusty notebook in it, snapped on a pair of latex gloves and picked through the sour-smelling pages. Something about mental family members. . .

'Sarge? I said, where are we going?'

'Hmm? Oh. . . Cove: got to help DI Steel search for signs of Knox.'

Butler wilted slightly. 'Oh God, not more tramping about in the snow.'

'Might have to make a little diversion on the way. . . Nip upstairs and get us a pool car, will you?'

She stomped off as he worked his way backwards through the notebook, looking for his visit to Danny Saunders's caravan. Then Logan went into his other pocket for the pilfered CV he'd been scribbling notes on since yesterday afternoon, and compared the two.

He closed his eyes and groaned. What a bloody idiot.

Logan's rusty Fiat bumped to a halt outside the part-completed steading. PC Butler hauled on the handbrake and killed the engine, then sat there, looking at the peeling steering wheel, the dented dashboard, the passenger-side window covered in a patchwork of black plastic bag and duct tape, the buckled bonnet. 'Bet you pull *all* the girls in this thing.'

'Should have tried harder for a pool car then, shouldn't you?'

'I was doing fine till I told Big Gary it was for you.'

Logan peered out through the chipped windscreen. Danny Saunders had managed to cover all the roof joists with a skin of marine-ply. Right now he was balancing at the top of a long ladder, nailing batons down over some sort of black material.

'Like driving an oil tanker. You never heard of power steering?'

413

'Lucky the damn thing's still going at all.' Especially after being shunted into a ditch by a dirty big Transit van. At least the duct tape and string was still holding the bonnet in place. . . though the engine had developed a worrying burning smell to go with the growling exhaust.

Logan clambered out onto the crunchy snow. The sky was a bright blue lid with dark-grey clouds massing over the North Sea. Probably going to be another horrible night.

Especially if DCI Finnie had anything to do with it. The lecture on not attacking your colleagues from Chief Inspector Young had been bad enough, but the one from the head of CID would be a lot worse.

Logan slammed the car door.

Standing on top of the ladder, Danny flinched, the hammer and a plastic pouch of nails skittering down across the marine-ply, then off the edge of the roof. 'Ah, shite!'

He turned, the expression freezing on his face when he saw who it was.

Logan picked his way through the snowy tufts. 'Morning, Danny.'

'I didn't rob that jewellers on Huntly Street!'

'Yeah, I know. I arrested someone for that yesterday.'

Behind him Logan could hear PC Butler climbing out of the car, scrunching over to back him up.

'Oh aye?'

'Funniest thing, but the guy was called "Alan Gardner". Ring any bells?'

Danny coughed, then glanced over the ridge of the steading roof at the moss-streaked caravan, just visible around the corner. 'Never heard of him.'

'You told him you'd break his daughter's legs if she didn't pay off her drug debt.'

'Got to get back to work. The roof gets all warped if it's not—'

'Danny? Why can't I hear hammering?' A woman's voice, coming from the caravan. Logan turned to see the pregnant fiancée standing there with her hands on her hips, face flushed, mouth a hard line. 'You know we need that roof waterproofed before it snows again. Don't make me come up there!'

'Oh Jesus. . .' He straightened up and shouted back. 'It's the police.'

Logan clumped through the snow towards her. 'Stacy Gardner?'

'You know fine well it is. What do you want?'

'I had a very interesting chat with your dad, Stacy. Says he's sorry he hasn't come up with more money, but he kind of got arrested doing over a jewellery shop on Huntly Street. He hopes your dealer,' Logan nodded at the man balancing on the roof, 'will give him a bit more time before hurting you.'

Stacy throttled the dishcloth in her hands. 'No idea what you're talking about.'

Danny sighed. 'Stacy, love, it's not—'

'You shut up, Danny Saunders, *I'm* dealing with this.' She took a step out onto the snowy ground. 'The old man can't cope since he got mum killed. Lives in a little world of his own.'

'Stacy, we—'

'I said I'm *dealing* with it!' She turned a cold smile in Logan's direction. 'So you see, you can't trust a word he says. He's lost it.'

Logan nodded. 'But you still trust him to look after Nicole, don't you? What is she, two, three? We had to put her into care.'

The pregnant woman stiffened. 'She's not my daughter any more. I'm making a *new* life.'

'He's sold everything for you, you know that don't you? Car, furniture, telly, cashed in his pension – even the house is up for sale, because he thinks you're in trouble.'

Stacy turned and reached back into the caravan for something, keeping whatever it was hidden by her pregnant bulge. 'So he sends me money every now and then. Not like I don't deserve it, is it? Just my share of mum's inheritance.'

'It's extortion.'

She swivelled round, both hands behind her back, and sniffed as if fighting back a tear. 'It wasn't *my* idea. Danny made me do it!'

Up on the roof, her fiancé's mouth fell open. 'You lying cow!'

'Where do you think Daddy got the idea to use a sledge-hammer? That was Danny's trick.'

'I was the one tried to talk you out of it!'

Stacy took a step forward, biting her bottom lip. 'Sorry, Danny, but I can't cover for you any more. It was all his fault, Officer. He *made* me do it.'

Logan looked back at the roof.

Mistake.

Stacy lunged, hands coming out from behind her back – eight inch carving knife in one hand, steaming kettle in the other. The kettle lashed past, close enough for Logan to feel the heat on his cheek.

He staggered back, arms over his head as the knife slashed down, the point tearing through the sleeve of his jacket.

Logan's heel caught something buried in the snow and he went crashing down on his backside for the second time in two days. Looking up at someone who wanted him dead.

And then a blur of black and fluorescent yellow: PC Butler charged across the rutted ground, her peaked cap flying off. Stacy snarled and swung the knife again in a huge overhead slash.

Butler darted in, arm up. She blocked Stacy's stab, reached

416

through with her other hand in some sort of weird jujitsu limb origami, and pulled, forcing the pregnant women's arm to bend in ways it *really* wasn't designed to.

Stacy's eyes bulged, then she screamed and lurched back into the wall of the caravan. 'You're breaking my arm!'

'Drop the knife, or I'll pop it right out of the socket!'

'Get off me you *bitch*!'

One more twist and the knife thudded into the snow, blade first, the handle sticking up into the air.

'Danny! Danny, help me! They're hurting the baby!'

But Danny just sat on the roof of his house and stared at her.

There was a gunshot sound and Logan's manky little Fiat puttered to a halt on the rear podium car park, leaving a cloud of grey smoke behind. Should probably get that seen to.

PC Butler killed the engine, before it died on its own. 'Everyone out. Now!'

'If my baby's damaged by carbon monoxide poisoning, I'll sue!'

Butler turned and stared at her. 'Shut up. For *once* in your life. All the way into bloody town!'

Stacy Gardner pouted. 'You can't talk to me like that! I—'

'For God's sake!' Sitting next to her, on the threadbare back seat, Danny Saunders gritted his teeth. 'Give it a rest, Stacy.'

'That's right – shout at the pregnant woman in *handcuffs*! Oh yes, you're such a big man, aren't you Danny? Such a big—'

Logan climbed out and slammed the car door shut, cutting off the rest.

PC Butler stood on the other side of the dented Fiat,

417

massaging her temples. '*Why* are we not allowed to gag prisoners any more?'

'Just get them processed and we'll head out to Cove. Let someone else listen to her bitch and moan for a while.'

Butler glared at the sky for a moment, sighed, pulled on her peaked cap, then wrenched open the car door and folded the driver's seat forward. 'I said everyone out!'

Logan left them to it.

Logan had the Wee Hoose to himself while he waited for PC Butler to get Danny Saunders and his poisonous fiancée photographed, fingerprinted, DNA-sampled, and checked into separate cells.

He spread Danby's cases out across the desk. The PNC printouts weren't exactly heavy on detail, more summaries and status reports. A couple of unsolved murders: one drug addict found with a bullet hole in the back of his head; one prostitute kicked to death behind the bins at a nightclub. One Post Office job where the gang had got away with a pathetically small amount of cash after putting a pensioner in intensive care – solved. One blackmail: a bank manager with a thing for Filipino ladyboys – solved. A couple of demanding money with menaces. . .

Something started ringing. It took Logan a minute to realize it was his new phone. 'McRae.'

'*LoganDaveGoulding, Just heard back from your CSI boys about the old man who was attacked last night.*' Might have known the psychologist wouldn't mind using the wanky Americanism.

'What about him?' Logan kept on reading.

The last report in Danby's file was a drug seizure: a shipment of heroin and cocaine, smuggled in through the international ferry terminal in North Shields. Estimated street value of one-point-six million.

'*Knox didn't rape him. He bit him, he tortured him, he beat him, but there's no sign of penetration.*'

According to the summary three men were due up in court in four weeks' time, all of them connected to Michael 'Mental Mikey' Maitland's operation.

God rest his soul.

'*So it's exactly the same as the Sacro handler . . . Harry Weaver. I thought it might be because Weaver wasn't old enough, didn't fit the victim profile, but I'm beginning to wonder if Knox might be impotent.*'

Logan skimmed a list of charges. 'That's a good thing, isn't it?'

'*Causing pain is how Knox achieves arousal, it's what gets him off. If he can't get an erection, he's just going to try harder. The next victim's probably going to end up dead. And it won't be quick either.*'

Logan stopped reading. Not so good after all.

'Any ideas where he's heading?'

There was a pause.

'*Well . . . Aberdeen's been highly traumatic for him, completely out of his comfort zone. He'll want familiar ground, somewhere he feels safe.*'

All roads lead to Newcastle. Which was pretty much what they'd been thinking anyway. Logan thanked the psychologist and hung up.

Logan drummed his fingers on the desk, staring at the blank computer screen.

God: the idea that Knox could get even worse. . .

'You should eat more roughage.'

Logan turned to find Doreen settling in behind her desk. 'What?'

'You've got the same expression on your face my six-year-old gets when he's constipated.'

'*Actually*, I was thinking about Richard Knox.'

'Join the club. DCI Finnie's got everyone on either Knox

419

or Danby. It's an absolute nightmare trying to get anything else done.' She rearranged her cardigan. 'Do you know if our little fairy princess got to see her grandad again?'

Logan shrugged. 'I've been a bit—'

'Oh for goodness sake. *I'll* do it.' Doreen pulled the phone towards her and started dialling. 'Hello? Yes, I want to speak to someone about a little girl taken into temporary care last night. . .'

PC Butler stuck her head around the door. 'You ready, Sarge?'

Logan gathered all the files together and stuck them back in the folder. 'We got a pool car?'

Butler's expression soured. 'Guess.'

The Fiat groaned from second to third, then whined from third to fourth, and refused to do fifth at all. 'You know.' Butler hauled the gearstick back again. 'I've got some friends who could arrange a little electrical fire, if you like? Claim on the insurance?'

'I'll bear that in mind.' Not that he'd get much for it – the thing only cost him two hundred pounds. Logan ran his finger across the dashboard, leaving a clean grey line in the dust. 'Suppose you were a gangster—'

'Cool.' Butler grinned. 'Do I get to kneecap that sleazy git DS MacDonald?'

'Just shut up and listen, OK? Suppose you were a gang-ster and some police officer had just cost you over a mill and a half in drugs. He's got three of your men banged up waiting for trial, and if they turn Queen's evidence it's going to be bad news for your other business interests. What do you do?'

She didn't even pause. 'Kill them. Get a couple of mental-ists inside to shank the bastards. Sends out a message – no one squeals.'

Logan looked at her. 'What if they're loyal.'

'Not worth the risk. Got to cut out the cancer before it spreads.' She slowed down for a corner, the tyres rumbling over a lumpy mixture of slush and ice. 'Then you go after the pig.'

Logan turned back to the window. 'That's what I was thinking.'

'He awake yet, Babe?'

'Dunno. Think he's faking it?'

'One way to check.'

Pain lances through Detective Superintendent Graeme Danby's nipples. His eyes snap open and he roars. Or tries to. There's something over his mouth. Something over his head, making everything dim and muffled. He rocks back and forth, fire burning across his chest.

'Gotta love the titty-twister, like.'

Fucking hell that *hurts*.

Then the woman's voice is back again. 'Hello, Sweetheart, remember me?'

Graeme tries to shrink back, but he's sitting on something: can't move his arms or legs. . . A chair? And it's freezing in here.

He'd been. . . He'd been wearing the white fluffy dressing gown he'd found in the hotel room wardrobe – the one with the matching slippers in a little plastic bag. But now he feels a biting draught on his bare stomach and thighs.

Isn't even wearing any underwear.

He's tied to a chair, stark bollock naked, with a bag over his head.

With *her*.

Graeme tries to sit up straight, to bring his chin up. Not to tremble.

'You've been a naughty boy, haven't you, Danby?' A man's voice, Newcastle accent.

And then a fist slams into Graeme's stomach, wrenching him forwards. Or as far as he can go with his wrists tied to the seat. He tries to breathe through the aching stabs, air whistling in and out through his burning nose. Everything smells of burning copper.

'You see, Babe, we know what you've been up to. You and your pet rapist.'

Oh God, don't be sick. Be sick and you'll choke. Choke and die. Naked, tied to a chair with a FUCKING BAG OVER YOUR HEAD!

Slowly, he hauls himself back up, eyes scrunched tight shut. Swallowing it down.

'Neil? Do the honours will you, Darling, I hate questioning someone when I can't see their eyes.'

Fumbling. The whoosh of fabric against his face. Then a cool draft of air.

Graeme opens his eyes, blinks. Looks down at his pale, naked body – the big dent in his right leg where the bone poked through years ago.

'That's better, isn't it?'

Julie. She hasn't changed much since last time: still wearing the same cowgirl jeans-and-boots combo. That polished razorblade smile.

Someone looms into view over his shoulder – Elvis quiff, big nose, tufty eyebrows. 'Afternoon, Guv. Sitting comfortably?' Elvis has a tartan pillowcase in his hand. He drops it to the floor.

Julie pulls up a chair, wrong way round, and straddles it. Smiles down at Graeme's crotch. 'Didn't think it was *that* cold.'

He tries on his best Senior Police Officer Glower, but she just laughs.

'Neil?'

A fist slams into the side of Graeme's head. Ringing in his

ears. The taste of blood. Lights flashing on and off. Then a throbbing ache.

'Now, Babe, you need to think really hard about this, because if you get the answer wrong you lose ten points and we move on to the water round. And trust me, you *won't* like the water round. Understand?'

Graeme stares at her. Then nods.

'Good. Neil, you can take the gag off.'

A harsh ripping noise, eye-watering agony. 'Fuck. . .'

Elvis holds up the duct tape, grinning. 'Got half his beard off in one go! Can we do his eyebrows next?'

'Bastards. . .' Breath hissing through gritted teeth.

'OK, Babe: here's your starter for ten.'

He can hear her chair scraping closer.

'Where's Richard Knox?'

'No, I can barely hear you.' Logan stuck his finger in his ear as they juddered up the hill past the truncated concrete pyramid of the Shell building, heading south. A massive eighteen-wheeler passed them in the outside lane, sending filthy grey-brown spray all over the car, the windscreen wipers struggling to clear it, leaving two diarrhoea-coloured rainbows across the glass.

'*I said, where the bastarding hell are you?*'

'Nigg roundabout. Should be with you in ten minutes.'

If the car didn't die by then.

'Listen, I found a possible motive for abducting Danby – million-and-a-half in seized—'

'*I don't care. Just got a call from Susan, she's got these stomach cramps. . .*'

Oh no.

Logan swallowed. 'She all right?'

'*Course she's no', she's having bloody stomach cramps!*' Silence. '*What if she loses the baby?*'

423

More silence.

'I'm sure she'll be fine. It'll all be fine.' That was what you were meant to say, wasn't it?

Steel coughed. Sniffed. Cleared her throat. *'Sod it, I'm taking her to A&E. You're in charge: give the search another couple hours then wind it down. Make it look like we tried.'*

'Do you want. . .'

But Steel was gone. He was talking to a dead phone.

'Sod it.' Logan jabbed the car's cigarette lighter with his thumb, and when it popped up he pulled a cigarette from the packet and sooked it into life.

Butler immediately started making pantomime coughing noises.

'Fine. . .' Logan ground it out in the overflowing ashtray. 'Happy?'

'Bad enough I've got to drive this rattletrap without catching your second-hand smoke.'

'Just drive, OK?'

The gritters were out in force – two of them taking up both lanes of the dual carriageway, huge rusty yellow things topped with flashing orange lights, strafing the road with salt and sand. All the cars hanging back to avoid having the paint battered off their bonnets.

Butler took the second exit at the next roundabout, heading into Cove, weaving through the suburban streets for the south-east corner.

Jimmy Evans's house sat on its own at the end of a long, rutted driveway, potholes and ice making Logan's tatty little Fiat slither and jerk as Butler got them as close to the brightly lit house as possible.

A series of patrol cars and police vans snaked back from a snow-covered driveway, blocking the lane.

'We'll have to walk from here.'

*   *   *

Sunlight speared down from a crystal blue sky, making the fields glitter, the snow crunchy underfoot, the sound of dogs and police chatter ringing in the crisp air.

The Police Search Advisor met them at the front door, scratching an armpit. With thinning, scraggy blonde hair and a pointy nose, he looked a bit like a meerkat with mange. 'So.' He squinted at Logan. 'It true you're in charge now?'

'That a problem?'

'Hey, long as you sign off on the overtime, I'm happy.' He held out a stack of reports and Logan flicked through them.

'You want to summarize this for me?'

More scratching. 'No sign of Knox anywhere.'

There was a shock. 'IB?'

The POLSA took his hand out of his armpit for long enough to point at a familiar filthy Transit van. 'Still doing the guest bedroom. Family's cleared out, so we've got the run of the place.'

'Door-to-doors?'

He blinked, then did a slow three-hundred-and-sixty-degree turn, staring out at the snow-covered fields. 'Erm. . . There's no one living anywhere near, if you don't count the sheep, so—'

'Back there, where the lane joins the main road. There's houses overlooking the entrance – they might've seen a car coming or going.'

The rest of Constable Meerkat's face turned as pink as his nose and ears. 'Ah, OK. I'll get that organized. . .'

The Airwave handset clipped to Butler's shoulder started bleeping and she moved away a couple of paces to answer it, then came back and handed the thing to Logan. 'Control.'

'McRae.'

'Aye, hud oan, puttin' you through. . .'

Click.

'Sergeant, it's Dr Frampton, we met at the—'

'Steve Polmont crime scene, yes, I remember.'

'I tried getting in touch with DI Steel, but it seems she's unavailable?'

'Yeah. . .' According to the paperwork, there wasn't so much as a footprint beyond the back garden.

'We've got a result from the soil sample we took yesterday, from the flat where Knox escaped. A footprint just inside the hallway?'

'Uh-huh?' Logan handed the search reports back to the POLSA. Steel was right – the search was a waste of time, but at least it looked as if they were doing something. Knox was long gone.

'We ran it against the national soil database, and there's about a dozen places it could have come from in Aberdeenshire, I've emailed the results to you.'

'Hold on. . .' He pulled out the scrap of paper he was using as a surrogate notebook, and pinned it to the roof of the nearest patrol car with the side of his hand, pen poised. 'Want to give me the edited highlights?'

Pause. 'The sample has a pH of five-point-five and carbon's sitting around three-point-six percent. Add in silt at eleven percent and that makes it Cairnrobin. You see, the general SSKIB values for soils like these—'

'Place names. Honestly, it'll be quicker if you just give me place names.'

'Oh. I see.' She cleared her throat. 'Yes, well Cairnrobin is a pretty small series – there's only three hundred and ninety-five hectares in the whole of Scotland – in isolated pockets around Cove, Menie House, and near the mouth of the Ythan at Sleek of Tarty.'

Logan crabbed them out on the paper, then put his hand over the mouthpiece, leant over to the POLSA. 'Any signs of a break in?'

'Back door – the lock's been gouged with a screwdriver.'

He went back to the call.

'. . .time. You see, a soil sample is like a fingerprint—'

'Thanks Doctor. That's great. I'll be in touch.' He hung up before she could launch into anything else.

Logan stood there, tapping the handset against his chin.

Butler raised an eyebrow. 'Something?'

He turned to the POLSA, and slapped his hand on the roof of the patrol car. 'You got keys for this?'

Turned out it wasn't even locked. Logan slipped into the passenger seat and fired up the little grey laptop mounted on the dashboard, using it to log into his Grampian Police email address.

Half a dozen messages from Beattie – which he ignored – and right after them the one from Dr Frampton. He opened it, then clicked on the .jpg attachment, shifting in his seat as the picture file downloaded.

It was a high-resolution map that looked as if it was made from stitched together screenshots. The areas where the soil matched the print in the flat highlighted in red. One cluster of red blobs sat north of Balmedie, near Donald Trump's golf resort; one was about halfway to Peterhead; but the biggest concentration lay along the coast just south of Cove.

Logan frowned at the screen.

Most were just fields, but two of the blobs had houses in them.

Logan zoomed in on the Cove section. 'See this?'

Constable Itchy squinted. 'No, that's wrong.' He stuck his finger on the laptop's screen and drew a little greasy circle inside the red bit. '*That's* the search area: Steel only wanted a hundred meters. Are we meant to search the rest of it? Only it's bloody freezing out there, and it'll be dark soon.'

Why was there mud from around the victim's home on the carpet of Knox's Sacro flat?

Maybe whoever helped him escape stopped off on the way up to check on potential targets. . .?

Logan looked up at the house. 'I need to speak to the victim, Evans.'

The POLSA shook his head. 'Like I said – the family's cleared out. Son took the old man back to Sunderland, said they didn't want him being on his own, you know, with Knox on the loose.'

Couldn't blame them. 'Give him a phone: I need to know if Evans saw anything suspicious – cars, people – over the last couple of days.'

Mind you, they'd have to be pretty open-minded mobsters to find their accountant an old man to torture and rape. . .

'Sarge?'

Logan blinked. 'Right. . . You two go grab a cup of tea. I've got some calls to make.'

48

Richard Knox shivers, standing at yet another bedroom window, wrapped only in his granny's patchwork quilt. The one that smells of old woman and cat.

The back garden's pretty, like one of them Christmas cards with robins on it, all plants and snow and ice and that. Fresh flakes floating down like cigarette ash.

His hand hurts even more now. Can barely move the first three fingers, they're so swollen.

He pulls the quilt tighter around his shoulders, then creeps over to the door and puts his ear against it.

They're arguing again.

Arguing about him.

'. . .out in the middle of nowhere. Let the bastard freeze to death.'

'That wasn't the plan!'

'I'm just saying we don't have to—'

'You can't just. . .'

Richard goes back to the window. Gives the sash a one-handed tug, even though he knows it's locked. What's he going to do: jump down into the garden, clamber over the back fence and run away into the snow with his cock hanging out and a quilt round his shoulders? Like a pervert playing Batman?

The big bloke with the grey hair's right: he'd freeze to death.

So instead Richard settles back on the edge of the bed and clutches his granny's old bible to his naked chest.

He sniffs, wipes his nose with the palm of his good hand, then smears the silvery slime on the bare mattress. At least it's stopped bleeding.

Not exactly what he'd had in mind, is it? Naked in some strange bedroom, waiting for them to decide how they're going to make him suffer.

03:10, YESTERDAY MORNING

There's a knock at the door.

Richard stands there in the bedroom of his bland little Sacro flat, eyes closed, swearing. Then hauls his trousers up again.

Mood's ruined now.

He gathers his things – the quilt Granny Murray made, the suitcase with Grandad Joe's clothes in it, the plastic bag.

Lying on the bed, Harry just cries.

Richard hauls everything he owns to the front door and opens it.

There's a man standing in the corridor outside: pale leather jacket, black ski-mask over his head, sawn-off shotgun in his hands. Very sinister. Richard hands him the suitcase. 'You're early.'

Someone else steps up, done up in IRA chic like his mate. 'Where are they?'

'You can put the guns away. I've taken care of me minders. Now—'

A fist slams into Richard's stomach. His knees give way and he thumps to the carpet, arms wrapped around his aching innards. Breath coming in ragged gulps.

No – this wasn't the deal. This isn't right!

The first man shoves past, and his mate steps up and kicks Richard in the chest, hard enough to flip him over onto his back. It's like being shot, but all he can do is gasp, can't even struggle as they drag him back into the flat.

Clunk, the door closes.

Man Number Two stops dead, staring into the bathroom. Then he peels off his ski-mask, exposing a face like skimmed milk. His jaw falls open, eyes wide. Then he turns to Richard. 'You dirty. . .'

Another kick, this one hard enough to make Richard fold up like a fortune cookie, clutching his aching balls, moaning, tears streaming down his face.

The other one says, 'What the hell's wrong with you?'

'Bathroom. Look in the bathroom.'

'Fucking hell. . .'

Another kick.

'There's someone else in here!'

Silence.

'Fuck. . .'

And then they're back, dragging him through into the bedroom.

'Look what you've done! You sick piece of shit . . .' A punch in the kidneys, making him squeal. Then another one.

'Fucking hell, Evans. Is he. . .?'

They cluster around Harry – still tied to the bed, naked, face down, with his pasty backside propped in the air.

Richard closes his eyes. Grits his teeth. Then forces himself over onto his stomach. Waves of fire ripple out from the small of his back, groin aching, chest burning.

Get out of here. NOW. Arm over arm, crawling along the oatmeal-coloured carpet.

'HEY! Get back here you little sod.'

Rough hands grab him, haul him back towards the bed

and Harry's naked body. 'This what gets you off, is it?'

A backhand slap snaps Richard's head sideways and he starts to cry.

They're going to kill him.

They're going to beat him to death in some crappy council housing flat for sex offenders.

The one in the pale leather jacket backs up a step. 'You know what? This works. Fuck it, this works really well.'

'Got to call an ambulance, police—'

'Grab him.'

'Lowe, *look* at the guy on the bed. We have to—'

'Fine, I'll do it myself.'

Those rough hands again, dragging Richard across the carpet, shoving his face against Harry's naked thigh.

Richard struggles, but the guy digs his knuckles into the back of his neck.

'Bite him. Go on, bite him like you did my dad, you fucking *freak*!'

'I don't . . . don't. . . Please. . .'

He hauls Richard's head back, then rams it forward into the hairy, clammy skin.

'You do as your told, or so help me God I'll break every fucking bone in your fucking body.'

'I don't. . .' Pain, rips through his hand, bones grating against each other as the big man stamps on Richard's knuckles, crushing them against the carpet.

'Fucking *bite* him!'

Richard opens his mouth wide and sinks his teeth into Harry's cold flesh.

49

Logan closed the front door behind him. The beautiful blue sky was gone, replaced by a layer of featureless grey that hurled little shards of ice at him, stinging his ears and nose, cheeks and fingers. He shuffled into the lee of a police van, trying to get his lighter to work.

Fourth time lucky: it caught and Logan dragged in a lungful of smoke, then spluttered it right back out again. Only his second cigarette today, not bad for twenty past three.

Nearly an hour and three-quarters to go. Have to leave soon, or get caught up in the traffic heading back to town. Rush-hour was bad enough, but the snow would grind everything to a halt. And he *wouldn't* want to be late for his bollocking from Finnie.

That would be a dreadful shame.

The phone in his pocket rang, the vibration travelling through to his ribs.

'Bugger off.'

It kept on ringing.

'Bloody hell. . .' He dragged it out with numb fingers and hit connect. 'This better be bloody important.'

'Sergeant . . . er . . . I mean, Logan. Look we got off to . . . it was a mistake, OK?' Detective Inspector Beardy Beattie.

Logan huddled closer to the van, breath steaming out around his head before being whipped away by the wind. 'You're bloody right it was.'

'I didn't know this was going to happen! How could I know? I just . . . you said he had all this counterfeit cash and I thought. . . I thought it would—'

'What? What *exactly* did you think it would do?' He watched a patrol car slithering away down the lane, its headlights cutting through the blue-grey gloom, catching the whirling snowflakes. 'You hounded an eighteen-year-old boy till he tried to kill himself. And *then* you tried to pin it on me!'

'I just. . .' Sigh. 'Look, you're good at this policeman stuff, it's easy for you. I just wanted something to, you know, be a success. Crack the counterfeit case.'

There was a long silent pause.

Logan switched his phone to his other hand, dug the numb fingers into his armpit, smoking with his eyes screwed up.

'Can you understand?'

Logan held his cigarette out at arm's length and let go. The wind snatched it out of his fingers, sending it spiralling away to explode in a shower of orange sparks against the IB Transit van. 'Fuck off, *sir*.'

Logan hung up.

Richard Knox stands at the window, staring out into the falling snow. He shivers, watching as a car pulls into the driveway.

The house is one of them farm building conversion things: all natural stone, wood floors, and exposed beams. When what you really want is proper insulation, carpets, and central bloody heating.

The huge black Range Rover lumbers to a halt, blocking the other cars in. There's a pale grey Mercedes, a big black people carrier, and a little Clio.

It was the people carrier they'd used to transport him about – from the Sacro flat to the house where he had to bite the old man. And from there to here. Always blind-folded and gagged, trussed up like a joint of meat, on the floor behind the back set of seats. Well, you wouldn't want to get your nice Mercedes all dirty by stuffing a registered sex offender in the boot, would you?

The Range Rover's doors open and a small woman gets out, stands in the snow looking around. Oh God. . . It's *her*.

Richard shrinks back, hiding behind the curtain, peeking out around the edge.

Her sidekicks climb out, stomp round to the back and open the boot. Then they haul something out onto the ground. It's a man, big, wearing nothing but a dirty towelling dressing gown that flaps in the wind, hands fastened behind his back, something tartan over his head.

So they got Danby after all. . . It's almost enough to make Richard smile.

They drag the DSI to his feet, then towards the front of the house.

Down the hall, Richard can hear the 'gang' still arguing about what to do to him.

The doorbell's harsh artificial *Drrrrrrrrrrrrrrrrrrring. . .* echoes through the house.

'. . .*ever it is, just get rid of them!*'

Drrrrrrrrrrrrrrrrrrrrring. . .

'*All right, all right, I'm coming.*' That's Matt, the big man with the grey hair.

Richard presses his ear against the door. Muffled sounds. A clunk.

Matt says, '*We're not—*'

435

A painful grunt. A thump.

'Matt, for Christ's sake, can you not just. . . Who the hell—'

And then that Home Counties accent: *'Go get him.'*

'I don't know what you think you're doing, but I'm calling the police!'

'I SAID GO FUCKING GET HIM! KNOX – HERE – NOW!'

Logan's little Fiat made a grinding, rattling noise.

'You hear that?' Butler coaxed them around the round-about and onto South College Street. 'That's the sound of the transmission eating itself.'

There was a bang, and another cloud of grey smoke spiralled out into the dark afternoon. But the car kept on going.

He dug out his phone. Should really call Steel and find out if Susan was OK. Might not have her mobile on though, not in the hospital. And what if it was bad news. . .?

He called FHQ instead and asked for Constable Guthrie. There was a pause, then, *'Hello?'*

'Have you got that info I asked for?'

'The old bloke got attacked? The one from Cove?'

'What about him?'

'Did a full background check like you said – get this, according to a DS from Sunderland, his brother was one of Knox's victims. Almost went to trial, but the brother backed out after a visit from a couple of local heavies. . . Talk about your unlucky family, eh?'

About to get even unluckier.

'What about the man in the picture: Lowe?'

'Yeah, Bruce Lowe. His dad went missing for a week, turned up covered in bruises and bites. Wouldn't talk to anyone, ended up in a psychiatric care home. Died of bronchitis eight months ago.'

Butler hooked a left onto Portland Street, bypassing the long queue of traffic waiting at the lights, the Fiat towing a

436

growing pillar of smoke behind it. Even in a dying car they'd made pretty decent time. It wasn't even four yet.

'Did you do the property search?'

'Yeah, but it's not. . . Oh, hold on, just come in.'

'What's it say?'

'Dear Constable Guthrie. . . Blah, blah, blah. . . Right: Bruce Lowe bought a converted steading about half a mile outside Newburgh three years ago.'

Logan smiled. *Finally* something was going his way.

Richard Knox falls to his knees on the cold hard kitchen tiles. Tries not to cry out. The kitchen's all rosewood units, green marble worktops and stainless steel appliances. A big enough room, but it's already pretty crowded, you know?

The gang that snatched him from the Sacro flat are standing behind him – down the end with the cooker, where there aren't any exits. Matt: a tall, thin man with grey hair; Bruce: pale leather jacket, even paler skin; and a plain, dumpy woman called Ellen.

On the other side of the room are the three people Richard really hoped never to see again. Julie and her pet thugs. Not that she *needs* help, know what I mean?

A breakfast bar juts out of the wall, partitioning the kitchen in two. Danby's slumped over it. He doesn't move, doesn't say anything, just lies there, shivering, his legs a deep angry pink. That tartan bag still over his head.

Richard gathers the quilt around himself, hiding his shrivelled naked cock.

Julie smiles at him. 'Hey, Babe. You miss me?'

Matt steps forward. 'Look, I don't know what you think you're playing at but—'

Neil – the Elvis impersonator – takes a step forward and slaps Matt hard enough to send him crashing against the working surface. A mug shatters on the tiles next to Richard. He flinches, can't help himself.

Neil grins as Matt struggles upright with tears in his eyes, one hand clutched to his scarlet cheek.

'Anyone else fancy a go?'

Silence.

Bruce takes a small step forward.

Dumpy old Ellen puts a hand on his arm. 'Don't. . .'

He raises his pale chin. 'This is my home.'

'Good for you, Sweetheart; love what you've done with the place.' Julie perches on a stool at the breakfast bar. 'Now, you all know why we're here, so why don't we act like grown-ups and no one else needs to get hurt.'

Bruce balls his fists. 'He raped my father.'

'And you want revenge, correct?'

Bruce nods.

'And you're going to . . . what: kick him to death? Have yourselves a lynch party? Batter his brains in with a hammer?'

A voice from the doorway says, 'We're going to hand him over to the police.'

They all turn to look at the old man, standing there in his fleece and jeans. Face is a right mess, you know? All covered in bruises. He purses his lips, raises an eyebrow at Julie. 'Who the hell are you?'

'Well, well, well, if it's not Mr Jimmy Evans. We were reading all about your terrible ordeal in the papers this morning, Babe. Feeling better?'

The old man's chin comes up. 'We're handing him over to the police.'

'I see. . .' Julie smiles. 'And then what? They believe your trumped-up charges and he goes back to prison for the rest of his sordid little life? That the idea?'

'They won't have any choice, he's—'

'Oh Sweetie, he'll be out in six, seven years tops. Then

it'll all start up again.' She sighs. 'No, your young friends here have the right idea. Mr Knox needs to pay a much *darker* price for his crimes.'

'We won't—'

'She's right.' Ellen looks down at Richard, then backhands him across the face. The blow snaps his head around, smacking his cheek into a cabinet door. Hot stinging pain on one side, dull throbbing on the other.

They're going to kill him.

Richard bites his bottom lip. Tries not to cry. It's a test. It's all a test.

Oh God, they're going to kill him.

Julie winks. 'That's more like it!'

Ellen straightens her shoulders. 'He raped my grandad. An eighty-year-old man and this piece of shit tied him up in the basement and raped him.'

'Tell you what, why don't we make it nice and simple?' Julie thumps a huge handbag on the breakfast bar – like a leather mop cap with rope ties and big handles – and digs about inside. Four pairs of 3D glasses go on the worktop followed by a big bunch of keys, a packet of tissues . . . and a moulded leather holster. She unfastens the restraining strap and pulls out a black slab of metal.

A semiautomatic pistol.

Oh God.

Richard blinks. Tries to look away. But the gun's like a magnet.

She pulls back the slide and peers inside, then lets it go with a clack, ejects the magazine, and puts it in her pocket. Julie places the gun down in front of her.

It clunks on the marble worktop.

'One in the breech. All you have to do is shoot him in the back of the head.' She looks at Neil. 'Show them, Babe.'

He makes a gun of his thumb and forefinger and marches over – Matt, Bruce, and Ellen shrinking back as he gets close. Then Neil takes his position behind Richard, grabs a handful of hair, and forces his head down. The big man jabs his finger into the dip at the back of Richard's skull.

'Bang.'

Oh God. . .

He lets go and Richard scrabbles sideways against the cabinets, knees drawn up to his chest, hot tears dribbling down his cheeks.

Oh God. . .

'Isn't that fun?' Julie smiles. 'Best thing is, because it's a forty-five, when it comes out the other side it'll take most of his face off.'

Ellen licks her lips. Looks from Richard to the gun, then up to Matt. 'You do it.'

'I . . . with. . .' He rubs at the angry red handprint on his cheek. Looks up at his dad, then drops his eyes. 'Bruce. . .?'

The old man bangs his hand on the wall. 'This isn't right!'

'You're not in charge any more, Evans.' Bruce holds out his hand. 'I'll do it.'

'Excellent. Tony, get the patio doors would you, Babe? Don't want the nice man getting brains and bits of skull all over his nice new kitchen.'

Tony – the one who doesn't look like Elvis – hesitates a second, then does what he's told. Cold air floods the room.

The security light comes on at the back of the house. The garden's almost featureless, an expanse of crisp white. The trees and bushes bent under the weight of snow, more flakes swirling down from the dark sky.

'Oh God, please. . .'

Neil grabs Richard's arm.

'No, please, God no, please. . .' Richard snatches at the

cabinet handle, holding on, knuckles going white. He stares at the old man. 'Don't let them do it!'

But Jimmy Evans just turns his back.

'Please!'

Neil kicks Richard in the ribs.

He screams, but doesn't let go. 'Please! You—'

His head jerks backwards and hot copper fills his mouth; a ringing noise followed by a wave of fire. He lets go.

Neil drags him across the kitchen tiles, over the lip of the patio doors, and tumbles him out into the snow.

So cold against his naked skin it burns.

Richard scrabbles to his knees, hands clasped in front of him, tears and snot running down his face as they form a circle around him, looming. He chokes back a sob. 'Please, *please*, I didn't mean it. You don't have to—'

'SHUT UP!' Julie holds the gun out to Bruce. 'There you go, Babe. Just like we showed you: one shot to the back of the head and it's all over. We'll even help you get rid of the body.'

Bruce takes the gun.

Oh God.

'Please, it wasn't my fault. I've changed! *I'm not like that any more!*'

Bruce scuffs through the snow until he's standing directly behind Richard, then grabs a handful of hair and forces his head forward.

Something hot runs down Richard's frozen thigh, steaming in the frigid air. 'Please don't do this. . .'

The gun barrel presses into the skin of his neck, right where Tony's finger was.

Richard closes his eyes.

Father, why have you forsaken me?

Now the only noise is the roar of the wind, the groan and creak of the trees.

441

Neil sighs. 'Some time today would be nice, like.'

'I don't think I—'

'Shoot him.'

'I—'

'The fucker raped your old man! Do it!'

The barrel presses harder into Richard's skin.

Neil's screaming now. 'KILL HIM!'

Silence.

Then Julie says, 'Not so easy, is it, Bruce?'

Bruce drags in a huge breath and sobs. 'I want to. . . I really want to . . . but I *can't*.'

The barrel drifts away and Richard falls forward, vomiting into the snow. Oh thank you, thank you merciful God, thank you.

'You want me to do it, Sweetheart? I can if you like. It's no problem.'

Richard stares at her, warm bile cooling on his chin as she reaches out and takes the semiautomatic from Bruce's limp fingers. Takes a step, so she's standing in front of Richard, the gun barrel a supermassive black hole, sucking everything into it.

'Any last words, Babe?'

All Richard can think of is, 'Please. . .'

She straightens her arm and pulls the trigger.

50

Logan's Fiat gave one last almighty bang and died, juddering to a halt on Queen Street. PC Butler pursed her lips, pulled the keys out of the ignition, and pointed through the windscreen. 'You want to get out and push?'

FHQ loomed black and grey up ahead, all the windows shining bright through the swirling snow, less than two hundred feet away. Almost made it.

Logan shook his head. 'Never get it up the ramp.' He climbed out into the road, lurching as the wind buffeted at his back. 'Shove it to the kerb.'

Between them they managed to push the rusty corpse to the side of the road.

Butler pulled her cap down low over her ears, hunching her shoulders. 'What now?'

Logan checked his watch – just after four. Still an hour to go before he had to face Finnie. Or he could just avoid it altogether. . . 'Fancy some overtime?'

He jammed his hands deep into his pockets and crumped through the snow towards FHQ.

*   *   *

'Alpha Six One, we've got a mannie says his neighbour's killing her husband, Deansloch Crescent, can you attend, over?'

Logan turned down the police radio till it was barely audible over the car's rumbling diesel engine and the squeal of the windscreen wipers. 'Still don't see how you managed this.'

Sitting behind the huge wheel PC Butler grinned. 'Trust me, you don't want to know.'

The police Land Rover was kitted out in full mountain rescue livery, with ladders, shovels, flares, bull bars, one of those collapsible stretchers, and a set of spotlights strong enough to give polar bears a tan. But *most* importantly: four wheel drive.

Quarter past four on a Wednesday afternoon and the city was at a standstill, nose-to-tail traffic stretching ahead of them, all the way down King Street – taillights and head-lights making haloes in the driving snow.

Butler leaned over and thumbed a button. Blue and white flickered from the Land Rover's roof, then the sirens joined in. The cars in front inched over towards the kerb.

'That's more like it.' The constable sent the Land Rover roaring into the growing gap between the two lanes, the traffic parting before them. Twin streams of slush and snow fountained out from the wheel-arches, spattering the cars on either side of the road.

Logan wasn't exactly certain this was a 'lights and music' kind of trip, but what the hell. He was probably going to get suspended anyway, might as well go out in style.

Click.

Richard sprawls across the frozen ground, screaming, arms wrapped around his head.

And then he realizes he's still alive. The bullet hasn't ripped through his skull, spattering the pristine white garden with pink and red and grey like an angry Rorschach ink blot.

Feeling rushes back into his body – fingers and toes burning with cold, legs and arms aching with it, his torso raw. He opens his mouth, but all that comes out is a squeak.

Julie grins down at him, then looks off towards the knot of people huddled by the patio doors. 'Oh come *on*.' She waggles the gun at them, then reaches into her pocket and pulls out the magazine clip. Slots it back into place. Racks a round into the chamber. 'Do you *really* think I was going to give you a loaded gun? Might've hurt yourself.'

Richard shivers his way to his hands and knees, shaking so hard he can barely breathe.

Bruce's head is down, his skin even paler than before, crying.

'Tony, Neil, why don't you take Mr Knox back inside and clean him up a bit?'

The two heavies grab an arm each and drag him back into the house. Richard can't even stand, his legs aren't working, all he can do is tremble. Teeth clattering in his head.

Oh God, he's still *alive*. . .

Through the kitchen, down the hall, and into a huge bathroom, all done up in black slate and glistening chrome. They heave him into a big enamel tub, then crank open the taps. Water sputters in, cold at first, then steaming hot. Richard scrabbles back, his pink toes going bright red, the skin throbbing and groaning.

'Fuckin' hell.' Neil grabs the big mixer-showerhead above the shiny taps and thumps his hand down on the chrome button. 'Don't be such a bloody poof.'

The showerhead judders, and hot water spurts out. He curls his top lip and holds it over Richard. 'Stop wriggling! Your own fault for being a filthy little shit, isn't it?'

Needles, broken glass jammed into his cracking skin. . .

And slowly the feeling fades, the warm water leaching its heat into his bones. It's just starting to feel good when Neil twists the taps again, shutting it off. Leaving Richard shivering in the bottom of the tub.

Tony, the quiet one, settles on the toilet lid and stares at Richard's pink, naked body. 'We had a deal, Knox.'

Richard doesn't say anything.

'We had a deal and you fucked us over.'

'I didn't. . . I wasn't—'

Neil slaps him, hard across the face. 'Where's the money?'

Richard's mouth tastes of blood, sweet against the bitter tang of vomit. 'I don't. . . I don't have it. It—'

Another slap.

'Bad time to get a sense of humour, Knoxy, WHERE'S THE FUCKING MONEY?'

Richard wraps his arms over his head. 'I don't have it! Mr Maitland made me split it between his kids before he died. . .'

This time it's a punch, right in the stomach. 'Where's the money?'

He curls up in the bath, sobbing. 'I don't have it, I don't have it. . .'

One in the kidneys. 'Where's the money?'

'AAAAGH. . . *Please*, I don't have it!'

Then the door opens. 'Hey, Sweethearts, how's it going?'

Tony sighs. 'Says he hasn't got the cash any more. Mental Mikey willed it to his kids.'

'That's a bit of a pain.' She squats by the side of the bath and looks into Richard's tear-filled eyes. 'I'm disappointed in you, Babe. We bought you all that lovely Rohypnol and you used it a day early to disappear on us. You promised to give us Danby – you didn't. And now you don't even have the money. . . You're no use to me, Darling.'

She stands.

Neil: 'What you want us to do with him?'

Not the gun again. *Please* not the gun again.

Tony: 'Sell him.'

They all turn to look at the man sitting on the toilet. 'Sorry, Sweetheart?'

'Sell him. They're all scrabbling to claim Mental Mikey's empire back home, aren't they? Cunningham, Dawson, that violent prick Smithy. . . Bet any of them would pay good money to get their hands on Knox. 'Specially if we don't tell them he's not got Mikey's cash any more.'

Oh God, no. . . Smithy'll kill him. And not quickly, Richard knows, because he's seen it.

Julie smiles. 'Excellent idea. Might even give us a bit of leverage down south. Can't do it direct though – too risky – but we could go through an intermediary. Someone local.'

'What about that little weasel you've been getting info off?'

'Who, Polmont?' She shakes her head. 'Silly bugger went and got himself killed, didn't he, Babe? But I might know a man. . .'

She pulls out her phone and steps out of the bathroom, leaving him alone with Neil and Tony again.

Richard scrubs his hands across his damp, swollen face. 'Please, you can't—'

'Wouldn't fuckin' like to be you.' Neil throws a towel into the bath. 'Dry yerself.'

'I can get more money. I can—'

The slap sends him crashing against the black-and-silver tiles. 'I said, dry yerself!'

Richard keeps his mouth shut and does what he's told.

Tony sits there on the bog, watching him. 'Not the luckiest, are you? No cash, no mates, no one to protect you. . . Know how long Danby held out, before he told us where you were? Five minutes.'

Neil curls his top lip. 'Didn't even have to show him the pliers, like.'

447

'Can't believe you thought he'd get you out of the country. How thick are you?'

Julie comes back in, snapping her phone shut. 'All sorted. Shall we. . .?'

They drag him, limping, back through to the kitchen.

He stands there, both hands cupping his balls.

Bruce, Ellen, Matt, and Evans are down the other end, by the fridge, but the only ones who'll look at him are Ellen and the old man. The other two's eyes keep slipping away to the floor.

Julie smiles at them. 'Here's the deal: we're going to sell Knox's scrawny, trembling backside to some *really* nasty Edinburgh gangsters. That way he gets what's coming to him, and you lovely people get some compensation for what he did to your families. We split it fifty-fifty. Sound fair?'

No one says anything. Well, she's got that gun, hasn't she?

Richard sniffs. A tear falls to the tiles at his feet.

Ellen bends down, scoops up the quilt Granny Murray made and flings it at him. 'Here, you can take your shit with you.'

Richard grabs it, bottom lip trembling, breathing in the smell of the old lady and her house. If they're going to sell him to Cunningham or Smithy he'd be better off out in the garden with a bullet in his brain. At least that way it'd be quick.

He wraps himself in the quilt. And then Ellen snatches something off the working surface – a tatty Asda carrier bag. 'All of it.'

Richard catches the bible before it hits him, clutches the crackly plastic to his chest, closes his eyes and thanks God.

Evans steps forward and dumps the old suitcase on the kitchen floor. 'I didn't want it to end like this, but you deserve whatever's coming to you, Knox. I hope you rot in hell.'

Then Neil and Tony march Richard down the corridor,

and back out into the snow. They plip open the locks on the big Range Rover, haul the boot open, and shove him inside. They're back two minutes later with Danby, the bathrobe flapping open in the eddying snow.

After the warmth of the shower, Richard's hands and feet throb with the cold. Probably got frostbite, or hypothermia, or something like that.

Tony throws the battered leather suitcase in on top of them. 'Don't go getting sexy with your roommate, OK?' And then he slams the boot shut.

Danby still has that tartan thing over his head. His skin's cold, pale, and pebbled, like a supermarket chicken; his hands cable-tied behind his back. They haven't bothered to do that to Richard. Don't think he'll put up a fight. Don't care if he sees their faces either. Because they know he won't live long enough to tell anyone.

And he knows they're right.

Richard sniffs, wiping a tear away with his sore hand.

The doors clunk open, then closed again. A big petrol roar as the engine fires up, and something cheery burbles from the radio, then fades out so a DJ can say, *'Wasn't that great? We'll be having the news with Lorna Knight in eight minutes, but first here's a reminder from the Met Office, we've got a severe weather warning for the whole North East, so only travel if your journey is completely necessary, OK? In the meantime, curl up somewhere comfy-cosy and grab yourself another mug of hot chocolate. And speaking of Hot Chocolate, here they are with "You Sexy Thing"!'*

Richard lies down on the plastic boot liner and wiggles in close behind Danby, pressing chest to back, legs to legs, then wraps an arm around his chest, holding him close. Sharing what little body warmth he has as the car lurches away into the snow.

* * *

449

Logan scrambled down from the Land Rover. Its blue-and-whites barely dented the blizzard, headlights reaching no more than a dozen feet in front of the bumpers.

The house was isolated, a long rectangle of freshly pointed granite with a slate roof. Old-fashioned six-pane windows – that probably cost a fortune to reproduce in double-glazed wood-effect UPVC – glowing pale gold.

He staggered over to the door, clasping his collar around his throat with one hand and tried the doorbell. Then hammered on the door as well. Too cold for dicking about.

PC Butler slithered to a halt beside him. She was dressed in the full Grampian Police outdoor-ninja ensemble: black trousers, black boots, black fleece poking out from under a black waterproof, fluorescent-yellow high-vis waistcoat with 'POLICE' across the back, and a black peaked cap jammed on her head. She'd even managed to scrounge up a pair of gloves from somewhere.

'You want me to try round the back, Sarge?'

Logan nodded, then hammered on the door again as Butler disappeared from view.

It took nearly two minutes for someone to open the door, by which time Logan couldn't feel his feet.

A woman stood in the doorway: short, heavy-set, bleary eyed. It was *her* – the woman Wendy Leadbetter had picked out from the picture, the one with the 'DIE – KNOX – SCUM!' placard. She blinked at him a couple of times. 'Can I help you?' Geordie accent.

Logan hauled his warrant card out of his pocket. 'Police.'

She looked at it, then looked at him. Then sighed. 'Best come in.'

*   *   *

They were in the lounge. Three men sitting around a roaring gas fire, two in matching armchairs, one on the couch, an open bottle of Lagavulin on the coffee table between them. The peaty whisky smelled like disinfectant in the silent room.

One was the pale man from the crowd photographs – Bruce Lowe, the home owner. One was tall with grey hair and a red handprint on his cheek. And the third was Jimmy Evans.

Logan stared at him. 'Thought you were on your way down to Sunderland.'

The old man shrugged and took a sip of whisky. 'Surprise.'

'So, let me guess,' Logan turned to the third man, 'that makes you the son?'

'Matt Evans.' He drained his glass, then reached forwards and topped it up again. The bottle trembled in his hand. 'Knox raped my uncle.'

'Where is he?'

The woman slumped into the sofa, next to the old man, helped herself to a whisky. 'Gone.'

Jimmy Evans ran a hand across his bruised forehead. 'We were going to hand him over to the police—'

'Evans!' Lowe scowled at him. 'He doesn't know any—'

The woman waved her hand. 'Oh shut up, *Bruce*. It's over, OK?'

A shape lumbered into view through the window: Butler, her black jacket and hat already caked with snow. She rapped on the glass. Logan ignored her. 'What's over?'

Evans took a swig of pale-yellow whisky. 'My brother never got over what Knox did to him. Chained to a wall, tortured, raped. . . And then when he goes to the police, what happens? Two big bastards come round and threaten to cripple his grandkids if he doesn't change his story: say he lied about it.'

'Knox was here and you let him *go*?'

'Was never the same after that. Took Simon four years to die; just gave up in the end.' The old man drained his glass.

'Knox killed him, sure as if he'd stuck a knife in his guts. So when that policeman Danby called and said he wanted to—'

'Evans! Keep your big gob shut!' Bruce Lowe clambered to his feet and turned to Logan. 'I just asked them back here for a drink, offer a bit of support. He's drunk. You can't—'

'Don't talk to my dad like that!' Matt hauled himself out of his armchair. 'Least he had the guts to go through with it, you couldn't even shoot the little—'

'I had nothing to do with—'

'SHUT UP!' The woman slammed her glass down on the coffee table. 'Just . . . shut up.'

The knocking at the window got louder.

She sank back into the sofa. 'We didn't let Knox go, we sold him.'

Logan could feel his mouth hanging open. 'You *sold* him? Who the hell wants to buy—'

'Some bossy cow turned up with two thugs. She said she could sell Knox to some gangsters who're after him. Split the money with us. Supposed to be compensation for what he did.' Ellen gave a short laugh, then picked up her glass again, greasy beads of alcohol shimmering on the sides. 'They even had this. . . fat naked guy in a dressing gown with them, tied up with a bag over his head. Suppose they were going to sell him too.' She took a swig. Bared her teeth. 'Must be good money in perverts.'

She had no idea.

There was a clunk from the front of the house, a muffled voice saying, 'Oh . . . *boy* that's cold. . .' PC Butler letting herself in. 'Hello?'

Logan called back: 'In here.'

The constable bumbled in, nose and cheeks bright pink. 'What happened? I was knocking and everything.'

'Get your notebook out.' He pointed at Jimmy Evans. 'You abducted Richard Knox and made it look like he raped you.'

'We needed enough evidence—'

'Evans!' Bruce Lowe was on his feet again. 'I swear to God, if you don't—'

'—make sure he'd go back inside for life this time. He—'

'Don't listen to him! We didn't do anything, it was Knox!'

Logan grabbed Lowe by the scruff of the neck and hauled him back into his seat. 'YOU SIT DOWN AND KEEP YOUR MOUTH SHUT!'

The man shrank back into the armchair.

Logan loomed over him. 'What about Harry Weaver? Was he in on it too? Or did you put the poor bastard in hospital for fun?'

Lowe looked away. 'It. . . Knox had. . . He was like that when we got there. Tied up on the bed, naked, blood everywhere. The woman too. We never touched them.'

Silence.

Logan turned to the rest of the room, 'Where did they go? This woman who's going to sell Richard Knox for you?'

The old man topped up his glass again. 'She said there was some Edinburgh gangster who'd act as go-between. . .'

Logan stuck out his hand. 'Car keys.'

They looked at him. 'What do—'

'Give me your car keys. *All* of them.'

A minute later he had two sets for the Mercedes, and one for the big black people carrier. The woman dropped her Clio key fob into his hand and Logan stuffed the lot into his pocket.

'You will stay here and you will wait for a patrol car to collect you. Do you understand?'

51

'Babe, pull over and I'll drive.'

'I'm *doing* it, all right? Can't see a bloody thing out there, like.'

Julie sighs. 'We'll be all night at this rate.'

Richard Knox peers through the metal grille of the dog guard, over the back seats, and out at the road. Thick curtains of white, billowing down from the darkness.

He ducks back down.

The big car thumps over something and Danby groans. Turns out the tartan bag's just a pillowcase, held in place by a thick cable-tie round his throat.

Richard's hands are stiff from the cold, the left one barely working at all. Every time he moves the fingers it's like being stabbed, but he manages to ease the pillowcase out from under the cable-tie, and up over the big man's head.

Danby's face is pale . . . well, except for the bruises, the black eye, and the swollen lip.

Richard strokes the superintendent's face, feeling the stubble scratch beneath his fingertips.

Poor old soul. . .

Then the big man coughs, his whole body rattling, face going bright pink. A deep ragged breath and he slumps back. A thin stream of spit dribbles out the side of his mouth.

Richard takes a corner of Granny Murray's quilt and wipes it away. 'You sold us out. Said I could go away on me own, live me life somewhere.'

Danby closes his eyes, breath coming in deep wheezes. 'You . . . raped him. . .'

Richard hangs his head.

'You raped him, and he blew his head off with a shotgun.'

'You said if I shared the cash with you, you'd help us escape. 'Stead of which you set us up!'

Danby laughs, but it turns into another coughing fit. Big man like that, you'd think he'd have more insulation against the cold, wouldn't you? And he's got a dressing gown on, all Richard's got is a tatty old quilt.

'You. . .' Wheeze, shiver. 'You did the same to me, know what I'm saying?'

Got to admit he had a point there.

'Don't suppose it helps, but I'm sorry.' Richard lies down again, wrapping himself around the superintendent, holding him tight. 'They're gonna kill us, aren't they?'

The big man's head sinks back against the plastic boot liner. 'If we're lucky. . .'

Logan slammed the front door shut and hurried over to the police Land Rover. He clambered into the passenger seat. Where the hell was Butler?

She appeared from behind the Mercedes and hunched through the blizzard to the Renault Clio. There was something red in her hand. And as Logan watched, the Mercedes seemed to sink a couple of inches. A minute later the Clio joined it, then the people carrier.

Butler climbed up into the Land Rover, a grin stretching

her rosy cheeks as she folded a long blade back into a huge Swiss Army Knife. 'Just in case anyone's got a spare set of keys they're not telling us about.'

Logan pulled out his mobile phone while the constable cranked over the huge diesel engine.

'Yes, I want you to get a patrol car out to. . .' He frowned, turned to Butler. 'Where the hell are we?' Then repeated the address to Control as she drove them out into the blizzard. 'Three IC-One males, one female, I want them picked up and charged with perverting the course of justice.'

There was a pause. *'Are you are aware it's blawin' a hoolie oot there?'*

The headlights turned the world into a snow globe, with the Land Rover at the centre, shaken by the howling winds.

'Yeah, I kinda noticed.'

'Can you no' bring them in yoursel?'

'Don't have time. Tell Finnie I know where Richard Knox and DSI Danby are. I need an armed response unit to the McLennan Homes development south of Balmedie.'

'Jesus, yer no shy the day, are you? Hang on. . .'

Logan stuck the phone against his chest. 'Does this thing not go any faster?'

Butler didn't even look round, kept her face straight ahead, eyes narrowed, staring out into the driving snow. 'It's Scott of the Antarctic out there.'

The little country road twisted and turned, drystane dykes on either side disappearing under drifts of white.

'Do your best, OK?' Back to the phone. 'So am I getting my ARU or not?'

But the voice on the other end wasn't the wee Teuchter from Control any more, it was the head of CID. *'Sergeant McRae, tell me, was it my imagination, or did I instruct you to be in my office at five? Yet here we are at half four and you're asking for a firearms team?'*

Logan filled him in on his visit to Bruce Lowe's steading.

'Hmm. . . Where are you?'

Logan peered through the windscreen. A signpost flared in the gloom, reflecting back the Land Rover's head-lights. 'Just coming into Newburgh now. So: firearms team?'

'I'll get an ARU out to Camberwick Green as soon as I can. In the meantime, you are not authorized to take any action until they get there. If you get yourself killed just to avoid our meeting I will be highly pissed off, is that clear?'

'Yes, sir.'

Newburgh wasn't a big place. The A90 – the main road north to Ellon and Peterhead – ran through the middle of the little town, and as soon as they turned onto it Butler put her foot down.

Normally, at this time on a Wednesday, there would be a steady stream of traffic coming the other way, trying to beat the rush-hour out of Aberdeen, but today it was quiet. Just the occasional eighteen-wheeler crawling its way north.

Butler's Airwave handset bleeped into life as they reached the outkirts of Balmedie – Control calling to say that the firearms team had just left FHQ.

Then it was Logan's phone's turn. He checked the display: DI Steel.

'How is she?'

'They'll no' tell me what's going on. . .' A sniff. Silence. 'Should arrest the whole bloody lot of them.'

He tried to force a smile into his voice. 'I'm sure it'll be—'

'So, have you sodded up all my cases yet?'

'Of course not. It's fine.'

The Land Rover slowed, bouncing to a halt at a break in the central divide, opposite a sign saying 'McLennan Homes

– SITE TRAFFIC ONLY'. Then they rumbled across the other carriageway and up to the site gate.

'*Anything else going on?*'

Logan looked out at the high chainlink fence and the signs caught in the Land Rover's headlights: 'SITE PATROLLED BY GUARD DOGS', 'NO ENTRY TO UNAUTHORIZED PERSONNEL', 'WARNING: RAZOR WIRE', 'DANGER OF DEATH'.

He swallowed. 'Yeah, no, everything's fine. Tell Susan we're all asking for her, OK?'

They said an awkward goodbye, then Logan slid the phone back in his pocket.

The gate was open, not all the way, just wide enough for a large car to squeeze through. Butler drove the Land Rover in. On the other side, the road was virtually invisible, a set of rutted tyre tracks disappearing into the gloom.

Logan turned and peered into the back of the vehicle. 'We got any weapons?'

'Sarge? I thought we were meant to wait for the cavalry?'

If this was America they'd have shotguns and tear gas and riot gear and ammo. Instead of which they had a big first aid kit, some road flares, and enough rope to build a bouncy bridge over the River Dee. Fat lot of good that was going to do.

The car lurched to a halt, throwing him backwards against his seatbelt. 'Hoy! Careful.'

Butler tapped him on the shoulder. 'We've got company.'

She was right. A set of headlights glowed in the darkness, getting closer.

'Sod. . .' Logan glanced left, then right. 'Block the road.'

The constable wrestled with the steering wheel, three-point-turning the Land Rover until it was parked side-on, then Logan reached into the back, grabbed a couple of the road flares, and clambered out into the snow.

It was like being punched with a fistful of ice. He staggered, letting the car door slam shut in the wind.

Fuck it was *cold*...

He lurched over the rutted surface to a point about six feet from the Land Rover's bonnet, pulled the plastic cap off the first flare and struck the igniter across the end. It sputtered, then sent out a gout of lurid scarlet flame. Logan jammed the other end into the snow, then hurried around to the other side and stuck the second one behind the car.

With the blue-and-white lights flashing in the middle, there was no way you could miss the police Land Rover.

He hobbled back to the driver's side. Butler wound down the window and said something Logan couldn't hear over the howling wind.

'What?'

'I said, we're supposed to wait!'

Logan pointed through the whipping snow to the approaching headlights. 'You want to let them just drive right past you?'

Butler thumped back against the headrest, sighed, then undid her seatbelt and climbed out into the snow. She hauled on her gloves and hunched her shoulders up round her ears. 'Must be bloody mad...'

The headlights got bigger and bigger and then a huge black rectangle growled out of the snow. It stopped ten feet from their makeshift roadblock and sat there, with the engine idling.

Logan wiped the snow from his face and stumbled through the gusting wind to the huge car, PC Butler swearing along behind.

It was one of those massive Range Rover Sports jobs. The kind that looked as if they'd been designed out of Lego. Three people: two in the front, one in the back.

Logan knocked on the driver's window. It buzzed down and the driver smiled at him. She had blonde hair cut in a bob and jazz on the stereo.

'Can I help you, Officer?' English, probably from somewhere posh.

The man in the passenger seat scratched his eyebrow, keeping his eyes on the road. The one in the back seat yawned, then ran a hand through his greying quiff. All very nonchalant.

'Can I see some ID?'

The woman's smile got bigger. 'I'll show you mine, if you show me yours, Babe.'

Logan gritted his teeth, unzipped his jacket and pulled out his warrant card. Trying to stop his pink fingers from shaking.

'Nice one.' She reached down between the seats, rummaged, then produced a black leather card holder. Handed it out of the window.

Logan flipped it open.

It was a warrant card, just like his, only where his said, 'GRAMPIAN POLICE' hers said 'SOCA'.

He checked it twice before handing it back. 'Care to tell me what the Serious Organized Crime Agency is doing on a building site north of Aberdeen, Sergeant . . . Bultitude was it?'

'Nope.'

Logan stared at her.

In the back seat, Elvis shifted from one buttock to another. 'Close the window, eh, Julie; getting a draft, like.'

The woman went to buzz the window back up again, but Logan slapped his hand on the sill. 'We're not finished here.'

'Yes we are, Babe.'

He stared at her. 'It was you, wasn't it? Two men and a woman – you're the ones who took Richard Knox from Bruce Lowe's place. Where is he? And where's DSI Danby?'

The man in the passenger seat sighed. 'Not again. . .'

The woman's smile became sharper. 'That's need to know, Sergeant.'

460

'Don't screw me about: where are they?'

She raised an eyebrow. 'Neil?'

'Fuckin' have it.' The back door popped open and Elvis climbed out into the snow. Typical Geordie, he didn't even have his coat on, just a black shirt picking up a dandruff coating of snow. He flexed his arms.

Jesus he was big: six-foot-two, six-foot-three, arms like a body builder's.

Logan's other hand dug deeper into his pocket, fingertips wrapping around the little canister of pepper-spray. Out of the corner of his eye he saw PC Butler take a step forwards, the harsh CLACK of her extendible baton clearly audible over the wind and the Range Rover's engine.

'Is there a problem, Sarge?'

The big man just looked at the pair of them, then smiled. Cricked his neck from side to side.

A gust of wind buffeted Logan. 'There's a firearms team on its way. You won't even make it back to town.'

Sergeant Bultitude clapped her hands. 'A firearms team? How, *exciting*! Will they have guns?' She dipped back out of sight, then came back with a semiautomatic pistol clutched in her hand. 'Like this one?'

She brought it around until it was pointing at Logan's face.

He felt his bowels clench. Held his hands out, palms open. 'Let's not—'

'This is how it's going to go down, Babe. You get back in your little plodmobile and drive away. Nice and peaceful. Otherwise. . .' She made a little circular motion with the gun barrel.

Logan stared up at her. Swallowed. Tried not to tremble. 'Where's Knox?'

Bultitude pursed her lips. 'Brave. I like that.' She nodded, back towards the building site.

'You actually did it? You *sold* him to Malcolm McLennan's mob? You're supposed to be police officers!'

A shrug. 'Your Malk the Knife's the tip of a Europe-wide smuggling iceberg: drugs, goods, people, weapons. Worth *millions* every year. Richard Knox is a nasty little rapist, but he's worth a lot to certain people down south. We sell him to Mr The Knife at a knock-down price, and we get an in with everyone.'

'You can't just—'

'You *know* what he did: what he got away with. Dozens of old men, tortured and raped. And you want to let him walk?' She snorted. 'Sweetheart, at least this way they get a bit of justice.'

Logan stared at her. 'What about Danby: you sell him too?'

The woman from SOCA sighed. 'I'm afraid Detective Superintendent Danby's been a naughty boy. We got a call from Knox a couple of weeks ago – Danby offered to smuggle him out of the country for a cut of Mental Mikey's rainy-day money. That's not nice, is it?'

Fuck.

Another blast sent Logan lurch-stepping, driving icy daggers into the back of his head. The big man glaring at PC Butler didn't even wobble.

'Where is he?'

'Sorry, Babe, that's need to—'

'Answer the fucking question!'

Her eyes narrowed, lips thinning over bared teeth.

The man in the passenger seat buried his head in his hands. 'Oh Christ, here we go. . .'

The gun had drifted away, now it was back pointing at Logan's face. 'I don't like your—'

'Julie. . .' The passenger leant over and touched her shoulder. 'Last thing we need is local plod on a mission, getting in the way, you know what I'm saying?'

'*Nobody* talks to me like that.'

'I know, I know.' He licked his lips. 'Look, we can't tie Danby to Mental Mikey's money, can we? Not if Knox has given the bloody stuff away. We've got nothing on him, like.'

'This Sweaty—'

'We're going to have to let him go anyway, know what I'm saying? It's not worth the aggro.'

There was a pause.

She pulled her face into a tight smile, eyes narrow slits as she stared at Logan. 'You want Danby?' The driver's door popped open and she climbed down, stomped through the whipping snow past Angry Elvis and around to the Range Rover's boot. She hauled the hatch up with one hand – the other still wrapped around the gun – reached in and dragged something out.

It hit the ground with a thud and a grunt. Just as Logan turned the corner.

'You want him? You can have him.'

Detective Superintendent Danby lay on his side in the snow, dirty-white bath robe rucked up around his middle, the skin on his legs and buttocks worryingly pale.

'What did you do?'

'When he wakes up, tell the corrupt bastard he's mine.' She slammed the boot shut again. 'Neil, get your arse back in the car. We're leaving.'

Elvis flexed his shoulders again. Curled his hands into fists. 'We going to let these Jock bastards—'

'Maybe you didn't hear me, Babe?'

The big man froze, eyes darting back towards the Range Rover. 'I . . .' He cleared his throat. Spat. The wind snatched it away before it got anywhere near the ground. He got back in the car.

She marched back to the driver's door and climbed inside. Buzzed the window up. Then put her foot down. The huge

463

four-by-four's wheels span, sending a spray of snow and ice across Danby's pale, crumpled body. And then it was off, swinging around the police Land Rover, over one of the road flares and away into the distance.

Logan let out the breath he'd been holding in, then bent over and clutched his knees. Dear God. . .

PC Butler appeared at his shoulder. 'Shame. I was looking forward to tearing that big bastard's head off.'

He looked at her. It was official – he was surrounded by nutjobs.

'Help me get Danby back to the car.'

They cleared a space on the back seat, then bundled the DSI inside. There was an electric blanket thing in a box in the boot with its own heavy battery pack. They draped it over him, then wrapped him in layers of space blankets, the crackly silver and gold sheets making him look like a baked potato.

Butler strapped the detective superintendent into place with both sets of seatbelts. 'Hospital?'

'Building site.'

'Damn.'

They left the road flares burning, and Butler did another slithering three-point-turn to get the Land Rover facing the right way. Then Logan told her to kill the blue flashing lights as they drove deeper into the development.

'You sure about this, Sarge?'

'Nope.' Logan pulled out his phone. No signal. He reached over and plucked the Airwave handset from Butler's shoulder.

Control still didn't have an ETA for the firearms team. The whole Bridge of Don was gridlocked after a bendy-bus slid sideways across all four carriageways between the bridge and Balgownie Road, trying to avoid a three-car pile-up. They were having to divert via Grantham in snow-laden rush-hour.

The message from DCI Finnie was to sit tight and not do anything stupid.

Logan hit the disconnect button.

PC Butler looked at him. 'We're going to do something stupid, aren't we?'

'Yup.'

52

The development loomed out of the blizzard – skeleton houses, the hunched shapes of machinery. First stop the site office.

The lights were on, but when Logan sent Butler out to try the door it was locked. No one inside.

A little after five and the sun was long gone, now everything beyond the reach of the headlights was enveloped in darkness.

The Police Land Rover bumped over something in the snow, the front end rearing up, then the back. Behind them, Danby groaned again. At least he was still alive. Probably more than they could say for Richard Knox.

Butler let the four-by-four rumble to a halt. 'Think we've run out of road.'

Logan peered into the whirling white and inky black. Last time he was here with PC Martin and her cadaver dog, Wardrobe, the further away from the site office they got, the more complete the houses were. Assuming they hadn't just staked Knox out to freeze to death in the great outdoors, he'd be in something that at least had a roof on it.

The Land Rover was fitted with a roof-mounted spotlight. Logan grabbed the handle and flicked the switch. A crack sounded above his head and the harsh white beam leapt out through the snow.

He fiddled with the handle, swinging the spotlight about, trying to get a feel for it, then did a slow sweep left to right. Didn't matter how strong the light was, it could only penetrate so far before the whirling flakes consumed everything.

He pointed towards the nearest property with a roof. 'That way.'

The Land Rover bumped and rolled its way slowly through the drift-covered landscape. The first house was dark. So was the second one, blue-and-white 'POLICE' tape snapping and writhing outside it. The third was dark too. But a pale glow oozed out from the downstairs window of house number four.

'There.'

Logan snapped off the spotlight. Butler killed the engine and the headlights. Darkness. Now the only sound was the howling wind and the creak of springs as the Land Rover rocked with each blast.

'Right.'

They both stayed where they were, in the dark, watching the house through the windscreen.

Butler cleared her throat. 'We got any sort of plan?'

No.

Logan licked his lips. Melting snow plastered his hair to his head, trickling down the back of his neck and into his collar. 'I'll take the front, you go round the back.' He pulled his damp sleeve back, exposing his watch. 'What time have you got?'

She checked. 'Quarter past.'

'Right, we go in at twenty past. *Quietly*, understand?'

Butler nodded and they synchronized watches. 'You sure about this, Sarge?'

'Nope. You?'

The constable pulled out her extendible baton, undid her

seatbelt. Took three deep breaths. Opened the door, and jumped out into the night.

Logan gave her a couple of minutes to get into place, then climbed into the darkness, sinking up to his knees in a drift of soft grey.

He waded his way forward, clambering upwards until the snow only came as far as his ankles, leaching the heat from his damp socks, making his trouser legs stick to his skin. His whole head burning with the cold.

The front door was painted some dark colour, indistinguishable in the gloom, but the little portico offered a bit of shelter from the whipping snow.

Logan checked his watch. Twenty past in: three, two, one. . . He grabbed the handle.

Thank God it wasn't locked.

He threw the door open and stumbled into the house.

A tiny hallway, door leading off to one side – probably a toilet – stairs leading up to the first floor, set of glass doors to the right. That was where the light was coming from.

He looked through into a small lounge.

They were obviously still finishing off the property. A stack of skirting boards lay beneath the front window; two or three boxes of bathroom tiles; a table-mounted circular saw; rolls of silver-backed Rockwool; a nail gun; drums of thick, grey electrical cable; some stuff for fitting carpets; a toolbox; a plastic bag of screws, the shiny thorns of metal glinting in the glow of a big battery torch that lay on the floor.

Richard Knox was curled up next to it, naked on a rectangle of plastic sheeting, hands behind his back, silver duct tape thick around his ankles, another strip across his mouth.

Where the hell was PC Butler?

Logan checked his watch again. Twenty-one minutes past. Butler should've been here by now.

Logan reached for the glass-panelled door and froze. There was someone in the room with Knox. A man, dressed in a thick padded jacket – goatee beard, glasses, comb-over. The project manager: Brett.

Brett crouched down beside Knox with his back to the door, and Logan caught a flash of needle-nosed pliers.

And then Knox writhed, screaming behind the gag as Brett twisted and pulled and shoved.

Damn it. . . Now he didn't have any choice.

Logan eased the door open and crept inside, matching his footfalls to Knox's muffled yells, eyes darting around the room in case Brett wasn't working alone.

The project manager sat back on his haunches, staring down at Knox. 'I'm going to keep doing this until you tell me where the money is. You may have the rest of them fooled, but I *know* you've still got something hidden away, haven't you?' He opened the pliers and something metal fell to the floor. 'Shall we take another one out? I think—'

Logan battered him over the head with the torch.

The project manager slumped sideways, the pliers bouncing out of his hands.

Not the most heroic rescue in the world, but it worked.

He rolled Brett over onto his front and cuffed his hands behind his back.

The plastic sheeting Knox lay on was spattered with droplets of scarlet. About a dozen little dark spines stuck out of his upper arm and shoulder, surrounded by angry red welts, oozing blood. About the same number again were just empty, bloody holes. Just like Steve Polmont.

Logan shifted around until his back was to the wall, then crouched down and patted Knox on the cheek.

The little man's eyes snapped open. He flinched back, screaming behind his gag.

Logan slapped him, and hissed, 'Shut up, you idiot! Not

going to hurt you.' He stole another look around the room. 'Are there any more of them?'

Knox drew a shuddering breath in through his nose and nodded.

Bugger. Where the bloody hell was Butler?

Logan reached down for the edge of the duct tape gag and froze. Might be a better idea to leave it where it was. Get Knox out of here as quietly as possible, before the rest of Malcolm McLennan's thugs got back.

'Can you walk?'

No response.

'I said, "Can you walk?"'

The thin, naked man just blinked at him.

One way to find out.

Logan sneaked over to the toolbox, looking for anything with a decent blade to cut through the duct tape. There was a battered Stanley knife in one of the trays with SP scratched into the handle. Perfect.

The mechanism was stiff, but he managed to slide the rusty triangular blade out, then squatted over Knox's ankles and started sawing.

'Wouldn't bother if I was you.' A Glaswegian accent, right behind him.

Logan froze.

Where was Police Constable Fucking Butler when you actually needed her?

17:18, SIX MINUTES AGO

PC Vicki Butler edged her way around the corner of the detached house. She'd abandoned the standard fluorescent-yellow high-vis waistcoat back in the car. Can't sneak up on anyone when you glow in the dark, can you?

470

She flexed her fingers around the handle of the extended truncheon. Feeling the weight.

Dear Lord it was cold.

She crept along the back wall – ducking under the kitchen window – making for the French doors.

Vicki peeled the cuff of her glove back and checked the time. Thirty seconds to go. Twenty-nine. Twenty-eight.

Her feet were going numb, even through two pairs of socks.

Seventeen. Sixteen. Fifteen.

She tightened her grip on the truncheon.

Twelve. Eleven. Ten.

Vicki inched closer to the French doors.

Six. Five. Four. Three.

She placed a black-gloved hand on the door handle.

Zero.

And then she heard it. A low growl, coming from right behind her.

Oh . . . crap.

She turned, slowly.

There was a dark shape slinking through the snow towards her. Big, muscular – snow sticking to its black fur.

Jesus, that was a *big* dog.

Vicki backed off, nice and slow. 'Good doggy?'

The growl became a snarl.

Fuck. . .

Andy Connelly, AKA: Mr Big-and-Bald, wiped his hands on a wodge of blue paper towels. From above Logan could hear the sound of a cistern filling up again. Completely missed the flush.

Connelly dropped the towels on the floor as Logan stood.

'Andrew Connelly, I am arresting you on suspicion of the murder of Steven Polmont—'

'He doesn't have the money any more.'

Logan pulled out his pepper-spray. 'Face down, on the ground, *do it*!'

'That's what you're after, right? Mental Mikey's little eighteen million pound nest egg?'

'Eighteen million?'

Shrug. 'So they say. But the little shite's frittered it all away, hasn't he?'

'On the floor.'

'Transferred into the offshore bank accounts of Mikey's successors.' Connelly frowned. 'Shame, could've done with a couple million, you know? Set me up somewhere warm and sunny till the heat dies down on that Polmont prick.'

Connelly nudged the unconscious project manager with his foot. 'Course this crawly wee fuck wanted to give it all to the boss, didn't he? Wanted to make up for all the dodgy goods and drugs you bastards seized.'

'I'm not telling you again: on the floor, *now*!'

'See, if Knox doesn't have the money any more, he's fuck-all use to nobody. You want him, you can have him.'

Lying on the floor behind him, Knox mumbled, kicking the floor.

'Yeah, I want him.'

Shrug. Connelly turned and walked through the lounge door. 'He's yours.'

Logan frowned. That was a lot easier than he'd been expecting. He glanced back at Knox, lying trussed up on the floor, opened his mouth to say something, and then Connelly hit him – a side-on rugby tackle that sent them both crashing against the wall. Hard enough to crack the plasterboard.

They went down in a tangle of limbs, Logan gasping for breath as his scarred stomach screamed at him, swinging fists, elbows, knees, *anything* to get the bastard off.

Only Connelly was bigger, heavier, and a hell of a lot stronger.

Less than thirty seconds and he had Logan pinned to the chipboard, face down, with his knee in the middle of Logan's back. The big man grabbed a handful of Logan's hair, hauled his head up off the floor, then slammed it down again.

Logan threw an elbow back, but all he got from Connelly was a grunt.

His forehead battered into the chipboard again.

Bright lights chasing darkness. Jackhammers in his brain. Thumping.

And then a hand grabbed his flailing wrist and pinned it to the floor.

'Never, *ever*, take your eyes off the prize.' Connelly reached out with his other hand, and Logan watched him drag the nail gun over.

'Fucking get off me!'

The nail gun's nozzle was cold against the back of Logan's hand.

'See, it's got a pressure safety trigger, have to press down to fire.'

THUNK.

Logan screamed, even though the pain hadn't kicked in yet. It. . . He stared at his hand. The nail was sticking through his sleeve, pinning it to the chipboard.

THUNK. Another nail on the other side.

Kneeling on top of him, Connelly laughed. 'What? You thought I was going to put a nail through your fuckin' hand? What kind of animal do you think I am? Sides, get blood on the floor, have to hack up that whole chunk of chipboard and replace it. . .'

'GET THE FUCK OFF ME!'

'Ah well, it's only chipboard.'

473

THUNK.

Silence.

There was a half inch of dark grey metal sticking up out of the back of Logan's hand. Fire raced up his arm. 'FUCK! AAAGH! FUCKING . . . FUCK!'

'Fancy another one? Piercin's all the rage these days, but.'

THUNK.

'FUCK!'

'See: did that one at an angle so your hand's stuck. Chippies call it dovetailin' the nails. Is that no' interestin'?'

Warm red trickled out between Logan's palm and the chipboard.

The weight shifted on his back.

'We going to do your right hand next? Or shall we just stick a couple through your forehead?'

Logan whipped his head to the side, eyes raking the floor for something to. . . *The rusty Stanley knife*. He threw his right hand out, groping for the handle.

Connelly leaned down and grinned in his face. 'No fuckin' way, big man. Nice try though—'

Something dirty-pink slammed into Connelly's bald head. He lurched forwards and the feet hit him again, both together, heel-first, cracking his nose. Then again, bouncing his head off the flooring.

It was Knox, writhing on the blood-streaked plastic sheeting, driving his feet down on Connelly's head again, both legs still duct-taped together at the ankles. Face screwed up, hissing behind the gag.

One more time and that was it – he collapsed back against the plastic sheeting, sobbing. But Andrew Connelly wasn't moving any more.

The kitchen door nearly exploded off its hinges, the handle making a deep gouge in the plasterboard wall.

PC Butler lurched in, left trouser leg torn and tattered,

blood oozing down her shin, little flecks of red all over her face, waving her extendible baton. 'POLICE! Nobody fucking move!'

She stood there, wobbling for a moment, frowning at the scene. 'What did I miss?'

53

Logan dry swallowed another couple of ibuprofen, chased them down with an amoxicillin, gagged, then washed everything away with a mouthful of lukewarm tea.

His hand throbbed, all wrapped up in white bandages and feeling like it was twice the size. Could barely move his fingers. Lucky both nails missed the tendons, or he'd have been buggered – that was the technical term the surgeon had used.

Two days later and it still hurt like hell.

PC Guthrie slouched through into the Wee Hoose, waved a brief hello, then settled onto Biohazard Bob's desk. 'You got a minute?'

Logan checked the clock, it was surrounded by Post-it notes with arrows and 'BEER O'CLOCK?' scribbled on them.

'You can have three. Got Goulding coming in, we're off to see Knox at half past.'

'Finnie tells me you're the man for the graveyard flasher case?'

Logan closed his eyes, slumped in his seat, head dangling over the backrest, arms hanging by his sides. 'What *now*?'

'He got his knob out again this morning – showed it to a

nice young lady who used to kickbox for Scotland. She beat the living crap out of him.'

'He downstairs?'

Guthrie nodded. 'His black eye's even better than yours.'

'Stick him in an interview room and leave him to sweat for a while. You can do a bit of looming if you like?'

'Yes, Guv.'

Soon as the door clunked shut, Doreen swivelled her chair around. 'You know, you should really go home with that hand. You don't *need* to be here.'

'Course he does.' DS Mark MacDonald grinned. 'Our lad here can't leave in case they decide to give Beardy Beattie's job to you, me, or Bob. It's OK, Laz, we'd be kind to you, wouldn't we?'

'I'm just saying it's not right to be in work with a serious injury like that. . .'

Logan gathered up his files in his good hand and excused himself. Pausing on the way down the corridor to sneak a look into Beattie's office. They'd already taken the name plate down, and now it was just the idiot himself, hunched over a file box, tidying away his personal effects so the next occupant could move in.

It was a miracle they hadn't just fired his useless beardy backside.

Logan even managed to whistle a happy tune on his way down to reception.

The meeting with Knox was pretty straightforward. The rat-faced Geordie was in a private room at Aberdeen Royal Infirmary, with a plainclothes officer from the Offender Management Unit stationed outside – just in case.

Logan settled back against the wall, letting Dr Goulding take the single seat.

Knox's belongings were piled on the wide windowsill,

the battered leather suitcase on the bottom, his granny's quilt folded on top of that. The man himself lay in the bed, beneath the institution-grey covers, family bible clutched to his chest.

'So you see, Richard.' Goulding reached forward and patted Knox on the arm – the one that wasn't swathed in bandages. 'While they admit faking the attack on Jimmy Evans, they're still denying they had anything to do with the Sacro team.'

Knox nodded. His face looked even worse than usual – covered in a dark web of purple, green and yellow bruises.

'But, the police have found fibres and DNA from Bruce Lowe, Ellen Hill, *and* Matthew Evans in the Sacro flat. The Procurator Fiscal's charging them with both attacks.'

A tear spattered on the crumpled bed sheets.

'Now.' Goulding drew his chair up closer. 'We need to talk about what you're going to do when you get out of here.'

Knox looked at Logan. 'What about Danby?'

'Gone back to Newcastle. Discharged himself yesterday, said he wanted to be with his family.'

'That's good.' The bruised man took a deep breath and fiddled with the bible's cover. 'No offence, like, but after Aberdeen it'd be nice to go somewhere hot. Can I do that? Spain, or something?'

Goulding tilted his head to one side. 'Normally no, but given your actions in helping save DS McRae's life. . . We'd need a few more sessions to confirm you've got everything under control.' The psychologist smiled and patted Knox on the arm again. 'We'll see. You're making great progress.'

'Somewhere hot, with no *snow*.' He even smiled, hugging the bible to his chest. 'How great would that be?'

Logan pushed himself off the wall. 'We'd better be off.'

The chair creaked as Goulding levered himself out of it. 'Yes, right. You call me if you need anything, OK?'

Logan hovered by the door when the psychologist had gone, staring at the bruised figure on the bed. He cleared his throat. 'I wanted to say, thanks. Again. For stopping Connelly.'

Knox shrugged a shoulder – the one without the bandages on it. 'Thanks for not giving up on us. Again.'

Nod.

Silence.

'Yeah, well. . .' Logan backed towards the door. 'Bye.'

He caught up with Goulding at the lifts. 'You want to go on ahead? I need to see someone.'

'Ah.' The psychologist nodded. 'Of course. Would you like me to wait? I've cleared the afternoon to write up Knox's evaluation reports anyway.'

It wasn't as if Logan could drive anywhere by himself – not with his hand full of stitches and swollen up to the size of a small balloon. He chewed on the inside of his cheek for a moment. 'Actually, you're OK. Thanks, but I can get a lift back with a patrol car. Not a problem.'

'Well, if you're sure. . .'

'Yeah, thanks anyway.'

They said goodbye on the ground floor, Goulding getting out of the lift to walk to the exit, Logan staying on to the first sublevel. He wandered the old familiar chipped and faded corridors to the Maternity Hospital. It wasn't visiting time for nearly two hours yet, but a flash of his warrant card and some puppy-dog eyes got Logan through the security doors and into the post-natal ward. Where a chubby nurse with squeaky shoes escorted him to a little double room. The curtains were drawn, leaving just the flickering light from a TV mounted above one of the beds, a worn-looking woman staring dark-eyed at the screen. DI Steel was sitting beside the other – empty – bed, one of those plastic nicotine inhaler things clamped between her teeth.

'How is she?'

'Off having a pee.' Steel looked up, her face a roadmap of wrinkles and creases, dark purple bags under her eyes. 'You look like shite.'

Logan sank into the chair next to her with a grunt. Everything ached. 'Not exactly page-three material yourself.'

'Cheeky wee shite.' But she was smiling as she said it. 'Any news?'

'Been on the phone to SOCA – said they couldn't comment on any ongoing investigation, assuming there actually *was* one. Which they refused to confirm or deny. Wouldn't even tell me if Sergeant Julie Bultitude really exists or not. The bastards could've been anyone. . .'

'Aye, that sounds like SOCA all right.' Steel creaked her way out of her seat, rubbed the small of her back. 'Come on, I'll introduce you.'

The little intensive care ward was dim behind the glass partition, green lights winking in the gloom on half a dozen microwave-oven-sized plastic incubators.

Steel cupped her hands to the glass, then leaned her head into the hollow.

Logan did the same. 'Which one?'

'Second from the right, third row. Jasmine.'

A little pink bundle of wrinkled skin with a tube up her nose – taped to her cheek with a white strip. Little fingers. Little toes. Wires stuck to her chest with sticky pads covered in printed teddy bears. 'God, she's *tiny*.'

'Nine weeks preterm. That's sod all these days. Before you know it she'll be nicking fags and necking Bacardi Breezers round the back of the shops.' Steel straightened up and slapped

Logan on the back, hard enough to make him wince. 'Who knew your knob would turn out useful for something, eh?'

'This is a last and final boarding call for flight SZ515 to Plymouth, would all remaining passengers please go to gate number six where this flight is now closing.'

Detective Superintendent Graeme Danby shuffles another step forward in line. Fast bag drop his arse. What's the point of doing everything online when it takes half a bloody hour to get your stuff checked in?

He leans left, favouring his gammy leg, and peers around the two chavs in Nike tracksuits. Looks like the only exercise this pair get is waddling to the door to pay for their home delivery pizza, know what I'm saying?

Graeme checks his watch. Twenty to three. Plenty of time.

He shuffles forward another step, teeth gritted, even after half a dozen painkillers.

Should really be flying business class, bypass all this standing in line crap. Still it's a lot of money. Hard to break the habit of a lifetime. Even when he's got four-point-six *million* split between various offshore bank accounts. That bitch Julie and her thugs tried to beat it out of him, get him to fess up to taking the cash, but he kept his mouth shut, didn't he?

Four-point-six million's worth a couple of broken ribs.

Mr and Mrs Athletic get to the front of the queue with their overloaded trolley.

Graeme checks his watch again.

Always like this when he's got to fly somewhere. Especially if he's got to make connections. Newcastle to Charles De Gaulle; Charles De Gaulle to Shanghai; Shanghai to Auckland. Over thirty hours sitting in economy.

He tries not to think about it. Bad enough flying anywhere – that's why he's got sleeping tablets. Pop two when they board in Paris, wake up in the Far East eleven

481

hours later. Valerie and the kids meet him at the airport in Auckland. Tearful reunion. And they all live happily ever after.

The Tracksuit Twins are arguing with each other about who's got the passports. Morons. Should have a couple fake ones stashed away, shouldn't they?

Never know when you need to get out of the country without those bastards from the Serious Organized Crime Agency finding out, you know what I'm saying?

Preparation – that's the key.

'This is a general boarding call for flight BA1333 to London Heathrow. Would all passengers please come forward to gate number two with their boarding cards ready for inspection.'

Someone taps him on the shoulder, but Graeme doesn't look round. 'You can bloody well wait your turn like everyone else—'

'Now, Mr Danby, is that any way to talk to an old friend?' A deep gravelly voice, the words wafting into his ear on a cloud of extra strong mint.

Graeme keeps his eyes fixed on the fatties. 'Alfie. Thought you were doing a six stretch in Holme.'

'Very kind of you to take an interest, Mr Danby. But got out early, didn't I? Good behaviour.'

The mint smell gets stronger, making Graeme's stomach clench.

'Mr Cunningham wonders if you'd like to join him for a drink, Mr Danby? Discuss a certain shipment of his you . . . intercepted.'

He swallows. Keeping the bile down. 'Love to Alfie, but I've got a plane to catch, know what I'm saying?'

Something hard jabs into his back. 'RSVP, Mr Danby. We wouldn't want to make Mr Cunningham invite your wife and kids too, would we?'

He'd do it too, no matter how far away they were.

482

Fucking hell.

He'd been so *close*.

Head down, Graeme picks up the handle of his trundle case and follows Alfie out of the queue.

What other choice does he have?

The canteen was quieter than the Wee Hoose, so Logan grabbed a table there. Tin of Irn-Bru, Tunnock's Tasty Caramel Wafer, making little chocolate shrapnel while he copied notes out of his vomity notebook and into the new one he'd just signed out of stores.

Took a while to cross reference it all back to the original, with page numbers and everything, but at least now he could leave the stinky thing in its plastic bag, buried away in a filing cabinet in case it was ever needed. Instead of carting it about the whole time.

That done he moved onto the scrap of paper he'd liberated from Douglas Walker's bedroom. Copying the notes he'd made on Jimmy Evans, the Mackenzie and Kerr jewellery heist, and Douglas Walker's attempted suicide. He flipped it over and gave the art student's CV a scan. Mediocre pass marks in Maths, French, Physics and English, top marks for Art and Design. Summer job at a graphic design agency. Part time at a printers in Bridge of Don, paying his way through university. . .

Logan stared at the name written in for a reference. 'JAMES CLAY'. The same name that was on the yellow stickie that came with the last envelope of cash from Wee Hamish Mowat.

Logan closed his eyes, leant forward, and banged his bruised forehead off the tabletop.

Bloody idiot.

It's important for the local economy that we all do our bit, don't you think?

It wasn't a bribe, it was a tip-off.

* * *

483

Two patrol cars, one police van, and Dildo Mair's Vauxhall Vectra sat in the little car park outside an unremarkable industrial unit in the Bridge of Don. The sign above the big roller doors proclaimed: 'JAMES CLAY ~ PRINTING WITH STYLE' next to a big cartoon exclamation mark with glasses, a cheesy grin, and its hands full of papers.

Classy.

Inside, a huge printing press sat towards the back of the unit, the smell of hot dust and oil-based ink drifting out into the cold afternoon. Reams of paper were stacked on pallets along the walls. A big electric guillotine. A collating and folding machine. In the corner, a kettle was finally coming to the boil, watched by half a dozen of Aberdeen's finest in full uniform.

A little breezeblock office was built against one wall, full of desks, drawing boards, filing cabinets and paper samples. Logan poked the scan button on a digital radio again and the display cycled round to *Original FM*. An old Crowded House song bounded out of the speakers.

Sitting on the edge of a half-sized filing cabinet, Susanna Frayn, from Her Majesty's Revenue and Customs, leant forward and tapped Logan on the shoulder. 'Turn it up, I like this one.' Then settled back, singing along quietly.

She did the same for the next song. And then it was the news – a bit about Richard Knox; investigations proceeding into the body discovered at McLennan Homes' Balmedie development earlier this week; a new goalkeeper signed for Aberdeen Football Club; weather – more snow on its way; and then the travel. According to which, Friday afternoon rush-hour traffic was terrible. Surprise, surprise.

A large window separated the office from the print shop. Dildo gazed out at the constables searching the place. He stuck his hands in his pockets, rocking back and forth on his heels. 'We got a call today, from this bloke who wants us to get him a refund from a prostitute calling herself "Big Eleanor", works down the docks. Says he entered into an oral contract with her in good faith.' Dildo made hand-and-mouth gestures, poking his tongue into his cheek to sell the mime. 'Only now he's heard a rumour that she's really a man, thinks he's been a victim of misrepresentation and fraud.'

Susanna smiled. 'What does he want, his deposit back?'

Logan shook his head. 'Thanks for lowering the tone.'

'Hey, could be worse.' Dildo grinned. 'At least I didn't tell you about the DVDs we seized last week. There was this one with two midgets, a redhead, a jar of Vaseline, and a Shetland pony they—'

'Dildo!'

The man from Trading Standards sighed. 'You were a lot more fun before you became a dad. Remember that time we. . .'

Dildo drifted to a halt. There was a constable standing on the other side of the window holding a sheet of A1 paper against the glass. It was covered in a rainbow of bank notes: pink, purple, brown, and blue – fifties, twenties, tens, and fives. Had to be three or four hundred quid's-worth on the one sheet.

The constable stuck his head around the door. 'Found a huge stack of them under a pile of annual reports. We're millionaires! Bwahahaha. . .'

Susanna was staring at him with one eyebrow raised.

'We'll . . . erm . . . start loading them into the van.'

Dildo wrapped an arm around Logan's shoulder. 'Laz, my man, I may just have to buy you a pint tonight.'

'Can't.' He held up his bandaged hand. 'Antibiotics.'

And by the time he was off them it'd be three weeks without a single drink. One by willpower, the rest by doctor's order. Now if could just cut out the cigarettes and learn to eat meat again, he'd be back where he was two and a half years ago.

Still, it was better than nothing.

Richard Knox stands at the window of his hospital room, looking out at the snow-covered world. The car park's busy, so are the roads, gritted from pristine white to glistening black.

Richard smiles – been a while since he's had a good day. And OK, it feels like he's been run over by a minibus and the antibiotics turn his stomach. . . But he's getting better, you know? That psychologist Goulding said so: responding to therapy. Changed man.

Been telling them that the whole time.

Found God, didn't he. Or God found him.

Doesn't really matter in the end.

Long as you tell them what they want to hear.

He hugs the threadbare bible to his chest. All those notes and scribbles. Exodus 29.45, 18.20; Nehemiah 9.12; Ezekiel 38.03. Doesn't take long till you've got bank account numbers, sort codes, authorization passkeys. Everything you need to hide large sums of money. Ten million pounds worth, even after expenses and buying that double-crossing bastard Danby off.

Jet off to Spain, disappear after a couple of months, start a new life somewhere exotic. Aberdeen's ruined the northern hemisphere for him. He wants somewhere warm to get back to God's work.

Richard smiles down at all the little people scurrying about beneath his hospital window.

He'd been telling the truth when he'd told them getting caught was a lesson. It taught him he wasn't ready. Danby only found him cos Billy Adams went crawling to him, covered in bruises, his pants full of blood. Stupid mistake: he'd let Adams live.

Simple.

And that was God's *real* lesson: he'd been sloppy. Lazy. So God sent him to prison with all the killers and perverts and paedos and rapists. People who could teach him how to break into houses. How to dispose of bodies. How to kill and torture and rape and not leave any traces for them CSI bastards to find.

A seven-year masterclass in how to get away with murder. And Richard Knox is a fast learner.